MURDER
AT
ASHGROVE HOUSE

by Margaret Addison

A Rose Simpson Mystery

Rose Simpson Mysteries (in order)

Murder at Ashgrove House
Murder at Dareswick Hall
Murder at Sedgwick Court
Murder at Renard's

Chapter One

'Oh, William, I am so frightfully worried about our house party this weekend,' said Lady Withers floating into the library at Ashgrove House, where Sir William was seated on a Chesterfield sofa reading *The Times*. 'I'm afraid that it's going to be a disaster. I'd invited all the right people, that's to say the ones that go together so to speak, but now I'm awfully afraid that it's not going to work at all.'

'There, there, Constance my dear, it can't be that bad,' said Sir William, soothingly. Such an announcement had not worried him unduly for he was well used to his wife's exaggerations. Indeed, to her annoyance, as far as Lady Withers could tell he was carrying on reading his newspaper.

'Darling, I'm being absolutely serious.' Lady Withers perched herself beside him on the sofa and fought with the newspaper until, with a sigh, he closed it and put it on the coffee table resigning himself to giving her his full attention.

'What can you mean, my dear? I can't imagine anything nicer than having young Lavinia down for the weekend. It seems an age since we last saw her.'

'It *has* been ages, William. She's been working in that awful little dress shop. How she can possibly bear it, I don't know. I don't think they even usually give her Saturdays off, can you imagine. But you know what young girls are like these days. I blame it on the war, don't you? All that ambulance driving and men's jobs, not of course, that Lavinia did any of those things, being just a child at the time, but still it made women feel they could do all sorts of things and I expect it's still in the air. Now, what was I saying? Oh, yes, it's not Lavinia I'm worried about, because of course I want to see her. It's who she's bringing down with her that worries me. Of course, when she asked me if she could bring down a friend, I had no idea that she meant a girl who worked in the shop with her! So of course I said yes, and then when she told me who it was, well it seemed rather churlish to refuse and—'

'Connie,' said Sir William hastily interrupting his wife's flow, 'I'm sure there's really nothing to worry about. Lavinia said in her letter that this Rose Simpson friend of hers is very nice and perfectly respectable. Actually, I think it will make quite a nice change from our usual sort of guest; I was getting a bit bored of them to tell you the truth.'

'William! You know what Lavinia's like. She's never been a very good judge of character, she just sees in people what she wants to see. Do you remember that awful girl that she brought down with her a couple of years ago, you know, that one whose face was covered in freckles and ate with her mouth open! And this one's bound to be worse. She's probably a common little thing covered in make-up, thinking she looks like one of those American screen goddesses. I bet she's got an awful cockney accent too and she won't know how to behave with the servants, she'll probably upset them dreadfully and then they'll all give in their notice and walk out and then where will we be? And,' carried on Lady Withers quickly, seeing that her husband was about to protest, 'can you imagine what Marjorie will say when she hears about it, as she's sure to?'

Marjorie was the Countess of Belvedere, Lady Withers' older sister and Lavinia's mother. 'She's never forgiven me for Lavinia working in that blasted shop. She blames me, as if it had been all my idea. Just because it was here at Ashgrove that Lavinia and Cedric made that silly bet that she couldn't earn her own living for six months, and Cedric only did it because Lavinia said that she was sure he didn't do any work at Oxford, just flounced around pretending to be intellectual and copying everyone else's essays. They really can behave like a couple of children sometimes, the way they wind each other up. I tried to explain it to Marjorie, that I hadn't even known that they had made a bet until she told me about it, but she was not impressed and I could tell she didn't believe me. You know how she can be sometimes.'

'I do,' conceded Sir William. Much as he loved his wife, he often found her endless rambling conversation infuriating, but then he had only to remind himself how much worse things would have been if he had married her sister. Poor Henry. He didn't know how the Earl of Belvedere stuck it, but he would never admit as much to his wife.

'"Ladies from our class do not work in dress shops, Constance." That's what she said to me as if I didn't know it already. Apparently even Mrs Booth, who in Marjorie's opinion is totally middle class even if the lady in question considers herself to be from the top drawer, said to her that it would be totally unthinkable for anyone in *her* circle to serve in a shop, even in the smartest couture house in Paris, which of course Madame Renard's certainly is not, as it's in a little London back street and sells ready-to-wear dresses, not even bespoke. Really, William, Marjorie can be so cruel sometimes. She said that it was all my fault, that they would never have made that silly bet if they hadn't been here at Ashgrove. So can you imagine what she'll say if she finds out about this Rose girl? She'll say that I'm condoning Lavinia's bad behaviour … no … worse, she'll say that I'm encouraging it.'

'There, there, Constance, my dear, you're worrying far too much.' Sir William patted her affectionately on the arm. 'Stafford will make sure that everything goes all right.'

'Yes, dear Stafford, I don't know what we'd do without him. But that's not all, William, if only it was. Cedric's coming down this weekend as well. He wired to know if we could have him and you know what boys his age are like. He didn't wire until it was too late and he'd already set off, so I couldn't wire back and say "No".'

'Why on earth would you want to say no, Constance. It will be nice to see Cedric again, and it will be nice for Lavinia to see her brother. Let's just keep our fingers crossed though that they don't make any more bets while they're here.'

'Well, I expect that's why he's coming down this weekend. Not to see Lavinia or to make any more bets, but to see what this shop girl of hers is like. Oh …'

Lady Withers broke off what she was about to say as a sudden thought flashed across her mind and absentmindedly she clutched onto Sir William's arm, digging her nails into his flesh until he winced.

'Oh, William, I've just had an awful thought. What if this girl decides to set her cap at Cedric! He can be such a silly boy, so very young and impressionable, just the sort to fall into her trap. He's probably never come across a scheming little minx before. Whatever will Marjorie say if they elope to Gretna Green while they're here? It will be such a scandal, Marjorie will never speak to me again what with Cedric being heir to the title and the estate and …'

Lady Withers looked up and caught the pained expression on Sir William's face.

'I know, dear, that you think I'm over reacting and being a dreadful snob, but really, I'm not. You see the *real* reason that I'm so worried about Cedric

3

coming down this weekend is that Edith's coming down as well. We arranged it weeks ago, so you see I can't really do anything about it without offending her. You know how sensitive Edith can be, William. I do so hope there won't be any well *unpleasantness*, this time. You do remember what happened last time, don't you, when they both happened to come down at the same time. Of course it couldn't possibly have been foreseen, not by anyone, but it was still very unfortunate.'

'Yes, yes, I do.'

For the first time during their conversation, Sir William sounded concerned.

'It's likely to be damned awkward my dear, but if there's nothing we can do about it we'll just have to manage it the best we can. Make sure that they sit at opposite ends of the table and all that, and that they see as little of each other as possible while they're here.'

'Yes, you're quite right. I suppose we'd better explain the situation to Stafford, although I'm sure he'll already have everything in hand. You know how awful I am, darling, at trying to work out whom to place next to whom at dinner. I do hate those awful uncomfortable silences which one is obliged to fill by saying the most silly, trivial things. Nowadays I just tend to leave it to Stafford to put out the placement cards at dinner parties because he never gets it wrong.'

'Indeed, Sir William, m'lady.'

Neither Sir William nor Lady Withers had heard their butler enter the room. At times Sir William wondered whether Stafford actually walked like other people, because he seemed always to glide noiselessly from one room to another.

'Oh, Stafford, I knew you would', said Lady Withers, sounding relieved. 'Although I do wish you wouldn't creep up on us so, it's most disconcerting. But I should have known that you'd have everything under control.' She clapped her hands. 'Oh, I feel so much better about things already. Everything's going to be all right, nothing will go wrong, nothing to worry about …'

And she drifted out of the room in very much the same manner as she had floated in, humming a tune softly to herself, blissfully unaware that her original migivings were to prove quite founded.

'Oh, Mr Stafford', said Mrs Palmer, the Withers' cook-housekeeper, as she relaxed with her after dinner coffee that evening in the 'Pugs' Parlour', a sitting-room-cum-dining-room used by the upper servants, 'I fear we have quite a weekend in front of us. I suppose everything's been done as much as can be, to avoid disasters?'

'Indeed, Mrs Palmer, it has.'

Mr Stafford's voice, as always, so Mrs Palmer thought, was wonderfully calm and reassuring. Indeed she was sure that she had never seen him look ruffled or flustered.

'Spencer has been instructed to unpack Miss Simpson's suitcase as soon as she and Lady Lavinia arrive, and then Spencer and Miss Crimms will cast their eyes over her dresses and check that they're all suitable, especially the dress that Miss Simpson is proposing to wear to dinner.'

Miss Crimms, Lady Withers' lady's maid, who was also sitting in the parlour, nodded in agreement between sips of her coffee, careful not to spill any in front of the butler.

'And what if they're not?' Mrs Palmer asked, intrigued. 'What then?'

'We have contingency plans in place, Mrs Palmer,' replied Stafford solemnly. 'Miss Crimms has already looked out some old gowns of her ladyship's that we can give Miss Simpson to wear if necessary, gowns that her ladyship is very unlikely to remember that she ever owned.'

'Yes, we don't want her ladyship to turn around and accuse Miss Simpson of stealing one of her dresses from out of her wardrobes, now do we!' Miss Crimms said, unable to suppress a giggle.

'No, indeed not, Miss Crimms,' Stafford glared at her, 'that would never do. Her ladyship is not to be distressed or inconvenienced in any way, not if it is within my power to prevent it. As I was saying,' *before I was so rudely interrupted*, he would have liked to have added, but didn't, although the look that he gave Miss Crimms said exactly that, 'if necessary a suitable gown will be given to Miss Simpson to wear in place of her outfit, and then it will merely be a case of persuading her to wear her ladyship's gown instead of her own.'

'And how will you do that, pray?' asked Mrs Palmer, enjoying the lady's maid's obvious discomfort at being admonished by the butler.

'We have our ways,' replied Miss Crimms, wishing to redeem herself as quickly as possible. 'Gentle persuasion in the first instance if Miss Simpson appears amenable, and then if not more rigorous measures can be adopted if necessary, such as accidentally spilling a vase of water or pot of rouge over her dress when she is about to go down to dinner or, if the dress is too awful, offering to press it and then scorching it with an iron!'

'No!' Mrs Palmer looked appalled. She was quite sure Lady Withers would not approve of such drastic measures.

'I only ever did that once, Mrs Palmer,' confided Miss Crimms, leaning forward, 'When I was lady's maid to a very young lady who shall not be named, but who was going to go to a ball in a *very* unsuitable dress, that would have brought much distress to her mother and shame on the whole family if she had ever gone out in such a thing. But there was no reasoning with her, I can tell you, for she was a headstrong young madam if ever there was one, stubborn as a mule. So I said to myself, there's only one thing to be done, my girl, you'll have to ruin that dress so it can't be worn. So I told her that I'd just go and press it, and then I scorched it good and proper with the iron, right down the front!'

'You never did!' exclaimed Mrs Palmer. 'And how did the young lady take it? Did she guess that you had done it deliberately?'

'Of course she did! And she was that angry that she went as if to slap me across the face! But I said, "If you do that m'lady, I'll take this dress here and show it to your Mama and say as how you were intending to wear it out and I was only trying to stop you making a right spectacle of yourself, that I had tried everything else, but that you'd just not listened to me." Well, that soon took the wind out of her sails, I can tell you. Became as meek as a lamb, she did. Scared of losing her allowance from her parents, I've no doubt!'

'Yes, well, Miss Crimms,' said Stafford, gravely, 'hopefully we will not have to resort to such drastic measures in this case!'

Chapter Two

Fortunately unaware of the concerns expressed by Lady Withers and her servants regarding her possible character and wardrobe, Rose Simpson studied her reflection in her dressing table mirror. She sighed and, not for the first time, wondered whether she would pass muster with Lady Withers and, perhaps more importantly, with her servants.

She made a face at herself in the mirror and turned her gaze away from her reflection and then turned back again to the mirror and tried to imagine what Lady Withers' first impression of her would be, based on her appearance. She tried to view herself objectively, as if seeing herself for the first time, her dark brown hair arranged in finger curls and her figure which, although it could never be described as slender like Lavinia's, was not altogether unpleasing. Her face, she thought, was pleasant without quite being pretty, although she hoped few would be so unkind as to describe her as plain. How unfair, she thought, that Lavinia should have it all; not only was she rich and a peer's daughter, but she was also startlingly beautiful in that cool, aristocratic way. Lavinia's beauty was the sort that made both men and women stare. With her tall, willowy figure, that made her look both aloof and fragile at the same time, her platinum dyed hair and her face with its even, delicate features; she could easily have passed for a film actress.

Rose thought back to when her friend had first suggested that she accompany her on a visit to her aunt's.

'Don't worry,' Lavinia had assured her, finding it hard to contain her excitement, 'it will be fine, an absolute hoot. Dear old Aunt Connie can't wait to meet you. You'll absolutely love her. She *is* awfully old fashioned and a bit vague, of course, but an absolute sweetie just the same, do say you'll come.'

Rose had agreed that she would, because everyone always said yes to Lavinia; she could be awfully persuasive when she set her mind to it for she was someone used to getting her own way. How else had Lady Lavinia Sedgwick, only daughter of the fifteenth Earl of Belvedere, managed to defy her parents to work in a clothes shop, but still retained her monthly allowance? Much to the surprise of her brother, shock and dismay of her mother, and obvious delight of Madame Renard, the proprietor of the shop where both she and Rose worked, Lavinia had stuck it out so far for some four months or so and showed no signs of quitting. How much of this was because she actually enjoyed the work, and how much was because she did not want to lose face with her younger brother was hard to tell. Although it must be different for Lavinia, Rose acknowledged, knowing that the situation was only temporary and that in two months' time she could walk away from it all, head held high, back to her pampered, upper class life.

Rose sighed again. If only the same could be said of her. If only she was not destined to earn her living working in a shop. Still, at least for one glorious weekend, she could pretend she inhabited Lavinia's privileged world. But she was beginning to feel nervous. What if she did not manage to pull it off, even though, so Lavinia had told her, it was to be a very small house party. Besides themselves there was to be only one other guest, Edith Torrington, a distant relation and old school friend of Lady Withers', so really there was nothing to worry about. Thank goodness for the recent wave of reasonably priced ready-to-wear copies of the Paris fashions that meant that even a girl on a low income, such as herself, could afford clothes made in the style of the top fashion houses. Working in a dress shop had helped too for one of the perks of her job was having the option to buy clothes at a discounted rate. Unlike some of the other girls, who opted for the up to the minute fashion items, Rose chose more classic styles that would not date so quickly.

'I can always lend you something to wear,' Lavinia had said. But despite the exquisiteness of Lavinia's gowns, Rose knew that she could never have worn one to Ashgrove House. It was not just that she was afraid of ripping them or spilling something down the front, but more it was the imagined embarrassment she would feel, and she could feel her face going red and hot just thinking about it, if Lady Withers were to say: 'Oh, what a lovely dress, Miss Simpson, where did you get it?' and she was forced to tell her the truth or, even worse, if Lady Withers was to look at her curiously and say nothing, leaving her wondering whether or not Lady Withers had recognised her dress as being one of Lavinia's.

Rose started practising her make-up. Usually she applied just a touch of rouge to her cheeks because foundation creams were so expensive, but for going to the Withers' she had decided to splash out on it. Expense being no issue for Lavinia, Rose had marvelled at the 'Gardenia' look her friend wore each day to the shop; it gave a white and waxen look to Lavinia's face much favoured by the Hollywood silver screen stars of the time, but Rose hesitated at trying the look herself. Instead she had opted for the more natural 'tea rose' shade of foundation, ivory with a touch of pink. She applied it carefully and sparingly. When she had finished, she thought that there was a slightly surreal look to her face that she was not sure she liked. No, it didn't look quite right. Sighing, she applied lipstick in a light rose shade which seemed to soften the effect.

'That looks better, more like me,' she whispered to her reflection. Still, she thought, I'd better take the rouge along as well, just in case. What a pity there isn't time to ask Lavinia for a lesson in applying foundation.

Lady Lavinia Sedgwick flung open the door of her wardrobe and surveyed its contents, with something approaching satisfaction. True, it held nothing like the vast array of dresses that hung in the massive wardrobes in her dressing room at Sedgwick Court, but even so, she had managed to bring with her to London a few of her favourite outfits. She giggled suddenly as a thought struck her. Eliza, her lady's maid, would have had a fit if she had seen the way she had shoved and crammed all her clothes into this tiny little wardrobe in her lodgings. She had given absolutely no thought to creases or whether the delicate fabric of her dresses would be crumpled and ruined beyond repair by such harsh treatment. Instead she had just leaned against the door to make it shut, and Eliza had not been there to give her a disapproving stare.

It hadn't seemed quite right to bring her lady's maid with her somehow. She couldn't imagine Eliza dressing her just to go to work in a shop serving others, and she certainly could not imagine any other shop girl being dressed by a maid. Eliza wouldn't have approved anyway, far better to let her maid stay at home with her parents and attend to her mother's numerous house guests. Still, it would be nice to get back home and be pampered again, to have someone else lay out her clothes for her, run her bath and dress her hair.

If she were honest, and she would admit this to no-one but herself, she was getting a little bit bored with it all now, this working in a shop business. It had all been quite fun when she had first started, a bit of a lark, something to write and tell her brother and friends about. And to begin with she had not had a moment to get bored because her friends had kept popping in to see her, even though the shop was certainly not located in the most fashionable of addresses and the clothes tended to be ready-to-wear or semi-made scaled-down from the Parisian designs, not at all the bespoke outfits they were used to. Even so, her friends had bought one or two small items, which had gone down very well with Madame Renard, who she knew was hoping that, by employing a member of the aristocracy, she might attract a more elite clientele to her establishment, which might eventually enable her to move to a more up market premises, even perhaps in time Regent Street itself, where she could stock the genuine Paris fashions, not just cheap replicas that almost any woman, regardless of her financial circumstances, could afford to buy. She might even be able to employ a few more expert stream-stresses who could produce gowns from scratch for her more favoured, well-heeled clientele …

After some deliberations Lavinia selected a brightly coloured silk twin-print ensemble consisting of a sleeveless, drop-waisted dress with contrasting winged collar and matching three-quarter length coat. It was one of her favourite outfits because of the vividness of the colour and pattern, a deep royal blue background, decorated with red and white roses, which looked quite wonderful with her bright red, lacy Italian straw hat. When she put this on, she would feel more like her old self again, a moneyed, young woman about town with no cares but to shop, not a nondescript shop girl disappearing into the background while all attention was given to pleasing the customer.

She sighed. She had found it hard work. Not so much choosing suitable clothes for her customers to try on, or giving fashion advice for which she prided herself on being something of an expert. No it had been the being nice to customers bit that she had found so hard. To be polite and seem interested in people with whom she would not normally have passed the time of day, she had found particularly trying. And then when they wouldn't take her advice and insisted on buying something that did not, in her opinion, suit them at all, oh, to have to bite her tongue! And it was not even as if Madame Renard had given her the more mundane tasks to do. She had been protected from doing the most boring aspects of the work; Madame Renard was not a stupid woman, she wanted to hold on to her key attraction, her prize possession, as long as possible.

So Lavinia had not been asked to sweep the floor or pack the dresses into boxes and wrap them in brown paper with string to be sent to customers on approval, or been expected to wait on the most insignificant or dithering customers. Madame Renard had asked her only to attend to her most fashionable and wealthy customers, who could be persuaded to spend a considerable amount of money on outfits if they knew that they were being recommended by a fashionable member of the aristocracy, and they were informed by Madame Renard of Lavinia's identity straightaway for fear that they might be tempted to be rude to her if they thought that she was just another shop assistant, so it had been all: 'Oh, do let me introduce you to Lady Lavinia, daughter of the Earl of Belvedere, don't you know. Lady Lavinia's helping me out in my shop for a while, a little bet she has made with her brother, Lord Sedgwick, so funny don't you think, ha, ha! Lady Lavinia has cast her eye over my new season stock and would be absolutely delighted to give you her recommendations as to what the fashionable young lady will be wearing this season …'

If Lavinia was honest, she had found it all rather embarrassing and sick making, not helped by Sylvia, another of the shop girls who particularly resented her presence at Madame Renard's, rolling her eyes and then looking at her with daggers in the background. But she had liked the look of shock on the customers' faces as they had become aware of her as a person, and an important one at that, rather than dismissing her as just another faceless servant. They had engaged with her as if she were their equal, although of course she was far above them. That had not stopped them thinking she was interested in them, asking her opinion on which clothes would suit them and going with her choices.

On the odd occasion, just for wickedness and because she could, or just because she was bored and thought she could not possibly last out the day, she would advise them to buy something that did not flatter them at all, and they would go with her recommendation just so that they could say to their friends: 'Lady Lavinia helped me choose this outfit, don't you know, it's going to be all the rage this season.' Still she had stopped doing that now ever since she had overheard Sylvia saying to Mary, another of the shop girls, that for someone with all her money and breeding, she had absolutely no taste in clothes at all.

Oh, she could hardly wait to be at Ashgrove again, to be spoilt and pampered by Constance's array of servants, many of whom had known her since she was a small child. Of course, it was a pity that dull old Edith was going to be there too. She'd have much preferred it if it was just going to be Sir William, Lady Withers, Rose and herself. Never mind, Edith was bound to still be moping around, keeping herself to herself so she needn't hinder their enjoyment. Just as well Ceddie wasn't going to be there, because how embarrassing it would be to have a repeat of all that. Lavinia shuddered just thinking about it. No, it was going to be goodbye Lavinia, drab little shop girl, and hello Lady Lavinia Sedgwick, the beautiful, much photographed debutante and favoured style icon of the women's weeklies. She would have to get up especially early so that she could spend time making up her face and dressing her hair before they set off on their journey, which she always found so fiddly and time consuming these days with no maid to help. After all they must make the most of Madame Renard allowing them to take the day off on Friday as well as Saturday. She could just imagine Sylvia's face when she heard the news. She giggled.

Rose was the only real friend that she had made in the dress shop. The other shop girls had not known what to make of her and were definitely working class, whereas Rose had appeared at ease in her presence. She would even hazard a guess that Rose was originally from the middle classes although, from what she could gather, her family had now fallen on hard times. Horrid Sylvia had made a point of either ignoring Lavinia completely or being rude to her when Madame Renard's back was turned, and Mary had gone to the other extreme, hanging on her every word and trying to show her everything and do everything for her, when all she had wanted was to be treated like just any other shop girl, well not quite, of course, she didn't want to do anything too boring or back breaking or mundane. Only Rose had treated her normally and had been genuinely friendly. She had probably been as fascinated by her as Mary had been but, unlike Mary, she had not felt intimated by her, or felt the need to try and please her. No, she liked the friendship she had with Rose because she felt that Rose liked her for herself.

'Excuse me, m'lady,' Stafford gave a little cough and half bowed towards her ladyship. Lady Withers, who had been in the process of arranging some flowers rather haphazardly in a vase, jumped, knocking the vase over, water and flowers spilling out on to the table and floor.

'Oh, Stafford, now look what you've made me do! I do wish you wouldn't creep up on one so, it isn't natural. Why can't you make a noise like everyone else?'

'Quite so, m'lady, please forgive me. I'll arrange for Martha to clear up straightaway.'

Although certainly not his intention to make her ladyship start, he thought on reflection that the outcome was not disastrous. After all, he always sent Martha to rearrange the flowers whenever Lady Withers took it upon herself to start flower arranging. Her ladyship, in his opinion, had many fine qualities, but arranging flowers in a vase was not one of them. Of course, when only Sir William and Lady Withers were at Ashgrove it did not matter so much because Lady Withers always thought her flower arrangements looked wonderful and Sir William was not one to notice such things, but when guests were staying, and titled ones at that … Stafford almost grimaced despite himself, that would never do at all. 'But I thought you'd like to know m'lady,' he continued, 'as soon as I had been informed.'

'Informed of what, Stafford? Oh, do stop talking in riddles or drawing things out.' Lady Withers sunk into a nearby chair and dabbed ineffectually at her wet hands with her handkerchief. 'Out with it, Stafford. What was this thing that was so important to tell me that you had to sneak up on me and worry me half to death?'

'Yes, m'lady, very sorry m'lady.' Had Lady Withers looked at him instead of busying herself with drying her fingers she would have seen that, despite his tone, he did not look particularly contrite. 'I thought you'd like to know, m'lady, that I've just taken a telephone call from Sedgwick Court. It appears that the Earl and Countess of Belvedere are on their way down.'

'On their way down, whatever do you mean, on their way down?' Lady Withers had stopped dabbing at her fingers, her handkerchief now clutched in one hand that was beginning to tremble.

'It appears, m'lady, that the Earl and Countess have it in mind to stay the weekend, here at Ashgrove.'

'What!' The handkerchief was flung to the floor as Lady Withers sprang up from her seat with a speed that surprised even Stafford, although he was careful as always not to show it.

'William! William!' Stafford was just in time to rush over to the door and hold it open for Lady Withers as she fled from the room in search of her husband. Such was her distress that she did not wait until she had found him, before starting her conversation. 'Oh, William, William, it's so awful. Stafford has just brought me the most dreadful news …'

Chapter Three

'Mr Stafford, you could have knocked me down with a feather when I met with her ladyship this morning to go through the menus!' Mrs Palmer was sitting at the highly scrubbed kitchen table, a steaming cup of tea before her and Edna, the little scullery maid, standing beside her, fanning Mrs Palmer's face with pages from a day old copy of *The Times* newspaper.

Stafford secretly thought that the effect created was a little melodramatic, even by Mrs Palmer's standards. She was a short, dumpy woman who always looked hot and flustered as a result of standing over a hot stove all day and barking orders at the scullery and kitchen maids. Today, however, he had some sympathy for her predicament.

'Not only does her ladyship say that she thinks it likely that Master Cedric will bring his friend down with him from Oxford, you know, Lord whatsit, but she tells me that the Earl and Countess of Belvedere are coming to visit as well!'

'Indeed, Mrs Palmer. I did try and forewarn you as soon as I had taken the telephone call from Sedgwick Court,' Stafford said, biting his tongue as always to stop himself from reprimanding Mrs Palmer in front of the lower servants for calling Lord Sedgwick, Master Cedric, as if he was still a small boy come creeping in to her kitchen to snatch a freshly baked sausage roll, not a grown man who in the fullness of time would inherit an earldom. 'But it was your afternoon off yesterday and I didn't want to trouble you when you returned, given the lateness of the hour.' Stafford broke off from what he was saying to give her a pointed stare. Really, he thought, Mrs Palmer should set an example to the maid servants. 'And then this morning, I thought I'd leave it until after breakfast before telling you, but her ladyship was herself a little unsettled by the news and took it upon herself to rush to see you to make sure that you had the necessary stores in, and if you didn't to give you the chance to order more in.'

'It's just as well we've got a large kitchen garden, Mr Stafford,' Mrs Palmer said recovering a little and flapping Edna away with instructions to pour her another cup of tea. 'We shan't have a problem with the vegetables, it's the meat and fish I'm worried about, because of course I've had to change my menus, it'll have to be fancy cooking now, what with the countess coming.' She looked up sharply at the scullery maid. 'Stop that gawping girl and go and fetch Mr Stafford a nice cup of tea.'

'Yes, Mrs Palmer,' the girl looked as if she could not get away quickly enough.

Mrs Palmer started thumbing through her copy of *Mrs Beeton's Book of Household Management*. Like most cooks of her generation she considered it her cooking bible and, when alarmed by news of an impromptu dinner party, she was in the habit of clutching it to her breast to provide her with the necessary moral support.

'Her ladyship said she would come down again in half an hour or so once I'd had time to put together some dinner party menus. Perhaps I could pass some ideas by you, Mr Stafford, if you don't mind? As you know, I do like a nice dinner party, gives me a chance to be creative and stretch myself a bit, can make a nice change from the usual plain cooking that her ladyship likes, but of course, it would have been nice to have had a little more notice to get prepared like. I'm not just thinking of the food, neither. I could really do with some more hands in the kitchen. I'm going to need more help than I'll get from those two dolly daydreams.' She pointed vaguely at the scullery and kitchen maids. 'Heads in the clouds most of the time they have, Mr Stafford, boys, dresses and dancing is all that fills their heads most of the time. But like as not I'll have to make do with them. Too short notice I expect to get help in from the village.'

'I expect you're right, Mrs Palmer. But I'm sure you'll cope magnificently, you always do,' replied the butler soothingly as he and the cook-housekeeper made their way to her sitting room. 'I think her ladyship feels a little overwhelmed too. She was expecting to be entertaining just a small house party this weekend, her old school friend and Lady Lavinia and her friend and instead she is being bombarded by the gentry! Still, I'm sure we'll get through it, Mrs Palmer, as we always do.'

'And of course, Mr Stafford, what with me being housekeeper as well as cook, I've all the bedrooms to sort out, decide who's having what. I suppose we'd better make sure that we give the best room to the countess otherwise she's sure to complain, and then there will have to be doubling up between

16

the housemaids and footmen to act as ladies' maids and valets as I'm sure they won't be bringing down any with them.'

Edna and Bessie, the kitchen maid, stole towards the sitting room and listened at the closed door with bated breath. They could just about make out what Mrs Palmer was saying.

'I was thinking, Mr Stafford, clear beef consommé to start with, can't go wrong with that, followed by cheese soufflés, and then the fish, of course. A whole dressed salmon followed by a meat course of chicken in aspic with duchesse potatoes? Then, for pudding, peaches and raspberry mousse. And then just in case any of them is still hungry, you know what an appetite Master Cedric's got, I'm sure they don't feed him properly at that university, I'll send up savouries – eggs stuffed with prawns, angels on horseback, chicken liver on toast, curried shrimps and sweetbreads and suchlike. What do you think, Mr Stafford, will that be posh enough for the countess? I don't want to show up her ladyship.'

'Indeed it will be, Mrs Palmer, indeed it will. I don't think the earl and countess could expect a better meal if they'd been invited to dine with the King himself at Buckingham Palace!'

'Oh, Lor,' said Bessie snatching Edna's hand and dragging her back to the kitchen before the butler and cook-housekeeper came out of the sitting room and caught them eavesdropping. 'This weekend's going to be something dreadful for us. You've not been here when we've had a proper house party before, have you? You won't believe the amount of additional work that's involved, we'll hardly have time to catch our breath or go to the lavatory even, and Mrs Palmer will be that flustered and bad tempered, she'll be about to blow a gasket any minute and she'll probably cancel our half day off on Sunday as well!'

Edna's face crumpled and there was clearly the threat of tears spilling down her young face.

'Don't worry, Edna,' Bessie said, kindly, holding her hand and pushing a black curl, that had come loose, back under Edna's mop cap. She was only a few years older than the scullery maid, but Edna suddenly looked so young and frail that instinctively Bessie felt pity for her. 'No need to give on so, Edna. Happen I did speak rather hasty like. All I meant was that it's going to be a lot of hard work for the likes of you and me, but it'll be exciting too. There'll be a real buzz around the place, loads of comings and goings.

17

They'll be delivering the fish and meat and Mrs Palmer will be examining them, super critical like, she'll be very exacting in what she'll accept and she'll give them an earful I can tell you if it's not of the very best quality. And Ernie will probably be delivering stuff as well.'

At the mention of the delivery boy, Edna blushed and started to brighten.

'And Mrs Palmer will be creating the most wonderful dishes, Edna, they'll be a sight to behold. If you watch and listen you'll learn such a lot. That's what I'm going to do. And I'll offer to give her a hand with some of the trickier dishes, because it's the only way to learn, Edna. You know I've set my heart on being a cook before I'm thirty. And when I am, you'll be my kitchen maid and we'll have so much fun.'

With that, in something approaching high spirits, they raced to lay up Mrs Palmer's table with all the utensils she would need to cook from scratch; two chopping boards, one big, one small, two graters, several sieves, including a hair one and a wire one, five mixing bowls and an impressive range of knives and forks, spoons and whisks. By the time Mrs Palmer had thumbed through a few pages of her cooking bible to double check recipes she already knew by heart, the table was fully laid.

'Well girls, that's what I like to see,' Mrs Palmer took a deep breath and rolled up her sleeves. 'Let's make her ladyship proud, shall we? Let's show them what the kitchen at Ashgrove is made of!'

'My dear, whatever are you doing hiding yourself away in here?' enquired Sir William, wandering into his wife's morning room which was situated on the first floor of Ashgrove House, next to the linen cupboard.

'I'm keeping out of the way, William,' Lady Withers replied closing her copy of *The Lady* magazine, the pages of which she had been flicking through listlessly in an attempt to try and keep herself occupied. 'You should have seen Mrs Palmer's face when I told her Marjorie and Henry would be staying this weekend. She looked as if she was going to explode, I was so worried, I almost called out for Stafford; you'd have thought I was telling her that the King and Queen were coming, the way she kept going on, saying as how she'd have to change all the menus and bring extra staff in.'

'Well, I've been thinking, my dear,' Sir William said, 'about Edith and well, I think you were right to be worried yesterday. I think it really would be best for all concerned if you put her off.'

'Oh, William, how very tiresome of you,' Lady Withers said, giving her husband a stare of exasperation. 'If only you'd shown half as much interest in everything yesterday, when I was tearing my hair out with the worry of it all. I can't possibly put Edith off, it's simply much too late now. Why, Harold's probably bundling Edith into a train carriage as we speak. And besides, now that I know Marjorie and Henry are coming down too, I think it might prove rather useful having Edith around, it might help to defuse things.'

'How so, my dear?' Sir William looked distinctly puzzled.

'Well, as soon as Stafford told me that my sister was on her way here, I knew the weekend was going to be an absolute disaster. Marjorie has obviously got wind somehow about Lavinia coming down and probably intends to have it out with her about this shop work business once and for all. Well, of course, I realised that would mean that it was going to be absolutely awful for us all, Marjorie doing her usual bull in a china shop routine and Lavinia is bound to be all stubborn and tearful and sulky. We'd probably have been left to entertain her friend and Marjorie would have been paranoid that Cedric was going to take a shine to her and then Cedric probably would, just to annoy her ... oh, I could hardly bring myself to think about it.'

'I still don't see, my dear, how Edith being here will make things any better. Surely it will only make things worse.'

'Oh, William, you really are a typical man. Of course it will make things a whole lot better. No matter how angry Marjorie is with Lavinia, she won't want to wash her dirty linen in public, will she? She may have been quite happy to have a go at Lavinia in front of us, what with us being family and she holding me responsible for Lavinia working in that shop in the first place, which of course is very unfair ... but she won't want to make a scene in front of Edith. She's always rather turned her nose up at Edith what with her being a poor relation and all that, no, she won't think it the done thing at all to have a row with Lavinia in front of her. And then, of course, Edith did go to school with Marjorie and me, so we will be able to reminisce about the old days when things start to get a bit heated. We'll have lots to talk about because I don't think Marjorie has seen Edith since we all left school. But, best of all though, Edith will be able to occupy Miss Simpson, what with them coming from the same sort of class and everything, they're bound to have loads in common. And that will keep Miss Simpson out of harm's way so that she can't get up to any mischief with Cedric.' Lady Withers was looking relieved. 'All in all, William, I think things have turned out very well indeed, all things being considered.'

'That may be so, my dear, but I think for poor Edith's sake she must be put off from visiting us this weekend.'

'But, William, I have just explained to you that it will all be fine.'

'Not for Edith, Constance.' There was a sharpness to Sir William's voice that made Lady Withers look up at her husband both in surprise and with a degree of curiosity, for she was not used to him speaking to her in such a tone.

'I'm sorry, William, but it's really too late now to change anything. You really should have spoken up sooner if you objected to it so much.'

'I really wish I had. Can't you understand, Constance, I'm *afraid*.' Sir William sat down beside his wife on the sofa and took her hands in his. 'I'm really worried that something dreadful might happen this weekend, Constance. You see, it's all so *dangerous*.'

Edith Torrington sat at the breakfast table surveying the remains of her half eaten slice of toast and half-drunk cup of tea, both of which she had forgotten about entirely and allowed to get cold.

'Oh, for goodness sake, Edith,' said Harold Torrington, gently but with obvious frustration, looking up from his morning newspaper. If he were a different sort of man he might have cursed. 'That's the second cup of tea that you've let get cold this morning. What on earth are you thinking about, my dear? You seem far away today, lost in your own thoughts.'

'I'm sorry, dear,' Edith looked up guiltily, 'I'm sorry if I'm not quite with it today.' Or any other day, she could have added. She studied her husband as if she was seeing him for the first time. She saw a middle-aged man with once very dark brown, almost black hair, now predominantly turned to grey and which was receding at the temples. He had been handsome once, she thought, or at least she had thought so and her mother had considered him quite a catch, she remembered, particularly in the circumstances; the answer to their dreams. But now his looks were going, as were her own and he looked just like any other bank manager dressed for work in the City. She found her mind drifting away again until she discovered herself considering how many other such men there were, living in the suburbs of London, having their breakfast, just like Harold, before going off to work. And then she felt her mind float off to think about herself and what she must look like to a stranger looking on. I'm faded, she thought, a sob catching in her throat, a washed up, worn out version of the woman I used to be. If only I could live again, if only I could feel something other than this numbness, if only ....

'Edith!' She looked up sharply. Harold was beginning to lose patience now, she could hear that irritated edge to his voice. 'You didn't hear a word I said, did you. You always seem lost in a dream world these days, I can never keep your attention. Sometimes I don't think you'd notice if I wasn't here, indeed,' he added bitterly, 'perhaps you'd prefer it that way.'

No, she wanted to say, no, I wouldn't. She wanted to get up from the table, overturn it and watch the breakfast things scatter and hear the satisfying smash of crockery. She wanted to look at the mess of egg yolks and toast as they congealed together on the floor, to see the tea spilling out of the cups and staining the slightly faded emerald green rug that she had always hated, but which Harold's mother had given them for a wedding present and so she'd always felt she could not get rid of. But most of all she wanted to rush over to her husband, to take his two hands in hers and hold them to her as if she would never let him go. But she couldn't, she knew, because he would see it as another sign that she was unstable. She wanted to shake him and scream that she would be all right if he would only let her talk about *him*, the person she had loved more than anything else in the world. If only he wouldn't pretend that he had never existed, that what had happened had never occurred, oh, if only he would talk about it!

She looked at him, her lips trembling and wondered, what do you *really* feel? You must care. Why do you have to keep it all bottled up. Why don't you scream and shout and cry and be angry with me? Why don't you either tell me you hate me; that I ruined your life, or take me in your arms and tell me that everything is going to be all right, that it will get better? Why don't you tell me that at least we have each other?

But he didn't say or do anything, he never did, that was the trouble. Instead he just looked hurt, hurt and concerned. She could see the tell-tale vein throbbing in his forehead. If only he would stop being so nice, so nice but so very dull.

'It will do you good, Edith,' Harold was saying, trying hard now to make light of everything, trying to pretend that they were a normal married couple and that their marriage wasn't falling apart around them.

'What will?'

'Going to Ashgrove to stay with Constance. You hadn't forgotten, had you? You're going this weekend. You arranged it a while ago. The country air will do you good, bring a bit of colour to your cheeks, you've been looking awfully pale you know, old girl.'

'Am I? Yes, I suppose I am.' She put her hand up to her face as if she could feel the greyness of her skin. If I go to Connie's I can walk and walk, she thought, walk and walk in the gardens, in the parkland, in the woods beyond, go down to the river ... I can walk and walk until I'm so tired that I can't walk anymore, and then perhaps I will collapse with exhaustion and forget, just for a few glorious moments, and if I do then perhaps I will be able to sleep, a deep sleep untroubled by dreams.

She sighed and closed her eyes for a moment as she imagined the blessed relief. But her eyes flew open almost at once. No, of course it wouldn't be like that at all. She would have to listen to Constance, or at least pretend to listen to Constance, as she talked on and on about her silly pointless things: how good Stafford was, and how difficult it was to get and keep decent servants these days since the war, how the gardens never looked quite as good as they used to in the old days when they had an army of gardeners not just the head gardener and garden boy, how cold it was considering it was September and it looked so sunny, and a hundred other useless, trivial, meaningless things.

'I wish you were coming with me, Harold, couldn't you? It would do you good too to get away from London. It would give us a chance to talk about things like we used to, do you remember?'

'No, Edith, I'm sorry, I can't. It's quite out of the question, I'm afraid, I'm far too busy at work.'

She felt him recoiling from her. What he means, she thought bitterly, is that he won't. It's got nothing to do with work. He won't come because he doesn't want to and he certainly doesn't want us to talk about it, he wants to forget and he wants me to forget too. He wants me to forget that *he* ever existed, to act as if nothing happened, as if our lives have not been shattered, as if we are not living a sham.

'I had better go, old thing, I don't want to be late for work; can't give them an excuse to lay me off, can I, not with jobs being so scarce nowadays.' He was trying to make her laugh, she knew, and she managed a feeble smile. He got up from the table then, and came over and patted her awkwardly on the shoulder and bent down and kissed her fleetingly on the forehead; just a gentle peck, she thought, no hint of passion. If only he wasn't so nice and reasonable about it all. If only he showed her that he was hurting too. 'Take care of yourself, old thing. I'll see you Sunday evening and then you can tell me all the news from Ashgrove.'

With that he left the room. She heard him stop briefly in the hall outside to exchange a few words with Alice, their maid; no doubt, she thought bitterly, to warn her that her mistress was feeling particularly fragile this morning and to treat her with care. Then she heard the bang of the front door as he closed it behind him and then he was gone and she was left alone with the remains of the breakfast things.

Edith waited a few moments in case he returned. But all was still and quiet, except for the faint echo of Alice humming a tune to herself in the distant reaches of the house. When she was quite certain she would not be disturbed, Edith took the photograph from the pocket of her blouse. She studied it; it was getting so creased now, too much handling, of course. She'd have to be careful from now on in case it ripped, because there wouldn't be another one quite like it, could never be another one. The thought hit her so forcibly, as if it was an actual physical blow, that she clenched her hands together suddenly feeling choked. She stared for a long time at the face of the young man in the photograph and then, as she had done a thousand times before, she bent and traced the features of his face gently with her fingers and touched her lips to the photograph, the paper receiving the kiss that she could no longer give to the flesh and blood man. How long she sat there, she did not know, could hardly hazard a guess even. Vaguely she became aware that tears were now trickling effortlessly down her face. How was it possible to weep so silently, so unconsciously? She shuddered and then with a hopeless shrug she surrendered to her grief.

Chapter Four

After much deliberation, Rose selected an all silk flat crepe dress in rose beige with a symmetrical column of bows and a normal waistline, made up of rippling flares and tiny pleats and with a longer skirt than was usual for the time. It was one of her favourite dresses, understated, but hinted at quality and taste, just the sort of dress she considered Lady Withers and, perhaps more importantly, her servants would approve of and consider appropriate for wear to a weekend country house party. Not though, of course, that it was to be much of a party as such with just one other guest besides themselves. However, she still wanted to make a good impression. Yes, she would wear this dress, together with her petal trim hat in dove grey. She had also packed her one good tweed suit, together with a couple of white silk blouses, one with a peter pan collar and the other with a pussy bow, just to be on the safe side because nobody could complain about those, and a couple of bright summer dresses in small flower-patterned material with co-ordinating cardigans for good measure.

She had been less decided about evening wear. She knew that Sir William and Lady Withers always dressed for dinner regardless of whether they had guests or not, and Lavinia was sure to wear some ridiculously expensive, stunning gown. Backless ones were all the rage and, with her stunning figure, Lavinia was bound to look utterly gorgeous. It was tempting to try and compete. Rose had contemplated telling her mother about the visit earlier, for she would have insisted on running her up a couple of dresses in the latest fashions, made from the leftover bits of material from the gowns she made for her more affluent customers. However, her mother's worsening eye-sight, coupled with their ever dwindling finances which made their financial situation ever more precarious, meant that Mrs Simpson could ill afford to waste her time making outfits for which she would not be paid. If only she, Rose, had inherited her mother's sewing skills, but alas she had not. Besides, if Rose was honest with herself, she knew that she could never really hope to compete with Lavinia.

She had been tempted to pack her synthetic gold satin dress but it would look very inferior to Lavinia's gold lame gown, a fabric incorporating metallic threads, which gave the overall effect of liquid metal. So instead she had settled on her old black silk velvet bias-cut dress with its cap sleeves, and a draped bodice gathered at the high waist which, while it might prove a little warm for a summer's night and was rather plain, had the advantage of looking both tasteful and elegant. While she was sure Lavinia would wear different gowns on the Friday and Saturday nights, she had resigned herself to wearing the same dress twice but with different accessories; on the Friday night her mother's pearls, which she felt would lift the outfit and give it a touch of class, and on the Saturday night, a flower, scoured from the flower gardens at Ashgrove, which she intended to wear as a corsage.

She had, of course, packed her own case because neither she nor her mother employed a maid who could do it for her. It would be different, of course, at Ashgrove; there would be a housemaid assigned to her as lady's maid, to unpack her case and hang up her clothes and even press them if necessary before she wore them, and in the morning her clothes would be laid out for her and a bath run. She looked at the clothes in her case, frowned and took them out again and repacked them as carefully as she could. Her cheeks flushed as she imagined the maid tutting to a fellow servant. 'Of course you can tell she's only a shop girl. You should have seen the way she packed her clothes, something shocking it was. Talk about creases, it will take me half the night to press them to make them look half decent...'

Although no-one else was in the room and the conversation was entirely inside her own head, Rose found that she was blushing. She could not help but think that things could have been so different if... but no, she must not go there, she must not dwell on what could have been, but instead focus on the here and now....

'Oh, Rose, I don't know how to tell you.' It was the day after her father's funeral and her mother had clutched at her sixteen year old daughter's hand and led her into her bedroom to sit down on the bed beside her. This in itself was unusual, for her mother regarded her room as her own private sanctuary to which Rose was rarely invited. So Rose had known instinctively that something was wrong, more horribly wrong even than the death of her father which, if truth be told, though it was too awful to admit, was almost a relief for them both. Worryingly, whatever her mother wished to say, she wanted to keep from their servants, Dobson, the cook and Doris, the daily help. She remembered afterwards the smell of lavender which had filled the room and remained with her long after her initial feelings of devastation, caused more by her shock at the obvious wretchedness of her mother than by the news she had to impart, the implications of which she had not fully comprehended then.

It was only later, when she had been alone in her room, turning her mother's words over and over in her mind that it had slowly dawned on her that what had hitherto been a relatively comfortable and naïve middle class existence, was about to become unravelled. Much later still, when she thought back on that day, she remembered also the blackness of her mother's mourning dress which mirrored her own, casting dark shadows across the rooms like crows.

'It's too awful, Rose. It's even worse than I'd feared.' In the privacy of her room, away from the prying eyes of servants, her mother had given way to tears and wept freely. Rose, still very much a child in some ways, had felt awkward and afraid. She had pressed her handkerchief into her mother's hand and stood and waited for the sobbing to cease, or at the very least subside, not sure whether she wanted her mother to explain what she meant, or to be left in blissful ignorance.

'We're destitute, Rose,' her mother had said, mopping at her eyes with the piece of cloth, 'totally destitute! Your poor, dear father, God rest his soul, has left us with nothing but death duties and his gambling debts.'

Rose had stood there, not taking in fully her mother's words. Mrs Simpson was not prone to exaggeration and so Rose had known that it was right to fear the worst; it was not simply going to mean a few less treats; their very way of life was threatened.

She had been six when her father had gone off to fight in the Great War. Her recollections of him were somewhat hazy, but she had remembered that he had been a tall, strong mountain of a man, always laughing as he teased her mother while he stole a kiss, or bent and scooped the young Rose into his arms, the little girl giggling and wriggling as he lifted her up to sit on his shoulders, she all the while clinging on to his hair and his ears least she should fall. She had felt so high up, sitting there on his shoulders, peering down at the world beneath, that sometimes she had pretended that she was sitting astride an elephant like the pictures she had seen of people in India.

It had come as a shock when she found that he was gone. She could not understand why he would leave her, her mother telling her that he was a brave hero gone to fight for his country, had meant nothing to her. She had wanted him to be there with her. The years had passed and she had grown up. When he had returned she was no longer the little girl he remembered and he was no longer the big, strong, laughing man that she had idolised. She suspected later with hindsight and an adult's understanding, that they had both felt a little disappointed in one another and somehow cheated knowing that they could never get back those lost years.

From both Rose's and her mother's perspective, Mr Simpson had returned from the war a broken man. Physically he had been intact unlike so many other poor wretches who had returned with missing limbs and scarred faces, or not at all, and initially his mind had seemed undamaged. But it soon became clear by his brooding silences and inclination to be alone that he was a different man from the one who had left home. Rose's mother had explained to her that during the war her father had seen some terrible things that still haunted him and that, while he did not wish to talk about them, he was finding it difficult to forget. Her mother had clung on to the hope that in time things would change, and she would eventually get back a resemblance of the man that had gone away. Instead things had got worse as her husband had found it difficult to concentrate and keep a job and had sought solace instead in drink and gambling, the knowledge of which Mrs Simpson had tried in vain to keep from her daughter. Rose and her mother had both watched helplessly as, in equal measures, the family's money was squandered and Mr Simpson sunk into a rapid decline, his health deteriorating until, barely six years after he had returned from the front, he had died, and the full desperateness of the Simpsons' financial situation was revealed.

Rose's mother had gone to pieces and so it was the girl herself who was forced to be the practical one and find a solution to their financial crisis. It had not been easy. Mrs Simpson had initially refused to even contemplate giving up their servants or their home even though they had barely a penny to their name. Rose's suggestion that they take in paid lodgers was met with an outright refusal. It was only when faced with the stark ultimatum that they do so or lose everything, that Mrs Simpson had relented, but it had not been a success. Rose had chosen the lodgers carefully, a Mrs Partridge and her unmarried daughter; they were quite respectable and Rose had hoped that her mother might find some things in common with the older woman which would make the sharing of her home more palatable. But Mrs Simpson had not liked strangers living in their house; the loss of privacy and the giving up of the use of rooms had jarred with her; in addition she complained to her daughter that Mrs Partridge was inclined to be rather loud and too talkative, whereas Miss Partridge was painfully shy, barely uttering a word and was inclined to start when spoken to. The situation had become tense and uncomfortable for all parties, and it was something of a relief to both Mrs Simpson and Rose when the Partridges had left to live with some distant relations.

The Simpsons had been forced to sell their house. Mrs Simpson had cried bitterly and Rose had moped around the place touching doors and walls one last time, trying to commit the rooms to memory, knowing as she did so that she was saying good bye to more than just her childhood home. She could not help but dwell on "what ifs". What if her father had been killed in the war? What if he had returned the man that he had left, laughing and smiling and not felt compelled to turn to drink and gambling? Although she tried not to, Rose could not help resenting her father's behaviour, which had ruined both hers and her mother's future.

They had bought a much smaller house in a poorer part of town and had let go of Doris, who had sobbed uncontrollably at their reduced circumstances. Dobson had been the next casualty, although Rose's mother had fought to keep her and Dobson herself had seemed just as reluctant to leave.

'I'm that sad to go, Miss Rose,' she had said taking the girl aside. 'I've seen you grow up from a little babe to a fine young woman and I've been with your mother since the day she left her parents' home to marry your father. It breaks my heart it does, to think of you and your mother as you are now. If I could afford to, I'd stay on with you both and take no wages. Whatever are you going to do? You've absolutely no money as far as I can tell. Why, I don't think you've even got a brass farthing between you.'

'You're right, Mrs Dobson, things are looking awfully grim right now. Neither my mother nor I want to let you go, but we've simply got no other choice. Of course we'll provide you with a very good reference and if our circumstances ever change, I'll be sure to write to you. I'm going to leave it a day or two and then I'll break it to Mother that I'll have to get a job.'

In the end Mrs Simpson had been the first to get work. For the sake of her daughter, she had reluctantly pulled herself together, finally facing their situation. The thought of Rose financially supporting her, while she sat home alone in their mean little house doing nothing but dwelling on what had been, was abhorrent to her. Dressmaking had seemed the obvious answer for it was something she was both very fond of and good at; she could also do it in the privacy of her own home. At first she had approached some of her more affluent friends for work, or former friends as they had now become as their paths now seldom crossed. As time went on, word of mouth brought her more business although the work was often irregular and could not be relied upon to provide a living wage for them both. Almost as soon as her mother had embarked on her dressmaking business, Rose had gone out and sought work herself to supplement their income. Madame Renard's was the second shop she had approached. Five and a half years later, Lady Lavinia Sedgwick had entered the same establishment to satisfy an adolescent bet.

Chapter Five

I must remember this weekend, Rose thought, every tiny detail of it because there will never be another one like it, not for me. With that she sighed contentedly and settled back into the luxurious leather seats of the yellow Rolls Royce that Lady Withers had sent to collect them from the railway station. How strange it felt to be seated next to Lady Lavinia Sedgwick in a chauffeur driven car about to enjoy the weekend at a country house, the guest of the local landed gentry. She really must try and savour this moment, this wonderful feeling of excitement and anticipation and just a little apprehension.

Rose looked over at her friend and wondered if Lavinia had any idea how much this all meant to her. But she seemed totally oblivious, smiling and laughing at their recent exploits at Madame Renard's, how they had managed to convince a particularly odious customer to spend far more money on clothes than she had intended and mimicking the way Madame Renard spoke when she introduced Lavinia to her more up market customers. She caught Lavinia's eye and they both threw back their heads and giggled like a couple of school girls, each finding the other's laughter so infectious that they did not know if they would ever be able to stop. Rose, who initially had been very aware of the presence of the chauffeur up in front, idly wondered what he must think of them laughing as if their sides would burst. But she could not help it, and she soon gave up caring what he thought.

Indeed, to Rose, Lavinia suddenly looked very young and carefree, the lack of worries or responsibilities showing in her face as she suddenly whisked the red straw hat from her head and let the wind tug at her hair until it had come tumbling down around her shoulders, becoming a mess as stray wisps of hair blew in the wind around her face. Rose thought Lavinia suited the windswept look, which gave a warmth to her cold aristocratic beauty; in contrast, Rose had never felt so plain.

'We are going to have such a wonderful time, Rose,' Lavinia had assured her earnestly, grabbing hold of her hand. 'Of course, while I love Ashgrove absolutely to bits, I would have suggested that we go to Sedgwick Court, but it's too far away to go just for a weekend and besides there's my mother which is enough to put anyone off. She'd be quite impossible, you know. She wouldn't leave me alone for a moment trying to make me change my mind about the shop and she's such a snob. I'm afraid she'd be rather horrid to you. It's much better that we go to Aunt Connie's. You'll adore her, I know you will, because she has that effect on everyone, everyone simply worships her, even the servants. I can't think why really, because sometimes she comes out with the most outrageous things, you know says what everyone is really thinking but are too polite to actually say.' She became aware of the look on Rose's face which had been one of alarm. 'Oh, I've made her sound a bit intimidating and I didn't mean to at all. You'll absolutely love her. Do you know, when Ceddie and I were little, we used to pretend that Father had married Aunt Connie instead of Mother because it would have been absolutely magical if he had done, and I think it could have happened because from what I've heard, Connie and Daddy used to be sweethearts when they were young. But Aunt Connie married Uncle William instead and I must say he's an absolute sweetie too.'

Rose was suddenly aware that they had turned off the road. She looked up quickly at her surroundings and caught a first glimpse of Ashgrove House through the trees which lined the long drive along which she found they were driving, and which eventually led up to the house. Ashgrove House sat deep in its own land made up of gardens, including a croquet lawn, pasture land and woodland, the predominant trees in the latter being ash from where the house had derived its name. Level fields enclosed with fences or hedges gave way to steep banks down to the river and the house itself, made of red brick, dated from the late eighteenth century, although some later Victorian alterations had been made to it by a previous owner. It was three-storied and five-bayed, with a fine pillared entrance portico and roofs of slate from which protruded a number of ornate gothic chimney stacks. Rose caught her breath. Ashgrove House was more imposing and impressive than she had expected. When Lavinia had spoken of it, she had been almost dismissive. 'It's quite delightful, absolutely lovely,' she had assured her, 'but of course it's not a patch on Sedgwick.' To Rose, whose experience of such residences was admittedly limited, it looked very grand indeed. Its owners were clearly affluent as both the house and drive were in a good state of repair and the gardens, she was to discover later, were well-kept and tended by gardeners.

'The only bit of a downside,' Lavinia was saying, 'is that Edith will be here. She's a distant relative of ours, or something, although I don't think my mother likes her much as she's never been invited to stay at Sedgwick even though she and mother and Aunt Connie were all at school together as girls. The odd time I've seen her at Ashgrove, I've always found her deadly dull and depressing, although to be charitable she does have reason to be upset. It must have been awful for her, but it's all so long ago now and it isn't as if she was the only one to have been affected by the war.

And then, of course, there was that awful episode a couple of years back when she made an absolute fool of herself over poor Ceddie. She just wouldn't leave the poor boy alone. She threw herself at him and started shrieking that she'd never let him go again, that he was safe now. It was absolutely awful. Uncle William and old Stafford had to forcibly drag her away from Ceddie and all the time she was kicking and hitting out and wailing. Aunt Connie had to send for the doctor to give her a sedative. It was absolutely horrible, I'd never seen anyone behave like that before, you know, totally out of control ... Brewster, why ever have you stopped the car?' Lavinia looked about her suddenly aware that the Rolls Royce was stationary. 'Surely you don't mean us to walk the rest of the way up to the house carrying our own luggage!'

'No, no Lady Lavinia, of course not,' replied the chauffeur looking awkward. 'I'm just following orders. Her ladyship asked me to stop here, before I drove you up to the house. I'm not sure why, but she was most particular about it, she was; I'm sure she had her reasons.'

They waited, Lavinia sitting upright in her seat gazing straight ahead of her and looking distinctly put out, Rose, slightly nervous and self-conscious, wondering what to expect. The chauffeur, Brewster, busied himself fiddling first with his steering wheel, then with the wing mirror and then with his gloves until it seemed to Rose that they had sat there for some time. She was beginning to feel fidgety herself and, from out of the corner of her eye, she could tell that Lavinia was getting more and more irritated.

'This is ridiculous, Brewster. Surely you don't expect us to wait here forever. Just...'

'Psst!'

'Good gracious whatever *is* that noise, and where's it coming from?' Lavinia demanded, looking all about her wildly, before climbing out of the car quickly to have a better look around. Brewster, taken unawares by the quickness of Lavinia's actions, scrambled out of the car after her to open the door for Rose. Following Lavinia's example, Rose looked about her but both girls had trouble locating from where exactly the sound had come.

'Psst! Over here.' From out of the trees that lined the drive up to Ashgrove House emerged a woman of over fifty, her hair pulled back in a bun that looked as if it was coming slightly undone and which was squashed under a wide brimmed straw hat decorated with artificial fruit, the red cherries of which were gleaming in the mid-morning sun. She wore a calf length beige skirt and white cotton blouse over which at her throat was tied haphazardly a flower-patterned silk scarf. The overall effect was one of dishevelment and that, coupled with the fact that the woman was wearing gardening gloves and carrying a pair of secateurs in her right hand, led Rose to believe that she must be some kind of gardener.

'Connie!' Lavinia rushed over to her and embraced her warmly. 'Whatever are you doing, Aunt, lurking in the shadows and making poor Brewster stop the car for secret assignations? And what on earth are you dressed up in this get up for, is it your gardener's day off?'

'My dear, I wanted to catch you before you arrived at the house and pretending to have to prune the roses gave me the excuse I needed. I slipped out of the rose garden, and came around the house and have been hiding behind this tree for the last twenty minutes or so. If only I'd known that the train was going to be late. Either that or Brewster was driving far too slowly. If only William would allow me to take the wheel, I'm sure you'd have got here much quicker.'

'I can't quite believe you've been waiting here for us that long, Aunt Connie. We've been stopped here an age, I was beginning to get frightfully cross with poor Brewster but....'

'That's because I got rather distracted by a red admiral butterfly that I happened to spot, haven't seen one for ages, just usually see those boring cabbage white ones and so I forgot to listen out for the car, but please don't interrupt my dear, we must be quick in case we're caught. What I wanted to tell you, warn you really, is that your mother's here. She invited herself for the weekend. Well, actually she didn't even do that. Just got her butler to ring up Stafford and tell him she was coming, she and your father, although how on earth she managed to persuade him to leave his library, I can't imagine. Anyway, they arrived not long after breakfast. They must have set off at the crack of dawn, either that or they set out yesterday and broke the journey somewhere last night.

'Somehow she's got wind that you'd be down at Ashgrove this weekend and she wanted to catch you as soon as you arrived. I think she wants to have a word with you about this working in a shop business and seeing as you rarely go home ...' Lady Withers looked at her niece somewhat reproachfully as if she held her responsible for the arrival of her unwelcome guest '... she thought she'd better come down here if she wanted to catch you.'

'Oh, but this is awful,' cried Lavinia and Rose thought that for once her friend may not be exaggerating, for she had never seen her looking so genuinely upset. 'Oh, she'll spoil everything. She won't leave me alone for a minute, she'll badger me, going on and on at me until she has managed to get me to promise not to return to Madame Renard's. Well, I shan't. I won't let her get her own way, I won't, not this time.' Rose began to feel anxious and just a little disappointed. Perhaps it was not going to be such a wonderful weekend after all.

'That's the spirit, my dear,' Lady Withers was saying, looking impressed. 'This working in a shop lark seems to have toughened you up a bit. But I thought it only fair to give you the heads up, so to speak. Fore-warned is fore-armed as they say.' And with that she attempted to swat at a wasp with her secateurs.

Up close Rose could see that, although now a little faded and wrinkled, when she had been young Lavinia's aunt must have been a beautiful woman. There was still something proud and majestic about the way that she carried herself that showed breeding; at the same time there was something rather fragile about her, that Rose was sure brought out the protective instinct in men, which she felt was the desired effect and wondered idly how much of this sense of fragility had been deliberately cultivated by Lady Withers.

'It must have been Ceddie. He must have let it slip. Oh, the silly boy, I should never have told him we were coming to Ashgrove this weekend.'

'Quite probably, my dear, especially as Cedric's wired to say that he's coming down too, although he hasn't arrived yet and we're not quite sure when to expect him, you know how vague young men can be these days. I'm sure that you'll be delighted to see *him*, of course; it will be nice for you two young things to have someone else young about the place rather than having to make do with us old things, but it does make things all a little awkward with Edith coming down. I didn't want to put her off, you know how careful you've got to be with poor Edith, she does feel things so dreadfully being so highly strung and sensitive, what with everything that's happened, but it's going to be all rather awkward. I just hope that we don't have a repeat of last time. You remember how awful it was, absolutely dreadful and made more so because one just didn't know what to do. If it hadn't been for dear William and Stafford, I'm not sure what we would have done. I mean, it was so unexpected, one couldn't possibly have foreseen that it was going to happen. I'm just worried that Edith will give a repeat performance in front of your mother, oh, I can't even bear to think about it. Marjorie won't be at all understanding. She's likely to give poor Edith a piece of her mind and then the poor woman's bound to go all to pieces.'

'Oh, Aunt Connie, what a weekend it'll be. But at least Ceddie will be down. As well as being good to see him, at least if he's here I will have a bit of peace from Mother. She'll have to divide her time between lecturing me and talking to Ceddie. You know he's always been her blue-eyed boy while I've been rather a disappointment to her. She won't pass up a chance to find out how he's getting on at Oxford, because he goes home to Sedgwick almost as infrequently as I do. In fact, I think he only goes back to ask Daddy for money to pay his debts, oh what frightful and ungrateful children we are. Why … whatever is the matter, Rose? You don't look quite right at all, your face is all pink. Was it the journey? I have to say it has made one feel frightfully hot.'

'I'm fine, Lavinia, really I am,' Rose said trying to pull herself together, although she did not feel at all fine. If truth be told, she was beginning to feel quite queasy about the whole weekend. It was bad enough that Lady Belvedere was going to be there and likely to put a dampener on proceedings, but for Viscount Sedgwick to be there as well. Lavinia had always spoken warmly of her younger brother and she was sure he would prove delightful, but from Rose's point of view it changed the weekend completely. It was one thing to pass the weekend at Ashgrove with Lavinia's delightfully eccentric old aunt and her old school friend, but quite another to find that a young and, from what Rose could tell from the society pages, extremely attractive and eligible member of the aristocracy was also going to be present. Instinctively her thoughts went to her wardrobe. She thought of her sensible tweed suit, her faithful silk velvet evening dress and her mother's pearls; she should have been more adventurous with her clothes because, especially compared with Lavinia, she was likely to look distinctly dowdy.

Lady Withers assured them that she would make her own way back to the house through the gardens and asked that they give her ten minutes' start before they set off along the drive in the car so that she was there to greet them. Rose and Lavinia got back into the car, the doors opened for them by the diligent Brewster. Rose could tell at once that her friend was in an agitated state.

'Oh, Rose,' said Lavinia clasping her friend's hand excitedly, 'it's going to be a bore, of course, having Mother here and you mustn't mind a thing she says to you because I'm afraid she's bound not to like you at all, what with you working in the shop with me, but it's so wonderful that Ceddie is going to be down. You'll find him great fun and think him awfully nice, although he can be rather an annoying little brother at times. But that's not why I'm excited, Rose. I'm excited because of who he may bring with him.'

'He'll be bringing down someone else with him? But Lady Withers didn't say anything about there being another guest,' Rose said, anxiously.

'Well, I doubt whether she knows. Ceddie can be awfully vague and irritating at times. He'll think nothing of bringing down a friend with him without asking Uncle William and Aunt Connie first. And he needn't really, because they're always delighted to see us and they have got loads of servants and bedrooms and things, so it's not as if they'd be caused any inconvenience although, of course, they weren't to know that my parents were coming down, and if Mother doesn't bring her own lady's maid with her and Daddy his own valet I suppose there might be ....'

'Lavinia,' Rose interrupted, 'who do you think your brother will be bringing down with him?'

'Why, Hugh, Marquis Sneddon, of course. He's the only surviving son of the Duke of Haywater and he's recently become a great friend of Ceddie's, they're quite inseparable. He's quite a few years older than Ceddie, but still quite young, about twenty-eight or nine, I think. Mother will be delighted because she's quite set her sights on him for me. There aren't that many eligible heirs to a dukedom around these days of the right age, I can tell you.

Because of the war and everything, they're either much too old or still children, and mother doesn't really want me to marry below a marquis although, at a push, I think she'd settle for an earl, like Daddy. But she's got her heart set on my being a duchess. Normally I don't fall in with her wishes, as you know, but Hugh is exceedingly handsome, all dark and brooding, you know the type. He'll quite take your breath away, Rose.'

It was clear to Rose then that the weekend was likely to prove more eventful than she had been expecting. While she was beginning to approach it with a feeling of trepidation, she was excited too. It never occurred to her for one minute that the mix of people that the weekend was throwing haphazardly together, might result in murder.

Chapter Six

The front door was opened to Rose and Lavinia by Stafford who, to Rose's mind, seemed to embody respectability and have every attribute that a good butler should. He was tall and thin and suitably deferential, but he also had a certain authoritative air about him as if one could expect him to be knowledgeable on every matter of importance. She could well imagine that a person like Lady Withers would defer to him on decisions affecting the smooth running of the house. Lavinia seemed delighted to see Stafford and Rose thought that she could detect the shadow of a smile cross his face, as he bowed at them slightly. She remembered what Lavinia had told her in preparation for her visit, about herself and Cedric almost growing up at Ashgrove, because they had visited so often in their childhood, and how Stafford had been with Sir William since a young man. She noticed that Stafford's bow had encompassed them both and, when he looked up, Rose was relieved not to detect in his eye any sign that he thought her beneath his respect or considered her presence there inappropriate, either as a friend of Lady Lavinia's or as a guest at Ashgrove.

Behind them Brewster was unloading their luggage and a footman dressed in tailored livery, who Rose found out later was called Albert, sprang forward to take it up to their rooms.

'I must apologise, Lady Lavinia, that neither Sir William nor her ladyship is here to greet you. Her ladyship was in the rose garden, but unfortunately we have been unable to locate her exact whereabouts and Sir William is engaged on an important telephone call in his study, but will be with you in a moment.'

'Don't worry Stafford, you're here to greet us and we passed Aunt Connie on the drive. She'll be here in a moment,' Lavinia assured him with an air of confidence that showed that she felt very much at home at Ashgrove. 'And it isn't as if I don't know the way. This is Miss Simpson, a very good friend of mine, she works in the shop with me, don't you know, but she is ever so much better at it than I am. Which rooms has Mrs Palmer given us? Do say it's the Snug and the Silk Room.'

'It is indeed, Lady Lavinia; Mrs Palmer knows how you love the Silk Room and she thought you'd like Miss Simpson in the room next to you.'

Rose looked around her trying to take it all in. The ground floor of Ashgrove House consisted, as far as the residents and guests were concerned, of a large square hall, drawing room, dining room, library, study and most conveniently a lavatory. What lay beyond the green baize door, the domain of the servants: the long corridor, which led eventually to a back door; the rooms opening off the corridor which included the servants' hall, the housekeeper's parlour, a pantry, a large kitchen, a scullery, the service door to the dining room, the male servants' bedrooms, a back staircase of linoleum steps off the corridor which finally led up to the female servants' bedrooms way up in the attic and the staircase leading down to the cellar, boot room and coal cellar, she was not aware of on her arrival, although she was to become unexpectedly acquainted with a few of these rooms during the course of her stay. At the moment, however, she was taking in the rather grand, old, highly polished wooden staircase leading off from the hall to the first floor and admiring the oil paintings on the wall encased by heavy, ornate gilt gold frames.

'Well, Stafford, I understand the old battle axe is here?'

'I beg your pardon, Lady Lavinia?' The butler stared looking ever so slightly taken aback.

'My mother, Stafford, I understand she has invited herself down for a visit.'

'Ah, indeed, Lady Lavinia, the countess is here and I gather most keen to see you.'

'Well, I'm not at all keen to see her. I suppose it's too much to hope for that she's having a lie down after her journey, so that we can just sneak in?'

'Indeed, m'lady, Lady Belvedere was most anxious to see you as soon as you arrived and is waiting for you in the drawing room.'

'Oh, fiddlesticks! Well, I suppose we had better get it over with. Rose, you mustn't let her intimidate you. She'll try and talk down to you, as if you were one of her servants. You mustn't stand for it. Pretend she's one of those awkward customers that we get in the shop sometimes; you're ever so good at knowing how to handle them.'

Rose took a deep breath and followed Lavinia into the drawing room.

Perhaps not surprisingly, given Sir William's and Lady Withers' position, it was the grand décor of the room, rather than the rather matronly figure of a woman perched very upright on a striped patterned regency chair, that initially caught Rose's attention. The drawing room, with its almost double height ceiling, plasterwork frieze over the doorway and fine marble fireplace framed by a large, highly ornate gilt mantle mirror, was papered in a duck egg coloured damask wallpaper. The room was dual aspect with two sets of double French windows, each opening out onto a stone terrace which, as far as Rose could tell, went all the way around the house. Heavy gold brocade silk curtains, complete with swags, framed the French windows. The room itself contained a selection of richly upholstered armchairs and sofas in raw silk or velvet. Highly polished mahogany occasional tables were scattered around the room, on which were displayed a selection of photographs in silver frames and bunches of freshly cut roses and other in season flowers from the grounds in lead crystal vases. Paintings by one or two of the lesser known masters decorated the walls; the overall feel of the room was of elegance and understated opulence.

It was only when Rose had fully taken in the splendour of her surroundings that she focused her attention on the Countess of Belvedere. Lavinia had advanced forward to greet her mother and while Lady Belvedere was berating her daughter, Rose had the opportunity to take in the countess's appearance, relatively unobserved. Lavinia had spoken often of her mother having been considered a great beauty in her youth, but in Rose's view there was little evidence of this now. She could see that there was a faint family resemblance between Lady Belvedere and her sister in that they had the same colour of very dark brown, almost black, hair which had mostly turned to a shade of iron grey, but whereas Lady Withers was slender and almost doll like in physique, Lady Belvedere was stout with a plump face and sagging jaw line. Even had she remained silent, Rose could have told by the sour expression on her face that her nature was cold and spiteful; clearly there did not seem much love lost between mother and daughter as Lavinia approached her cautiously, as if anticipating a trap and Lady Belvedere in turn looked at her with annoyance. To Rose's eye, Lady Belvedere was dressed in a fashion more associated with the Edwardian era with her lace cuffs and high-necked collar, complete with straw hat decorated with ribbons and feathers. In her right hand she clutched a cane although it was not to aid her in walking, for Rose was to find that she was surprisingly agile and quick for a woman of her age and build, but rather she used her cane for emphasis by tapping it on the ground to make her point or show her disapproval.

'Mother, how are you?' Lavinia had crossed the room to bend and kiss her mother's cheek as the woman in question remained sitting. 'I did not expect to see you here, what made you decide to come and stay with Aunt Connie this weekend of all weekends?'

'Obviously you did not expect to see me otherwise you would have changed your arrangements, and my intention in coming here was to see you, as well you could have guessed.'

Rose hovered by the door somewhat taken aback by the exchange between the two women. Clearly there was to be no pretence by either that they were particularly pleased to see the other. Lavinia, Rose noticed, was agitated, first looking down at her shoes to avoid her mother's eye, then glancing around the room as if seeking salvation, and then fiddling with her enamelled mesh bag, obviously wanting to be anywhere than where she was.

'Mother, if you've come here to –.'

'Quiet, Lavinia; now you listen to me.' Lady Belvedere tapped her cane on the floor for emphasis and the sound was clearly audible throughout the room, notwithstanding the rug. 'This nonsense has gone on for quite long enough. I want you to stop it now. You have had five seasons as a debutante and you are still to find a suitable husband. How are you to marry a man of equal, if not senior, rank to your father if you go about working in a dress shop? You know I have my heart set on your becoming a duchess or a marchioness. What man of title will be interested in marrying you now? You must put these ridiculous, childish games aside and act like a young lady. Have you any idea of the ridicule you have opened us all up to as a family with your antics? Why, even Mrs Booth had the audacity to tell me that it would be quite unthinkable for anyone in her circle to serve in a shop, as if somehow she was above me because my daughter did just that; the very cheek of the woman!'

'I'm sorry, mother, but I –.'

'Don't interrupt, Lavinia, or try to make excuses for your behaviour. It all stops now, do you hear me? And who is this *person loitering by the door* who you have failed to introduce to me? I assume it's one of your fellow shop girls?'

41

'Yes, yes, oh, Rose ….*Rose*, I'm sorry I forgot...' Lavinia, in a clearly distracted state, turned and beckoned Rose to come over and be introduced to her mother. Rose wondered why the countess had even enquired after her, because the way she was speaking to her daughter clearly indicated that Lady Belvedere considered the two of them alone, or as good as alone, in that Rose was somehow invisible or not worthy of consideration. This impression was not altered when Rose walked over and Lady Belvedere looked her up and down with a look of barely disguised contempt. The countess, with a very slight tilt of her head, gave her the briefest of acknowledgments, so brief in fact that Rose half wondered whether she had imagined it.

What would have happened then, whether Lady Belvedere would have dismissed her or ignored her completely so that she could continue to berate Lavinia, Rose was not to know because at that moment the door opened and a middle-aged man in a tweed suit sporting a trim moustache walked in. There was something very self-assured about the way that he entered the room, a quiet self confidence that revealed him to be the owner of the house. More importantly, there was a jovial, good humoured air about him that had the effect of making Lady Belvedere pause and hesitate as if, for the first time, she was suddenly aware that she had an audience and that admonishing her daughter in front of it might not be entirely appropriate.

'Uncle William!' Lavinia ran over to the man and hugged him warmly and Rose wondered how Lady Belvedere must feel to see her daughter look so pleased to see her sister's husband and yet so disappointed to see her own mother. Looking over at her, it was hard to tell what the woman was thinking because the sour look on her face, which appeared to be her usual expression, remained intact. Despite the breath of fresh air that Sir William had brought with him into the room, Rose was aware of a certain coldness that radiated from Lady Belvedere which made her shiver. For the first time, she felt afraid, but of course that was ridiculous, for there was nothing to be afraid of. It was true that Lady Belvedere's stay at Ashgrove was likely to put a bit of a dampener on the weekend, but that was all. Rose still intended to enjoy herself and Sir William seemed most welcoming. As if on cue, Sir William disentangled himself from his wife's niece and introduced himself.

'How do you do, Miss Simpson? You are most welcome. Lavinia has told us all about you. You must forgive me for not being here to welcome you when you arrived. I had a few important telephone calls to make, I'm afraid, which just wouldn't keep. I can't think where my wife's got to. It's not like her not to be here to greet our guests. I say, Marjorie, is anything wrong?'

'William, entertain Miss Simpson, will you. I'd like to have a private word with my daughter.'

'Oh, Mother, not now, surely. We want to go and freshen up before lunch, and I want to show Rose her room.'

'Better get a move on girls, Stafford will be in here shortly with the sherry.' Sir William watched as Lavinia and Rose made their escape. 'Don't worry so, Marjorie, you'll have ample time to talk to Lavinia after lunch. We're not expecting Cedric until mid-afternoon.'

'Ah, Cedric, at least it will be a joy to see him, although I fear he is rather neglecting his studies. I suppose it's what young men do nowadays, or perhaps they always did?' Lady Belvedere, still seated, looked about the room. 'Where *is* Constance, William? She barely stopped to say hello to me when we arrived before she disappeared out through that window mumbling something about having to prune the roses. Stuff and nonsense! Since when has Constance known anything about gardening, I ask you. You'd better hope that that head gardener fellow of yours doesn't catch her chopping bits off his rose bushes, they can be awfully possessive about their gardens and Constance is bound to make an awful mess of the pruning.'

The two girls ran into the hall and up the stairs giggling, almost colliding as they did so with one of the housemaids, who had emerged from a bedroom carrying fresh linen. On the first floor, in addition to Lady Withers' morning room and the linen room, there were six principal bedrooms and dressing rooms and two bathrooms and lavatories overlooking the hall. Lavinia did not stop on this floor, however, but continued up to the second floor where there were a further six secondary bedrooms, one of which had formerly been a nursery and another a schoolroom. Two rooms, which had also previously had other uses had been made into a small bathroom and lavatory.

'This is your room, Rose,' said Lavinia stopping at the door to one of the bedrooms, 'it's called the Snug, because I'm afraid it's rather small, but it does have the advantage of being next to mine. My room's called the Silk Room and I always stay in it when I visit, even though normally there's plenty of room for me to have one of the bedrooms on the first floor if I wanted, but I love having a floor to myself and there's a great view of the gardens. 'Hopefully we won't be bothered too much by my mother. She and Daddy are bound to have been given rooms on the first floor next to Uncle William's and Aunt Constance's. I expect that they'll put Cedric and Lord Sneddon on that floor too; the bedrooms are far grander than the ones on this floor and they've all got dressing rooms.'

Rose was surprised to find that not only had her suitcase been brought up to her room, but it had also been unpacked and her clothes hung up in the wardrobe, and her toiletries laid out on the dressing table. Lavinia had followed her into her bedroom and had opened her wardrobe and was leafing through her clothes with interest. Lavinia paused when she came to Rose's black, silk velvet evening dress and scrutinised it; Rose had wondered at the time whether her friend considered it too plain, later she thought Lavinia had just been relieved that it had not outshone her outfit.

'Of course, it's an awful bore Mother being here,' Lavinia said finally, perching on Rose's bed. But I'm jolly well going to make Cedric keep her occupied. I don't know how he could have been so stupid as to let her know that we'd be coming to Ashgrove this weekend. He must have known what she'd do.'

'I don't think she likes me very much,' Rose sighed and sat down on the bed beside her friend.

'My mother doesn't like anyone very much,' admitted Lavinia with surprising conviction, 'not even me, her own daughter. You mustn't take it personally, Rose. I would be far more concerned if she liked you. Why on earth my father ever married her, I can't imagine, although she was very beautiful when she was young, and rich, of course, both her and Constance. But Daddy and she have absolutely nothing in common. They hardly see anything of each other, he's always shut up in his library with his books or in his study tied up with estate affairs and my mother's busy with her fund-raising efforts and lecturing our poor vicar on how he should be dealing with the poor, most of whom she thinks are quite undeserving. If only Daddy had married Aunt Connie instead. I'm sure she wouldn't have minded a bit about me working in a shop for a bet, she would have seen it as a bit of a lark.'

'You're fond of your father though, aren't you, Lavinia?' Rose, who adored her own mother, could not bear the idea that Lavinia should not be fond of at least one of her parents.

'Daddy's an absolute sweetie, what Cedric and I see of him anyway, but that's not much as he always shuts himself away. I think he's a bit of a recluse. How on earth my mother managed to persuade him to come down to Ashgrove, I can't imagine. Oh, if only he wouldn't let my mother walk all over him all the time, if only he'd stand up to her once in a while. I'm sure if he did, she'd be so much more bearable, she's too used to getting her own way.'

Rose suppressed a grin; the same could be said of her friend.

'Oh, I suppose we can't put it off any longer, we'd better go down. Hopefully Aunt Connie will be there and Daddy, of course. I'd like you to meet him.'

'Oh, there you are at last, Constance. Wherever have you been, you can't have spent all that time dead heading roses,' Lady Belvedere sounded quite annoyed. 'And do tell me you're going to change. It really would be too much if you come to luncheon dressed liked that.'

'Naturally I'm going to change,' retorted Lady Withers, looking quite red in the face, whether as a result of her efforts in the garden or because she was put out by her sister's comments, it was hard to tell. 'But may I remind you, Marjorie, that this is my house and if I choose to lunch in my gardening clothes, then I will.'

'Now, now,' said Sir William trying to smooth things over. 'Stafford will be in here any minute with the sherry and he tells me that Mrs Palmer has put on a very good spread for lunch, quite excelled herself, I believe.'

'Well, that wouldn't be difficult,' replied Lady Belvedere, 'her cooking's not up to much at the best of times. If she's excelled herself this time, it will just mean that it's just about acceptable, certainly nothing to write home about.'

Unfortunately, while Lady Withers just stood there gaping in amazement and Sir William chose to ignore this slight on his cook's culinary skills, his butler chose this very moment to enter the room; although his face remained as impassive as ever, the faintest of twitches revealed to Sir William that he had heard Lady Belvedere's unkind remark and Stafford, he knew, was not a man to take insults to the staff lying down.

Lunch was something of an uncomfortable affair for Rose as she was faced with a vast array of cutlery and courses. Rather to her surprise, she noticed that the women, in particular, tended to eat only small amounts of each course and she followed suit, determined not to look out of place. She wondered what happened to the food that was left on the plates, whether it was thrown away, or resurfaced in the servants' meals or even in later dishes for the household. Fortunately, she had found herself next to the kindly Sir William who asked, with what appeared to be genuine interest, after her work in the dress shop. He in turn gave her a potted history of Ashgrove House and also described the grounds. Lady Belvedere, she was relieved to see, was seated at the other end of the table so Rose was subjected only to the odd contemptuous look from the countess, who clearly disapproved of her presence in the house. Lavinia, who was seated next to her mother and so was suffering the full force of her conversation, was looking distinctly irritated and miserable in equal amounts, and trying with much endeavour to ignore what Lady Belvedere was saying, by concentrating her attention on playing restlessly with her napkin.

The Earl of Belvedere had joined the party very late, just as they were about to receive their first course. This in itself did not seem to surprise anyone other than Rose. It appeared that Stafford had been sent to prise Lord Belvedere out of the library and he had entered the dining room looking slightly disorientated, as if his mind had been left behind in the books. He had seemed surprised to see his daughter, as if he had forgotten that she would be there, but equally he looked pleased in a quiet, reserved manner. Following introductions, he had acknowledged Rose with a smile and Rose had felt kindly towards him, perhaps more so than was strictly warranted, because of the relief that she felt at his appearing to be nothing like his wife. In appearance, he was very similar to Sir William, in that he had similar colouring, was about the same age with the same style trim moustache and like Sir William was wearing a tweed suit. It was only after the meal, when the two men had risen, that Rose saw that the earl was taller than Sir William by a head or so, and somewhat slighter in build.

After lunch, it appeared that Sir William had important correspondence to deal with in his study and that Lord Belvedere was keen to return to his books. Lady Withers made a half-hearted attempt to engage all the women in conversation, but failed spectacularly as Lady Belvedere cut her dead with a glance and demanded the use of her morning room for half an hour or so in order that she could continue her one-sided conversation with her daughter. Lavinia initially looked minded to refuse to go with her mother, but then seemed to think better of it, as if it was best to get it over and done with as soon as possible so that she could get on with enjoying the weekend. She gave Rose a resigned look and followed her mother out of the room.

'My sister really is too bad,' said Lady Withers, looking after the retreating figures, 'if only she'd leave poor Lavinia alone and stop trying to dictate to her all the time. Then the poor girl wouldn't feel so obliged to constantly rebel. I do so feel for Lavinia. William and I, not having been blessed with children of our own, have always rather thought of Lavinia and Cedric as our son and daughter, rather than as our niece and nephew. Oh, I was so hoping that we'd all have a nice quiet weekend together. We do so like meeting Lavinia's friends, but I'm afraid my sister does have a tendency to spoil things. She was just the same when we were children, always bossing everyone around, determined to get her own way.'

'I'm sure we'll have a wonderful time, Lady Withers,' replied Rose feeling rather awkward that Lady Withers had spoken to her so frankly. 'Sir William was just telling me over luncheon all about your lovely gardens. It would be so wonderful to see them, if you don't mind, of course. It's so nice to be out of London and such a wonderful sunny day.'

'Of course, my dear, I don't suppose you're used to seeing such things,' replied Lady Withers, looking relieved and proceeding out of one of the French windows. 'I expect that you live in a ghastly little house with absolutely no garden to speak of. If we just go along the terrace here we'll get to the rose garden and then I'll take you to see the other gardens. They are rather beautiful I can tell you, although, of course, I know absolutely nothing about flowers or gardening really. We're so fortunate to still have Bridges; you won't believe how many families around here have lost their gardeners. They went off to war and never came back, or those who did decided that domestic service was beneath them. Yes, I suppose we are lucky, really, what with having Bridges and Stafford and Mrs Palmer. Perhaps it's going to be all right after all. Perhaps I was wrong when I thought that something dreadful was bound to happen this weekend.'

Chapter Seven

'It's no use, Mother, I'm not going to –,' began Lavinia, as she followed Lady Belvedere into Lady Withers' morning room and closed the door behind her.

'Oh, do be quiet, Lavinia,' said her mother impatiently, turning around and giving her daughter such a glare that the words froze on Lavinia's tongue, and she was forced instead to give her mother her full attention. 'I am tired of this. In my day girls were always obedient to their parents' wishes. Nowadays young people seem to think that they know best; in that, I can tell you, they are very much mistaken. You are not going to go back to that awful little dress shop and that is that; there is no discussion to be had on the matter. If necessary, I'll see to it that your father stops your monthly allowance and that you remain a virtual prisoner at Sedgwick until you learn some sense and do as you are told.'

'Father would never allow –'

'Oh, don't talk nonsense, Lavinia, you know full well that your father will do exactly as I say. We both want to do what is best for you even if you yourself are quite determined to ruin all your chances. But enough of this, we'll talk about all this shop nonsense later. What I really want to talk to you about now concerns a chance to redeem yourself.'

'What do you mean, Mother?' Lavinia found that she was curious despite herself.

'Constance tells me that Cedric is expected down this weekend. And if he comes down, it's highly likely that he'll bring Lord Sneddon with him. You must make the most of this opportunity, Lavinia, while their friendship is still strong. When else are you going to find yourself the only eligible woman at a house party where the heir to a dukedom just happens to be present? You know as well as I do, that even for a woman like you with every privilege and beauty, the only way to true freedom is through an advantageous marriage. If you continue to behave in the way you have been, shut away in your dress shop and attracting all sorts of the very wrong kinds of people, you will deter any appropriate suitors. This weekend you will act demurely and do everything in your power to secure Lord Sneddon's affections. It can't be a hardship for you after all. Why, there must be a hundred aristocratic young ladies who would give anything to be in just such a position. And besides, Lord Sneddon has the additional benefits of being young and handsome. What more can you ask for, Lavinia? Do not disappoint me.'

'Very well, Mother,' said Lavinia, secretly very pleased that for once her mother's wishes mirrored her own. For, ever since she realised Lord Sneddon might be joining them, she had been busy planning how to secure the marquis's affections in the snatched moments between being lectured to by her mother and entertaining Rose.

'It is a pity that you brought that girl with you,' Lady Belvedere was saying, 'she's bound to be an unnecessary inconvenience and an absolute embarrassment; her sort of women always are, they always think they are above themselves but they don't know how to behave in our sort of company. Did you see the way she simply stared at the dishes we had for luncheon? She's probably never seen so much food, for one moment I thought that she was going to try and eat it all and then lick the plates clean!'

'You're being very unfair, Mother,' replied Lavinia, suddenly feeling defensive of her friend, not least because she was feeling rather guilty having been half wishing herself that she had left Rose in London this weekend so that she could give Lord Sneddon her undivided attention. 'She knows exactly how to behave in company, or I wouldn't have brought her with me. Her family has simply fallen on hard times, that's all. Why, if her father was still alive, she wouldn't be forced to go out to work at all.'

'Even so, she's hardly from our class. However, it could prove to be a blessing in disguise,' admitted Lady Belvedere rather grudgingly. Seeing the bewildered expression on her daughter's face, she went on to explain. 'Well, fortunately she is a very plain creature which by comparison will only help to accentuate your looks. And I expect, if her present attire is anything to go by, that her clothes will be cheap and a little vulgar. What a pity you didn't know Lord Sneddon was going to be here and then you might have packed some of your finest gowns and diamonds.'

'Well, actually, I did, Mother', admitted Lavinia rather sheepishly. 'I wanted to impress Rose; she's only seen me in those awful shop clothes.'

'Excellent, that's my girl,' said Lady Belvedere grinning with obvious delight; it was not a pretty sight.

'It's a pity Edith is going to be here,' said Lavinia more to herself than to her mother, 'although I suppose Aunt Connie will keep her occupied. She'll probably wander about in the gardens daydreaming and go to bed early, thank goodness, her sort always do. I just hope that she doesn't behave all silly over Cedric again, it was too embarrassing last time. If you had been there, Mother, you'd have been absolutely horrified.'

'Edith?' said Lady Belvedere sharply. 'Edith Settle, that was? Edith Settle is coming to Ashgrove *this* weekend?'

'Yes, but she's Edith Torrington now, Mother. I think she married a bank manager or someone like that. She quite often comes to stay with Aunt Connie. I think Aunt feels sorry for her, you know, after everything that's happened to her. It is rather sad, after all. I suppose we should be charitable....'

'Edith is coming *here*?' Lady Belvedere repeated the question slowly to herself and seemed suddenly oblivious to her daughter's presence.

Lavinia eyed her curiously, somewhat alarmed, for she was not used to seeing her mother behave in such a way.

'What is it, Mother? I know it'll be a bit awkward and we'd both rather she'd not be here. But she is an old friend of Aunt Connie's and Aunt's bound to occupy her and keep her away from Cedric. I bet Constance's as worried as we are that there might be a repeat performance of Edith's behaviour the last time she laid eyes on Cedric. I'm sure she'll do everything in her power to prevent it from happening again. She's probably roped in poor old Stafford and Uncle William –.'

'Be quiet, child, let me think,' snapped Lady Belvedere.

'What about, Mother? I'm sure everything will be all right. I know Aunt Connie is a bit absentminded and flaps around a bit, but I expect between her and Uncle William they have got everything sorted out. I know you've never liked Edith very much and I have always wondered why, what with you all being at school together when you were young and everything.'

'What makes you think I don't like Edith, Lavinia?' the countess said sharply, eyeing her daughter suspiciously, as if she thought she might have an ulterior motive for saying what she had done.

'Well, I don't know exactly, I just, well, assumed you didn't, Mother,' replied Lavinia, beginning to feel uncomfortable under her mother's unflinching gaze. 'I mean you never speak of her, or ask her to stay, even though she is some sort of distant relative of ours and quite poor in comparison to us. Why else would she have married a bank manager of all people?'

'You're right, Lavinia,' said her mother, noticeably relaxing a little. 'I didn't like her very much when we were children. Her family hardly had two pennies to rub together and yet she was always going about giving herself airs and graces and saying as how we were all related and so must be friends. You know what Constance is like. She was totally taken in by her. I think she felt rather sorry for her even then, even before … but I could see right through her, I can tell you, I knew exactly the type of person she was and what she was after right from the start.'

'And what was that, Mother?'

'What?' Lady Belvedere looked up quite startled.

'What did she want? What was she after?'

'Oh … um, well nothing, nothing important anyway,' replied the countess hurriedly and she started to change the subject, reprimanding Lavinia again for working in the dress shop and bringing ridicule on her family. But her reactions had not been quick enough, for Lavinia had caught a look on her mother's face, and although it had been there very briefly, seconds at most, she recognised it for what it was. It was a look that she had rarely, if ever, seen before on her mother's face. And as she tried to take in its significance, for she was both shocked and surprised in equal measure, she was sure of one thing. The look she had caught on her mother's face, brief and fleeting though it had been, had been one of fear.

'Well, Miss Crimms, do we know what the situation is with regards to our guest's dress?' enquired Stafford accosting the lady's maid once the dishes and the remains of food had been cleared away from the dining room, and the presence there of the butler and the footman was no longer required. 'Has Spencer had time to unpack the luggage and go through Miss Simpson's wardrobe?'

'Indeed she has, Mr Stafford, and I made sure that I was on hand to look through Miss Simpson's clothes with her myself. Martha, as I'm sure you're already aware, Mr Stafford, is going to have to act as lady's maid to both Lady Lavinia and Miss Simpson on top of her usual duties as upper housemaid; I myself am going to have my hands full, I can tell you, standing in for Lady Belvedere's lady's maid. Why the countess couldn't bring her own lady's maid with her, I can't imagine.'

'I'm sure you'll manage very well, Miss Crimms, although I know Lady Belvedere can be very exacting. It's probably just as well that none of the guests have brought their servants with them, as there may have been a shortage of accommodation and certainly it would have been very cramped in the servants' hall, to say nothing of all the additional cooking the kitchen and scullery maids would have been required to do on top of helping Mrs Palmer prepare the dishes for the household. It's unlikely Lord Sedgwick will bring his valet with him, or Lord Sneddon, if he accompanies him; Albert will have to double up as valet to both the young lords and Briggs will have to valet for Lord Belvedere as well as for Sir William.'

'It does seem an awful lot of additional work, Mr Stafford, if only we'd been given a bit more notice, we could have brought in some help from the village.'

'I am sure her ladyship feels the same,' replied Stafford, 'she was given very little warning herself.'

'Oh, and I almost forgot Mrs Torrington, I suppose I'll have to act as lady's maid to her too, although perhaps Martha and I will be able to do her between us, because if I remember rightly, she's very undemanding.'

'We were talking about Miss Simpson's wardrobe, Miss Crimms,' reminded the butler, feeling that the conversation had been allowed to digress somewhat.

'Oh, indeed,' replied Miss Crimms, enthusiastically. 'Well I'm pleased to say that it won't be necessary to raid her ladyship's wardrobe or bring a hot iron into play, Mr Stafford. Miss Simpson's wardrobe seems quite appropriate, very proper; in fact one might even go so far as to say it's a little boring for one so young. Why, I could see her ladyship wearing Miss Simpson's evening gown, black silk velvet, it is, a little old and a trifle worn in a couple of places, I'll admit, but it's quality dressmaking all the same.'

'I'm glad to hear it. Well, that's one less thing to worry about, Miss Crimms. Right, I think we'd better get back to our duties, we have more than enough to be getting on with.'

52

Lavinia left her mother on the first floor landing and made her way down the grand wooden staircase. Lady Belvedere had claimed to be tired after her journey and wanted to have a rest before Cedric joined them, although her daughter thought it more likely that she had wanted to be alone so she could think.

Lavinia pondered over the look that she had seen on her mother's face. It had crossed her face only fleetingly, but Lavinia was sure that she had not been mistaken, that for one brief moment Lady Belvedere had revealed she was afraid. And if her mother was frightened, then so was she. Much as she disliked her mother and was constantly anxious about causing her displeasure due to the inevitable unpleasant consequences of such an action, she was confident of her mother's authority, which conversely she found rather reassuring in that, by association of being her daughter, she felt herself comfortably safe.

It seemed to her incredible that her mother could be afraid of Edith Torrington, a mere distant relation who was poor in comparison with the Belvederes. She led a different life from them and mixed in different, lesser circles; not only that, she was so pathetic, so insignificant, and yet it had been the mention of her name that had caused the look of fear to cross Lady Belvedere's face, Lavinia was sure.

It occurred to her then that she did not really know very much about Edith. She had met her occasionally at Ashgrove if their visits happened to coincide. However, Edith had tended to keep herself very much to herself on those occasions, withdrawing from the body of the group to sit on the edges. Then Lady Withers would whisper, none too quietly Lavinia always thought, and cringed least Edith heard, that they must be kind to her after everything she had been through, after her great tragedy. And even Lavinia, who always tended to think of herself before others, was hushed into obeying because it all seemed so awful somehow, that something so terrible could have happened to someone so insipid.

As she entered the drawing room where she had expected to find Rose, she looked out of the French windows and saw that her friend was walking amicably through the formal gardens with Lady Withers who, every now and then, was pointing out a flower-bed or shrub that she thought might be of interest to her guest. Even from where she was standing well inside the room,

Lavinia could just make out her aunt's vague, rambling words as they carried on the wind. It seemed to be very much a one-sided conversation with little opportunity given to Rose to contribute, for Lady Withers did not pause for a moment for breath. Lavinia laughed. How very typical of dear old Connie, she never changed, nothing ever seemed to at Ashgrove. With that thought she ran to join them and forgot all about her mother being afraid. It was only later that she remembered.

Edith came to with a start. She must have been daydreaming. She did that so often now, that she was not even conscious that she was doing it. She found it hard to remember how her days had been before, when she had participated in the world around her and not found the need to retreat into her own thoughts.

She turned her head and looked at the wooden clock on the mantelpiece, her eyes widening in surprise as she realised that somehow two hours had gone by since her husband had left for work. How had that happened? It seemed only a few minutes ago. If she didn't get a move on she would not arrive at Ashgrove until just before dinner and that really wouldn't do, it would be much too late and Constance was bound to telephone to see where she was and Alice would let slip to Harold about her very late departure and then he would know that she had been going over her memories, thinking of a time when she had been happy ... She could see his face now, creased up with all that pent up hurt that he was trying so hard not to show in case he exploded.

Oh, why did she have to cause him so much pain? He was a good man who deserved better, a better wife than her, anyway. He should never have married her, she realised that now; he could have been happy with a different wife, a wife who wasn't her. Poor Harold, if only things had been different, if only ... but no, she must not allow herself to dwell on "if onlys". When she thought about it, her life had been full of "if onlys", really nothing else but "if onlys", but she must not allow herself to think about it now otherwise she would drive herself mad. A little voice inside her head told her that she was already half mad. But one had to go on, everyone expected one to go on, Harold expected her to go on and she was trying so hard not to disappoint him any more than she had done already. She owed him that much at least, it was just that she found it all so difficult, this going on.

Reluctantly she roused herself from her chair and went to pack her suitcase. If she asked Alice to do it for her, it would take all day because Alice had no idea what one wore in the country, she was such a townie. It would be nice to see Ashgrove again, the lovely gardens, the woodland, the lake. If only she could have been there alone to enjoy it, to take in the sunshine and the glorious flowers with perhaps only the faithful and unobtrusive Stafford and Mrs Palmer on hand to see to her few needs. She didn't want Constance to be there. She didn't want to endure Constance's endless chatter and catch her every so often looking pityingly at her out of the corner of her eye, while all the time knowing that Constance thought that she should have got over it all by now, that was the British thing to do after all, keeping a stiff upper lip.

But it was easier said than done and it was all very well for Constance to think like that, Constance who had been pretty and rich and popular and had never longed or wanted for anything in her life, but had got everything handed to her on a plate. Sometimes she hated Constance. She tried not to, because really it wasn't fair of her, it wasn't Constance's fault after all and Constance was so kind to her, even if it was in a rather absentminded, patronising way.

Well, at least there weren't going to be any other guests, except for Lavinia and her friend, of course, and Edith could easily keep out of their way by walking in the gardens and in the woods because they would hardly want to bother with a middle-aged woman like herself. It might prove a blessing in disguise because hopefully Constance would spend most of her time fussing over them and subjecting them to her trivial chatter. Perhaps it wouldn't be so bad. And after all, there was always William, if things got too bad, there was always William.

Chapter Eight

'Mrs Palmer, I wondered if I might have a quiet word.'

The cook-housekeeper had rarely seen the butler look uncomfortable, if ever, and she was immediately intrigued.

'But of course, Mr Stafford, shall we go to my sitting room or to your parlour?'

'To my parlour, I think, Mrs Palmer. Hopefully I won't keep you .a minute because of course I know how busy you are with all this extra work associated with our additional guests; young Bessie told me you weren't able to get much help in from the village today.'

'No indeed, Mr Stafford, I'm afraid it was too short notice, we'll have to cope the best we can today, but I'm hoping that we'll have more luck tomorrow otherwise we'll all be working all hours,' replied Mrs Palmer, following the butler to his parlour. 'You'd think with the amount of people out of work these days, we'd have no problem getting people in to help out for a few hours. Now, what did you want to talk to me about, Mr Stafford, I'm assuming that it isn't about labour shortages?'

'No, indeed not, Mrs Palmer. It's really rather a delicate matter, I'm afraid,' said Stafford, closing the door behind them, 'and I'm not sure exactly how to put it without shocking you. 'It concerns young Lord Sedgwick's friend, Marquis Sneddon. I wouldn't have mentioned anything until I was sure that he was definitely coming, but I was afraid that things would get too busy later on to discuss things properly, so I thought we should deal with the issue now.'

'Indeed, Mr Stafford, you intrigue me,' Mrs Palmer was all ears. 'Is there an issue with this friend of Master Cedric's? A marquis, you say he is, Mr Stafford?'

'It's a courtesy title, Mrs Palmer. He's the only surviving son of the Duke of Haywater and so is heir to the dukedom. But I'm afraid there is an issue, Mrs Palmer. I am sorry to say that the gentleman has a certain, how shall I put it delicately, a certain *reputation* for leading young servant girls astray in the houses he is staying in.'

'No!'

'Indeed, Mrs Palmer, I'm afraid so. You may recall that I am on quite friendly terms with Mr Gifford, the butler at Beswick Hall, and when he discovered that Lord Sedgwick had struck up a friendship with the marquis, he saw fit to warn me of what happened when Lord Sneddon stayed at Beswick Hall last summer. I'm sorry to say that when he was in drink he got one of the young housemaids into trouble and she had to be sent away. When Gifford looked into the matter further, he discovered that a similar thing had occurred the previous year when Lord Sneddon was a guest at another country house.'

'Oh, Mr Stafford, how awful, think about our poor girls!' wailed Mrs Palmer. 'Young Annie has got her head screwed on all right, but what about Bessie and little Edna. They are daft as can be about boys; they're just the sort of foolish young girls to be impressed by a duke's son taking an interest in them. And then one thing will lead to another, they have no sense these young girls, no sense at all.'

'I *am* thinking about our young girls, Mrs Palmer,' replied Stafford solemnly, 'and that is why I'm suggesting putting certain measures in place in order to deter his lordship from making any unsuitable advances to them. The families of these young girls entrust us with their daughters' wellbeing. It is our duty to provide them with moral guidance and to keep them safe from harm while they're under this roof. And I cannot tell you what shame it would bring on this house, or how much I would feel I had failed, if a servant from Ashgrove were to leave in disgrace.'

'Ay, that's the trouble of it, isn't it, Mr Stafford? Everyone will say that the girl has done what she shouldn't have done and ought to have known better, and if she takes her trouble home, likely as not it'll be the threat of the workhouse for her. But no-one ever thinks less of the man who got the girl into trouble, they don't blame him for it, he's just seen as a bit of a lad, especially if he's a duke's son. It isn't fair, Mr Stafford, I can tell you that, there's one rule for men and another for women.'

'That's as may be, Mrs Palmer, and I don't say as I don't agree with you, but I'm afraid that, while society thinks the way it does, there is nothing that we can do about it except do everything in our power to make sure nothing of the sort happens at Ashgrove.' The butler looked both sad and solemn, but Mrs Palmer fancied underneath both those emotions she could also see a look of steel and determination. 'It would seem that these occurrences happen late at night when the household is asleep and the young lord is the worse for drink. We must make sure that he is given no opportunity to roam about the house and visit the servants' bedrooms. He won't be able to get to them through the attic door because we can easily keep that locked. What is worrying me, Mrs Palmer, is what we do about the green baize door off the hall. That's the only other way he can gain access to the servants' quarters. But we can hardly keep that locked, not with her ladyship the way she is.'

'Mr Stafford, we'll have to. I'm sure that her ladyship will be far too tired from all her entertaining to think about getting up in the middle of the night to come down for a midnight feast. I mean, it isn't as if she does it that regularly any more after all, just on the odd occasion when she hasn't eaten much at dinner. But that's hardly going to be the case this weekend, not with all the dishes I'll be producing.'

'Even so, Mrs Palmer, it's just possible that the mood will take her and then what'll her ladyship think if she can't get into the kitchen because we've locked the door?'

Mrs Palmer sighed. She knew there was no reasoning with the butler where Lady Withers was concerned, for he would never hear of her being inconvenienced or put out in any way. Personally she thought that Lady Withers should have been discouraged, long before now, from roaming the kitchen in search of food. She was very much of the view that the household should remain their side of the green baize door and she could not stop herself from conjuring up images in her mind of her mistress poking around in cupboards and inspecting the work surfaces for dust or dirt, which was irrational because she knew that Lady Withers was quite oblivious to such things. But her ladyship was not above poking about in the refrigerator for food, as Mrs Palmer knew to her cost. On one fateful occasion, the cook-housekeeper had come down one morning to find a plateful of cold roast beef, earmarked for that day's luncheon, gone and had blamed all the servants in turn before discovering that Lady Withers had been the culprit. After that an informal arrangement of sorts had been put in place whereby each evening, before retiring to bed, Mrs Palmer would leave out some food covered with a cloth for Lady Withers to sup from if she found herself hungry in the middle of the night.

'There is no way around it, Mrs Palmer, we will have to leave the door unfastened. The only solution, as I see it, is to ensure that someone is on watch all through the night.' He raised his hand as Mrs Palmer looked as if she were about to protest. 'No, I'm not suggesting that it be left to just one person to do. I'm proposing that Briggs, Bridges and I take shifts. I'm not intending to use young Albert; he's a good lad but I doubt he'll be able to hold his tongue about it. It makes sense for Bridges to take the first shift and then he can go off to his cottage, I'll take the middle one and then Briggs can take the last. That way none of us will lose too much sleep so we'll still be able to undertake our duties satisfactorily and I'll always be on hand, my bedroom being just off the kitchen, should Lord Sneddon decide to grace us with his presence.'

'Well, if you're sure, Mr Stafford, but it seems a lot of unnecessary trouble to me. I'd sooner you lock the green baize door,' replied Mrs Palmer, wiping her hands on her apron. 'There is something else that occurs to me though.'

'And what is that, Mrs Palmer? I thought I had covered every eventuality.'

'With regards the maids, yes you have, Mr Stafford. But it occurs to me that if Lord Sneddon has an eye for girls of a lower social class to himself, then there is another girl at risk that we haven't considered.'

'You mean –.'

'Yes, Mr Stafford, I mean Lady Lavinia's young friend, Miss Simpson.'

Rose Simpson was, at that moment, walking around the formal gardens of Ashgrove House with Lavinia and Constance, herself worrying about the imminent arrival of Lords Sedgwick and Sneddon. Her concerns, however, regarding these two young gentlemen were concentrated on what they would think of her, and how she would come across to them, rather than of any untoward motives they might have towards her. The thought that one of them might want to ruin her, certainly had not crossed her mind. She was beginning now to have serious reservations about accepting the invitation to Ashgrove. It was true that both Sir William and Lady Withers had been welcoming, but the unexpected presence of the countess had cast a shadow over the visit. Rose was already a little scared of Lady Belvedere, who had left her in little doubt that she disliked her and regarded her beneath contempt. The countess probably held her responsible for her daughter's continued employment at the dress shop and, if Rose was honest, there was probably an element of truth in this for, if Lavinia had not found a friend there but had had to make do with the resentful company of Sylvia or the sycophant attentions of Mary, then in all likelihood she would not still be there.

But all that paled into insignificance at the prospect of Lord Sedgwick's and Lord Sneddon's arrival. She knew she was ill prepared to come face to face with two of the most handsome and eligible young men in England, to say nothing of the richest. While she had never met them in person, she was familiar with their looks from the society pages of magazines and newspapers, which seemed to contain photographs of one or other of them almost every day. She was suddenly very aware of her own shortcomings, not only of her relative poverty and her far lower social position, but also of her insignificant looks and the cheapness of her clothes that would make her stand apart. She wondered too, why they had chosen this weekend of all weekends to visit Sir William and Lady Withers. She did not think it was a coincidence, for Cedric knew that Lavinia meant to visit Ashgrove. Rose felt her cheeks grow warm. The only explanation was that they had wanted to meet her, this shop girl that Lavinia had befriended. They would surely see her as a source of amusement to liven an otherwise dull visit to middle-aged relatives.

She suddenly felt wretched, it was too awful. She wanted to be home, sitting by the fire with her mother in their little sitting room with the last few pieces of remaining furniture salvaged from their old house. She saw the two of them sitting there in companionable silence, half listening to a programme on the wireless, while her mother worked away with a needle, straining her eyes as she tried to finish a dress that she was making for one of her clients. Rose herself would be pretending to read a book or magazine, while all the time she would be surreptitiously studying the household accounts, trying to calculate how long they had before another painful decision had to be made about their accommodation and whether there were any further economies that could be made to prolong the inevitable. Usually such a scene made her feel depressed, but now she found herself longing for it, the dull familiarity of it all.

60

Rose looked up. Amid the idle chatter between aunt and niece she could see Stafford coming towards them across the lawn. She could feel her heart beating faster and her hands becoming moist. She wanted to dash back into the house, race up the stairs and shut herself in her bedroom. Once there, she would focus all her attention on studying the plate glass covered dressing table in her room, with its valance of floral chintz, until the beating of her heart grew more regular and she felt able to pluck up the courage necessary to meet the visitors.

'M'lady, Lord Sedgwick and Lord Sneddon have just arrived.'

'Ah, very good, Stafford; show them into the rose garden, will you, it's much too nice to go back inside. In fact, I think we'll have our afternoon tea outside, we might as well make the most of this good weather, so welcome after all those rains of late spring.'

'Very good, m'lady.' Stafford gave the slightest of bows and retreated across the grass.

'Dear old Stafford,' Lady Withers said, fondly. 'I really don't know what I would do without him. He and Mrs Palmer run this whole house between them, I really don't have to do a thing. In fact, when I do try to do something, it always goes wrong, like inviting Edith down for the weekend at the same time as inviting you down, my dear. I should have known Cedric would want to see you and having Edith and Cedric here together is the very worst thing. And of course,' she added as an afterthought, 'it will be rather a nasty surprise for him to find that your mother is here too.'

'I wonder whether I should go and warn him before he bumps into Mother,' Lavinia enquired, more of herself than of anyone else.

'Oh, don't worry my dear, I'm sure Stafford has already done that, he thinks of everything. I really don't know what I'd do if he ever decided to leave. I suppose there will come a time when he's too old to remain in service and wants to retire, but I do hope that won't be any time soon.'

'Nonsense, Aunt Connie, he's not that old,' replied Lavinia laughing. 'And even if he is, I can't see him ever stopping work, he's much too devoted to you.'

'Bless you, child,' beamed Lady Withers. 'Oh look, here are the young gentlemen now. My, how handsome Lord Sneddon is, Lavinia, I believe he's quite a catch.'

'Shush, Aunt,' replied Lavinia hurriedly, 'he'll hear you, but yes he does look absolutely divine, doesn't he. Don't you agree, Rose?'

'Yes,' replied Rose dutifully, although it was not Lord Sneddon who had caught her eye. Even so, she could see why Lavinia found him attractive. He was tall, a good head taller than his companion who was himself by no means short or even of middle height, and was very dark with almost jet black hair. He carried himself well, very upright, and there was a look approaching arrogance about him as if he were fully aware of his own importance which, given that he was heir to a dukedom, the highest hereditary title in the British aristocracy, was not insignificant. His eyes, when he turned to focus his gaze on Lavinia, could be described as nothing less than smouldering and Rose heard a small intake of breath from her friend as she luxuriated in his attentions. It was a few moments before he turned his head to acknowledge Rose's presence because Lady Withers had intervened herself to welcome him, clasping his hands in hers and fussing around him like a bee around a honey pot. When at last he directed his look to Rose, there was an altogether different expression on his face, although Rose thought that probably only she herself had seen it.

Lord Sneddon's look towards her was clearly mocking. It seemed to Rose that he took his time to look her up and down as he might a horse he was considering purchasing and a smile crossed his full, rosebud lips which was by no means kind. It made her for a moment feel vulnerable and alone. Both Lavinia and Lady Withers were totally oblivious to her discomfort, she was sure, just as she was equally certain that Lord Sneddon's intention was to make her feel ill at ease.

'Miss Simpson, or may I call you Rose?' the marquis drawled. 'How wonderful to make your acquaintance at last. Cedric and I have heard so much about you from Lavinia and I can see that she did not write a word of a lie about you, for you are exactly how I pictured you would be from her description of you.' He turned to Lavinia and they both laughed. Rose stood there feeling awkward. She thought it unlikely that her friend would have said anything outright unkind about her, but the way Lord Sneddon insinuated by his manner, it was as if she had.

'I say, you there,' Lord Sneddon flicked his fingers and Albert, the young footman, came hurrying over. 'Have you got one of those modern domestic refrigerators here?'

'Yes, your lordship, we've an electrically operated one. It has a storage capacity of twenty-two cubic feet and Mrs Palmer, she's the cook-housekeeper, is right proud –.'

'Splendid. Take these,' Lord Sneddon handed the footman what looked like some small metal balls. 'Put them in the refrigerator, they need to be made ice-cold and then bring them out to me this evening when we have cocktails.'

'Very good, my lord,' said Albert, taking the balls gingerly.

'Whatever are they, Hugh?' enquired Lavinia.

'Wait and see,' replied Lord Sneddon with a gleam in his eye. 'If you're lucky I might put one or two in your glass.' Lavinia giggled.

The man who had caught Rose's attention was still a little way off and appeared engrossed in conversation with Stafford. This in itself seemed remarkable to Rose, more so because the butler appeared to be smiling, having seemingly forgotten his usual impassive air; the combination of these two things roused Rose's curiosity. The man came closer and, as he strode across the gardens towards them, she took in his appearance for the first time. He was tall and slender and his hair, which was slicked back from a side parting, was blonde. He had chiselled features which almost made his face look more beautiful than handsome, Rose thought, as if he were a Greek god rather than a mortal man. His skin was tanned a golden brown as if he spent much time out of doors. Like his friend, he carried himself well and while he looked imposing, there was nothing about his manner that was aloof. To Rose, his looks rivalled those of a matinee idol. She could not help but stare at him.

Two things happened then. Later she wondered if everything would have ended up differently if they hadn't. The first thing was that Mrs Palmer, who had come out of the house presumably to ask a question of Lady Withers about the tea or to welcome the guests herself, slipped and fell heavily on to the ground. In an instant, the fair-haired young man was at her side, helping her up and appearing genuinely concerned as he made sure that she was not hurt. The two of them had looked at each other with mutual affection and it was obvious that the young man was a favourite among the servants and that they held him in high esteem. The second thing was that, having satisfied himself that Mrs Palmer was all right, Lord Sedgwick had looked up and spotted Rose looking at him shyly and he had smiled, a genuine smile, of that she was sure, a smile that had lit up his face and made his eyes shine. And in that moment, Rose, who was not a romantic by any means, being too much of a realist to believe in fairy-tale endings and dreams coming true, had fallen in love.

Chapter Nine

'How do you do, Miss Simpson?'

'How do you do, your lordship?'

'Oh, don't call me that, Cedric, please. But don't call me Ceddie, I beg of you. Only Lavinia calls me that, and I am trying so very hard to persuade her not to. It was all very well when we were children and she was my big sister, but now that I am a man, I find it a trifle embarrassing.'

Rose laughed. 'If I am to call you Cedric, then you must call me Rose.'

'I should be delighted to, Rose, especially as roses are my favourite flower by far.'

'Enough, you two,' interrupted Lavinia coming over. 'My brother can be a bit of a charmer, Rose, you must take no notice of him and certainly don't encourage him. But, Ceddie, you haven't said hello to me yet and I haven't seen you for absolutely ages. I suppose you know Mother's here? Whatever possessed you to tell her that I would be down at Ashgrove this weekend?'

'Stafford told me as soon as we arrived. He was very discreet and conveniently looked away so as not to see me grimace. But I didn't tell Mother that you'd be here, Sis. Why ever would I do such a thing, especially as Hugh and I decided to come down too? Hope you girls don't mind us being here. We thought it would be fun and I'm so tired of studying, I can't tell you. Don't look at me like that, Lavinia,' Cedric gave his sister's shoulder a playful nudge. 'I do heaps of work, you know, despite what you may think. It's not just a round of parties, I want to get a decent degree.'

'I'm sure you do, little brother. Oh, but why does Mother have to be here to spoil everything?'

'I suppose it's our fault for not going home enough. Try to look on the bright side, it won't be too bad and I understand from Stafford that father has come down with her. I don't know how she's managed that. I can't remember the last time he left Sedgwick. Mother usually has to make his excuses.'

'It's all very well for you, Ceddie, you're her favourite and can't do any wrong in her eyes. But it's awful for me. Why, we hadn't been here five minutes and she was already badgering me about working in the dress shop.'

'How's that going, Sis? I must admit that I can't imagine you being particularly nice to customers that you don't like, or putting clothes away or anything.'

'Oh, it's all right, I'm quite enjoying it and of course, I've met Rose.'

'Yes.' The word hung in the air as Cedric turned and smiled at Rose. Rose felt her stomach do a somersault as she returned his smile. And all the while she realised that Lord Sneddon was following their exchange with some interest, the way she lowered her gaze and could not help herself from blushing. And a tiny part of her, that was not focused solely on Cedric, warned her of danger and told her to be afraid.

'So you see, Rose, it really is lovely to be here at Ashgrove. Despite what my sister thinks, I really have been working desperately hard and I always find it so relaxing here. Uncle William and Aunt Connie are always so pleased to see us but in a quiet, unassuming sort of way so that one feels one can just be without having to put on a show of any kind. I say, does that make any sense or am I just talking a lot of old rot?'

Lord Sedgwick and Rose had been wandering aimlessly around the grounds for a quarter of an hour or so, Lord Sneddon and Lady Lavinia always a few feet behind, equally engrossed in conversation.

'I understand what you're saying perfectly, Cedric.' *Cedric*! She, Rose Simpson, a simple shop girl, was on first name terms with the heir to an earldom and it had felt to her, in these last fifteen minutes or so, that she had been waiting all her life for Cedric to appear, that while she felt excited and agitated by his presence, she also felt relieved and reassured as if it was supposed to happen, as if it were fate. 'I've only been here a few hours myself, but it is so tranquil and peaceful here. I feel as if I have left my old life behind and stepped into another world where anything might happen. I'm going to find it a very hard wrench to leave on Sunday afternoon.'

'So shall I, Rose, but we have the whole weekend in front of us, so let's not think about that yet.'

'My lord.' Stafford had somehow managed to appear, totally unobserved until he had spoken. 'Begging your pardon, but the Earl of Belvedere has requested your presence in the library.'

'Really, what now, Stafford? Miss Simpson, Rose, will you forgive me if I abandon you for a while? I don't like to keep Father waiting. He doesn't often ask to see me. Truth be told, I had completely forgotten that he was here.'

Rose watched his retreating back and felt a sense of loss. She was not left to her own devices for long however, for Lady Withers, who had been occupied in another part of the garden, came hurrying towards her.

'I say, Miss Simpson, are you into roses like your namesake? We have some wonderful rose bushes here at Ashgrove that you simply must see. Of course, green fly has been particularly active on our roses this year, so Bridges, our head gardener, tells me anyway. He syringes the infested plants with a nicotine wash which he simply swears by. It's effective against all aphids and caterpillars, so he tells me. This way.' Lady Withers, who apparently did not think it necessary to wait for an answer, led Rose across the lawn and through an archway into a small garden which was obviously the rose garden. As soon as they had gone a few yards into the garden, Lady Withers turned around abruptly to look behind them and Rose followed suit, noticing as she did so that Lady Withers looked relieved.

'Ah, good, they haven't followed us, I was afraid they would. Oh, no need to look alarmed, Miss Simpson, I haven't got something to say to you that I didn't wish to be overhead. No, on the contrary, I'm afraid I've rather asked you to come in here on a false pretence; not that our roses aren't rather splendid, because they're really rather good. No, it's just that I wanted the two young people to have some time together, get to know each other, so to speak. I'm very fond of Lavinia, of course, but she does have a tendency to be a bit headstrong and apt to do her own thing, which is all very well in a girl of seventeen, but not the thing at all for a woman almost twenty-three. It's high time she was married and although she still has her beauty, her looks will fade soon enough like her mother's looks have done, mark my words.'

It seemed to Rose that there was nothing much to say to that and that it was probably better if she did not volunteer an opinion, although she found that Lady Withers' comment about marriage had irked her, for she herself was only a year younger than Lavinia.

'So she needs to strike while the iron is hot, so to speak. And it really is rather fortunate that my sister is still having her lie down because I'm afraid to say that she is likely to put off any potential suitor. I'm sure she doesn't mean to, but poor Marjorie can be rather fierce at times and she very rarely smiles or is even in good humour come to that. Oh dear, that makes her sound quite dreadful and I really don't mean to, but all in all I think it's probably best for Lavinia's sake if Lord Sneddon sees as little as possible of her mother. Wasn't it Oscar Wilde who said something about all women becoming like their mothers? What an awful prospect, we don't want Lord Sneddon to be put off, do we? My goodness, Stafford,' Lady Withers broke off at the reappearance of her butler. 'How on earth did you get there? If I didn't know better, I'd swear that you had wings. Whenever I look around, there you are. Well, what is it now?'

'Mrs Torrington has just arrived, m'lady.'

'Edith, oh, I had quite forgotten about her. How tiresome, not that I don't want to see Edith, of course, or I would never have invited her here, it's just rather awkward that's she's coming now when my sister and especially Cedric are here, we really don't want another scene. I say, Stafford,' Lady Withers raised her voice slightly as if she thought her butler was rather hard of hearing, 'I was just saying to Miss Simpson that we really do not want another scene.'

'No, indeed not m'lady,' agreed the butler, 'which is why I took the liberty of putting Mrs Torrington in the morning room on the first floor. I was afraid that if I put her in the drawing room or brought her out into the gardens, there was a possibility that she might inadvertently come across Lord Sedgwick and the earl coming out of the library and I thought that such an encounter would be unfortunate, until Mrs Torrington had been told the situation.'

'You were quite right, Stafford, as always,' sighed Lady Withers. 'Well I suppose I had better go and see Edith and break the news to her. Why she does have to be so silly about Cedric, I really don't know, I mean, it was such a very long time ago, one would have thought that she would have got over it by now.' She turned and looked at Rose as if she had suddenly remembered that she was there and did not know quite what to do with her.

68

'Ah, Miss Simpson, now what about you? Should I leave you here to amuse yourself or would you like to accompany me to see my old school friend? I think, on reflection, you had better come with me, if you have no objection.' Rose did not for she was rather curious to make the acquaintance of the mysterious Edith who seemed to have such a thing for Cedric despite the very large difference in their ages.

She followed Lady Withers into the house and up the stairs to the morning room which had, earlier in the day, been used by the countess to berate her daughter. On the landing just outside the door, looking as if he were trying to pluck up the courage to enter the room, stood Sir William.

'Darling, whatever are you doing here?' enquired Lady Withers, obviously surprised to see her husband there. 'I thought you were tied up in your study answering your business correspondence.'

'Ah, yes my dear, I was,' replied Sir William, looking rather awkward. 'But just as I finished I heard Stafford greeting Edith in the hall and I thought I'd take the opportunity to forewarn her about ... er ... Cedric, before she happened to bump into him. But by the time I had put my papers away, I found that she was no longer in the hall but had been shown up here into your morning room.'

'Well, Stafford thought it would be safer and I have to say I agree with him. But you thought *you'd* warn her?'

'Yes, seeing as I was here, so to speak, and you were in the garden.'

'I see.' There was a certain coldness in the way Lady Withers uttered these two words that resulted in an uncomfortable silence. Rose averted her gaze, suddenly finding the pattern on the wallpaper very interesting.

'Constance, please, it's not what ...'

'Don't say another word, William, we won't discuss it here and now. I take it that you haven't had a chance to actually speak to Edith yet? In which case Miss Simpson and I will go and tell her. I say, my dear,' Lady Withers said turning in that instant to both dismiss Sir William and to address Rose, 'is there any chance of my calling you "Rose", I can't keep calling you "Miss Simpson" while you're a guest in my house, it makes you sound too much like a servant.'

'Yes, of course, "Rose" is fine, Lady Withers.'

'Oh, and do stop calling me "Lady Withers" dear, "Connie" will do.'

Before either of them could venture into the room, however, the door opened and Edith appeared in the doorway, the sound of their voices having drawn her out.

'Oh, Connie, I didn't know you were there, and William too.' To Rose, who scrutinised her with some interest, Edith looked slightly flustered as if she found the whole experience of being greeted by three people, one unknown to her, quite overwhelming.

Rose did not know what she had been expecting, but Edith certainly was not it. She realised that she must have been assuming that a woman who was sufficiently attracted to a man half her age to make such an apparent spectacle of herself, would go to great lengths to retain her youth and beauty. But this could not be said of the woman standing before her, who looked to Rose's eyes quite nondescript. Her blonde hair was showing grey in places and her face was faintly lined with either worry or sickness, Rose was not sure which; it was only later that she knew it to be grief.

'Now, Edith,' Lady Withers was saying, 'I'd like you and me to go back into the room and sit down. I've something to tell you which I'm afraid you might find a bit upsetting at first but I'm sure that once you have got over the shock you'll be all right and it needn't spoil your visit here at all. Why, it will be just like old times with us all back together. Rose, here, who's a young friend of dear Lavinia's, will summon the servants and arrange some tea for us,' she paused to glance over her shoulder at Rose, 'won't you my dear, I'm sure you won't mind.'

'No, of course not Lady Withers ... er ... I mean, Connie.'

'Such a sweet girl; would you believe, Edith, that she works in a dress shop? William, what are *you* doing still here? Go and entertain the gentlemen. I'll see to Edith.'

'Yes, my dear, it's just that –.'

'Oh, for goodness sake, William –.'

Unexpectedly, in the air of tension that had suddenly sprung up between husband and wife, the library door opened below. It was a welcome diversion to all those present on the landing and, almost as if they had been one, they stepped forward together and peered over the banister.

Later, when Rose thought back over it all, it seemed that everything then happened in slow motion. Firstly, Cedric came out into the hall followed by his father the Earl of Belvedere; secondly, Sir William flung himself quite

70

unceremoniously in front of Edith, as if to shield her from the view; thirdly, Edith half stumbled forward and half pushed Sir William aside as if determined to see what she was being sheltered from; fourthly, both father and son had looked up to see the cause of the kerfuffle; and lastly, Edith had let out a gasp that was clearly audible, even to the men below, and she had clasped her hands to her chest as if experiencing a sudden pain, before her legs had buckled up beneath her and she had crumbled onto the floor.

There was a moment of silence when no-one moved or uttered a word as if they did not know quite what to do. And then, as if to make up for the delay, everything, to Rose, seemed to happen very fast indeed. Sir William sprang forward and took Edith by the shoulders and helped her to her feet. Lady Withers threw open the morning room door and between them they half carried, half steered, Edith inside. Rose, left alone on the landing, looked down at the upturned faces of the men below. Their expressions showed a mixture of shock and bewilderment as they stood stock still, unsure whether or not they should offer some assistance.

But what struck Rose most forcibly was the atmosphere. It was as if something sinister and threatening lurked somewhere in the air, just out of sight but clearly there. She fancied that out of the corner of her eye she may even have caught sight of a door further along the corridor closing softly and she wondered suddenly whether it had been Lady Belvedere, roused from her afternoon nap by the commotion on the landing. Whatever was causing her feelings of unease, it made Rose shiver. She put out a hand and clutched the banister to steady herself, as she tried to take it all in. She had just witnessed surprise, shock, even sadness, yes, but they were all emotions that she would have expected given the situation. However, there seemed to her other stronger emotions in the air that were engulfing Ashgrove House. And when she cast her eyes below, both Cedric and Lord Belvedere were looking distinctly nervous, which made her think that she was not alone in imagining it all, that others felt as she did, that the house was haunted by something else. But what was it? What was causing her feelings of dread? She was finding it difficult to put her finger on it, although it seemed almost within her grasp, and then it came to her all at once, suddenly and forcefully, this thing that had been eluding her. She knew now what it was and part of her wished she did not. As clear as day she knew what permeated Ashgrove; it was fear and hatred.

Chapter Ten

'It appears,' said Lord Sneddon, strolling idly over the well-kept lawns, 'that we have been quite abandoned; we are all alone.'

Lavinia looked about her and felt a thrill of excitement. The weekend, since she had first heard of her brother's intention to visit, was so far going even better than she could have hoped for. Lord Sneddon appeared quite enchanted with her, hanging on her every word, and Lady Withers had very obligingly taken Rose away so that there were no unnecessary distractions. Lavinia congratulated herself for having had the foresight to pack two of her best evening gowns. She was bound to outshine poor Rose; what was a dress of plain black silk velvet after all compared with one of gold lame or silk satin. Already, while half her attention was focused on Lord Sneddon's conversation, enabling her to nod, murmur agreement and giggle in all the right places, she was already considering in her mind how to dress her hair that evening and which of her jewels would best show off her gown. What a pity that her mother had not seen fit to bring their ladies' maids with her, Eliza was so very good at dressing her hair.

'I have to say, Lavinia, I'm most impressed that you've managed to stick out this shop lark. When Cedric first told me about your bet, I'm afraid to admit that I didn't think you'd last a week, indeed, I hate to tell you, but I entered into a little wager with your brother to that effect.'

'You never did, Hugh!' Lavinia tapped him playfully on the arm with her glove. 'I hope you lost a packet because it will have served you jolly well right for having so little faith in me. I would have you know that when I put my mind to something, I rarely give up; I always get what I want.'

'I'm sure you do.' He looked her directly in the eyes, almost as if he was issuing some sort of challenge and she could not help blushing. It occurred to her then that she might be being a little too obvious in her intentions. She knew that she was beautiful and that some men found her manner charming, she was also very aware that a number of seasons were behind her and that, despite her wealth, her mother was beginning to have concerns about her finding a suitable husband.

'What about you, Hugh, what are you up to these days?'

'Oh, this and that, Lavinia, this and that,' replied Lord Sneddon, in a vague sort of way. 'I'm afraid my father's health is not so good. I fear it won't be long before I come into the dukedom and have to oversee the estates and then my life will be quite taken over with duties and responsibilities. I intend to make the most of my freedom while I have it. So I'm afraid that I've just been rather enjoying myself.'

'And you find my brother good company?'

'Oh, exceedingly. Although Cedric is apt to take his studying a little too seriously, I am sure I never did when I was at Oxford. I'm always trying to encourage him to let his hair down a bit and have some fun once in a while. I'm afraid that you must consider me a very bad influence on your brother, Lavinia, but he has a very good influence on me and I must say, he does have the most charming family.'

'I trust you're not referring to my mother?' Lavinia smiled. How easy this all was. Lord Sneddon was making absolutely no attempt to hide the fact that he was attracted to her.

'Indeed not, although I understand that she is a most charming woman. No, I was thinking –.'

'I say, Lavinia, Lord Sneddon,' Sir William was making his way over to them across the lawns, 'Constance has decided that we should have tea on the terrace. She's tied up with Edith just now in the morning room, but she will be down in a minute; the servants are bringing the tea things through now.'

Lord Sneddon, Lavinia noticed, was annoyed by the interruption although trying not to show it, while she found that she herself felt a surprising sense of relief. If she were honest, things between her and Hugh were going a little too fast for her liking. She took a sideways glance at him to reassure herself. Yes, he was very handsome and indeed charming company as well as being the heir to a dukedom, in fact everything she could want in a husband.

'Edith, my dear, how are you feeling now?' enquired Lady Withers, patting her friend's hand in a vague sort of way which she meant to be comforting. Edith was lying full length on the settee. 'I realise that it must have been quite a shock for you. We did try to warn you, but unfortunately we weren't quick enough. I hasten to add that Cedric invited himself down, I

73

would never have dreamed of inviting him to stay this weekend of all weekends. Indeed, it seems to be quite a weekend for people inviting themselves down or just turning up, what with Marjorie and –.'

'Lady Belvedere's here too?' asked Edith, sitting up abruptly.

'Yes, although don't worry, I'm sure Cedric and his father won't say anything to her about this little … er … well, you know, they are both awfully discreet, quite the gentlemen, both of them.'

'Yes, I'm sorry, Constance, to have made such a fool of myself. It was just the shock, you see, I thought I was over it all years ago, but it seems I'm not. Please don't fuss over me, you don't need to, you know, I'll be right as rain in a few minutes. You must go down and see to your other guests. I'll just sit here for a while, if you don't mind, gather my thoughts. Perhaps I could take some tea here, if it's not too inconvenient? I don't think I can quite face the others just yet, but don't worry I'll be absolutely fine by dinner, I really will, I promise.'

'Well if you're sure you'll be all right, my dear,' said Lady Withers who, if truth be told, was eager to get back to her guests if not least because she was rather uncertain as to how best to deal with, or indeed what to do about, Edith. 'Now, you rest a little, my dear. I'll send the parlour maid up with your tea. It's just what you need, I think, a nice cup of strong tea with lots of sugar in it, just the thing for a nasty shock.' Even to Constance's eyes, Edith still looked dreadfully pale. Lady Withers wondered if it was really the done thing to leave a guest alone in such a state. She suddenly noticed Rose who had remained on the landing and was hovering uncertainly in the doorway, wondering whether she should return to the gardens, or whether she ought to offer some assistance.

'Oh, Rose, I didn't see you there,' said Lady Withers, looking relieved and, coming over to the doorway, lowering her voice a little, although she was still clearly audible to Edith. 'Would you mind awfully staying with Mrs Torrington a little while, my dear, to make sure that she's quite all right. I don't like to leave her all alone, but I must see to my other guests. My sister's probably down there now wondering where I am, and I'll need to chase the servants for tea. I'll send yours up here too, shall I? I expect you and Edith have a lot in common and it will be such a relief to me, quite a weight off my mind to know my friend is being looked after.'

'No, of course not Lady ... eh ... Connie.' In truth, it was the last thing Rose wanted to do, as she could already imagine the uncomfortable silence that would ensue between herself and Mrs Torrington as they both sat there waiting for their tea to be brought up, wondering what on earth to say to one another. However, it was the ideal opportunity to find out once and for all about the cause of Edith's fascination with Cedric, and why seeing him brought her so much pain.

Rose chose an easy chair covered in glazed chintz positioned at an angle to the settee on which Mrs Torrington had previously been half reclining, but on which she was now sitting very upright, her hands firmly balled as if she were willing herself to be calm. Both women looked at each other every now and then and when they happened to catch each other's eye, they smiled shyly. It occurred to Rose that, notwithstanding her long friendship with Lady Withers, Edith felt as much a fish out of water at Ashgrove as she did herself.

'I feel I must apologise to you, Miss Simpson, for your being called upon to keep an eye on me when I'm sure you'd much prefer to be outside with Lavinia and the others taking in the splendours Ashgrove has to offer, to say nothing of this glorious sunshine,' Edith said, at last. 'You must think my behaviour just now very strange; I feel I owe you an explanation least you think too badly of me.'

Rose looked up expectantly. It was hard to know what to say, so she said nothing, just smiled, but it appeared that a response was neither required nor expected from her.

'Tell me, did Constance and the others say how I might behave if I saw Lord Sedgwick?'

'They inferred that you were likely to be very upset, that you had encountered Lord Sedgwick a couple of years ago when you had been down at Ashgrove, and that the encounter had left you distressed.'

'Did they say why?'

'No, and I thought it impolite to ask.'

'What a sweet child you are. Lavinia is lucky to have you for a friend. Will you pass me my handbag please, it's to the right of you.' Rose did as she was bid. 'Thank you. Look at this, and tell me what you make of it?' Edith passed Rose a black and white photograph that was severely creased.

The subject matter was a young man with blonde hair, dressed in an army officer's uniform of the Great War.

'It's Cedric,' said Rose, confused, 'but no, it can't be. He'd have only been a child when this photograph was taken, but it must be him, it looks exactly like him.'

'It's not him,' said Edith, quietly, 'although it does look a lot like him, doesn't it? I'm sure though, that if you were to put them side by side, you would be able to see a number of differences, but we'll never know now.'

'Who is he?' Rose noticed that Edith's eyes were filling with tears.

'He was my son, Robert. He was killed in the war, not long after his eighteenth birthday. It was near the end of the war. If only he'd been born a few months later, he'd have been spared the fighting altogether and he'd be alive now. He'd probably be married with a family of his own.'

'I'm so sorry, Mrs Torrington.' Rose leaned forward in her chair and half stretched out her hand to Edith.

'Thank you, my dear, that's very kind of you. I know that I'm not the only one to have suffered because of the war. I know that there's probably not a family in Britain that hasn't lost someone. But you see, Robert was my only child and I loved him so much. I've tried and tried for the sake of my husband to get over it, but I just can't. Part of me doesn't want to get over it, you see. It would seem disloyal somehow, as if I never loved him. I'm so afraid of forgetting what he was like, the way he wore his hair, even the sound of his voice.'

'I understand,' Rose said gently, moving to sit next to Edith on the settee and taking her hand in her own, 'it must be very hard, especially when it must seem that everyone else has moved on.'

'I'm so sorry,' said Edith sobbing quietly. 'I've only just met you, and here I am making a complete fool of myself, and pouring out my life story to you. But you seem so very kind and I find it all so difficult at home. I don't really have anyone to talk to about it, you see. I've tried and tried to talk to Harold, my husband, but he just doesn't want to know. He likes to keep his emotions buttoned up, you see, you know, stiff upper lip and all that. He thinks it best if we both try and be strong. It's tearing my marriage apart.'

'I can understand how hard it must be to see Cedric. He must remind you awfully of your son and what you have lost.'

76

'Yes. When I saw Cedric here a couple of years ago, he was the same age as my son was when he went off to war, just a couple of months before he was killed. I found it all too much. I convinced myself somehow that he was Robert come back from the grave. I made a frightful scene, I'm afraid, I blush even now to think of it. I must have frightened Lord Sedgwick dreadfully, but I'm better now. It was an awful shock to see him just now because I wasn't expecting to, but I'm sure I'll be all right at dinner. You never know, my dear,' continued Edith, drying her eyes on her handkerchief, 'this might be exactly what I needed.'

Without warning, the door opened. Both women looked up expecting to see the house-parlour maid coming in with the tea. It was with something akin to alarm then, when Rose saw that the newcomer was not the maid but the Countess of Belvedere. Both women scrambled hastily to their feet, but not before Edith had snatched the photograph of Robert back from Rose's hand, almost tearing it in the process as she stuffed it into her bag.

'Hello, Edith, Constance said you were expected.' Lady Belvedere had followed Edith's actions and turned her gaze to Edith's handbag as if she thought it held some wild animal.

'Hello Marjorie. It's been a long time since we were all together, hasn't it? It's hard to remember that we all used to be inseparable.' There was an icy coldness to Edith's voice which made Lady Belvedere look wary and, Rose was sure she had not imagined it, afraid.

'I'll see you again at dinner, Marjorie. Rose and I are having our tea in here. We must catch up later, I've so much to tell you.'

Lady Belvedere looked for a moment from one to the other, nodded and then retreated, closing the door softly behind her. Rose looked at Edith in awe, there was obviously more to this old school friend of Lady Withers than met the eye.

Chapter Eleven

'Oh, there you are, Rose, I've been looking for you everywhere,' Lavinia said as Rose came out onto the terrace. 'Aunt Connie said that you'd kindly offered to look after Edith and have your tea with her in the morning room, but that was ages ago. It really is too bad Edith making another scene. Poor Cedric, it quite shocked him, you know, although he tried not to show it. It was awful for Daddy too; he wasn't there last time it happened so he had absolutely no idea what to expect and so was very shaken by it all. He was as white as a sheet when he and Cedric came out to join us, you'd have thought he'd seen a ghost.' Lavinia sighed. 'I do hope Edith's not going to ruin the weekend, it really is too bad of her. I mean, it's awful enough having Mother here lecturing me all the time, without having Edith having hysterics.'

'Mrs Torrington's been through a lot, Lavinia, losing her only son in the war. It can't have been easy for her. She showed me a photograph of him and he did look jolly like Cedric, you know. It must be hard for her when she sees him. It must remind her of what she's lost.'

'Aunt Connie said that they didn't really look that much alike, that it was just in Edith's imagination,' said Lavinia dismissively. 'You know, just two young men of approximately the same age with a similar build and the same hair colour.'

Rose blushed as a thought suddenly struck her. Was it possible that in her own mind she had exaggerated the extent of the resemblance in the photograph between Robert and Cedric, because her thoughts were on Cedric at the time?

'But anyway, that's enough about her,' Lavinia was continuing, 'we've come here to enjoy ourselves and we jolly well will, we won't let Edith spoil it. The boys have gone for a walk to the village; I said I'd wait for you. What shall we do now? We could follow them or go for a walk around the grounds; you haven't seen it all, there's parkland and a lake and woodland, but we'll probably explore that all tomorrow with Hugh and Cedric, they were talking about taking a picnic. Or we could go to my room and have a good old gossip and decide what we're going to wear tonight for dinner,'

Lavinia looked distinctly excited at this prospect, 'we never really get the chance to have a good old chat at work, do we, and I'm always so exhausted by the end of the day to go out, that I'm no good to anyone.'

Rose would have preferred to go for a walk for she felt she had been cooped up inside enough, but she could tell that her friend wanted to talk to her about Lord Sneddon. So instead they returned to the house and went to Lavinia's room which, Rose noticed, was decorated far more extravagantly than her own. For one thing, Lavinia had a canopy over her bed made from a soft glazed gold chintz, with the curtains looped over wooden arms fixed in the wall. At the windows, there were curtains in a floral chintz of regency pattern, complete with covered, shaped pelmets and the dressing table, considerably larger than the one in Rose's room, was kidney-shaped with a drapery of muslin over chintz complete with a three-sided, gilt-framed looking glass fixed on the wall above, originally intended, Rose felt sure, for use over a mantelpiece in a small drawing room rather than in a bedroom.

'What a lovely room.'

'Yes it is, isn't it? I always have this bedroom when I come to stay; it has great views over the garden and parkland, being so high up, as your does too, of course. I say, I hope you're finding your room all right, I know it's pretty small and not quite as lovely as this one, but I thought it would be such fun if our rooms were next to each other and we're far enough away from Mother. It would be just so awful if her room was next to mine, she would be coming in all the time telling me how to behave and what to do and how to dress. Honestly, she treats me just like a child sometimes, you wouldn't think I was twenty-two the way she goes on. I really think she thinks Cedric and I are still in the nursery. Poor Daddy, she treats him rather like that too. Still, he can always seek refuge in his library and I don't think he listens half the time to what she's saying to him. Oh, but enough about Mother. I want to talk to you about, Hugh … Marquis Sneddon,' Lavinia giggled, 'what do you think about him? Isn't he gorgeous, just about the most handsome man you have ever seen?'

'He is very good-looking,' admitted Rose, 'but I didn't really get a chance to talk to him much. You two seemed to be getting on like a house on fire though', she laughed.

'Yes, he really couldn't have been more attentive to me if he tried. And he is so fascinating; he knows lots and lots and has an opinion on simply everything.'

'Do you know him well?' enquired Rose curiously.

'Not really,' Lavinia flung herself down on her bed. 'Cedric and he haven't been friends that long, but Cedric's brought Hugh to Sedgwick a couple of times when I've been there, but there've always been other guests there too. Before that I had seen him at the round of parties during the season, of course, but he was always surrounded by loads of people that I never really had the chance to make his acquaintance. This really is proving to be an unexpected opportunity. I just thought it would be a quiet weekend, just the two of us and Aunt and Uncle and Aunt's dull old school friend. But I must say, I'm going to try and make the most of it. For once Mother and I are in perfect agreement; she's desperate for me to marry someone like Hugh. Oh, to be a duchess. Just think, I could even lord it over Mother.'

Rose looked at her friend with some concern. It would do no good though, she thought, to tell Lavinia of her feelings of uneasiness when she had first met Lord Sneddon. It was difficult to put her finger on exactly what had unsettled her and Lavinia certainly wouldn't thank her for it, she'd probably think Rose was just being jealous and perhaps she was right. No, it was better to keep quiet. She'd probably discover that she was being very unfair to the gentleman and he couldn't really be that bad, not if he was a friend of Cedric's.

Cedric. The name definitely had a certain ring to it. A few hours before it had been a very ordinary name which meant absolutely nothing to her; now it meant everything. Lavinia had spoken frequently of her brother and Rose, having seen his photograph in the society pages, had been interested to hear about his latest exploits. But everything was different now, now that she had actually met him. She couldn't think or imagine any other man but Cedric. His presence seemed to fill the house and she knew that, whenever she thought back on this weekend, it would not be Lavinia that she would remember or Sir William or Lady Withers, or even the splendours of Ashgrove House itself and being waited on by servants; no, she would remember it as the moment when she had met Cedric. Her life would forever be split into two parts, the time before she met Cedric and the time after. Right now she did not feel that she could ever be interested in any other man.

It was so silly, of course, and so very unlike her. She was being totally irrational and idiotic, for she knew that nothing could ever come of it, even if he happened, unlikely though it was, to feel the same way about her as she did about him. Suddenly she wanted desperately to be alone so that she could give herself up fully to her thoughts. So strong was the urge that she had to bite her lip to stop herself from leaving the room with Lavinia, totally oblivious to her internal turmoil, still in mid conversation.

'…. so you see, Rose,' Lavinia was saying, 'I say, are you all right? You don't look quite yourself, you're all flushed.'

'It's nothing, I'm just a bit tired that's all. I thought I might have a quick lie down before we have to dress for dinner.'

'Jolly good idea, I might do the same. We're bound to stay up late with Cedric and Hugh being here. We'll be sharing Martha, who'll be acting as our lady's maid. She's a house parlour maid really, but quite good; she's acted as lady's maid for me before when I've not brought Eliza with me. Do you mind if she sees to me first? My dress is a bit fiddly to do up and I need her to arrange my hair. I'm desperate to look my best tonight. I want to make the right impression, after all. You're used to dressing yourself anyway, aren't you, although I dare say you don't usually dress for dinner?'

When Rose got to the door she hesitated and turned back.

'Your brother's awfully pleasant, Lavinia.'

'Yes, he is, isn't he?' Lavinia had now moved to sit in the chair in front of her dressing table and was scrutinising her face in the mirror. 'He's nice to simply everyone; he has an absolute knack of putting everyone at their ease, everyone's always talking about it. Mother finds him a complete godsend when she has some awkward guest come to stay at Sedgwick and all my girlfriends simply adore him. They're all quite sure that he's in love with them, it's an absolute scream. And the funniest thing is, Cedric has absolutely no idea the effect he has on women; he really is a complete innocent. Mother's always convinced that some very unsuitable girl is going to take advantage of him.'

'Goodbye, I'll see you later, Lavinia.'

'Yes, absolutely, I'll knock on your door and we can go down together. The dinner-hour here is a quarter to eight because Aunt and Uncle are terribly old-fashioned, I'm afraid. They'll want us all to meet beforehand in the drawing room before we go in to dinner. But Cedric and Hugh mentioned the four of us meeting twenty minutes earlier so we can have cocktails.

As the door closed behind Rose, Lavinia abandoned looking at her reflection in the mirror and looked instead at the closed door, her thoughts on her friend. She frowned, notwithstanding her constant fear that pulling such a facial expression might cause wrinkles. For one brief moment, the gesture obliterated her beauty.

'My dear,' said Sir William walking into his wife's room while dressing for dinner that evening, 'how is Edith now? Did she get over her shock?'

'Oh, for goodness sake, William, how you men do fuss over her,' replied Lady Withers, slamming her hairbrush down onto the dressing table. 'Why, I think that woman's got you all wrapped around her little finger with her helpless act. I appreciate it must have been a bit of a shock to see Cedric again, but really, she does make such a song and dance about everything. I knew she would, which is why I was so anxious about Cedric coming to stay in the first place, but when I told you, you didn't seem that concerned about it. There's no point worrying about it now, William, it's far too late.'

'You're quite right, my dear, but even so I'd like to know she's got over the shock.'

'As far as I know, she has. I left Lavinia's little friend to sit with her a while. According to her, Edith soon rallied and intends to join us for dinner.'

'I see.' Sir William sounded hesitant, even to Lady Withers.

'Oh, do stop fussing, darling. She'll have to do it sometime. If it's not tonight, it'll be breakfast tomorrow or lunch or dinner. She'll have to get it over and done with sometime, so she might as well do so now. And Cedric will be quite sweet about it all, you know he will. The dear boy will probably go out of his way to be especially nice to her so that she doesn't feel embarrassed.

'And the precedence for dinner has all worked out rather well. Stafford's sorted it all out for me, because you know how confused I get about who you as host should be escorting to dinner and who should go next and suchlike. He's written it out for me, least I forget. Now let's see.' Lady Withers picked up a piece of paper from her dressing table and peered at it short-sightedly, 'I really must have a word with Stafford about his writing, it's much too small, one can hardly read it; now let's see. Yes, you as host will take in Marjorie, because she'll be the lady of highest rank present. Next I, as hostess, would have been taken in by the gentleman of highest rank, but unfortunately we are going to end up with a partnerless lady as there is an odd number of guests. I did try and think whether there was anyone among our acquaintance that we could ask to dinner as a stop-gap, who would also be a good conversationalist, but I could only think of Doctor Marsden and he is otherwise engaged. Next time I really must insist to Edith that she brings Harold. It really is most unfortunate because really the number of men and of ladies should be equal and Stafford told me that if the number must be unequal, it is better to have more men than women.

'Anyway, the upshot is that Stafford thinks I should follow everyone in alone. I did suggest to him that perhaps Miss Simpson wouldn't mind going in by herself, but he told me that wouldn't be the done thing at all. Now let's see who goes next after you and Marjorie. Ah yes, we found this rather tricky, or Stafford did, I should say, because you see the younger son of a duke comes after an earl in the order of precedence but, as Lord Sneddon is now heir to his father's dukedom, Stafford thought he should be treated as if he was the Duke's eldest son, which means that he'll come before Henry. So, Lord Sneddon will be taking in Lavinia, which should please her very much, Henry will be taking in Edith and Cedric, Miss Simpson, which is likely to upset Marjorie, but really that can't be helped, and then I'll just follow them in. Stafford's worked out the seating at the table as well, which he's written down on the back of this bit of paper for you to familiarise yourself with.' Lady Withers turned over the paper. 'Ah, yes having an odd number makes it jolly difficult, of course, but he's managed to arrange it so that Edith is sitting as far away from Cedric as possible. She shouldn't even be able to see him unless she leans forward and peers around Henry and Miss Simpson.'

'Even so, Constance, I think –.'

'No, William,' Lady Withers said firmly. 'I'm not going to think or talk about it anymore. Lord knows I've got enough on my plate as it is, making sure that all the servants do everything properly so as to avoid Marjorie complaining or making one of her nasty, snide little remarks.'

'Very well, Constance, but on your head be it.' The seriousness of Sir William's tone startled her and she turned to stare at him.

'William, everyone, especially that husband of hers, needs to stop mollycoddling Edith all the time. It's been twelve years. She can't expect everyone to keep walking on egg shells around her forever. Of course I feel very sorry for her, we all do, but everyone lost someone they loved in the war, she's got to start getting over it.'

'There are times, Constance, when you can be quite heartless,' said Sir William coldly. 'You haven't a clue what Edith's been through. You've no idea of how much she's suffered.' With that, Sir William walked out of the room and Lady Withers was left staring helplessly at the empty space where he had been standing, half wondering whether she should call out to him. She was so very unused to them arguing over anything that her eyes immediately welled with tears. Before she had decided quite what to do, she heard him marching across the landing to the stairs.

Constance turned and looked at herself in the dressing table mirror. 'He's still in love with her,' she said softly to her reflection, 'after all this time, he's still in love with her.'

A few doors down the corridor, Lady Belvedere walked into her husband's bedroom.

'Henry, did you know Edith would be coming to stay at Ashgrove this weekend?'

'What's that, Marjorie?' The Earl of Belvedere stood in front of the mirror trying to tie his bow tie. It was no good, however much he tried, he could never tie it properly himself. He sighed. In the early days of their marriage, Lady Belvedere had used to do it for him; nowadays he had to resort to his valet.

'I said, did you know Edith would be here?'

'What? I say, what the devil makes you ask that?'

'You were so insistent that we come down to Ashgrove this weekend. It's not at all like you. Usually I can't tear you away from your library. Anyway, it's a simple enough question, did you know that woman would be here?'

'Of course not, Marjorie. I just wanted to see the children, that's all. Lavinia hardly ever comes home to Sedgwick, as well you know. I just thought this would be a good opportunity to see her. Wonderful that Cedric's come down as well, jolly pleased to see him too, of course.'

An uncomfortable silence lingered in the air. Both knew, although neither said as much, that the reason Lavinia and Cedric came so seldom to Sedgwick Court was because they did not wish to encounter the countess.

'Does it matter so much, Marjorie, Edith being here?'

'I can't stand the woman, I never could when we were girls, and I doubt whether she's changed. But it's not me I'm thinking of. I thought *you* might mind.'

'Me? No, of course not, why should I mind?' Lord Belvedere stopped fiddling with his bow tie and looked at his wife curiously. 'It'll be nice to see her after all these years, it'll just be like old times, what.'

'All the same, I wish she wasn't here.' Lady Belvedere took a deep breath and closed her eyes for a moment. I'm scared, she thought, I'm scared about what might happen.

Chapter Twelve

By the time that the house parlour maid, acting as lady's maid, had finished dressing Lavinia and doing her hair, Rose was fully dressed and ready to go down.

'Oh, I'm awfully sorry, miss,' Martha said, puffing a little as she came into Rose's bedroom. 'It took me longer than I thought it would to see to Lady Lavinia and now I see that you've managed quite well without me.'

'No need to worry. But tell me please, will I do?'

'I think a *demi-toilette* is highly appropriate for country-house visiting, miss, and I see as you're wearing real pearls and your hair is done all nice and simple, so I'd say as you're turned out very well.'

'You don't think I'll look a bit underdressed, do you?'

'Well, perhaps a little compared to Lady Lavinia but, and I may be talking out of turn, I'd say as she's a little overdressed. Of course, I know as the aristocracy is amongst our guests at Ashgrove what with the earl and countess and the heir to a duke being here and all, but while Sir William and m'lady always observe the custom of dressing for dinner even when dining alone, I would say that Lady Lavinia's evening-dress were probably more suited to a ball. I might say that I did try and discourage her from wearing such large diamonds, but she was most insistent.'

'Is she wearing her pale gold silk satin gown,' enquired Rose, her heart sinking, 'the one that's backless?'

'Indeed she is, miss, although I managed to persuade her not to wear gloves which she seemed quite happy about seeing as she would have to remove them anyhow as soon as she had seated herself at the dinner-table.'

'Oh, dear. I suppose you've been put to a lot of additional work with so many guests coming for the weekend?'

'That we have, miss, and with so little notice we haven't been able to get in much help from the village today, so we're all having to double-up with regards to what we do. Still, I can't say as I mind much myself, like, as it means I get some practice hairdressing. You see, miss,' the maid bent forward and lowered her voice as if she intended to impart a great secret, 'my dream is to be a lady's maid one day to some grand mistress. I'm trying to save up to put myself through a hairdressing course and I'm teaching myself a little French because I'm hoping to have an opportunity to travel, that's my dream, like.'

'Well, I wish you every success,' Rose said, sincerely. Before she could add anything further, they heard the door of the room next door open, followed by a rapid tapping on Rose's own door.

'Lavinia, you look wonderful.'

'Do you think so?' enquired Lavinia, throwing back her head and striking a pose, the diamonds she was wearing glittering in the light from the room. 'I must admit that I do think I look rather good in this dress which obviously I didn't get from Madame Renard's shop!' She looked at Rose and smiled. 'You look awfully good too, you know. That dress really suits you and I love your pearls, are those your mother's, the ones that you were telling me about? Aunt will thoroughly approve.'

Together they descended the stairs and went into the drawing room where Lord Sneddon and Lord Sedgwick were awaiting them, the cocktails prepared and put ready in wine glasses on the drinks tray. Both gentlemen, Rose thought, looked handsome in their dinner-jackets and black bow ties. The old rule which had stipulated white tie, tail-coat and white waistcoat be worn at all dinners at which ladies were present, had generally now been abandoned except by the old school.

'Here they are,' declared Lord Sneddon. 'I say, Lavinia, you look swell as they say in America and of course you too, Rose' he added almost as an afterthought. 'Cedric, where's that footman? I want him to get those things out of the refrigerator that I gave him earlier. Ah, there you are,' as Albert appeared, 'have you got them, my man? Good, and are they ice-cold? Put one in each of the glasses and then hand out the drinks will you.'

'Goodness, Hugh,' exclaimed Lavinia, 'whatever are they, they look just like silver balls.'

'That's exactly what they are, silver-plated hollow metal balls. They're called "silverice" balls and they come from America. One uses them in place of ice cubes, the advantage being that they don't dilute one's drink.'

'Oh, how clever, Hugh. Don't you think so?' asked Lavinia turning to Sir William who had just entered the drawing room, 'how would you like to put them in your whisky, Uncle William?'

'I think I'd prefer to stick with ice cubes, my dear, I'm not very good with these new-fangled ideas,' replied Sir William, good humouredly. Rose saw that he was dressed in full evening dress of white tie and tails. 'Ah, here's Constance.'

'Henry and Marjorie are just coming down,' said Lady Withers as she entered the room. 'No sign of Edith, I see. I assume she's still intending on coming down for dinner. No doubt she'll let one of the servants know if she intends to take dinner on a tray in her room instead. Most unfortunate if she decides to, as it will completely upset the seating plan, but Stafford's made up another one just in case and both he and Albert are on hand to re-arrange the table settings if required. Ah, what lovely pearls, my dear,' Lady Withers said turning her attention from her husband to Rose, 'are they your mother's? They look just the sort of necklace I would wear. Really, Lavinia,' she said, looking reprovingly at her niece, 'are all those diamonds really necessary, you're not going to a ball, my dear.'

Lord and Lady Belvedere entered the drawing room and Rose thought that both looked rather ill at ease. The earl especially, she noticed, looked restless and fidgety; she wondered whether it was the result of being in his wife's company. Lady Belvedere made a beeline towards her son whom she had not seen since his arrival. A look of reservation crossed Cedric's face as he moved forward. For a moment his eyes met Rose's and the two of them exchanged a smile. Cedric had to walk past her to get to his mother and as he did so, he turned to her briefly. 'I say, Rose, you look jolly nice in that dress if you don't mind my saying so,' he said quietly, so that only she could hear. She flushed with pleasure and noticed that his cheeks had also gone a subtle shade of crimson.

Instinctively Rose looked up and saw that the countess was watching them closely. The expression on her face showed that she was not best pleased by what she had witnessed. Just then, Edith entered the drawing room and everything stopped and went quiet. All eyes were turned on the newcomer, even Lavinia's and Lord Sneddon's, despite the fact that up until that moment they had been engaged in eager conversation, seemingly oblivious to everyone else. A chilly atmosphere appeared to have invaded the room with Edith's entrance and Rose gave an involuntary shiver. Edith seemed fully aware of the effect of her arrival on the assembly, because she hovered awkwardly by the door. Her eyes sought out Sir William and she looked at him, Rose thought, almost pleadingly. He came to her side at once and this had the effect of breaking the tension in the room. Lavinia and Lord Sneddon took up their conversation and Lady Belvedere commenced her interrogation of Cedric, who stood before her looking uncomfortable. Only Lord Belvedere and Lady Withers continued looking at Edith, who was now engaged in conversation with Sir William. She happened to be smiling at something that he was saying and Rose caught the expression on Lady Withers' face. It took her by surprise because it was one of pain. Rose turned back to look at Edith and Sir William, and wondered.

'Dinner is served', announced Stafford and they all filed out of the drawing room to the dining room in precedence, each gentleman offering his arm to the lady whom he was taking to dinner, followed by Lady Withers. Once they had arrived in the room, the servants drew the ladies' chairs out a little from the table for them and Sir William, as host, remained standing until all the guests had taken their seats. It being a small gathering, there were no name cards on the table. Instead Sir William directed the gentlemen to their seats and each lady sat on the right hand of the gentleman that had taken her to dinner. This resulted in Sir William sitting at the head of the table with Lady Belvedere on his right and Edith on his left. Lord Belvedere sat next to Edith and opposite Lord Sneddon. On the earl's left sat Rose and next to her Cedric, and Lady Withers, at the other end of the table to her husband, sat next to her nephew. Rose was pleased to find herself seated opposite Lavinia who in turn, with no-one sitting on her right with whom she was expected to converse, felt that she was fully justified in focusing her attention on Hugh, with the occasional remark made to Rose for good measure.

Rose herself, could hardly believe her fortune. Not only had she been taken in to dinner by Cedric, her arm resting on his which had caused a delicious shiver to run up her back, but she found herself seated next to him. As in the gardens, she found him delightful company and, while the dinner itself was rather daunting with its many dishes and courses, she had no difficulty in engaging Cedric in conversation for he seemed to find her comments and observations amusing. The same could not be said of Lord Belvedere, seated on her right, who appeared silent and uncommunicative throughout the meal, disinclined to speak to anyone other than to exchange a few words with Edith, out of politeness. Rose noticed that Lady Belvedere

89

was watching her husband keenly, as if she found his behaviour in some way worrying. Every so often, the countess cast a glance at Rose and Cedric and if she happened to catch Rose's eye, she positively glared. This was in direct contrast to the look she bestowed on Lord Sneddon and Lavinia when she saw them engaged in animated conversation. Every so often Lord Sneddon broke off his conversation with Lavinia and conversed with her mother as manners dictated. The gist of their conversation from the snippets that Rose overheard suggested that their discussions centred on what his parents, the duke and duchess, were doing and also news concerning their mutual friends, many of whom appeared to be titled.

Rose looked up the table towards Sir William. He had just finished a conversation with Lady Belvedere to his right and now turned to his left to address Edith. Whatever he was about to say to her froze on his lips and remained unsaid as he glimpsed her face. From where Rose was sitting, it was difficult to see the expression on Edith's face, but it seemed sufficient to alarm Sir William, for he lent towards her slightly and spoke to her in a voice hardly above a whisper. This action caught the attention of both Lady Belvedere and Lady Withers. A look of anguish shot across Constance's face before she turned to Cedric to enquire after his studies.

Mrs Palmer had stuck to the menu that she had put forward to Stafford earlier in the day, which the scullery and kitchen maids had overheard her describe and which had subsequently been agreed with Lady Withers. Rose found that each course seemed to bring with it the offer of a different beverage. Sherry was served with the clear soup, Hock offered during the fish course before the champagne, which was served throughout the dinner along with port. For those not drinking wine, there was the choice of whisky and soda, lemonade, orangeade or barley water. Rose, unused to consuming vast amounts of alcohol and conscious that she had indulged in a cocktail before dinner, moved to lemonade after the sherry and one glass of champagne. Lord Sneddon, she could not help but notice, was drinking rather heavily, as was Lady Withers. Lord Sedgwick kept pace with the various beverages offered with each course but did not appear the worse for drink. Edith, Rose noticed, left her glasses untouched and instead requested a glass of water which was brought to her by Albert, the white-gloved footman, and which she sipped at eagerly.

Once the final course had been served and eaten, Lady Withers gave the signal for the ladies to leave the dining room by catching the eye of Lady Belvedere, as the lady present of the highest rank, who threw one last glance at her husband before rising from her seat. Rose and the other women present followed their example and left the room in the same order in which they had entered it, Lady Withers bringing up the rear. The gentlemen had risen and remained standing by their chairs until the ladies had left the room and Sir William, having opened the door for the ladies to depart, then shut it behind them and returned to his seat. The other gentlemen closed up as near as possible to him so that they could talk to one another more easily.

'Help yourself to port, Cedric, and then pass it around.'

There ensued a period of contented silence as the gentlemen indulged in their fortified wine and cigars and cigarettes.

'My sister seems to have made quite an impression on you, Hugh,' Cedric said at last, quietly enough so that neither Lord Belvedere nor Sir William could hear what he said. This precaution, however, appeared unnecessary, for both seemed lost in their own thoughts. 'If you're not careful, my mother will have you both married off in no time.' He spoke jokingly, with obvious affection for his sister, but when Lord Sneddon replied, he appeared serious.

'Would that be such a bad thing, Cedric? Wouldn't you like to have me for a brother-in-law?'

'I wouldn't have thought that Lavinia was really your type, old man. As for having you for a brother-in-law, I wouldn't mind so long as you promised to treat my sister well.' There was a slight edge to Lord Sedgwick's voice, which implied that he might have certain reservations about such a connection; this was not lost on Lord Sneddon, who looked annoyed.

'Enough of this marriage talk, Cedric. We're here to have fun, aren't we? Harmless fun, of course,' he added as he saw the warning look on Cedric's face. 'Anyway, enough about me, now what about you and Miss Simpson? Made quite an impact on you, I wager.'

'She certainly seems to be a remarkable young lady.'

'Really? I would have said that her sort are two a penny, but I suppose there's no accounting for taste. You, on the other hand, are quite a catch. Not so much as me, of course,' he laughed and Cedric decided to take what he was saying as a joke rather than to take offence. Not for the first time, however, he wondered whether their friendship had run its course. Hugh might be a good nine or ten years older than him, but Cedric was beginning to consider him rather shallow and irresponsible.

'Right,' said Sir William suddenly coming out of his reverie, 'shall we join the ladies? I say, Henry, are you feeling all right?'

'What?' enquired Lord Belvedere, clearly startled. 'Oh, yes of course, just feeling a bit tired after the journey, don't you know. Marjorie would insist that we set off at first light. Couldn't see the need for the rush myself, but you know what women are like.'

'How did she know we'd be down at Ashgrove this weekend, Father?' asked Cedric. 'I was careful to keep Lavinia's impending visit from my letters and Hugh and I only decided at the last minute to come down.'

'You know what your mother's like, she has her ways of finding things out. If you and your sister came to Sedgwick more often, she wouldn't resort to such measures. Really Cedric, your mother misses you dreadfully when you're away; Lavinia too, of course.'

'Well she has a funny way of showing it,' retorted Cedric.

'I suppose it was *her* idea that you come down to Ashgrove this weekend,' queried Sir William, sharply.

'Of course. What are you saying, William?'

'I just wondered,' said Sir William, 'whether it might have been yours.'

The coffee cups, which had previously been heated, had been placed on a tray with the cream jug, milk and basin of sugar. The footman entered the drawing room with a smaller tray, on which were coffee and liqueurs. The women helped themselves to coffee and seated themselves comfortably on the various settees and chairs dotted around the room. Only Lady Belvedere remained standing, clutching her coffee cup. Lavinia and Rose not surprisingly had chosen to sit together, as had Lady Withers and Edith.

'I do hope the men will be joining us shortly,' whispered Lavinia, 'I'm worried that any second now Mother will wander over and have another go at me about working. At least when Cedric's here he can distract her, he's her golden boy.'

'Edith, are you quite recovered now, my dear?' enquired Lady Withers, half-heartedly. 'I'm so glad. Now tell me, did you happen to go to Chelsea Flower Show this year? I didn't manage to, I'm afraid, what with one thing and another. I understand that it didn't have any outstanding features, but that the general standard of floral collections and the variety of plants shown were both excellent. I read somewhere that this year the main exhibits were housed in one large marquee instead of the usual two tents, such a good idea, far more convenient for viewing them and much more space. Bridges, our gardener, is particularly interested in novelties in roses; he's always trying to persuade me to introduce new roses to our rose garden, but I keep telling him that I like the old-fashioned ones, don't you?'

'Poor Edith,' said Lavinia looking over towards them, 'Aunt seems to be boring her to tears. I can't understand why she's prattling on so much about the most boring things. Of course, with Edith it is always difficult to find something to talk about, she's always so jolly sensitive about everything.'

'And how is that husband of yours, Edith? What a pity he couldn't come down this weekend. William and I are always saying what a very nice chap he is and of course he's absolutely devoted to you, anyone can see that.'

'Harold Torrington is one of the most dull men you'll ever meet, Rose,' said Lavinia, 'I'm jolly glad that he hasn't come down with Edith. Aunt is talking absolute rubbish. I know for a fact that she finds Edith's husband insufferably boring. As do we all. I imagine that Edith's quite glad to get the chance of a weekend away from him. Oh do look at Mother. Why does she have to look so disgruntled all the time? You'd think she'd make the effort to go over and talk to Edith, even if they did have a bit of a falling out years ago. Really, it's absolutely ages since they last saw each other.'

'Lavinia, everyone seems a little wary of Mrs Torrington, do you know why?' enquired Rose.

'Do they?' Lavinia looked surprised. 'I can't think why. I've always found her rather ineffectual and insipid myself. She always looks so fragile, as if she's about to break or burst into tears. I do hope she won't spoil the weekend for us. But enough talk about her. I'd much rather talk about what we're going to do tomorrow. I told you, didn't I, that Ceddie and Hugh were talking about taking a picnic to the lake? Oh, I say, I've just had a thought. Aunt?' Lavinia raised her voice so that Lady Withers could hear. 'Have you still got your circular croquet garden? It's just occurred to me that it might be fun to have a game or two of croquet tomorrow.'

'Yes, dear, we still have it, although it hasn't been used for absolutely ages. I think the last time was ten or so years ago on an occasion when you came to stay, Edith. But Bridges is very diligent. He always keeps it closely mowed so there shouldn't be any problem if you wish to play.'

'Yes, I remember it now,' Edith said. They were the first words Rose had heard her utter since she had come in to the drawing room. 'It's quite far from the house, isn't it?'

'Yes, a fair walk I suppose,' agreed Lady Withers, rather vaguely. 'One can't see it at all from the house; it's quite hidden by the yew hedge. You know what they say, out of sight, out of mind, what.'

'Yes, exactly,' mumbled Edith, and no-one else was near enough to see the gleam in her eye.

Chapter Thirteen

The gentlemen joined the ladies in the drawing room and helped themselves to coffee and liqueurs. Their arrival helped to encourage the guests to mingle and the atmosphere in the room to lighten, although Rose thought that she still detected a tension in the air. It was almost as if everyone was trying just a bit too hard. She herself felt like an observer, watching from the shadows to see how those in another world behaved. She watched as Lord Sneddon gravitated towards Lavinia, and saw how her friend giggled in delight as the countess looked on. Of all those present, Rose found Lady Belvedere's demeanour most unnerving, for gone was the strongly opinionated woman of the afternoon and instead, in her place, was a woman who was watchful and calculating, a woman who feared the worst. She remembered Lady Belvedere's expression when she had first encountered Edith in the morning-room and the way timid, quiet little Edith had stood up to her and that the countess had backed away as if she were afraid.

Lord Belvedere was deep in conversation with his son and Lady Withers took the opportunity to come over to Rose.

'He is very handsome isn't he, my dear,' Constance said, 'Cedric I mean, not Lord Sneddon, although he is a very good looking young man as well.'

'Yes, indeed.'

'My sister has high hopes for Cedric, of course. As the only son he will inherit his father's title in due course and manage his great estates. She'll want him to marry the eldest daughter of a duke or else money, which in these times means an American heiress as likely as not. I don't mean to pry or interfere, my dear, but I cannot help but notice the way you look at him. Cedric is a dear boy, he is always very pleasing and attentive company, it is his way, but you must not read any more into it than that.'

Rose felt her cheeks burning with embarrassment and humiliation. Had she really been so obvious? Lord Sneddon had gone over to speak to Cedric. Lavinia, catching Rose's eye came over, apparently concerned.

'Are you all right, Rose? You do look awfully flushed; I suppose it has been a long day. I was going to suggest that we stay up but I'm tired too, so when Aunt announces that she is going to retire for the night, I think we should too. I want to have loads of energy for tomorrow. Oh, its suddenly got cold in here, hasn't it, I wish I'd brought a wrap down with me. I suppose I could ring for a servant, but I expect that they've all retired to bed by now. Still, I expect if I pull the bell pull – '

'I'll get it for you, Lavinia,' offered Rose, eager for the chance to be by herself for a few minutes.

'Would you? Oh, you are a dear. I think it's laid across the chair in my bedroom, you can't miss it.'

Rose quickly left the room. A few moments later, another guest who had watched her departure with interest, also made his exit.

'You truly excelled yourself, Mrs Palmer, as you always do on occasions like this,' the butler assured the cook-housekeeper.

'Oh, do you think so, Mr Stafford?' Mrs Palmer beamed, obviously pleased by his praise. 'The meal did all seem to come together in the end, despite us being so short staffed. I'll say this for Bessie and little Edna, they certainly pulled their weight today, no stopping to gossip. Well, we'll find out tomorrow morning whether her ladyship was pleased when I go through the menu for the day with her. However, I couldn't help but notice, Mr Stafford, by the dishes that were brought back that one diner seemed hardly to have touched their food. Perhaps it wasn't to their liking?'

'That would be Mrs Torrington,' replied the butler. 'But I wouldn't read anything into it with regard to your food, Mrs Palmer. The lady in question appeared quite off-colour and out of sorts tonight, the effect of seeing Lord Sedgwick again I would imagine, most unfortunate.'

'Poor woman, she's been through a lot, as you and I well know, Mr Stafford.'

'Indeed. I would of course say this only to you, Mrs Palmer, but there seemed rather an odd atmosphere at dinner tonight. It was almost as if everyone was waiting for something to happen.'

'It's not like you to be fanciful, Mr Stafford. I expect that it's more to do with that they're such a strange assortment of guests. If her ladyship had had more of a choice in the matter, I doubt whether she would have thought to invite them all down together.'

'I'm sure that must be it, Mrs Palmer. All the same, I think I'll just take a last stroll into the drawing room and check that all's well before I call it a night.'

The wrap was not on the chair, as Lavinia had described, but lay discarded across the bed. Rose picked it up, cast a quick glance around the room, noticing once again the opulence of it in comparison with her own and left. She walked across the landing and went quickly down the first flight of stairs to the landing below. She was just making her way towards the main staircase down to the hall when an imposing figure appeared from out of the darkness, barring her way.

'Lord Sneddon, you startled me. I didn't see you there.'

'Evidently not. Come, Miss Simpson; may I call you Rose and you must call me Hugh. There's no need to look so alarmed, you know, I'm not going to eat you.'

'Please let me get past, Lord Sneddon, er, Hugh. I must get back to the drawing room. Lavinia will be wondering where I am.' It was evident from his speech that Lord Sneddon had had a fair amount to drink and Rose could feel herself becoming anxious.

'What's the rush? I think dear Lavinia is far more likely to be concerned about my absence than yours, don't you? But I'd rather like to have a chat with you just now. You've certainly made an impression on young Cedric. Was that your aim? I can't see what he sees in you, myself, but perhaps you have some hidden qualities that you'd like to show me.'

'Let me pass, Lord Sneddon.' Rose tried to keep the panic out of her voice.

'You needn't play hard to get with me, giving yourself airs and graces,' Lord Sneddon said, angrily. 'You're just a common little shop girl; two a penny, my dear. I can get a girl like you, anytime, anywhere; they're queuing up for me.'

'Well, I'm not. So I suggest –.' Rose broke off suddenly as she heard a cough. Both she and Lord Sneddon swung around to see from whence it came. From out of the shadows on the far side of the landing, emerged the butler.

'Excuse me my lord, Lord Sedgwick was just asking where you were.'

'Good God, man, where did you spring from? You weren't there a moment ago, I'd swear on it. I'll be down in a minute. Miss Simpson and I were just having a nice little chat.'

Stafford did not move.

'Well, get on man,' said Lord Sneddon, irritably.

'No, sir, I don't think so. Not unless I am accompanying Miss Simpson to the drawing room.'

'Why you impertinent –.' Lord Sneddon glared at them both. 'You'll pay for this, Stafford, see if you don't.' He turned on his heel and marched down the stairs angrily.

'Thank you, Mr Stafford, I don't know what I would have done if –.'

'Think nothing of it, miss. Not wishing to speak out of turn, but I would suggest that you lock your door tonight.'

'Oh, there you are, Rose,' said Lavinia when Rose returned to the drawing room. Lord Sneddon, Rose noticed, was making a show of talking to Sir William as if nothing had happened. 'I thought you'd got lost. Wasn't the wrap where I said it would be?'

Later that night when Rose retired to bed, she made sure to lock her door. For good measure, she also leaned a chair against it, but thought moving the dressing table as well was perhaps going a step too far.

Chapter Fourteen

Rose awoke early the next morning, her head heavy due to having slept fitfully during the night. Her sleep had been peppered with dreams of someone trying to get into her room, which had caused her to awake with a start on several occasions, the fear still with her so that she had felt compelled to get out of bed each time and try her door to reassure herself that it was well and truly locked.

Looking at her wristwatch, which lay on the bedside table, Rose saw that it was only a quarter to six and that, while the day was just beginning for the servants, indeed for some it was probably well underway, she had a full two hours before she needed to think about getting up. Reason told her that she should stay in bed and try to make up for the sleep she had lost. She had been informed by Lavinia that breakfast was served at nine at Ashgrove and that the maid would wake her at a quarter to eight with a cup of tea, so there was no fear of her oversleeping. Her clothes for the day would be laid out for her and the maid would tap discreetly on her door to advise her when her bath was ready. She was unused to such luxury and felt that she should make the most of it. Accordingly, she settled down in her bed and willed sleep to come, or at least to be only half awake.

Sleep, however, would not come and after twenty minutes had elapsed, Rose gave up trying. It seemed to her then that the best thing to do would be to take a walk around the grounds, which she hoped would help to clear her head. It was still so early that she did not fear coming across Lord Sneddon lurking half hidden behind a rose bush, and so she stole out of her room and down the staircases, across the hall and out through one of the French windows, which she closed carefully behind her. She walked out on to the terrace and around the perimeter of the formal gardens, skirting the courtyard garden and the kitchen garden with its espaliered fruit trees, until she came to the circular croquet lawn. This lawn, she discovered, was enclosed by a yew hedge which, together with the lawn's distance from the house, provided it with a degree of privacy which was lacking in the formal gardens. Lady Withers, she remembered, had remarked only the evening before how seldom the croquet lawn was used and it occurred to Rose that, given the early hour, it might be a good place for her to stop and gather her thoughts in preparation for the day ahead.

Uppermost in her mind was Lord Sneddon's conduct towards her the evening before. That he had been drunk, she was in little doubt, but it did not excuse his behaviour towards her. The most worrying aspect she found was imagining what might have happened had not Stafford come to her rescue. Despite the sunshine and the fact that she was wrapped up in a thick coat, she shivered. The possibility that her friend might marry such a man filled her with dread, and she felt duty bound to warn Lavinia before it was too late. However, she did not relish the prospect for she was afraid that her friend was likely to be dismissive and consider her in some way to blame.

She walked the perimeter of the yew hedge, marvelling at both its height, which meant that she was unable to see over it even on tiptoes, and also how thickly grown the hedge was so that she could not see through it to the croquet lawn beyond. She was just approaching the entrance to the croquet lawn when she heard voices. Instinctively she stopped, hesitating as to what to do next. It was still only a quarter to seven which seemed to her a strange hour to arrange a meeting, and the voices she realised now were raised, not so much in argument but more as if the speakers were each trying to get their own points over and were fearing interruption from the other.

Chapter Fifteen

Edith, talk sense,' said a man's voice that Rose could not immediately recognise. 'Think what you're suggesting. If you do what you're proposing, you'll hurt a number of people, is that really what you want?'

'It's no good, my mind is quite made up. Do you think I have done anything but think and think since I arrived and saw who was here? This is my one chance to reveal the truth and hold that woman to account. She has destroyed our lives and now I am going to make her pay.'

'Edith, I know you want justice –'

'Justice? Why, if there was any justice in this world, she'd be dead! I want to make her pay for what she did and I'm going to make her, even if it means killing her myself!'

'Edith! Don't say such a thing, even in jest.'

'Who says I'm jesting? I mean it. I'll do whatever it takes and to hell with the consequences. For all these years I have done exactly what everyone has told me to, to make amends for my great wrongdoing. And God knows I have suffered for it. I have lost my only child in a war that was supposed to end all wars, but what a sacrifice!'

'I know, Edith, you've been through much and it's not fair. But think what you'd be giving up. You have a husband who loves you –'

'Harold, dear Harold, he deserves so much better than me. But I've got to do it; this might be my only opportunity.'

'Is there nothing I can say that will stop you?'

'No. If I don't do it now, I shall die.'

'Then there's nothing more to say. On your head be it, Edith.' These words were said so decisively, that Rose knew instinctively that the gentleman was on the verge of leaving. This placed her in a dilemma for she had little doubt that the conversation that she had unwittingly overhead was intensely private and she did not want to be taken for an eavesdropper. She retreated further back from the entrance and, spotting some densely planted shrubs, she crouched down behind them hoping that she would be hidden.

As it happened, though she was not to know, the gentleman in question was so engrossed in his thoughts that he did not look about him once, but instead strode across the grass back in the direction of the house. Rose waited a couple of minutes before she stood up cautiously. Edith evidently had decided to remain where she was on the croquet lawn a little longer, no doubt to avoid a casual observer from witnessing them returning to the house together. Confident now that she would not be seen by Edith, Rose looked back towards the house and to the man striding towards it. He was quite some way away from her by now, but even so she could tell at once who it was. She thought back to the night before and the look of anguish that had crossed Lady Withers' face. It seemed to Rose now that her look of distress had been justified, for the man who had arranged what must surely have been a secret assignation with Edith, was none other than Sir William.

Rose made her way back to the house in a daze, hardly able to believe what she had just overheard. Had it not been for the fact that she had seen Sir William with her own eyes, she would not have believed him complicit in such deception. He had seemed to her genuinely fond of his eccentric, absent-minded wife, but it appeared that this was not the case and that Lady Withers herself had her own suspicions.

Rose thought back to dinner the previous night and remembered how Sir William had bent forward to make sure that Edith was all right, a gesture Lady Withers had correctly identified as one of affection. She deduced from what she had heard that Edith intended to confront Lady Withers with the truth and now presumably it would be up to Sir William to decide whether he should tell his wife about his relationship with her old school friend or wait for Edith to do so. Either way did not bode well, but while it was a tragic situation, Rose told herself that she must remember that it was not her tragedy. Even so, she could not help wondering what would happen when the truth was out, whether the marriage would survive or end in divorce, and her thoughts turned to Lavinia and Cedric and the effect that it would have on them, given that they regarded Sir William and his wife as parent figures, making up for the deficiencies of their own.

Whatever happened in the future, at this moment in time she did not want to run the risk of bumping into Sir William as they both made their way back to the house. To ensure that this did not happen, she decided to veer off into the kitchen garden and stay there a few minutes; she could always count the different types of herbs. She strode on with renewed purpose, turned a corner and ran straight into a servant who was weeping bitterly.

'Oh, I'm sorry, miss,' sniffed Edna, mopping ineffectually at her eyes with the back of her hand to try and disguise the fact that she had been crying. 'I didn't see you there. I didn't think anyone would be about at this hour, certainly not one of the guests, like.'

Rose studied her curiously. Edna made a pitiful sight with her tear stained face and strands of black hair escaping untidily from under her mop cap. She was probably fourteen, Rose guessed, although she looked little for her age and her uniform was a couple of sizes too big as if she was still expected to grow into her dress. There were smudges on her apron too of what looked like black-lead.

'What's the matter?' asked Rose, kindly.

'Oh, it's nothing, miss, really, but it's awful kind of you to ask. It's just Mrs Palmer, she's the cook-housekeeper here, well she's always down on me like a ton of bricks, she is. Nothing I do is ever right. It's bad enough when it's a normal day what with her going on about me not polishing the grate enough, or the legs of the kitchen table not gleaming even after I've scrubbed them down with soap and soda for all I'm worth. Me hands are that red and raw miss, what with scrubbing the steps and the kitchen dresser and kitchen cupboards and the floors. .And I've got all the washing up to do, including the pots and pans, and what with this house party, Mrs Palmer's got me preparing all the vegetables too and working all hours to help her get the meals ready. She's said that everything's got to be just right on account of the countess and Lord Sneddon being here. Lady Belvedere's awful fussy about her food, miss and Mrs Palmer says how we aren't to let her ladyship down, that Lady Withers, miss. But I've got so much to do, I just don't know where to start and I'm that tired miss, I really am.'

Edna gulped and her eyes filled with tears again. Visibly moved by her plight, Rose felt compelled to put her arm around her shoulders. 'There, there, I wish I could help in some way, but I'm not sure what I can do. What's your name?'

'Edna, miss. There's nothing you can do miss; I expect I'm just being silly. My mother says that if I buckle down and work hard I can be a cook myself someday, that's my dream, like. Oh no, is that the time?' Edna exclaimed, suddenly catching sight of the time on Rose's wristwatch. 'I must go or Mrs Palmer will have my guts for garters, she will. Thanks awfully, miss, for putting up with all my moaning. I feel a whole lot better now, truly

I do. You won't tell anyone, will you? I know I'm awful lucky to have this job really, what with all those people out of work.' And before Rose had even had a chance to say goodbye, Edna had hitched up her skirt and was running full pelt back to the kitchen and to Mrs Palmer's sharp tongue.

Rose was dreading breakfast and having to see Lord Sneddon again. However, it soon became apparent that the gentleman in question either had no recollection of his conduct of the night before, or wished to act as if nothing untoward had occurred. This suited Rose's purpose, for she had now resolved to say nothing of the incident to Lavinia and wanted instead to focus on enjoying the weekend. So she helped herself with relish to bacon, eggs and devilled kidneys from the silver chafing dishes on the sideboard, supplemented by coffee and hot toast served by the footman.

Besides herself and Lord Sneddon, Lavinia, Cedric and Sir William were the only other members of the household and guests present. Lady Withers, Lady Belvedere and Edith, as married women, were enjoying the privilege of breakfasting in bed. Once or twice Rose sneaked a glance at Sir William, but although he seemed a little preoccupied, he did not appear unduly anxious or worried. It was only when she was halfway through breakfast that Rose realised Lord Belvedere was not there.

'Father breakfasted earlier this morning,' explained Cedric. 'He was keen to continue with his cataloguing of Uncle's books. You'd think he'd get bored of it, wouldn't you. It's a pity to be cooped up indoors on a day like this. Speaking of which, Hugh and I were just discussing whether or not to play croquet this morning. Do you play at all? It's much more fun with four than two and you're always up for a game, aren't you, Sis?'

Rose admitted rather sheepishly that she had never played croquet before and wouldn't know where to start.

'Not to worry,' said Cedric, reassuringly. 'The rules are very straightforward. You have a ball and a mallet and the aim of the game is to be the first to hit the post having gone through a series of hoops. Of course you do try to croquet your opponents to advance your progress around the course and send them back, but I'll explain all that once we get out there, as well as telling you what it is to roquet someone.'

It transpired that Sir William had some affairs of business to attend to in his study and Lady Belvedere, Lady Withers and Edith all had letters to write, so only the four young people made their way to the croquet lawn, which Rose was relieved to find quite deserted. A wooden croquet set was produced made by Jacques, which Cedric informed her was reputedly the oldest sports and games manufacturer in the world, with a long-established reputation for producing high quality croquet equipment and it was hardly surprising given that they had invented the game, unveiling it to the world in 1851 at the Great Exhibition, for which they had received a gold medal.

Cedric explained to her that croquet was a game that encompassed the need for tactics, strategy and skill in equal measure, although he himself, he assured her, was rather lacking in all three categories.

'You'll have to watch out for Lavinia,' he warned her, 'she's utterly ruthless and totally devious, aren't you, Sis? She'll think nothing of croqueting you, even though it's your first time playing.'

'Absolutely,' agreed his sister, 'it's the only way to play if you want to win. So I'm afraid I won't be giving you any slack, Rose. What about you, Hugh, how's your game?'

'Oh, I think I can give you a run for your money,' Lord Sneddon replied, confidently. 'I'm quite a dab hand at this game, actually. I warn you, I'm particularly good at croqueting, I can send a ball for miles.'

'I'd like to see you try,' giggled Lavinia and there ensued a hectic game of croquet in which Lavinia and Hugh seemed to gallop up the course leaving Cedric and Rose behind. Once she had mastered holding the mallet correctly and getting a feel for how to strike the ball, Rose discovered that she was actually quite good at getting the ball through the hoops and keeping to a straight line. Cedric, she was sure, was deliberately not playing well in order not to leave her trailing behind. Both Lavinia and Lord Sneddon, she noticed, were quite reckless in the way they played the game, taking risks and trying to croquet each other at every opportunity, sending the other's ball charging down to the other end of the course and off the lawn into the yew hedge. It was all done very good-naturedly however, and for a couple of hours or so, all that could be heard was the satisfying strike of wooden mallets on croquet balls and the sounds of laughter.

In due course, Stafford appeared and advised them that the others intended to join them on the lawn for an al fresco lunch. Rose assumed that this meant that they would be eating a simple lunch of sandwiches, but various servants appeared carrying out tables, chairs, hampers and wine coolers, followed by Sir William, Lady Withers, the earl and the countess and Edith, the latter looking pale and agitated. Every so often, Rose noticed, Sir William turned his gaze on Edith and a worried look crossed his face, although it did not seem to her the look of a man on tenter hooks waiting for his world to come crashing down around him. The earl and countess also appeared preoccupied and, in the case of Lord Belvedere, fidgety; he got up several times and wandered across the lawn idly picking up a croquet mallet and swinging it, or stopping to engage in conversation with his children. Lady Withers was prattling away to Edith, something along the lines that many people, including herself, considered that putting the milk in first produced a better cup of tea, but that Stafford was really too tiresome about it, and kept insisting that it wasn't done, which meant then, of course, that she as hostess was expected to hand the milk-jug to each guest, which really did create such a lot of additional, unnecessary work.

'I wonder what on earth's the matter with Aunt Connie,' whispered Lavinia to Rose, 'she really is talking a lot of old nonsense to Edith. Did you notice that she did the same thing last night after dinner in the drawing room, before the men joined us? Poor Edith, she must be bored witless. I wonder whether one of us should go and rescue her.'

'I'll go,' offered Rose, although she did not think that it was Edith who needed rescuing. Lady Withers is just scared, she thought, of having her worst fears realised. She thinks that if she keeps on talking, Edith won't be able to get a word in edgeways to tell her what's been going on between her and Sir William. There was definitely a tension in the air, now that they were all present, which had not been there during their game of croquet. But was Edith really the cause of it? Rose certainly did not find her the most frightening woman there; that was Lady Belvedere, who sat a little apart from everyone else, as ever watching, her eyes flicking between them all, resting for a few moments on each by turn. Rose guessed that she was pleased to see the relationship developing between her daughter and Lord Sneddon, less so Rose's developing friendship with her son. The countess's eyes rested every now and then on Edith, who on one occasion looked up and caught her eye. Rose found herself recoiling in alarm, for the look that Edith gave Lady Belvedere was one of pure hatred. A lesser woman would have paled and left the assembled group feigning a headache. But Lady Belvedere stood firm. She answered the look with one of her own. If Rose was not mistaken, the countess was issuing Edith with a challenge; she was throwing down the gauntlet and calling her bluff.

Chapter Sixteen

When looking back over the next few weeks, at the tragic events of that weekend, Rose felt with hindsight that it had been almost inevitable that the tension that had appeared on the Friday and steadily built up would eventually explode, although few of those present, she felt sure, could have anticipated such disastrous consequences.

At the time, Rose was aware only that the arrival of the others at the croquet lawn for luncheon had brought to an end what, up until then, had been a bright and relaxed day. It was difficult to identify what exactly had marred the day, how the atmosphere had become strained for, despite the sunshine and the sumptuous banquet served by Lady Withers' attentive servants, gone were the tranquillity and laughter. Lord Sneddon was positively scowling, Lavinia was sulking and Cedric looked only worried.

It seemed to Rose that it must be due to the presence of someone in the party and that if that were the case, it was likely to be only one of two women. Reason told her that it must surely be the countess with her ill temperament, bullying manner and sour expression, but at the same time she could not help but remember the illicit conversation that had passed between Edith and Sir William, or the hurt expression on Lady Withers' face and the look of fear on her sister's when each encountered Edith. It seemed too farfetched that someone as nervous, timid and insignificant as Edith was, could cause one strong woman anguish and the other to be afraid. And it was because Edith appeared almost pathetic and yet seemed to yield so much power, that Rose found herself regarding the woman warily, tempted herself to give her a wide berth.

Even so, she found herself drawn to sitting next to Edith, as if the woman held some strange fascination that she could not resist.

'I feel that you and I are alike, Rose,' said Edith, 'watching on, so to speak, looking at the way people who are titled and have money live. See how many servants they have to look after their needs, doesn't it make you envious? Wouldn't you like to change places with Lavinia instead of going back to work in your shop? They were always lucky, they always got exactly what they wanted, even then.' Edith bent her head to Rose's and lowered her voice. 'They were the Bellingham sisters, you know?'

'Bellingham sisters, you mean Lady Withers and Lady Belvedere?' enquired Rose, somewhat confused.

'Yes, I still think of them as that, silly isn't it? It dates back to when we were all at school together. We used to spend the school holidays together too. We were quite inseparable, although I always knew I was different from them, the poor relation, I mean.'

'That must have been quite hard.'

'As a small child it didn't seem to matter, but as we got older, it became more apparent. They became more aware of their wealth, I think, and what it could get them. Did you know that their family made its money from coal mining? It both owned and operated the collieries, that's to say, their family owned both the mineral royalties and the coal, which isn't usual; it put them in a very strong position. I'll say this for the Bellingham's though, they had a good record in ensuring the safety of their workers as well as providing them with good housing. Theirs was one of the pits that the King visited during his Royal Tour of the North in 1912. Anyway, it was obvious that with that amount of wealth behind them, both sisters were destined to make good marriages. They had looks too; they were considered the most beautiful debutantes of their time. Yes, they had everything going for them.' A touch of bitterness had entered Edith's voice, which Rose resented. How could Edith just sit there and berate their wealth while at the same time enjoying Lady Withers' hospitality and engaging in an illicit liaison with her husband?

'You and Lady Withers are obviously close. Lavinia says you often come to stay at Ashgrove.'

'Yes, as much as anyone can be close to Constance.'

'And Sir William, you must be close to him too given that he's the husband of your old school friend?

Edith looked at Rose suspiciously for a moment, and then looked away.

'They seem a very devoted couple, don't they, Lady Withers and Sir William?'

'Do they? Yes, I suppose they do, I've never really given it much thought.'

'Well, perhaps you should,' Rose blurted out before she could stop herself.

'I –.'

'I'm sorry, I didn't mean ….it's … oh, I don't really know what I mean,' Rose said helplessly. It was not any of her business after all.

'It's all right, it's the atmosphere here. You feel it as I do. You can cut it with a knife. It's because of her you know.' Rose followed Edith's glance. She was staring intently at where Lady Withers and Lady Belvedere stood, engaged in conversation. Rose was pleased to see that Lady Withers' servants were at the other end of the lawn, loading up the hampers with the used cutlery, glasses and crockery and so were unlikely to overhear their conversation.

'I am about to do something that I am loathe to do,' said Edith, and Rose saw that she had tears in her eyes. 'It will break Harry's heart, of course, but I've got to do it, I've got to.'

'Must you really?' asked Rose. She felt a sharp stab of guilt. Not once had she thought about the effect the discovery of his wife's affair might have on Edith's husband, Harold. Her thoughts had only been with Lady Withers and Lavinia and Cedric and how they would be affected. Now she thought about the man she had never met. Surely he had suffered enough with the death of his only son; it would be too cruel to hear that his wife had been unfaithful with the husband of her old school friend.

'Don't do it, Mrs Torrington…. Edith,' Rose implored. 'No good can come of it, after all. You'll hurt so many people. Is it really worth it, just to free your conscience?'

'But I've got to. I don't think I'll be able to live with myself if I don't. Don't you see,' Edith turned to look at Rose beseechingly, 'I might never get another chance. The truth must come out, it must.'

Edith was right in thinking that she might not have another opportunity, Rose acknowledged, for now that Lady Withers had suspicions about her husband's relationship with her old school friend, it was highly unlikely that Edith would ever be invited to stay again at Ashgrove.

'But please don't.' Rose took a deep breath. Edith appeared so adamant that there did not seem anything for it but to let on that she had overheard their conversation on the croquet lawn. 'Sir William doesn't want you to, does he?'

'William? Oh, oh, no ….' Edith stared at her and then realisation must have dawned, because her face seemed to collapse.

110

'Please,' said Rose hastily, looking around afraid that the others would notice Edith's distraught state. She was relieved to see that everyone, other than Lord Belvedere, who Rose thought was unlikely to say anything or draw it to anyone else's attention, appeared to be too engrossed in their own conversations to have noticed. 'I didn't mean to listen to your conversation, really I didn't, but if Sir William doesn't want you to, why do it?' She wanted to add, but thought it mean to do so, so didn't, that if Sir William did not want Edith to say anything, then surely that meant that he had no intention of leaving his wife to be with her.

'Don't you see, I've got to.'

'But why?' Rose felt as if she wanted to shake Edith. 'Why must you do it?'

'She's got to pay, don't you see that? She's got to pay for what she did to me, to us?'

Rose felt herself becoming cold towards Edith. Why should Lady Withers pay? What could she possibly have done to Edith, compared with what Edith had done, and was about to do, to her? Edith was thinking only of herself. Perhaps she felt that if she could not have Sir William, she would make sure that he and Lady Withers were not happy.

'When are you going to do it?'

'Today sometime, before dinner, I must do it today.'

'Why must you do it today? Can't you leave it to the end of the weekend, when everyone's about to leave?' She wondered if Edith could arrange to stay on somehow, so that Lady Withers was not told the truth until her guests had all gone.

'No, I want to get it over with. Besides, there might not be time tomorrow.'

'Do you really think so little of her that you would cause her so much pain while everyone is still here?'

'Think so little of her?' Rose was alarmed to find that Edith had raised her voice. 'I don't just think little of her, I loathe and despise the woman! Why, I positively hate her, didn't you hear me say as much to William? As far as I'm concerned, she should die for what she did, she certainly doesn't deserve to live. I'm half minded to kill her myself and to hell with the consequences!'

111

Rose was visibly shocked. It was not just the vehemence with which Edith had said such awful things which led her to believe that she truly meant every word, it was that she had managed to disguise her feelings so well so as to appear friendly towards Lady Withers. Why had she been chatting idly with Lady Withers as they made their way towards the croquet lawn for lunch if she despised her so?

'But she's your old school friend –'

'Pah! She and I have never been friends. She never liked me then and she dislikes me even more now.'

'But if that's the case, why do you come to Ashgrove? If you hate Lady Withers so much, why do you accept her hospitality?'

'Lady Withers?' Edith looked at Rose in amazement. 'I'm not talking about *Constance*. Whatever put that idea into your head? No, I'm talking about Marjorie, the Countess of Belvedere.'

Chapter Seventeen

Before Rose had an opportunity to question Edith further and ask her what she meant, Lady Withers had whisked her friend away on some pretext about seeing some gown or other that she had a view to wear that evening. In the few brief minutes before she herself was persuaded to play another game of croquet, Rose, although deeply puzzled at how she could have misunderstood everything so completely, felt a deep sense of relief that Edith was not about to tear apart the lives of her host and hostess. That Edith had some personal grievance against Lady Belvedere was obvious, but it was not her concern.

The rest of the day was spent playing yet more croquet, and with Cedric as a capable teacher, Rose felt by the end that she was becoming quite a master at the game and was even able to croquet Lavinia. The activities of the day, however, were constantly disrupted by Lady Belvedere summoning one or other of them to her presence. The first to be summoned was Lord Sneddon, much to the young man's surprise, who was followed first by Lavinia and then by Cedric. Lord Sneddon, Rose noticed, returned distinctly out of sorts, not wishing to speak to anyone and smashing the croquet ball with such force that Rose was surprised that it did not split in two. Lavinia returned in a sulky mood, every so often looking daggers at Rose, as if her friend had upset her in some way rather than her mother. When Cedric returned he was quiet and withdrawn, as if he had much on his mind but, when he happened to catch Rose's eye, he smiled shyly. Rose half expected to be summoned herself to appear before the countess, but was relieved to find that this was not to be the case. Even so, it had put a distinct dampener on the afternoon, casting a shadow that lasted until dinner.

Lavinia, Rose knew, planned to wear her gold lame dress that evening, cut on the bias and pleated on one side, complete with fishtail. While she herself considered that such a dress was more suited for wearing to a banquet, it put her black dress to shame, particularly as she had already worn it to dinner the night before. She had also completely forgotten to select a rose from the garden to wear as a corsage. Just as Rose was resigning herself to wearing her mother's pearls again, hoping that no-one would notice that her outfit was exactly the same as the one she had worn the night before, there was a gentle tapping at her door.

'Excuse me, miss,' said Martha, coming in. 'I hope you don't mind, I know it's taking a liberty, like, but I couldn't help noticing when I was hanging up your things that you'd only brought the one evening dress with you. I hope you won't take offence, but I happened to mention it to Miss Crimms, she who's her ladyship's lady's maid and who's also seeing to Lady Belvedere while she's staying with us, and a more demanding and ungrateful woman I can't imagine, the countess that is not Miss Crimms, begging your pardon, miss. But Miss Crimms suggested you might like a fabric flower to make your dress look a bit different, like. She's ever so good at needlework and sewing is Miss Crimms, makes all her ladyship's smalls she does, and her mending is invisible, makes outfits look as good as new. You should've seen what she did with her ladyship's blue, silk chiffon dress after her ladyship accidently caught her sleeve on the door handle. Almost ripped the sleeve in two did her ladyship, but Miss Crimms mended it so it looked better than before, so she did. Well, anyway, miss, here you are, with Miss Crimms' compliments.'

Martha handed Rose a large fabric flower made out of raw gold silk, decorated with beads.

'Oh, Martha, it's beautiful but she shouldn't have,' exclaimed Rose, 'it must have taken her ages to make.'

'Miss Crimms is awful quick with a needle, miss. It took her no time at all. And to tell you the truth, I think she enjoyed it. She don't get much call to try out her needle skills making new things, not here, she don't. She suggests as you should wear it on one shoulder. If you sit still there one moment, I'll just fix it before I go back downstairs. There now,' Martha stood back to admire the effect, 'now don't you look a picture, miss.'

'That maid looked awfully pleased with herself,' said Lavinia coming into the room and lounging on Rose's bed while trying not to mess up her hair. 'I say, I like that flower, it totally transforms your dress.'

'Yes, it's lovely, isn't it?'

'Mother wouldn't stop bending my ear about you this afternoon.'

114

'Oh?' Rose, seated at the dressing table and in the act of powdering her face, paused and looked at her friend's reflection in the mirror.

'She says that you have designs on Ceddie, that you only became my friend so as to get the opportunity to meet him.'

'What rot,' said Rose, blushing furiously and swinging around in her seat to face her friend, 'surely you don't believe her, Lavinia? Why, I didn't even know that he'd be here.'

'I don't know, Rose. I don't want to believe her, of course, but you and Ceddie have been getting on rather well and besides there's another thing.'

'What?'

'Well, Hugh agrees with Mother; in fact I think he might have put the idea into her head. But that's not all,' Lavinia added quickly as Rose made to interrupt. 'Hugh told me that you had made a bit of a play for him too.'

'Did he now; how dare he? I think you'll find that the opposite's the case, Lavinia. If you want to know the truth, he made a drunken pass at me last night.'

'What absolute rubbish.'

'It happens to be the truth. But if you don't believe me,' replied Rose coldly, 'then I suggest you talk to Stafford. He witnessed it all and rescued me from what was a very unpleasant situation. Ask him.'

'Don't be ridiculous,' said Lavinia, 'I'll do no such thing. I think you're just jealous about me and Hugh. Well, you can jolly well make your own way down to the drawing room; I'm not waiting for you.' And with that she stormed out of the room banging the door shut behind her, with Rose left wondering how it had come to this.

Not surprisingly, it was a very subdued party that met for dinner that evening. Rose and Lavinia were clearly not talking to each other, with Lavinia taking every opportunity to glare at Rose when she happened to catch her eye across the table. While she was making a great show of finding everything Lord Sneddon said to her highly amusing, that gentleman in turn, although acting totally enthralled with Lavinia, every now and then allowed himself to smirk unkindly at Rose when he was sure of not being seen by anyone else. Turning to her dinner companion, Rose found that she could not even find solace in his company, for Cedric looked distinctly unhappy and hardly spoke, picking at his bread roll miserably. On her other side, the earl was as quiet and uncommunicative as he had been the previous night and Edith's face was positively ashen; indeed she looked as if she might faint any minute. Rose shot a glance at both Sir William, who was clearly concerned about the state Edith was in, and Lady Withers, who, while watching them forlornly, was talking loudly about nothing in particular to try and hide the fact. Only Lady Belvedere, Rose noticed, looked unperturbed by the tension in the room. She would even go so far as to say that the countess appeared to glow, as if it was something that she positively enjoyed. There was a cruel gleam in her eye and a curl of her thin lips which seemed to spell out victory, as if she had been anticipating a fraught and unpleasant battle that she had now won.

'I'm afraid that I don't feel very well,' Edith said suddenly, clutching her head. 'If you'll excuse me, I think I'll go to my room.'

There was the noise of chairs being pushed back as the men stood up. Edith on rising to her feet appeared about to swoon. But it was a sharp intake of breath from the countess that made Rose turn her attention to Lady Belvedere. Afterwards, Rose wished that she had remained looking at Edith and not let her attention be diverted; then she might have had an inkling of what would happen later. But she had been transfixed by the expression on Lady Belvedere's face, her eyes wide open, her lips parted and formed into the letter 'o'; it was unmistakeable; the countess was in shock.

It was apparent to Rose that Lady Withers did not relish the prospect of having to entertain her sister in the drawing room after dinner with only herself and Lavinia for company, particularly as it was obvious that the two girls had had some disagreement.

'I say, darling, don't leave it too long before you join us, will you?' she said somewhat desperately to her husband. 'I know that you men like to enjoy your port and cigars and talk about things we women don't understand, but I think everyone is rather done in this evening. It must be all that sunshine, don't you think? Makes one jolly tired.'

'Of course, my dear,' replied Sir William, catching on straightaway and Rose found she liked him even more because of it. 'I say, you chaps,' he said turning to address the other gentlemen, 'what say we abandon convention and join the ladies in the drawing room now?'

The earl and the two younger gentlemen concurred and they all made their way to the drawing room to take their coffee and liqueurs. The atmosphere, however, did not improve, if anything, it seemed more strained.

'I say,' said Sir William, just as Rose was thinking that she could bear it no longer and must think up some excuse to escape to her room, 'I've just bought a jolly nice pair of antique, Queen Anne, flintlock duelling pistols. I expect you'll want to see them, won't you, Henry, you're interested in that kind of thing, aren't you?' The earl nodded, looking keen at an opportunity to leave the room. 'They're by Delaney. You too Lavinia, Miss Simpson; they're pretty attractive things and they've got something fun on the butt caps that I think you'll find amusing.'

In the end everyone followed Sir William to his study, with the exception of Lady Withers and Lady Belvedere who, feigning tiredness, retired to their rooms. Sir William went to an alcove at one side of the room and, pulling back a thick velvet curtain, revealed his gun cabinet, which he proceeded to open with a key that he took from the breast pocket of his jacket.

'I say, Sir William,' exclaimed Lord Sneddon, 'that's quite a collection that you've got there. You wouldn't want them getting into the wrong hands.'

'Indeed you wouldn't, which is why I always keep it locked and carry the key around with me on my person.'

'Do you keep the ammunition in the cabinet as well?'

'Yes, I keep it all together under lock and key, can't be too careful these days. Right, here we are girls, what do you think of these? Silver-mounted they are, but what I want to show you is this.' He pointed out the butt caps. 'What do you make of these, they look like some kind of grotesque mask, don't they?'

'Oh, I think they look just like the face of a King Charles spaniel, don't you, Daddy? Do come and look too, Ceddie. Do you remember Bouncer? They look just like him.'

Rose made her way miserably up the stairs to her bedroom. She had been totally humiliated. Not only was Lavinia not speaking to her, but the countess had taken her aside to tell her that she wished Rose to take a walk with her after breakfast the following morning. Lady Belvedere had spoken none too quietly, so that, without a doubt other members of the party had

117

overheard. With a heavy heart, Rose had shortly after made her excuses to Lady Withers and left the drawing room. Lavinia was flirting with Lord Sneddon and Cedric had appeared so deep in thought that she doubted whether either had noticed her departure. She wondered, not for the first time, how the weekend, which had started off so perfectly, could have deteriorated so completely. How were she and Lavinia going to be able to work together on Monday? Perhaps Lavinia would decide not to come back to the shop, in which case Madame Renard would surely hold her to blame. Or perhaps, worse still, Lavinia might only agree to come back to work if Rose was sacked.

'Well, well, quite deep in thought little Rose and looking so dejected.' Rose froze. She recognised the voice immediately and it sent a chill through her.

'What are you doing here, Lord Sneddon and how did you get here so quickly? You were busy talking to Lavinia when I left the drawing room.'

'Yes, you did rather sneak out, didn't you? But I saw you go and followed. You stopped to powder your nose, so I took the opportunity to come up the stairs and wait for you. It's awfully deserted on this landing, isn't it? Only you and Lavinia have your bedrooms on this floor, don't you?'

'Lavinia will be wondering where you are,' said Rose, trying to keep the fear from her voice, 'hadn't you better be getting back to her?'

'All in good time, we're going to have a little fun first. As to Lavinia, she won't notice I'm gone for ages, her mother has collared her for yet another one of her jolly little conversations.'

'If you come any nearer to me, I warn you, I'll scream.'

'Scream all you like, my dear, there's no-one to hear you. If you think that tiresome butler's going to intervene on your behalf again, then I'm afraid you're sadly mistaken. He's in the housekeeper's sitting room talking over the day with a glass of sherry, I checked; a cosier picture you couldn't imagine.' He moved out of the darkness and advanced towards her.

'No, please don't –.' Rose turned and looked down the stairs. She would never be able to outrun him, he would catch up with her before she was halfway down. She wondered if she had the courage to throw herself down the stairs, surely it would be a better fate than the one that awaited her. She clutched the banister, hesitating; she was afraid she hadn't the nerve. This

118

gave Lord Sneddon the opportunity to grab her arm and twist her around to face him.

'Not so fast, now, my dear. I know you've got a bit of a thing for Cedric, but –'

'Let her go, Sneddon.'

The voice came out of the darkness as if from nowhere and so unexpectedly, that both Rose and Lord Sneddon instinctively froze. Lord Sneddon slowly released his grip on her arm and Rose stumbled almost blindly down the stairs. Out of the shadows emerged Cedric. She thought, as she stumbled past him and caught sight of the expression on his face, that she had never seen anyone look so angry. Lord Sneddon, from the way he was now standing there looking scared, obviously felt the same.

'Listen, Cedric, it's not what it looks like. She led me on, just as she's been leading you on and then decided –.'

'Don't bother with explanations, Sneddon.' Cedric had advanced up the stairs and before Hugh had a chance to react, he had punched him squarely on the jaw and sent him flying backwards, hitting the wall and landing heavily on his back. 'I heard everything, Sneddon, and I mean everything,' Cedric said, crouching down besides his erstwhile friend and grabbing him by the collar, yanking him up towards him so that Lord Sneddon was now put into a half lying, half sitting position. 'Now listen to me. I want you to leave this house first thing tomorrow morning. I'll make some excuse to my aunt and uncle on your behalf, tell them you were called back to town urgently to do with some family business or some such thing. It doesn't matter, but I want you out of here.'

'You'll pay for this, Sedgwick,' spat Lord Sneddon, putting a handkerchief to his bleeding cheek, 'see if you don't. I only wanted from her what you want. You're just more smooth-talking than me, so the damned girl thinks you're in love with her,' He staggered to his feet and down the stairs to his room.

Cedric came over to Rose, clearly mortified.

'Rose, I don't know what to say. I had no idea that he was like that when he had drink in him. I've heard rumours, of course, about his exploits with servants, but I never gave them any credence. How can you ever forgive me?'

'There's nothing to forgive, Cedric.' Rose longed to touch his face, such a very handsome face, she thought. Lady Belvedere would seek to put a stop to their relationship developing; that was the obvious purpose of their walk tomorrow. Rose knew she would never see Cedric again; it was almost too much to bear. She wanted to run to her room right now and throw herself on her bed and cry.

'You weren't to know. And anyway, you came to my rescue. If you hadn't I'd be –.' Her face crumbled and she began to sob.

'Rose, please don't.' Cedric grabbed her hands in his own. 'I can't bear it. And tell me you don't believe a word Sneddon said about my feelings towards you, I'm nothing like him, I promise you. Oh, I know that it's far too soon and far too forward to say so now, but you must know how much I adore you, Rose, how much I admire and love you. I have never known a woman like you. You are so totally unique, so totally you. Tell me that you feel the same about me as I do about you. I don't think I could bear it, if you didn't.'

'Cedric, I –.'

'I'm being totally sincere, Rose. I'm no good at this sort of thing, but please don't think I'm out to ruin you, I wouldn't dream of it. I love you.' Rose looked up and simply stared.

'There,' he laughed, 'I've said it and I'll say it again. I love you, Rose Simpson. I want you to be my wife.'

Rose gasped, hardly able to believe her ears. She wanted to laugh in turn and throw her arms around him, but part of her held back.

'Cedric, it's no good, your mother will never allow it. She'll –.'

'Don't worry about my mother, Rose,' he bent and kissed her, 'She can't stop us, nobody can. I'll deal with her.' A new harshness had entered his voice. 'I won't let her destroy our happiness, not like she has my father's. I'll do whatever it takes, Rose, to ensure we are together; I mean it, whatever it takes.'

'She's awful nice, you know?' said Edna as the scullery and kitchen maids lay in their beds in the little sparsely furnished attic room that they shared, with its sloping ceilings enlivened by a flower sprig patterned wallpaper. Although they were exhausted by their day's labour, as always, especially this weekend with so many uninvited guests resulting in additional work, they still made time for a chat; it was part of their usual nightly routine.

'Who is?'

'You know exactly who I mean, Bessie Smith, unless you haven't been listening to a word I've been saying these last ten minutes; Miss Simpson, of course.'

'What about her, Edna?'

'She was awfully nice to me when she found me crying in the kitchen garden this morning. I felt that embarrassed, I did, but she was really kind and she promised not to tell Mrs Palmer and get me into trouble, which I bet Lady Lavinia would have done. And she must have kept her word, because the old bat didn't have a go at me and you know as she would have done, any excuse to tell us off.'

'Well, Miss Simpson's one of us, isn't she?'

'Whatever do you mean, Bessie?'

'She works in a shop; she's a shop girl, Edna. I overheard Mrs Palmer and Mr Stafford talking about it. She works in that dress shop Lady Lavinia's been working in, you know, to do with that bet with her brother. So she's no better than the likes of you and me, not really.'

'No!' Edna sat up in her bed, her eyes large with astonishment. 'Well I never. But she's got ever such nice manners and she talks quite posh, really you'd never know.'

'That's because her family's come down in the world. Apparently her father drank and gambled away all their money, that's what Lady Lavinia told Martha this evening. I say that's awful mean don't you think, her gossiping to us about her friend's ill fortunes.'

'I certainly do,' said Edna indignant. 'I don't care that she's just a shop girl, Bessie, I think she's a real lady. And I'm not the only one, neither. Albert says Lord Cedric's awful keen on her and she's pretty keen on him, too. Perhaps they'll get married and she'll be a countess one day.'

'Don't talk daft, Edna. You're an awful romantic, you are. Can you really see Lady Belvedere letting her darling son marry a shop girl? No, she'll do everything in her power to stop it, you mark my words. And there won't be anything that either of them will be able to do about it, neither.'

'Well I think love can conquer all, Bessie, like it does in the movies. You just wait and see, I think they'll find a way to be together somehow.'

Chapter Eighteen

Rose awoke the next morning feeling elated, but also with a sense of dread. Cedric loved her! She would in time become the next Countess of Belvedere, would be her own mistress; no more working long hours being polite to customers who were rude to her, or being bossed around by Madame Renard. The days of scrimping and saving would be behind her. She would no longer have to fret about her mother's ever failing eyesight, for Mrs Simpson would never need to lift another needle, save to do petit-point embroidery for her own amusement.

But it was no good. She could daydream all she liked, but Lady Belvedere would never let it happen. She wouldn't let her only son, destined to become sixteenth Earl of Belvedere, marry a penniless shop girl. Cedric had promised her that he would stand up to his mother, do whatever it took to ensure they were together. And last night she had been happy to believe him, but in the cold light of day she did not feel so confident. Cedric was dutiful and obedient, he knew that he had a responsibility to maintain his social position and estates and Lady Belvedere, Rose felt sure, would play on this. He wouldn't want to, but Rose suddenly knew with a sinking heart, that in the end Cedric would concede to his mother's wishes.

She threw back the bedclothes and began pacing the room. She couldn't let it happen, she couldn't lose him. She was too close to perfect happiness to have the countess snatch it out from under her. Rose looked at her reflection in the mirror. Determination showed on her face, she was resolute. Last night Cedric had told her he would do whatever it took. This morning she knew that she would.

When she went down for breakfast, she found that Sir William was the only person there. Her host informed her that, as on the previous day, the married women were breakfasting in bed and Lord Belvedere had already eaten and was in the library. Lavinia had a headache and did not require breakfast and Lord Sneddon, Rose felt sure, would not be coming down for he would find it difficult to explain away the damage to his face that was sure to have resulted from Cedric's punch. She was not disappointed to find Cedric absent. His presence would weaken her resolve.

She was just coming out of the dining room when Miss Crimms, who had obviously been waiting for her to finish breakfast, came rushing over to advise her that the countess was waiting for her by the French windows in the drawing room. The servant hoped that Rose did not mind but, because Lady Belvedere was keen for their walk to commence as soon as possible and following her instructions, she had taken the liberty of gathering together a hat, coat and gloves that she had taken from Rose's wardrobe, so as not to delay the walk by Rose having to go upstairs to get these items for herself.

It was with trepidation that Rose joined the countess in the drawing room. There was no outward acknowledgement of the other's presence or any attempt to exchange pleasantries. Lady Belvedere merely opened one of the French windows and walked through onto the terrace. Like an obedient child, Rose followed.

In different circumstances she would have enjoyed this walk, as she followed Lady Belvedere through the well-tended gardens, cutting across a corner of the parkland to the woods beyond. This was an area that they had failed to explore yesterday. She would have enjoyed it, she knew, if she had been here with Cedric or Lavinia, the Lavinia of before yesterday afternoon that was, the one she was used to in the shop who would giggle at a joke behind Madame Renard's back. Even with Lady Belvedere as her unwelcome companion, it was not lost on Rose that the day itself promised to be another fine one and, even in her apprehension of what lay ahead, she could appreciate the beauty of the greenness of the lawns and the countryside all around her, so different from the greyness of the London she was used to. She took in the sweet smell of freshly mown grass, the vivid colours of the flowers in bloom. It seemed so peaceful, so inviting, such an unsuitable backdrop in fact, for a confrontation.

Meanwhile the Countess of Belvedere was striding forward at such a pace that Rose was finding it difficult to keep up and had to resort to half running, half walking in an effort not to be left behind. She stumbled along as best she could. She knew she would arrive at her destination hot, flustered and out of breath, whereas this seemed to be Lady Belvedere's usual walking pace, for the lady herself seemed hardly aware of Rose's presence or the heat, certainly she did not turn around to make sure that she was following her; it was as if she had forgotten the girl's existence.

The woodland, when they reached it, seemed dark and uninviting after the fierce brightness of the gardens and Rose hesitated before entering, hovering on the edge. The countess seemed oblivious to Rose's unease for she marched right in, barely stopping to identify a path through the trees.

Their progress slowed as they walked deeper into the woods and had to negotiate the odd fallen branch and twigs. The gardens, the parkland and Ashgrove House seemed far away and Rose wondered if she would ever be able to find her way back without Lady Belvedere's assistance, or whether she would be lost in the woods forever going round and round in circles never being able to find her way out.

The countess stopped abruptly and turned to face the girl, drawing herself up to her full imposing height.

'Right, this will do, Miss Simpson, we have come far enough. I wanted to make sure that we wouldn't be overheard as no doubt we would have been if we had taken a walk in the gardens. What I have to say to you is for you alone.'

If the countess was awaiting a reaction to her words, she waited in vain.

'I will not beat about the bush, Miss Simpson. As you are no doubt aware, I speak my mind. You can be in little doubt as to why I wanted to have a talk with you.'

'Indeed, Lady Belvedere, I have absolutely no idea why you should wish to speak to me.' Rose clenched her fist to give herself more courage. Her voice, she was pleased to hear, did not sound scared. 'Ever since we have been introduced you seem to have gone out of your way either to ignore me completely or to snub me. To what I owe this current pleasure, I cannot imagine.'

'No doubt you think yourself very clever, Miss Simpson, and perhaps you are in your own way. But I will not have this insolence, this pretence at denseness. We both know what you are trying to do, what your goal is, but I can tell you here and now that you can scheme as much as you want, but you will not succeed.'

'Indeed, Lady Belvedere, I know no such thing,' replied Rose coolly. 'I am not aware that I have been scheming as you put it. My intention is just to enjoy a weekend in the country with my friend.'

124

'Enough of this pretence.' The countess was beginning to look annoyed. 'I know that you have gone out of your way to befriend my daughter, to encourage her in her idiotic game playing at being lower class. You imagine no doubt that such a relationship will bring you advantages, that you may use it to elevate your position in society. You have also set your designs upon my son. You think you can bewitch him with your charms. Do you really think Cedric could be interested in a girl like you? He finds you a curiosity, nothing more, something to enliven a dull weekend. But if you hope to become something more to him, you are mistaken. Unlike you, he is born for great things. In time he will become the sixteenth Earl of Belvedere and he will need a wife of his own class who is worthy of him. He will marry a member of the aristocracy, the daughter of a viscount or a baron perhaps, or even the daughter of a duke or marquis, but certainly not someone like you!' Lady Belvedere spat out the words in a disgusted laugh.

'If you believe that to be so, Lady Belvedere, that Cedric can have no real interest in me, then I'm surprised that you've taken the trouble to have a talk with me.'

'My son is young and impressionable, Miss Simpson and it is possible that in an unguarded moment you may manage to lead him astray, but, I warn you, before you do something that you may, no *will* regret, that if you are thinking of trying to trap my son, then you had better think again. Cedric will not be blackmailed into an undesirable marriage. Do you really think that the Belvedere family has never dealt with the likes of you before? Do you honestly think I am just going to stand back and let my only son ruin his life?'

'I think you have insulted me quite enough, Lady Belvedere. I'm not going to stay and waste my breath trying to argue with you. I could tell you that you have got it all wrong, that you don't know me at all, but I know you wouldn't believe a word I say.'

'You're right, Miss Simpson, on all accounts. How very perceptive of you. I want you to pack up and leave immediately. Go back to the house, make some excuse to Lavinia for your sudden departure and then summon a maid to pack your case, although,' Lady Belvedere broke off to look Rose up and down disparagingly, 'you are no doubt used to packing your own bags, I doubt very much whether your mother has a servant. So no need after all to trouble my sister's servants. However, I am sure if you ask politely enough they will arrange for the chauffeur to drive you to the railway station.'

'You mistake my meaning, Lady Belvedere. When I said that I would not stay here, I meant literally that. I meant I'm not staying in these woods to be insulted by you. I have no intention of leaving Ashgrove House.'

'But I demand that you do!' Lady Belvedere, who was not used to being contradicted, was beginning to go red in the face.

'You have no authority to demand that I leave, Lady Belvedere. I am here as the guest of Sir William and Lady Withers and, I might add', here Rose paused to pluck up the necessary courage, 'unlike you, I am an invited guest.'

'How dare you, Miss Simpson! Lady Withers is my sister. I need no formal invitation to come and stay here. Do you think this rudeness does you any favours? It certainly won't win me over. Do you really think that I'll back down?'

'I have no idea what you will do, Lady Belvedere. But if I am being rude, it is only in response to your rudeness to me. You have made it evident to everyone, including the servants, how much you resent me and my presence here at Ashgrove House. And today you have left me in little doubt as to your feeling towards me. So if I am being rude to you, it is no more than you deserve.'

Silence filled the woodland, an uneasy, almost eerie silence, in stark contrast to the raised voices just before. Rose found herself shaking; she was too shocked to speak further. Never before had anyone spoken to her with such hatred, and never had she felt driven to speak to anyone so rudely. How appalled her mother would have been if she could have heard her. Lady Belvedere's face was quite purple now with rage and she was trembling. During the course of her tirade her voice had risen until her last few sentences had been almost shouted, strands of her hair escaping from her bun. For the first time that morning, Rose was pleased that the conversation had not taken place in the gardens where there almost certainly would have been witnesses to this spectacle.

The quietness that followed the scene felt unnatural, more a lull before the storm than after it, and Rose almost wished that the countess would continue with her threats or turn and walk away, not just stand there and stare at her with obvious hatred. She realised suddenly that neither woman knew what to do to break the deadlock.

When she heard the twig snap, it did not surprise her unduly or seem of significance. It was so quiet, this unnatural silence, with the two women glowering at each other that she expected sound to be amplified. So she made the mistake of dismissing it as just some creature scurrying about amongst the undergrowth, although it had been loud enough to cause both women to inwardly start and look up, momentarily distracted from their confrontation. Later, Rose told the inspector she was sure that the noise had come from behind a clump of bushes or undergrowth some way off behind her, but at the time she had been too disorientated with shock following the row to be sure, and she had had her back to it whereas Lady Belvedere had had a clear view.

It was only later, when the reality of the situation hit her that she wondered whether Lady Belvedere had seen something that she herself had not. Rose herself had not turned around. She might have done so had it not been for the reaction of the countess which had distracted and alarmed her. For Lady Belvedere had seemed to draw a breath, as if she had been taken aback. The colour had drained from her face and she had suddenly looked afraid. This rapid transformation from a fierce woman to a cowering one had frightened Rose and she had instinctively taken a step towards Lady Belvedere, what her intention in doing so exactly was she did not know for it seemed strange and inappropriate somehow to try and comfort or reassure the woman who only minutes earlier had been berating her. As it happened it did not matter for at the last moment she had inadvertently stumbled and lurched forward. She had tried desperately to catch at Lady Belvedere's arm to stop herself from falling, but had failed. At the same instant that she had hit the ground she had heard the gun shot rip through the air. It had been very loud and she had lain there trembling, not trying to get up, knowing exactly what it was.

When Rose did at last look up, she could not see Lady Belvedere at first. Where she had been standing there was just emptiness, as if she had been swallowed up by the trees and disappeared. But then Rose had lowered her eyes to the ground and seen the figure lying prostrate on the earth amongst the twigs and leaves. For a moment she had been unable to take it in, wondering whether her own heart had stopped, and then she had tried to hurry towards the body. Due to the shock she found that she had insufficient energy to drag herself up on to her feet. Instead she had crawled forward on her hands and knees feeling the dry earth beneath her palms, vaguely aware that she was ruining her one good day dress but not caring.

Lady Belvedere was dead, she could see that straightaway by the frozen expression on her face and the eyes wide open but unseeing. Her hat had come off and lay a few feet away and Rose found herself thinking nonsensically how annoyed Lady Belvedere would be to see that it was covered with dirt. The countess was wearing an unbuttoned tweed jacket over a white blouse which was fast turning red as blood seeped out from the hidden wound. There was no need for Rose to search in the pocket of her dress for a handkerchief to try to stem the flow of blood and yet she did so because she did not know what else to do. The futility of the gesture hit her; it was too late, Lady Belvedere was past saving.

Rose was vaguely conscious that she was beginning to rock to and fro and then she heard a high pitched wail, a scream that was barely human and filled the air and made her start. It was only after a few seconds that she realised that the noise came from her own lungs and that she was clutching Lady Belvedere's hand. She let it go flinging it from her as if it were contaminated. Still rocking to and fro she clutched her head in her hands, shut her eyes tight to keep out the horror and, tearing at her hair, she gave way to hysteria.

Chapter Nineteen

'Detective Inspector Deacon and Sergeant Lane from Scotland Yard, sir', Stafford said in his usual deferential manner as he showed both gentlemen into Sir William's study.

'Ah, very good.' Sir William got up from the sofa where he had been sitting and threw aside the newspaper he had been trying to read to while away the time until their arrival. 'So good of you to come so quickly. Scotland Yard, huh? A tragic business, of course, what, damned unpleasant, but I'd hardly have thought it warranted a couple of detectives to be sent down from Scotland Yard.'

'We were in the area, Sir William,' replied Inspector Deacon, a tall, dark-haired rather handsome man dressed in a three-piece, pin-striped suit who had an authoritative air about him, which immediately revealed his profession and which Sir William found rather comforting. He might be a trifle younger than he had been expecting, but he'd do, yes, he'd do very nicely; just the sort of chap to sort out this spot of bother without making a song and dance about it. Probably had a gentle manner with the ladies too, which would come in jolly useful with poor little Miss Simpson.

'We were sorting out a case of embezzlement in the area, sir,' the Inspector continued. 'The Chief Constable thought it best to call in Scotland Yard over this unfortunate incident, being as we were on hand so to speak and it involves the wife of a Peer.'

'Quite so, quite so.' Sir William beckoned them to sit down. The sergeant chose a chair by the window, outside Sir William's direct line of vision, where he could take notes discreetly and relatively unobserved, while the Inspector chose an armchair facing the sofa.

'Coffee if you please, Stafford.' Sir William sank back down onto the sofa.

'Very good, sir.' Stafford left, closing the door gently behind him.

'It's a most unfortunate business, Inspector. Not the sort of thing one wants to have happen at a weekend house party. I think you'll find it was a very tragic accident rather than anything more untoward. I've done nothing but think about how it could have happened since I heard the news. The more I've thought about it, the more I'm certain there can only be one explanation. It must have been a poacher in the woods looking for a rabbit or such like to feed his family. Goodness knows, it wouldn't be the first time. And poor Lady Belvedere just happened to be in the wrong place at the wrong time. How the poor fellow came to shoot her by mistake I simply can't quite fathom. Most of them are pretty good shots, I can tell you, but perhaps he was the worse for wear and inadvertently let his gun go off. And then, no doubt as not, he panicked and ran off. I'm sure that in a day or so he'll come forward when his conscience gets the better of him. I don't think our British justice system will treat him too harshly. '

'Indeed, sir, that's a possible explanation,' Inspector Deacon admitted and tried to keep the scepticism from his voice. Nevertheless Sir William looked up sharply as if he doubted the policeman's sincerity. He's clutching at straws, poor old fellow, thought the inspector, he knows the scenario he's putting forward is highly unlikely but he doesn't want to face the alternatives, can't say I blame him.

'I suppose you'll be wanting to talk to Miss Simpson, Inspector? She was out walking with Lady Belvedere when the countess was shot; a dreadful thing for a young girl to experience, jolly nasty. She was in a totally hysterical state, I can tell you, when they brought her back to the house. I was tempted to send for the doctor to give her a sedative, but I thought you'd probably want to interview her straightaway, what with her being a witness so to speak, not that I think she saw anything. So I made do with giving her a little brandy and Mrs Torrington's sitting with her now because she was in no fit state to be left alone.'

'Thank you, Sir William, most thoughtful. I'll speak with Miss Simpson shortly, but before I do there are one or two things I'd like to get clear first. Perhaps you could give me a run through of who exactly is staying at your house this weekend.'

'Certainly, Inspector.' Sir William looked relieved at being given a question that he could answer easily. 'Let me see. Well, of course there's myself and my wife, Constance, Lady Withers,' he began crossing the names off his fingers, 'Henry, Earl of Belvedere, poor Marjorie's husband, their son, Cedric, Lord Sedgwick, their daughter, Lady Lavinia and Cedric's friend, Marquis Sneddon.' The sergeant caught the inspector's eye and raised

130

his eyebrows at the sound of so many what he called "toffs". 'And Lady Lavinia's friend, Miss Simpson of course,' ended Sir William.

'Just a moment, Sir William, you mentioned a Mrs Torrington earlier. How does she fit in?'

'Oh dear me, had I forgotten to mention Edith? I'm afraid one does rather forget about Edith. She's staying here too, of course. She's a distant relative of my wife's, one of her old school friends in fact.'

'And Lady Belvedere was your sister-in law?'

'Yes, indeed, Inspector. She was my wife's older sister.' Sir William appeared suddenly lost in thought as he looked over to the unlit fireplace. 'It's funny to think that we were all inseparable once, when we were young, Henry, Marjorie, Connie, Edith and I. Five friends who did everything together. A long time ago now, of course, a lot of water under the bridge since then as they say.'

At that moment Stafford entered the room noiselessly bearing a silver tray with a silver coffee pot and three bone china cups and saucers, a milk jug and a sugar bowl. The inspector wondered how his sergeant was going to manage the tricky task of trying to juggle his cup and saucer in one hand with his notebook and pencil in the other. Stafford however foresaw the difficulty, as every good butler would, and as soon as he had poured the coffee and distributed the cups and saucers to Sir William and Deacon, he pulled up a coffee table to Lane and placed his cup and saucer in easy reach, while ensuring that it could not be knocked over accidently. He gave a final glance in the direction of Sir William to ascertain if anything more was required of him and, getting no sign to indicate the affirmative, left the room as silently as he had entered it, closing the door behind him as quietly as if he had been drawing a curtain.

'Quite a house party then, Sir William?'

'Yes, I mean, no. It is but it wasn't intended to be. My wife had only invited Edith, Lavinia and Miss Simpson for the weekend. But then we received a wire from Cedric to say that he was coming down and he ended up bringing his friend with him. And then we had a telephone call to say that Henry and Marjorie were coming down as well. It quite upset my wife, I can tell you, she thought they were all the wrong mix of people to have together, that they'd get along terribly and that there'd be all sorts of rows and disagreements, and oh ....' Sir William stopped suddenly as he realised what he'd just said. 'It rattled the servants too,' he continued valiantly. 'They'd all the bedrooms to suddenly get ready and of course the food. Constance and Mrs Palmer, our cook-housekeeper were determined to impress them. I don't want to speak ill of the dead, Inspector, but Lady Belvedere could be very critical if everything wasn't exactly to her liking. It used to worry my wife dreadfully. She used to be on tenter hooks before a visit from her sister, not that she used to visit very often, and hardly ever with her husband.'

'I see,' said Deacon, studying Sir William closely. 'So was there any particular reason why they all decided to descend on you this weekend?'

'Well, yes, I suppose there was. Lady Belvedere no doubt had got wind somehow that Lavinia would be coming down and saw it as an opportunity to berate her on this shop work malarkey of hers, try and get her to give it up and all that. Of course, it just made the girl more obstinate and determined to stick it out. You know probably better than I do, Inspector, what young girls are like nowadays. See nothing wrong with going against their parents' wishes. And Lavinia has definitely got spirit. Anyway, coming here was the only way that Marjorie was going to see her, because from what I can gather, Lavinia has been refusing to go home for the weekend, not wanting to receive a lecture from her mother.

'And then of course I think Cedric, that's Lord Sedgwick, Lavinia's brother, was curious to meet the friend, Miss Simpson. Quite smitten he was as soon as he set eyes on her. I think he found her a welcome change from the young ladies he usually mixes with. She's got a good head on her shoulders, has little Miss Simpson. Nothing silly and frivolous about her and she knows the meaning of hard work. The two of them seemed to get on like a house on fire, which, as you probably can imagine, did not go down at all well with Lady Belvedere.' Sir William paused as he reflected and it seemed to bring a smile to his kindly face. 'Of course, no doubt Cedric also wanted to see how Lavinia was doing. If I'm honest I don't think that any of us thought that she would stick with the shop work, too used to having her own way and enjoying herself. It was the result of a bet, you know, with her brother that she couldn't earn her own living for six months. But I'll say this for her, she's determined when she sets her mind to something and I don't think she wanted to lose face in front of Cedric. They've always been rather competitive ever since they were children.'

'Thank you. Right, before I have a word with Miss Simpson, I'd be grateful, Sir William, if you could tell me what sort of a woman the deceased was.'

'Ah,' Sir William suddenly looked uncomfortable and disinclined to say anything further.

'Sir William, I know it seems in bad taste to say anything disrespectful about the dead', said Deacon gently, 'but we really do need to build up a picture of the deceased's character. It will help us get to the truth of how she happened to get killed.'

'I don't see why that's necessary, Inspector. If she was killed by a poacher, as I believe she was, I don't see that her character has got anything to do with it.'

'Even so, Sir William, I'd be grateful if you'd humour me.' There was something about the inspector's voice that persuaded Sir William that he would not take no for an answer.

'Very well, in that case, Inspector, just between ourselves,' Sir William continued, still looking rather ill at ease. It amused Deacon to note that Sir William appeared to have completely forgotten about Lane, who was seated not far behind him and was at that very moment scribbling furiously into his notebook. 'Lady Belvedere was quite a difficult woman. If I am quite honest, I would not call her a particularly nice woman. Quite frankly, she was spiteful, domineering and ruthless. She wanted her own way in everything and wasn't concerned how she got it, or who she trampled on in the process. I'm afraid she was rather a bully.' It appeared to Deacon that once Sir William had overcome his natural distaste about speaking ill of the dead and his sister-in-law to boot, there was no stopping him, the flood gates had opened and his words poured out. 'My wife was quite scared of her, you know, had been ever since she was a small child even though she had no reason to be now, of course. I think her own children were probably equally afraid of her. She had quite a temper when she was annoyed, I can tell you, she could be very vindictive when she put her mind to it.'

The inspector looked up and caught his sergeant's eye. He knew exactly what Lane was thinking: no wonder someone took a pop at her!

'Right, so I assume from what you've said that she may have had a number of enemies, people who may have wished her harm,' Deacon said aloud, trying not to be put off by Lane who was nodding his head vigorously behind Sir William's back.

'No, no, Inspector. She could be a trifle unpleasant, that's all.' Sir William looked suddenly alarmed, as if he wished to retract his words. 'I've probably exaggerated it a bit', he added quickly in an attempt to lessen their effect. 'Truth be told, although I didn't like the woman very much, it doesn't necessarily mean to say no-one else did. Probably a bit biased, Inspector, I was all set to marry her once, you know, a long time ago, had set my heart on having her for my wife. It's hard to imagine now, but she was a jolly beautiful woman when she was young and of course beauty can blind one to a woman's defects. Ah well, it obviously wasn't meant to be. Now I just thank my lucky stars that I married her sister instead, got exactly the wife I thought I would with Constance.' He spoke Lady Withers' name with affection, as if he had suddenly realised that he had had a lucky escape.

Deacon tried to hide his exasperation. If Sir William was now keen on back tracking, it was unlikely that he would express his feelings so freely again.

'The family's taken Lady Belvedere's death very badly, I can tell you, Inspector. My wife's naturally very upset at losing her sister in such tragic circumstances, Lavinia is bawling her eyes out with her now in the morning room, enough to sink a battle ship, and Cedric has shut himself up alone in his room and refuses to speak to anyone, even to his father.'

'And the Earl of Belvedere, Lady Belvedere's husband, how has he taken the news?'

'Henry? Well, he's ensconced himself in my library, just as he did yesterday and the day before and every time he comes to stay for that matter. Not sure the news has really sunk in. He's in his own little world most of the time, Inspector. Obsessed by old books, you know, collects them, he's quite an authority I believe. I have rather a few valuable and interesting ones myself which he's making a point of studying. I rather think he's hoping that I'll sell them to him, but I shan't, they've been in my family for generations.'

'So you don't think he's too upset by the news?'

'It's not really that, Inspector. It's rather hard to explain. I suppose it's more that he and my sister-in-law led rather separate lives. I'm not saying

134

that they'd fallen out, so much as they just had completely different interests and didn't really see a lot of each other except at meal times.'

The inspector looked thoughtful as he digested this information and he saw Lane's pen pause for a moment before the sergeant scribbled hurriedly, as if he was afraid that if he stopped writing for even a moment he would miss some vital piece of information before it evaporated. Before Deacon could ask any further questions of Sir William, Stafford appeared in front of his master as if he were some summoned genie, and the inspector marvelled at how a man of more than medium build like the butler could move so effortlessly and noiselessly in an old creaking house such as Ashgrove.

'Excuse me, sir, I am very sorry to interrupt, but if I may have a word with you in private a moment.' Sir William looked about to protest. 'It is of the utmost importance, sir,' said Stafford quickly, anticipating a refusal, 'otherwise, of course, I wouldn't have troubled you.'

'Go head, Sir William,' urged the inspector, 'I'd like a quick word with my sergeant anyway.'

'Well, if you're sure, Inspector.' Sir William looked hesitant. 'Can't think what it can be, but my butler's not a man to make a fuss about nothing. I'll be as quick as I can.'

Chapter Twenty

'Well, what is it, Stafford?' asked Sir William irritably, following his butler into the hall. 'I take it, it *is* important. Not the done thing at all, you know, to take me away from the police when they're interviewing me. It's a man's duty to help them, you know, and God knows we want this mess cleared up as quickly as possible.'

'Naturally, sir, but what I have to say I thought you'd like to hear first, before we inform the police. If I may suggest, sir, that we go into the drawing room, where we can talk privately, I don't think it's in use now.'

'Good God, man, what's with all this cloak and dagger stuff? It's not some game we're playing, you know, Lady Belvedere is dead and ....' He broke off as he caught sight of Edith Torrington looking over the banisters at him from the landing above. There was a desperate look on her face.

'Edith, I … Run along, Stafford, go to your parlour and wait for me, I'll be along in a minute.'

'But, sir …' Stafford began to protest.

'Go along, man, I'll be with you shortly. I must speak with Mrs Torrington a minute.'

As soon as Stafford had departed, Sir William was up the stairs at a pace hardly to be expected in a man half his age. He seized Edith's hands and dragged her downstairs and into the empty drawing room, being careful to close the door behind him, so that they could not be overheard.

'Edith, what have you done? You did it, didn't you, after all I said, you went ahead and did it.'

'William, I couldn't help myself. She was evil, you know she was. She destroyed our happiness, I couldn't let her get away with it. You don't know how it feels to keep a secret such as I have all these years, afraid to tell anyone; afraid to tell my own husband. All my life has been a pretence one way or another, trying to pretend I was what I wasn't. And then she destroyed my one chance of happiness. It eats away at one, you know, a pain like mine, until you're half dead. I have felt a dreadful numbness all these years. I didn't think anything could ever hurt me again and when I found out the Belvederes were here, and I knew I had an opportunity, my only chance to ….' She broke off and sobbed uncontrollably. 'Oh, what have I done, William. I wanted to hurt her, of course I did, but I never meant for this to happen, you must believe me. I just wanted to take away the happiness that she had taken away from me. But I never thought for a moment that it would end like this, you must believe me, I never imagined ...'

'Pull yourself together, Edith, and quickly. We haven't much time to decide what to do. We've got to think.'

'I've already thought, William. I've done nothing but think since it happened. I am going to go to the police and hand myself in. I'm going to tell them that I did it, I'm going to confess.'

'You're going to do no such thing, Edith. Enough lives have been ruined by that woman. She's got justice although the law won't see it that way, of course. I'm going to do everything in my power to make sure the police don't find out the truth. I've already put the wheels in motion, told the police a cock and bull story about how it must have been a poacher who shot her by mistake and is too frightened to come forward. Oh, Edith,' he clasped her to him for a moment. 'I feared as much, you know, that something would happen, but never this, no not this! If only I had managed to stop you, to convince you not to do it.'

'I'm sorry, William, I've let you down, I know.' She looked up into his strong, kindly face and stroked his cheek. 'You'll never be able to forgive me for what I have done, I know that. I don't expect you to, I don't deserve it. But I don't want you to become embroiled in all this. It would break Connie's heart if she found out the truth.'

'Nonsense, I've always been here for you, Edith, you know that, and I always will be, whatever happens.'

'Oh, William, you are too good to me, you always were.' Edith disentangled herself from him. 'But do you honestly think the police will believe your story about the poacher?'

'Well, I've told it to the inspector. A young fellow, but pretty astute I'd say, from Scotland Yard, more's the pity. A local chap might have swallowed the story better, whereas this chap, Deacon I think he said his name was, he looked pretty sceptical when I told him my theory. Still, I hardly think he can prove anything to the contrary, I can't imagine any of us have watertight alibis, so he'll have to go with it. He's in an awfully difficult position, you know, most of his suspects being peers of the realm, let's hope he won't know how to deal with it. I've just got to make sure that they don't arrest poor Archie Cutter, the fellow must have been carrying a gun if he was doing in the woods what I think he was doing.' He took her firmly by the shoulders and looked her in the eyes. 'Edith, promise me you won't do anything rash. Don't go confessing. You must give me time to think what to do. Now, I've got to go, Stafford wants to talk to me urgently about something, damn the man, although at least it did give me the opportunity to speak to you before the police interviewed you. But I must go, he probably already thinks it a little odd that I wanted to stop and speak to you when he had something of importance to tell me. Stay here a couple of moments after I've gone before you leave, and then it won't be obvious to anyone except Stafford that we've been together and he won't say anything.'

He made his way to the door but just before he opened it he turned, and looked back at her earnestly.

'Promise me Edith, whatever happens you won't say anything to the police, you'll leave it to me to sort out, promise me.'

Edith swallowed and said nothing, but she did smile briefly and which Sir William seemed to find a satisfactory response for he turned and left, shutting the door noiselessly behind him. Had he not been in such a hurry to go and see Stafford, he might have realised that Edith had crossed two fingers of the hand she held unseen behind her back, and he might not have been so content with her reply.

'Do come in, Miss Simpson.' Detective Inspector Deacon held open the library door and beckoned Rose towards the leather Chesterfield sofa.

The library, for once, was empty of Lord Belvedere, who had been persuaded to leave and take up residence instead in Sir William's study. The former room was considerably larger than the latter, and the policemen felt it made a more appropriate interview room.

'I'm Detective Inspector Deacon from Scotland Yard. Do take a seat. I appreciate that this must all have been a dreadful shock for you and you probably don't want to think about it, let alone talk about it, but I'm afraid that I'm going to have to ask you a few questions.'

Rose looked around feeling rather disorientated. She had not been in the library before and the man before her was a stranger. There was something in his manner however that put her at her ease, as if he was used to dealing with people in her condition, which she supposed he was, given his occupation.

She caught sight then of Sergeant Lane, who was hovering behind the settee. Rose realised, even in her befuddled state, that he had positioned his chair in such a way that when she was seated he would be quite hidden from view. To begin with during the interview, she imagined him scribbling down her every word but later, as the interview progressed, she almost forgot that he was there.

'I'd like you to tell me in your own words exactly what happened, Miss Simpson. Take your time. Perhaps we could start with how you came to be a guest here this weekend. I understand from Sir William that you're a friend of Lady Lavinia's and that it was she that invited you down to come and visit her aunt and uncle?'

'Yes, I work in the dress shop with her. I expect Sir William's told you all about that, the bet she had with her brother?' Deacon nodded. 'She and I got on well together, became friends, and so she invited me to come and stay for the weekend at Ashgrove; she sees it as her second home.'

'I see. And what about the other guests, were you expecting them to be staying here too?'

'Oh no, except for Mrs Torrington, that is, we knew she'd be here.'

'Right, before I ask you anything else, I'd like you to tell me in your own words about today, leading up to Lady Belvedere's death. Firstly, when did you arrange to go on this walk together?'

'Lady Belvedere told me last night after dinner that she would like me to come for a walk with her this morning.'

'I see. So you and Lady Belvedere got on well, then?'

'No,' admitted Rose looking, to Deacon's mind, uneasy, 'not exactly.'

'So why then would she ask you to go for a walk with her?'

'To warn me off, Inspector. She thought I had designs on her son.'

'And do you?' Rose averted her gaze seeming suddenly to find the pattern on the cushion immensely interesting; she did not answer.

'Who else knew you were going on a walk with the countess this morning?' asked Deacon, deciding not to press the matter.

'I'm not sure, possibly everyone for all I know. You see Lady Belvedere asked, no it would be more accurate to say commanded me, in rather a loud voice. I thought at the time that she did it deliberately, to try and humiliate me.'

'So you went on the walk and ended up in the woods?'

'Yes, she wanted to make sure we weren't overheard,' said Rose looking up. 'If you must know, she wanted me to pack my things and leave immediately. I refused to, and she didn't take my refusal very well.

'I see,' said the inspector, thoughtfully, 'so I take it your voices were probably raised at this point?'

'Yes.'

'And then what happened?'

'I'm afraid we were both rather rude to each other, and very angry. But you see, neither of us was prepared to back down and the countess is ... was ... very used to always getting her own way. Then there was this silence,' Rose shivered, 'I can hardly describe it, it was so eerie and quiet, you really could have heard a pin drop. And then a twig snapped. We both heard it, but I thought nothing of it at the time, I mean it's the sort of thing that you hear in a wood, isn't it?'

'It is,' agreed the inspector, 'and then what happened?'

'She ... she was shot, oh, it was so awful,' Rose covered her face with her hands. 'I can't get it out of my mind. One minute she was there glaring at me, and the next she was lying on the ground, dead, covered in blood. Oh, I can't bear to think about it, but I can't get the image out of my head, I –.'

'Did you see who shot Lady Belvedere, Miss Simpson?' Deacon interrupted, sharply.

'No, of course not, otherwise I would have told you straightaway. I had my back to whoever it was, I didn't see a thing. I wish now, of course, that I'd turned around, I wish I'd seen –.'

'Perhaps it's just as well you didn't, Miss Simpson, otherwise you might not be here now.'

Rose was silent, taking in the enormity of the meaning of what he was saying; she began to shake.

'Sir William thinks a poacher shot the countess by mistake.' The inspector watched her closely.

'Does he?' Rose sounded surprised.

'Yes, but you don't think so, do you, Miss Simpson?'

'No.'

'Why not?'

'Lady Belvedere saw who pulled the trigger. I'll never forget the look on her face. She knew what he was going to do before he shot her. It was deliberate, I'd swear it, and there's something else,' Rose's voice had fallen to a whisper.

'And what's that?' Deacon asked her sharply. Even Sergeant Lane seemed to be waiting for her reply, his pen poised above the page waiting to scribble down her answer.

'Lady Belvedere knew her killer, Inspector, I'm sure she knew whoever it was that killed her.'

Chapter Twenty-one

'Seems a nice young lady, that, sir,' said Sergeant Lane of Rose, as he took the opportunity to get up and stretch his legs and flex the fingers of his writing hand before the next interviewee was shown in.

'Yes, she seems to be,' said the inspector, not sounding wholly convinced. 'But she had a clear motive for wanting rid of the countess, she admitted as much herself. And from what we've heard about Lady Belvedere, she wasn't the sort of woman to stand back and allow her son to marry someone she didn't approve of. Still, it must have been a very nasty experience for the poor girl, having someone shot dead in front of her and being out there all by herself in the wood.'

'Do I take it, sir, that you are treating this as a murder investigation rather than as a tragic accident?'

'I am, Lane. I don't buy in to that poacher story of Sir William's for a minute and neither, if I'm not mistaken, does the gentleman himself. I don't blame him, of course, wanting it to be an accident, I would myself if I was in his shoes; the alternative will be jolly unpleasant for him and his wife. But there it is, Sergeant. There is no way that it could have been a poacher, even if Miss Simpson had not said what she did about Lady Belvedere recognising her killer.'

'I'm not sure I understand your reasoning, sir,' said the sergeant, looking slightly confused.

'Miss Simpson admitted that she and the countess were speaking in raised voices. They were having an argument, a pretty heated one by the sounds of it, one or other of them probably ended up shouting likely as not.'

'I still don't follow, sir.'

'Any poacher who happened to be passing in the wood at the time would surely have heard them having their argument long before he actually came across them. Think, man, if he was out to trap a couple of rabbits and didn't want to be caught doing so, the last thing he would have done would be to have made his way towards where the voices were coming from. No, it stands to reason that he would have given them a very wide berth and gone

142

off promptly in the opposite direction. Whoever shot Lady Belvedere killed her deliberately, Sergeant, mark my words. This was a premeditated act. We're looking for a cold blooded murderer.'

There was a moment's silence as neither man spoke.

'That's as may be, sir,' said the sergeant at last, thinking it over, 'but I can't see Sir William giving up on his theory about a poacher easily.'

'No, you're right, he'll cling to that notion for all it's worth. He's probably already convinced everyone staying in the house that is what happened, the most palatable explanation by far, mores the pity, because likely as not it will mean that they won't be very co-operative or inclined to answer lots of questions if they think it was just a very tragic accident.' The inspector paced up and down the room deep in thought. 'Well, there's only one thing for it, Lane.'

'What's that, sir?'

'We need to make sure that we find the murder weapon, and sooner rather than later. We need to knock this poacher nonsense on the head once and for all. I have a feeling that we won't get anywhere with this case until we manage to convince them all that this was indeed a murder.'

'How are you feeling now, my dear?' Edith tucked the blanket more closely around Rose's shoulders and handed her the half full glass of brandy that Sir William had poured for her an hour or so ago, but which Rose had not felt up to finishing. On leaving the library and her interview with the policemen, she had returned to Edith's room not knowing where else to go, aware only that she did not wish to be alone and left with her own thoughts lest the image of Lady Belvedere's blood stained body should return unbidden.

'Much better, thank you', Rose gave a feeble smile. 'I'm glad I've got my interview with the police over and done with, although I expect they'll want to speak to me again because they didn't ask me very many questions. You've all been very kind. I'm sorry to have put you to so much trouble, nursemaiding me, so to speak. It was the shock you see.' She took a large gulp of the brandy and almost choked.

'There, there, of course it was, my dear. Now why don't I just take that glass from you while you lie down on the bed and try to get some rest? You'll feel much better when you wake up, I'm sure.'

'No, no, I couldn't possibly, Edith. I must go and see Lavinia, has …. has she been told about … about –?'

'Yes, yes don't fret,' Edith patted her arm gently, 'Constance's with her now, they're comforting one another.'

'And … and Cedric?' asked Rose hesitatingly, blushing in spite of everything.

'I think he's shut himself up in his room. He wanted to be alone at first when he heard the news, but I think his father's with him now, just as it should be. Don't worry, he'll be all right, you'll see.'

'Yes, I suppose so,' said Rose, not totally convinced. She wondered how anyone could ever be all right again when one of their parents had been so brutally murdered. 'It's just so awful. How can such a dreadful thing have happened? It's like some awful nightmare. I keep imagining that I'll wake up and find that it's all been a bad dream. But it isn't, is it?' She could hear her voice beginning to break. 'I just want everything to go back to the way it was before this all happened.'

'I know it all seems awful now and that you feel you'll never be able to get over it, but you will, my dear, I assure you,' Edith said with surprising conviction. 'You're still so very young and you've your whole life in front of you. Now, you mustn't think about it anymore, Rose, do you hear me?' Edith sat on the bed and took the girl's hands in her own cool ones. 'Promise me that you'll try and blot it out of your mind and forget all about it.' She lifted a hand to gently remove a strand of hair from Rose's face and there was such an earnestness and sincerity in her manner and words that Rose was touched and her heart went out to this woman who had herself endured so much heartache and yet was striving to comfort her.

'I'll try later, I promise, to do exactly what you say, but right now the police want me to try and remember as much as I can about what happened. They'll want me to try to recall every single detail of what I might have seen or heard because they think it'll help them to identify who killed Lady Belvedere.'

'But you won't be able to help them, will you, my dear? You said that you didn't see anything, nothing at all, that's right, isn't it?' The voice that had been so kind, so soothing a moment before, now contained a sudden note of alarm that had not been there before. Rose opened her eyes wide, but Edith's face looked as sweet and caring as it had before. Perhaps she had just imagined the change in her tone. It was such a strange day after all, a day when anything might happen.

'Yes, it all happened so quickly and I wasn't looking the right way. I had my back to the ... the person that ... I was looking at Lady Belvedere at the time it all happened. She was so very angry with me and I with her, you see, and then suddenly the expression on her face changed and she looked afraid. And before I could .....' She broke off at the recollection; it was a moment or two before she could continue. 'She saw him, she saw the person who killed her before he pulled the trigger. And she knew what he was going to do before he did it. The look on her face frightened me so much. It was as if she'd seen a ghost. I went forward to grab her hand to see what was wrong. But I shouldn't have, should I? I should have turned around to see what she was staring at, who she was staring at, what had made her so afraid.' Rose began to cry hysterically. 'I could have saved her, I should have turned around.'

'It's probably just as well you didn't, Rose', said Edith, gently again.

'I know, that's what the police said. That if I had turned around, I'd probably have been killed too, because I'd have seen him too.'

'But you didn't see who it was, did you, Rose? You can't say for sure whether it was a man or woman, can you?' The urgency in Edith's voice could not be mistaken now. And then as if to avoid all doubt she bent forward and clasped Rose's shoulders roughly so that it made the girl wince. 'You didn't see who did it, did you, you didn't see who killed Lady Belvedere, did you?' It was more a statement now rather than a question.

'No, no, of course I didn't.' Rose pulled herself away from the older woman's grasp. 'Don't you think I'd have told the police if I had? So no, no I ... but, oh no, no!' She leapt from the bed, a sudden look of horror on her face. 'But, of course, I've just realised what that means. But, no, it can't do, it's too awful ...'

'What is it, what is it?' Edith was on her feet now too, a look of alarm on her face.

'I must talk to the police again, now, please.' Rose stumbled towards the bedroom door. Edith barred her way. 'You're confused, Rose, you've been through an awful ordeal. Come and lie down. The police can wait. They'll want to see the body first and talk more to Sir William. No need to rush to see them, there's plenty of time.'

145

'No, I've got to see them now. I must tell them, it's important.' Rose lurched towards the door. Edith stood firm. The girl stared the woman in the face and then suddenly, in one fierce movement, pushed her aside. Edith was taken off guard and slipped and fell against the dressing table. Rose did not stop to check that she was all right. Instead she tore open the bedroom door and made a run for it across the landing and down the stairs. Her legs seemed heavy and slow and she was afraid that she would trip and fall or be overtaken. It reminded her of dreams she had had as a child where she was running away from something, but the more she tried to run the more she stood still like a hamster going round and round on a wheel, never reaching its destination.

She slowed once to look over her shoulder fearfully, afraid that Edith would be just behind, ready to pounce and drag her back in to the bedroom, but there was no-one there. The knowledge spurred her on and she did not stop again until she had reached the library, where she found herself banging on the door with clenched fists for all she was worth, as if she feared that it was locked and would never open. It was opened abruptly by a surprised Sergeant Lane, and before she could stop and think what she was doing or how it must look, she found that in her relief she had flung herself into his bewildered arms.

Chapter Twenty-two

'Right, Lane, let's get the alibis sorted out,' said the inspector, looking at the list of guests that Sergeant Lane had jotted down. 'We'll have another talk with Miss Simpson later, when she's got over the initial shock. She may find that she remembers something that may prove useful. I'd like you to go to the servants' hall and interview the servants. We need to get a feel for the people in this house, who got on with who, who disliked who, that sort of thing. We need to know exactly who we're dealing with. Pick up any gossip you can, I know you've got a certain way with cooks and parlour maids; it must be those youthful good looks of yours. Maids want to flirt with you and the cooks want to mother you. Just don't take too long about it and try not to eat too many cakes, I don't want you to be too stuffed with food to run after the murderer in case he tries to make a run for it!'

Sergeant Lane laughed and grinned mischievously. This was a part of his job he enjoyed, the harmless flirting with the young servant girls, impressing them with highly exaggerated tales of his exploits as a policeman. In his experience, servants tended to know everything that was going on in a house like Ashgrove, all the secrets and idiosyncrasies of their masters and mistresses, and gossip about the guests. And if he was lucky, he'd manage to sweet talk the cook into giving him a cup of tea and a homemade sausage roll just fresh from the oven, he could feel his mouth watering just thinking about it, and then perhaps finished off by a large slice of Victoria sponge, light as anything ...

'Stop daydreaming, Lane, you're not stuffing your face yet,' Deacon said. 'Listen, man, I want to find out who found Miss Simpson in the woods and what she was doing. Was she crouched over the body crying her eyes out or some way away trying to hide the gun? And what sort of state was she in? Did she run back from the woods herself or did someone have to bring her back and, if the latter, who was it and what were they doing there? The more I think about it, the more I realise how little we got out of Sir William or Miss Simpson, the first time we interviewed her, as to what exactly happened ... Good God, man, what's that noise?' Deacon broke off abruptly from what he was saying, swinging his head around violently to stare in bewilderment at the library door. There was a banging on it which seemed deafening after the detectives' quiet deliberations. 'They'll have the door off the hinges if they're not careful, or at the very least put a hole in it if they go on like that much longer.'

Sergeant Lane leapt across the room and opened the door. Rose collapsed into his arms. After a moment of indecision, Deacon took the girl from him and led her into the library where he seated her gently on the settee. He strode to the door and whispered urgently to the sergeant. 'You go on, Lane, see what you can get from the servants.' He looked over his shoulder. 'The girl still seems distraught and I don't want to lose any more time. We must crack on and interview Lady Withers and the house guests.'

Lane nodded and departed, although he was very tempted to stay and hear what Miss Simpson had to say. Deacon had just closed the door behind him and was making his way back into the room when the door swung open and a very excited young constable stood in the doorway, hardly able to contain himself.

'Good God, man,' said Deacon, annoyed at yet another disruption, 'haven't you heard of knocking.'

'Sorry, sir,' replied the constable looking slightly abashed at the ticking off. 'It's just that we thought you'd want to know straight away …'

Deacon held up his hand to silence him and walked over to the constable so that he could tell his news out of ear shot of Rose.

'What is it, man, for God's sake tell me quietly, there's no need to broadcast it to the whole house.'

'It's the gun, sir,' said the constable in an excited whisper. 'As you instructed, we were making a search of the woods for the murder weapon and we've found it, sir. We found it in some undergrowth not far from the scene of the shooting.'

Sergeant Lane found himself seated comfortably in a chair in the servants' hall. Initially his arrival had caused a flurry of excitement with maids of all description – house, kitchen and scullery – staring at him in awe of a real life Scotland Yard detective being in their kitchen, marvelling at his good looks, giggling and nudging each other, trying to catch his eye and being rewarded with a wink or a grin when they did. Albert, the footman, who was used to having the girls' undivided attention, and Mrs Palmer, had been less delighted to see him, although the latter was being grudgingly won over by his charm and his saying how his mother had once been a house maid herself in a large house like this and he knew the amount of hard work that went into making sure that the household ran like clockwork and if only the master and mistress of the house knew the full worth of their servants they'd double their wages in a trice. Soon she was beckoning him be seated at the vast well-scrubbed wooden table and, wiping her hands on her apron, was pointing at the kitchen maid and scullery maid for one to quickly pour the gentleman a nice strong cup of tea and the other to cut him a generous slice of Victoria sponge, fresh baked that morning before all the kerfuffle, as she called it. And as light as a feather, the detective had assured her, quite melted on the tongue it did and, though he would never admit it to her face, it tasted even better than the cakes his mother made, if such a thing was possible.

'Well, I'm glad you're enjoying it,' Mrs Palmer had said, rolling up her sleeves in preparation for starting her next cooking task, revealing to Lane two mighty forearms in the process, muscular from years of beating and whisking, 'what with all that's happened, I'll doubt them upstairs will be wanting their afternoon tea and I do so hate to see things go to waste, don't you, not though that it will with all these greedy young mouths,' she said indicating the maids and footman. 'Mr Stafford and Miss Crimms have got something of a sweet tooth themselves so I dare say there'll be nothing but a few crumbs left before the day's out.'

It had seemed to Lane an awful lot of servants for a household of just two to have, especially as the general view was that since the war it was hard to get good domestic staff. It appeared that, as a result of fair wages and good working conditions, and because generations of the same families had been employed there, Ashgrove enjoyed an almost unnatural sense of loyalty amongst its staff, so that although all the able men had joined up as soon as war had been declared, and some of the women staff had become ambulance drivers, nurses and the such, as soon as the war was over those who were able to had returned and had been received back to jobs kept open for them. The sergeant looked at Mrs Palmer, called such because of her status as cook-housekeeper, not because she had ever been married. He wondered idly whether she had chosen to be a spinster, to devote her life to the service of her employers, or whether she had lost a sweetheart in the Great War as so many women had done. Instead of fretting over a soufflé for Sir William and Lady Withers, was she wishing instead that she was fussing over a husband, to say nothing of the offspring they might have produced. Instead she immersed herself in her cooking and running a large house, a poor substitute for loved ones, he thought.

Lane, noting her harsh words to them, wondered whether Mrs Palmer resented the kitchen maid and the little scullery maid for the love and happiness that might await them but had eluded her. If she had been affected by the war, she had not been the only one. Lane himself had lost a cousin and an uncle, and Deacon, he knew from police station gossip, had lost his only brother. He knew also that it was only because of the dearth left by a generation of men lost in the Great War, rather than by personal merit that both he and Deacon had been promoted so quickly and at such a young age to fill dead men's shoes. He felt always a sense of guilt that he had benefited in this way from the death of others, that his career had been propelled forward while those of others had sunk in the blood and mud in France. Instinctively, he knew that Deacon felt the same although they had never spoken of it, that the only thing that kept the two of them going, assuaged them from the guilt that they had survived while others, better men, had perished, was the belief that they could bring justice to the Britain that these men had fought for, could make it a land worth dying for. It did not matter that he and Deacon had not been old enough to fight, they carried the guilt with them like a heavy bag, men born a few years too young. Lane had known a few lads the same age as him who had lied about their age. They had signed up and gone to France and most had died, but one or two had survived although they had never been quite right. Williams was in a home and recognised no-one but sat and shook all day, his mind all blown to pieces, while Brown's body had been blown apart, he had lost his legs and an arm and sat in a chair with his only arm resting over a blanket knitted by his mother, a former shadow of himself, but with his mind intact so that he could witness the life he had lost, the kind of man he could have been.

'I'd just like to get an idea if I can, Mrs Palmer, as to the guests, get a feel for their characters,' began Lane. 'We find if we get an idea about the types of people involved, their likes and dislikes, what kind of people they are and such like, well it helps us to find out exactly what happened. And I know from the stories that my mother used to tell me, there's nothing that goes on in a house like this without the servants knowing, particularly in a well-run house like this one.'

'You're quite right, Sergeant,' agreed Mrs Palmer, 'although I won't have it said that we tells tales, because we don't.'

'Quite so, Mrs Palmer. But you'll have nothing against helping the police with their enquiries, will you? But before we go into all that, there's something that's been puzzling me. Sir William was called away otherwise we would have asked him. It was Miss Simpson, I believe, who was out walking in the woods with Lady Belvedere when she was shot. I was wondering whether she made her own way back to raise the alarm. The inspector and I have been to the woods where the incident took place and it's a fair distance from the house, quite a trek over the parkland and through the gardens. She must have been shocked and distraught; I'd be surprised if the young lady could find her way back unaided. We had some difficulty ourselves finding our way back onto the path.'

'You're right, Sergeant, she was in no fit state to do so. She was found by Archie Cutter and his son, Sid. Crouched over the body she was, so they said. Screaming for all she was worth, as you'd expect. Had to prise her away, they did. Archie stayed with the body while young Sid led her back here to raise the alarm and get someone to look after her. An awful job he had too. First she wouldn't leave the body, kept talking a lot of odd nonsense so Archie Cutter told me later. Said as how it was all her fault that Lady Belvedere was dead, said as how she'd killed her! Poor lass didn't know what she was saying, poor thing. I doubt whether she had ever picked up a shotgun in her life let alone shot anything. Anyway, in case you start wondering and adding two and two to make five, Archie assured me there was no gun anywhere. He checked the undergrowth and bushes nearby. Talking nonsense, he told me, he thought she must have been delirious with the shock like. Anyway, once they had managed to tear her away from the body, quite a two man job it was and Sid such a little fellow even for his age, she kept stumbling like and trying to turn back.

'But the two of them managed to get here eventually. Sid brought her to the servants' entrance and we brought her in here and sat her down on that there chair where you are sitting now, Sergeant. Quite a state they both were in, I can tell you. Could get no sense out of either of them until Mr Stafford had given Sid a drop of the master's brandy. Miss Simpson was as pale and white as a ghost and shivering as if she would never get warm again, so I gave her a nice hot, weak cup of tea with plenty of sugar in it, because of course she was suffering from shock. Young Sid seemed to pull himself together first, although his words came tumbling out on top of each other. Anyway, eventually we could just about make out a garbled message about a lady lying dead in the woods. Sid was awful scared about having left his father guarding the body, kept saying that he was afraid that he'd get shot, that he was sure the man was still out there and we had to hurry.

'Mr Stafford and me, we didn't know what to make of it all, I can tell you. Something dreadful had obviously happened, but we didn't want to waste the police's time.'

'Very considerate of you I'm sure,' said Lane, trying to look impassive while taking in the news of the confession. He wanted desperately to scribble down all the information he could, but, not wishing to appear too excited, limited himself to writing down the general gist in a slow and methodical manner.

'Well in the end, because young Sid was in such a state about his father, Mr Stafford got Albert to telephone for the police while he and Bridges, that's the head gardener, set out for the woods to see for themselves what had happened. They took a couple of spades with them just in case, although what good they'd have been against a man wielding a gun, I'm not sure. Anyway they found Archie standing guard over the body and Lady Belvedere dead as a dormouse just as Sid had said. And Archie had the same story as to how he and Sid had come across Miss Simpson crouching over the body and what she'd said but he said as how she was talking gibberish and that he'd put it down to shock.'

'I see. We'll have to interview Mr Cutter and his son ourselves of course. But what can you tell me about them. Are they reliable?'

'Archie's cellar man at the "Horse and Hound". His family have lived in the village for generations, so they have, and Sid's his son, just a young lad but pleasant enough, eleven or twelve, still at school.'

'You mentioned earlier that they said they were out walking in the woods, but from your tone I gather you didn't believe them. Why's that, Mrs Palmer?' The sergeant looked at the cook quizzically, and for the first time during their conversation she seemed a little uneasy.

'The woodland backs onto Sir William's parkland, Mr Lane. Like as not the Cutters' intention was to do a bit of poaching. As you know times are hard, Sergeant, there's not many a folk who can afford fresh meat to feed their families these days. And Sir William is awful lenient with them. He likes as not turns a blind eye to a bit of poaching, as long as folks don't take advantage, of course.'

'I see, very good of him. But it does mean, does it not, that if Mr Cutter and his son were after bagging a rabbit or two they'd have taken a shotgun with them?'

The servants' hall suddenly became silent as the general to-ing and fro-ing made by the servants undertaking their daily tasks, which had created a background noise to their conversation, ceased abruptly and Lane inwardly cursed himself for being too direct in his questioning. He had no intention of making them guarded in what they said, frightened of incriminating someone.

'You misunderstand me, Sergeant,' said Mrs Palmer, clearly flustered, wringing her apron between her hands as if it was wet. 'I didn't mean to imply that just because Archie Cutter is not above doing a bit of poaching, he'd kill someone. That'd be ridiculous!'

'I'm not saying that he did, Mrs Palmer,' said the sergeant trying to recover the situation and reassure all the anxious eyes that were turned to him. 'I'm sure he didn't, but he would have had a gun with him and I need to find out what he did with it. I'm thinking that despite Sir William's lenient approach to a bit of poaching on his land, Mr Cutter wouldn't want to be caught red handed with a gun in his possession. I take it he came back with Stafford to get his boy? He must have done something with the gun. Our men are out searching the woods now, I don't want them to find Mr Cutter's gun and confuse it with the weapon that killed the countess, it'll only delay things.'

'I see, Sergeant, you're quite right,' said Mrs Palmer looking relieved. 'Well he did come back with Mr Stafford, as you say, to get young Sid. I think that Mr Stafford thought it best if a member of the household, so to speak, was guarding the body until the police arrived, so he left Bridges. And, before you ask,' she continued, holding up her hand as Lane looked about to interrupt her, 'Cutter was carrying no gun. He was looking mighty shocked himself so I sat him down and gave him a cup of sweet tea. By this

153

time, I'd taken Miss Simpson up to her room to lay down. Mrs Torrington offered to keep her company, for she was in no fit state to be left alone. Meanwhile, Mr Stafford went to acquaint Sir William as to what had happened. He was that grateful to the Cutters for how they had dealt with the situation, Archie staying with the body and young Sid seeing Miss Simpson home, that he gave them a brace of pheasant to take home with them. If we'd realised you would be here so quick we would have made them stay put. But I'll give you directions to their cottage, it's just a couple of miles away at the edge of the village.'

'Thank you, Mrs Palmer, you've been most helpful. I'll just go and have a word or two with my inspector and then no doubt I'll be sent off to interview the Cutters. And then I'll come back and ask you a few more questions about the guests, if you don't mind. It'll be a chance to have another slice of that delicious cake if nothing else.' He beamed around at all the servants, but none caught his eye or smiled this time.

Chapter Twenty-three

'Sir, there's something that I thought I'd better come and tell you before I interview the servants further,' said Lane entering the library. Seeing that Rose was still there, he beckoned to the inspector to come over to the door so that they could confer without being overheard. He was surprised to notice that one of the constables was also there, sitting in the same chair that he had sat in when taking notes. 'Miss Simpson was discovered in the wood by an Archie Cutter and his young son, Sid. Apparently she was in no fit state to make her own way back to the house so young Sid escorted her while Archie Cutter kept watch over the body. Mr Cutter is a cellar man at the local public house. The servants think that he and his son were probably out poaching when they came across her, which obviously means that one of them was more than likely carrying a gun. When Stafford and Bridges, that's the head gardener, sir, went to relieve Cutter and ascertain the truth of the boy's somewhat garbled story, there was no sign of a gun. Cutter had no doubt taken the opportunity to hide it while he was alone with the body. Sir William is known to be rather tolerant of poachers on his land, but even so, I doubt Cutter wanted to risk it, particularly as Lady Belvedere had been shot with just such a weapon.'

'That explains it,' said the inspector, not sounding particularly surprised. 'The constables located a shotgun during their search of the woods. It had been partially hidden in the undergrowth close to the scene of the shooting. It seemed to me a bit too convenient, unless of course the killer had panicked, which would fit in with Sir William's theory of a poacher who had shot Lady Belvedere by mistake. I've just been to see the gun myself in situate and to me it doesn't look as if it's recently been fired, but I could be wrong. It's been photographed and tested for fingerprints; some were found, and I was just about to go and check to see if they matched those of anyone in the house. But, as it now seems likely that it's this Cutter's gun, take the gun with you and go and interview the Cutters and take their fingerprints. Hopefully they'll confirm straight away that it's theirs, but make sure you bring it back so that our gun expert can check it. It's just possible that they might have killed Lady Belvedere by mistake and then hung around when they saw the state Miss Simpson was in, but I think that's highly unlikely. I think we'll find that another gun altogether is the murder weapon.'

'Very well, sir, but what about Miss Simpson? You'll be wanting to take a statement from her won't you, she's obviously got something that she wants to get off her chest; you'll need someone to take notes.'

'That's all right, Lane, I'm sure the constable will oblige. I'm very mindful that I've kept Miss Simpson waiting. They brought me the news about the discovery of the gun just after you left to interview the servants, so I left the constable to sit with Miss Simpson while I went out to take a look for myself. She seemed in a particularly agitated state and I didn't think she should be left alone. But I'm very keen at the moment that we locate the murder weapon and eliminate these Cutters and their gun from our enquiries if we can. I know I can rely on you Lane, but try and find out if the Cutters heard or saw something. They must have been in the vicinity when Lady Belvedere was shot. Perhaps they saw a figure running away or they may have overheard Lady Belvedere's and Miss Simpson's conversation, anyway, see what you can find out.'

'Very good, sir.'

'Right, I really must get on with interviewing Miss Simpson now before I have any more interruptions. I'm anxious to find out what she's got to tell us. I suppose Sir William will be back any minute.'

'I don't think you have anything to worry about on that score, sir,' said the sergeant trying vainly to suppress a grin. 'Last time I saw him was when I was leaving the servants' hall. I had to pass the housekeeper's sitting room, and happened to look in; Sir William was partaking of a glass of sherry with his butler. They both looked very settled.'

'Well, what is it Stafford?' demanded Sir William, for the second time that morning, as he entered his butler's pantry, a service room located off the kitchen. Sir William looked around him, taking in the counters and the sink, the fine china that was stored there, as well as the family's silver, which was both cleaned and counted in this room. He caught sight on the desk of the wine log, written in Stafford's very precise hand, as well as the merchant account books, charge over which was Mrs Palmer's responsibility. Leading off from the pantry was Stafford's bedroom. Sir William had rarely ventured into his servants' domain, and he felt at once as if he were entering into another world.

'This had better be good,' Sir William continued, 'I can't have you drag me out of a police interview just to check the quality of Mrs Palmer's soup or to go through the menu for luncheon. Doubt whether anyone will feel much like eating anyhow, what with this dreadful business, what?' He wanted dreadfully to sit down and rest a while and think, he considered the butler's pantry rather restful and masculine, an escape from the feminine finery of the main parts of the house, but he did not think it appropriate for him to do such a thing without being bidden, as if he would be overstepping the mark, imposing the master-servant relationship into somewhere which was totally Stafford's domain, and so he stood there uncomfortably, aware of his aching bones. However, there was only a rickety old chair which looked distinctly uncomfortable.

'Quite so, sir,' said Stafford in his usual deferential tone, his face as impassive as ever. Sir William had always found his butler's lack of emotion disconcerting and wondered, not for the first time, whether Stafford was secretly laughing at him.

'I can assure you that luncheon is not an issue, sir. Mrs Palmer and I had exactly the same thoughts on the matter as yourself, sir. Instead of roast beef and Yorkshire pudding with roast potatoes, cabbage, carrots and gravy …,' Sir William found his mouth watering at the description of the meal he was to miss despite his fine words, 'Mrs Palmer, having already started to cook the joint of beef before we became aware of the catastrophe, is going to do rare roast beef sandwiches and, for those who are really not up to eating anything at all, a hot chicken broth that she usually reserves for invalids. She is still intending on serving the apple pie and custard, sir, for we both thought that the sugar would give much needed energy which we feel is very necessary at a time like this to see everyone through the shock.'

'Yes, very good,' agreed Sir William, secretly delighted that pudding was still on the menu.

'And for the policeman from Scotland Yard, sir' continued Stafford, 'we thought just sandwiches and coffee. Would you like to sit down, sir? What I should like to talk to you about may take a little time to discuss. If I may suggest, sir, going into the housekeeper's sitting room, there are rather more comfortable chairs to sit on in there. Besides, we are sure to be disturbed by the other servants if we stay in this room.'

'Oh, very well, Stafford, if you insist, lead the way,' said Sir William wearily, collapsing into a rather faded armchair as soon as they entered the room. He noted that Stafford remained standing and he felt immediately that this placed him at a distinct disadvantage having the butler loom over him. 'Now what is it, Stafford, what's so important, spit it out, man.'

'When Betty, that's the under housemaid, sir, was cleaning your study this morning just before the police arrived, your saying that it was probably the room that they would use as their interview room, although, of course, they've since decided to relocate to the library, it being bigger, but we weren't to know that at the time. Anyway,' Stafford continued quickly, aware that his master was looking both a little confused and bored, 'suffice to say, Betty went in there to clean and that if it hadn't been for the police, it probably wouldn't have been cleaned until Monday morning, sir, when you were partaking of breakfast because you don't usually use it on .....'

'Get on with it, man,' interrupted Sir William rudely, 'do you think I am interested in when my study gets cleaned, don't you think I've got more important things to think about just now what with one of my guests having been killed on my property, my wife's sister at that?'

'Indeed, sir,' agreed Stafford, impassive as ever, 'which is why I wouldn't have said anything only when Betty pulled back the curtain of the alcove to polish your gun cabinet she noticed that the lock had been forced.'

'What!' Sir William's eyes bulged and he covered his face with his hand. 'Don't tell me my shotgun was missing?'

'No, sir, it had been put back.'

'Ah, that's a relief, nothing to worry about then. What do you mean by put back? It was probably never used in the first place. I've always thought that lock was rather dodgy, probably just came apart, meant to mention it to you before; have someone mend it at once.'

'Yes, sir, of course. But before I do, I should mention that the maid came to see me straightaway about her discovery. In view of everything that had happened, I took the liberty of examining the shotgun and found that it had been recently used and put back uncleaned.'

'Good God, man, are you sure?'

'Quite sure, sir.'

158

'How many people know about this, Stafford?'

'Just me and the maid, sir, and you now, of course. I think the maid could be persuaded to keep quiet about it though, she's a little in awe of me, sir; to tell the truth, I think I remind her a bit of her father.'

'Let me think, let me think.' Sir William got up and started pacing the room. 'We shouldn't really withhold evidence from the police, Stafford. Not the done thing at all, but if we tell them about it, it will knock the theory that Lady Belvedere was killed accidently by a poacher completely on the head.'

'My thoughts exactly, sir. I doubt even the most audacious poacher would dare to break in to your study to steal one of your guns.'

'This is awful, Stafford.'

'Quite so, sir, which is why I thought I should tell you first, before we informed the police.'

'Absolutely, old man,' agreed Sir William scratching his head. 'Yes, I suppose we must tell them. Damned if I know what to do about it. Of course, my duty is to help the police with their enquiries, but if I do tell them about the shotgun then they'll think Lady Belvedere's shooting was premeditated and that the culprit was one of my ... oh, it's too awful to think about. Do you think the murderer left fingerprints on the weapon, Stafford, or do you think he wore gloves? It's not really cricket after all to rat on one's guests. One doesn't invite people to come and stay and then pass information onto the police which will confirm that they are a murderer.'

'Quite so, sir, which is why I took the liberty of wiping the gun of fingerprints. I thought it was a necessary precaution in the circumstances.'

'You did *what*, Stafford!' Sir William looked aghast. 'Why man, that's tampering with the evidence, you're an accessory after the whatsit, you could go to prison!'

'Yes, sir, but only if the police find out. I'm hoping that they'll think that the murderer wiped his fingerprints from the gun himself. It's what I would have done, sir, if I had decided to take one of your guns and kill Lady Belvedere.'

'Yes, I'm sure you would have, Stafford. Why man, I bet you'd commit the perfect murder.'

'I hope so, sir, not that I hope the need will ever arise.'

'Well, I wouldn't like to get on the wrong side of you,' said Sir William eyeing his butler with a degree of unease. 'Anyway, what's done is done.

Who knows about you wiping the gun of fingerprints? I take it you didn't do it in front of the maid?'

'Oh no, sir, that would have been most improper, sir,' said the butler looking horrified, 'she holds me in high esteem, as do all the servants here, of course. I see it as my duty to be an example to them.'

'Yes, I'm sure you do. Well I suppose we'd better get it over with,' said Sir William in a resigned way, although having re-seated himself in the armchair during the course of their conversation about the gun, he suddenly found himself reluctant to get up. 'I suppose I can't hold it off any longer. Come with me, Stafford, and we'd better bring the girl too, I expect the police will want to have a word with her.'

'Perhaps before we go, sir, you'd like a small glass of sherry to fortify yourself for the ordeal.'

'Jolly good idea, Stafford, just what I need only better make it a large one and given that there's just the two of us and after the risk you've taken, you'd better join me in a snifter yourself.'

Chapter Twenty-four

'Right, Miss Simpson, please accept my apologies for keeping you waiting, I hope the constable has been looking after you in my absence,' Deacon said, closing the library door behind the sergeant. 'Now what is it that you wanted to tell us, I take it it's pretty important given that you almost broke the door down.' He smiled, but it did little to mask his concern.

'I'm sorry, Inspector, now I've had an opportunity just to sit here and think, while you were called out, I feel much calmer, much more myself, and I'm afraid I may have overreacted a bit. I think I may have made a bit of a fool of myself in front of Mrs Torrington.'

'Indeed?' Deacon raised his eyebrows slightly, looking interested. 'Well, suppose we start at the beginning. What is it you wanted to tell me?'

'Well, and I don't feel any less worried about this and it sounds a bit silly when I say it out loud, but...'

'But?' Deacon prompted, encouragingly.

'I don't think Lady Belvedere was the intended victim, I think I was.'

The constable, who had been taking notes all the while in the sergeant's absence, pressed rather too hard on his pencil and the lead broke. Deacon now looked keenly at Rose, all ears.

'Suppose you tell me exactly why you think that, Miss Simpson.'

'Well ... I know it sounds awfully melodramatic and of course I might have got it totally wrong, but, well, I stumbled just as Lady Belvedere was shot. I'd forgotten all about it, you see, what with the shock of it all, and then I suddenly remembered while I was upstairs with Edith, trying to rest. I stumbled and tripped just as the gun went off. It was the look on Lady Belvedere's face that made me fall. I've never seen anything like it, seen anyone look so afraid. I suppose I was transfixed, but I put my hand out towards her and, not looking where I was going and the ground being so littered with twigs and bits of branches, well, I tripped. And then when I looked up, I couldn't see her, and I looked down and there she was ...' She faltered for a moment at the recollection but went on valiantly, before the inspector had an opportunity to interrupt. 'He must have panicked, mustn't

161

he? When he realised he'd shot the wrong person, he must have panicked and run away.'

'It's possible,' agreed Deacon, pondering. 'Of course, you weren't facing the shooter, so we can't be sure who he was aiming at, but it's possible that you were his intended target.'

'That's not all, Inspector. What made me really afraid, although I think now I might have read too much in to it at the time, was that Edith seemed to be trying to stop me from coming down to see you, she even went so far as to try and bar my way, but then again, perhaps she was just worried about me. But she was very anxious to know what I'd seen. It was almost like she was trying to make me promise that I hadn't seen who'd killed the countess.'

'Interesting. Well, we'll certainly be having a word with Mrs Torrington. Now to come back to this idea about you being the intended victim, Miss Simpson. I'd like to explore that further. Do you have any enemies here in this house, anyone you could think of who might want to cause you harm?'

'Enemies, Inspector? Enemies is such a strong word, isn't it? I hope that I don't have any enemies anywhere, let alone in this house. Why, I met most of the people here only the day before yesterday.'

'So you can't think of anyone, Miss Simpson?'

'Not really. Lady Belvedere obviously wasn't too fond of me, and Lavinia and I have had a bit of a falling out, but it's silly really, I mean it's over nothing. She's my friend. The only other person I can think of, but I'd rather not say....'

'Yes, Miss Simpson?' Deacon looked up and nodded at her encouragingly. 'I'm afraid that it's important that you tell us everything no matter how irrelevant you may think it is.'

'Well, Lord Sneddon made a sort of drunken pass at me on the Friday night. Fortunately Stafford came to my rescue. But then he did the same thing last night, although this time I don't think he had any intention of taking no for an answer ...' Rose shivered slightly, as she remembered how frightened she had been.

'So what happened, Miss Simpson?' Both policemen looked at her concerned.

'Cedric ..., Lord Sedgwick saved me.' As Rose said these words, she thought how romantic it had been, being saved by the man she loved and for a moment she was lost in her own thoughts. A discreet cough by the inspector brought her back to the present. 'He must have had his suspicions about his friend,' she said quickly, 'because he just appeared out of the darkness and told Lord Sneddon to let me go and then he punched him in the face and told him to pack his bags and go first thing this morning. Lord Sneddon was very angry about it and threatened to get his own back.'

'I see. It sounds as if you had a lucky escape, Miss Simpson,' said Deacon. 'Well, Lord Sneddon's still here, so we'll be speaking to him later as well.'

'Going back to Lady Belvedere, Miss Simpson, let's just suppose she was the intended victim after all. As someone meeting most of the people here for the first time, I'd like to hear your views as to who might wish the countess harm. From what I understand, she could be rather a difficult woman.'

'Yes, Inspector, she was. She was a woman who wanted her own way and was used to getting it. I don't think anyone liked her much. Cedric and Lavinia avoided going back to Sedgwick as much as possible, and even Lady Withers seemed a bit scared of her. Her own husband kept himself out of her way, although, if I'm honest he seemed to keep himself out of everyone's way, preferring the company of old books to people. And Edith ...'

'Yes. Mrs Torrington?'

'She told me yesterday that she hated Lady Belvedere. She said something about the countess having done her some terrible wrong and she didn't deserve to live. She said something about being tempted to kill her herself, but I don't think she was being serious, Inspector,' added Rose, hurriedly. 'At the time I'm sure I thought she was just saying it for effect, I didn't think she actually meant to do it and I don't now, Inspector,' she emphasised. 'It was, well, just a figure of speech, that's all.'

'Indeed. Even so, I'm curious to have a word with our Mrs Torrington.'

'Well, that's a turn up for the books,' Sergeant Lane said, when Deacon had filled him in on events on his return from the Cutters. 'Puts a completely different complexion on things I'd say, sir; looks like the Countess of Belvedere wasn't the intended victim after all.'

'Perhaps,' Inspector Deacon wandered over to the fireplace and picked up a framed photograph from the mantelpiece, which he studied absentmindedly before putting it back down again.

'You don't sound convinced, sir. But it certainly gives us other suspects. This Lord Sneddon, for instance, sounds a nasty piece of work.'

'Yes, Lane, and Miss Simpson went on to say that, during the course of yesterday afternoon, Lady Belvedere summoned Lord Sedgwick, Lord Sneddon and Lady Lavinia to her presence individually and that each one looked annoyed or upset on their return. It would be interesting to know what she said to each; we'll have to try and find out, it might give us some more motives.' Deacon began to pace the room. 'But going back to Miss Simpson, we've only got her word that things happened the way she said they did. And remember, she's in a very agitated frame of mind at the moment, probably suffering from shock and who's to blame her, after what she's witnessed. One moment she's having a heated argument with someone and the next that person is shot dead before her eyes. No wonder the poor girl's in the state she's in. I don't know what to make of her claim that Mrs Torrington tried to prevent her from speaking to us. Did that really happen, or was it imagined on her part? Either way, we need to keep an eye on her.

'Now, let's look at what we do know for sure. Lady Belvedere announces in a loud voice in the drawing room after dinner last night, when most of the guests are present, that she would like Miss Simpson to take a walk with her in the woodland the following morning. She reiterates her request, or command should I say knowing the type of woman she appears to have been, through her maid after breakfast this morning. No doubt some of the servants were present, serving up the dishes and taking away the empty plates and so forth. So the news, which must have been of interest to all, could and probably did go all around the servants' hall. Then, knowing what servants are like, it probably got passed on to some of the other guests in the form of servants' gossip when they were taken their morning cups of coffee or tea or breakfast in bed. We can assume then, that everyone in this house could have known that Lady Belvedere and Miss Simpson would be walking in the woods this morning.'

'Surely, sir, that backs up what Miss Simpson was saying.'

'Don't be so quick to jump to conclusions, Lane. It could have gone as Miss Simpson says. She might have stumbled on a stone or something on the path and Lady Belvedere might have leant forward to grab her or offer her arm to prevent Miss Simpson from falling. However, knowing Lady Belvedere as we are beginning to, it seems to me more likely as not that she

164

would have left Miss Simpson to fall and probably been quite happy about it.'

'It would have been an instinctive reaction, sir, I think, for her to grab Miss Simpson, even if she didn't like her one little bit. Even if that weren't the case, sir, the murderer could still have been aiming the gun at Miss Simpson. If she and the Countess of Belvedere were walking side by side or perhaps had stopped to take in the view, or her ladyship had stopped to stress some point, and then Miss Simpson had stumbled, couldn't the murderer, if he had been aiming at Miss Simpson at that moment, have pulled the trigger and hit the countess by mistake?'

'Yes, it's possible, Lane. But it could just as easily have happened very differently. As I've already said, we've only Miss Simpson's word for it that she stumbled. Yes, I know, Lane,' Inspector Deacon put up his hand as he saw that his sergeant was about to protest. 'I agree with you that Miss Simpson seems a very nice young lady, very well brought up and personable to be sure, just the sort of lady your mother would like you to marry, no doubt! But what if she's not really like that at all?

'What about if she's set her heart on marrying this Cedric fellow? She could see him as her way out of her current life of relative poverty and servitude, so to speak. And the only real obstacle to the match is Lady Belvedere. The earl seems to spend his life shut up with his books and to take little interest in his wife or children, so he might not have an issue with the match, we'll need to check. I'm sure there was much speculation between everyone as to why the countess wanted to speak with Miss Simpson, but I think everyone probably was of the view that it was to warn her off, whether it be her friendship with Lady Belvedere's daughter or her designs upon her son.'

'I'm not convinced, sir,' said Lane. 'For one thing, Miss Simpson had no idea that Lord Sedgwick would be here. And would she really have fallen in love with him and decided to kill his mother all in the space of a couple of days?'

'Let's just suppose for a moment that Miss Simpson is the murderer, Sergeant, and the countess the intended victim. What could be easier than for Miss Simpson to take a shotgun from Sir William's gunroom either last thing at night, when everyone has gone to sleep, or in the early hours of the morning when the servants are still sleeping? It was a moonlit night and she could have walked some way along the path until she had come to a convenient clump of bushes, loaded the gun and hidden it in the undergrowth. Then all she's got to do is remember where she's hidden it, walk with the countess along the path, stop and perhaps point to something on the horizon and then while the countess is busy trying to see what has been pointed out to her, Miss Simpson darts into the undergrowth, picks up the weapon, aims it at Lady Belvedere, calls to her so she turns around and then shoots. Then all she's got to do is start screaming, wipe the gun clean of fingerprints and hurl it as far away from her as possible so that it's not immediately found. It would be the work of seconds, a couple of minutes at most. And it takes a little while for the Cutters to reach her. Plenty enough time for her to arrange herself in a kneeling position over the body, sobbing, trying to stem the wound with her handkerchief. A perfect show of grief for when the Cutters come stumbling onto the scene.'

'You really think that's what happened, sir?' Inspector Deacon took in the sad look upon his sergeant's face.

'No, Lane, I don't. All I'm saying is that it could have happened that way and that we've got to keep an open mind.'

'I bet everyone in this house would like it to be Miss Simpson, sir, she being an outsider and all and not one of their class.'

'It's because it's better than the alternative.'

'What's that, sir?'

'That it's one of them. But we mustn't forget what Miss Simpson said when the Cutters found her, about it being all her fault. However, another theory did just cross my mind, Lane, unlikely though it seems. What if Lady Belvedere herself arranged for someone to kill Miss Simpson while they were out on their walk together; it doesn't seem that out of character, does it? From what we've heard, she was pretty ruthless and determined to get her own way by any means. Well, what if the person she engaged to do the killing changed their mind and killed the countess instead, or by mistake because Miss Simpson tripped and fell at the crucial time? You never know, Sergeant, perhaps the murderer was murdered!'

166

Chapter Twenty-five

On leaving the library, Rose made her way up to her own room where she intended to lock herself in and think further on the events of the morning or, if that felt too wearisome, to rest. Right now, she would have given anything to be at home, safe.

She had just got to the top of the first flight of stairs when a door was flung open and Edith appeared on the landing. Both women looked at each other for what seemed to Rose a few minutes, but in reality was probably only a few seconds, and then Rose broke the silence.

'I've been to see the police.'

'Yes.'

'I've told them everything, everything I can remember.'

'Very wise.'

'Why did you try and stop me just now?'

'I didn't,' began Edith, before seeing the look of disbelief on Rose's face. 'Well, I suppose it might have looked like that. But I did it for your own good. You were so tired and agitated, your face had gone so white, I didn't think you'd manage the stairs without falling down them. I wanted you to lie down and rest a while, that's all.'

'You're lying. You wanted to know whether I'd seen who killed Lady Belvedere and you wanted to stop me from telling the police.' There was a silence, disturbed only by the ticking of the grandfather clock in the hall below. 'Well, aren't you going to say anything, Edith, aren't you going to deny it?'

'No,' said Edith, finally, 'I suppose I'm not.'

'Get out of my way. I don't want you anywhere near me,' Rose said, aware that her voice was beginning to rise hysterically. 'Leave me alone, no, don't come any nearer to me or I'll scream, oh, can't you see I'm frightened of you?'

'Frightened of me?' Edith sounded incredulous. 'Rose? Rose, dear, you have no reason to be frightened of me, I promise you. I mean you no harm.'

'I don't believe you. Oh, I don't know what to believe,' Rose said, becoming distraught. 'I'm just so frightened, that's all.'

'William should have sent for the doctor to give you a sedative,' Edith said, coming over to Rose and putting an arm around her shoulders. 'It was very unfair of him not to, to hell with the police.'

'Edith, can I ask you something?'

'Yes, of course.'

'Will you promise me that you'll tell the truth?'

'Yes ...well, I ...'

'Did you kill Lady Belvedere?' There was another silence.

'No, I didn't,' Edith said.

'But you know who did,' persisted Rose, 'and you are trying to protect them, aren't you?'

'Yes, at least, I think I know who did it and I am trying to protect them. They don't deserve to hang, Rose, we mustn't let that happen.' She looked at Rose beseechingly. 'Please don't ask me any more questions, I'm not going to tell you who it is, and if you tell the police about this conversation, I'll deny it, so it'll just be your word against mine.'

'I didn't tell the police about your conversation with Sir William on the croquet lawn, it didn't seem relevant.'

'Thank you, it wasn't.'

'I didn't tell them either that I thought Lady Belvedere was frightened of you, and then you of her.'

'You just imagined it, Rose, that's all. You seem to have a very vivid imagination.'

'That's as may be, Edith, but I didn't imagine you telling me how much you hated Lady Belvedere at lunch yesterday, or how she deserved to be dead and you were minded to send her on her way yourself. I'm afraid I told the police that.'

'It was very silly of me to say what I did. With hindsight ...'

'Yes, hindsight's a great thing, isn't it? But you weren't to know, were you Edith? I mean, you didn't shoot the countess, did you, so you weren't to know someone would kill her today?'

'No.'

Rose left Edith standing on the landing and proceeded up to her room. When she happened to look back, she found that Edith was still looking after her. Their eyes locked for a moment before both women looked away. Rose continued to her room aware that both women were left wondering what the other was thinking and, more importantly, what the other one knew.

'You'd better lead the way, Stafford,' said Deacon, trying very hard to keep his temper in check and hide how very annoyed he was with Sir William, who was following the inspector and sergeant rather dejectedly. It had seemed quite a good idea at the time to take a sherry with his butler, particularly in light of what Stafford had been prepared to do to protect the honour of the house and guests, but now Sir William considered that he had been a trifle unwise. Neither policeman had appreciated him not informing them at once that someone had broken into his gun cabinet. Somehow they had known that he had been drinking sherry with his butler. He did not feel that either could tell by his manner for he did not feel at all light headed, just calm; a lot calmer anyway, than he had felt just after he had spoken with Edith. Edith! How could she have been so stupid, how could ......

'It's in here, sir,' said Stafford, pulling back the heavy velvet curtain, 'in this alcove. You probably didn't even notice it was here when you were in this room before, sir. The curtain's always kept drawn.'

'Thank you, Stafford,' said Deacon examining the gun cabinet. 'Yes, the lock's definitely been forced. Sergeant, take out the shotgun, will you, use a handkerchief in case there are fingerprints.'

'This gun's recently been fired, sir, and put back uncleaned,' said Lane, examining the gun carefully. He walked over to Sir William's desk and switched on the table lamp so that he could examine the weapon more closely. 'It looks as if someone's wiped off the fingerprints with a cloth, sir.' Sir William and Stafford exchanged glances surreptitiously.

'I see. When did you last open your gun cabinet, Sir William? Is it possible that it was broken into a little while ago?'

'No, Inspector. I opened it last night sometime after dinner, and the lock was secure then.'

'Indeed?' said Deacon. Both policemen looked interested.

'Yes', replied Sir William, rather uncomfortably. 'I was showing my guests a couple of antique duelling pistols that I'd recently purchased, pretty things they are too. I thought the girls would find the pattern on the butt caps amusing and the gentlemen would be interested to see them; they're in particularly good condition given their age.'

'Did you bring everyone in here to see them?' asked Lane.

'Yes, Sergeant. Everyone came in here. No wait, my wife and Lady Belvedere didn't. They retired to bed, but everyone else came in here; it was a bit of a squash, to tell the truth. I unlocked the cabinet with the key, the lock was intact then, I assure you.'

'Where do you keep the key, Sir William?'

'I carry it on me at all times, in fact, I said as much last night because someone commented on making sure that such a collection of guns didn't end up in the wrong hands; we made a bit of a joke about it in fact. Of course, Stafford here keeps a spare key in his butler's pantry in case I lose mine, but I didn't mention that. '

'And the ammunition, where is that kept?' enquired the inspector. 'Do you keep it in the cabinet with the guns?'

'Yes, Inspector, I keep it under lock and key as well, one can't be too careful. It's in this drawer here.'

'Well,' said Deacon, 'of course our forensic chaps will need to confirm it, but I think we can safely say that we've found our murder weapon.'

'But I thought your constables had found a gun in the woods,' protested Sir William. 'Surely it's much more likely that gun's the murder weapon.'

'That gun belonged to the Cutters, Sir William, they've confirmed as much to my sergeant here. They were out poaching in the woods when they came across Miss Simpson. They panicked, particularly when they realised that Lady Belvedere had been shot, and so Archie Cutter decided to hide the gun before anyone found it on him. They were going to come back for it later when all the fuss had died down. Anyway, they were very forthcoming. When Sergeant Lane examined the gun, he noticed a small defect in the barrel. If the Cutters' gun was used to shoot the countess, we'll soon know because it will have left a distinctive mark on the bullet.'

'I see,' said Sir William. He suddenly looked very old and tired and the sergeant pulled out a chair for him to sit down on. He sat down heavily, his head in his hands, and for a moment no-one spoke.

'Come, Sir William,' said Deacon, gently, 'you knew as much. You never believed in that story you told us about a poacher shooting Lady Belvedere

170

by mistake, did you? It was just wishful thinking on your part. The murderer was bound to be one of your guests or a member of this household.'

'Yes, of course you are right, Inspector, I just hoped ...'

'Right, Sir William, now that we're all quite clear that this is a murder investigation rather than some tragic accident, I would like you to arrange for all your guests to be brought to the dining room. They can have a quick lunch there.' The Inspector turned to the butler. 'The sergeant and I will have ours in the library, thank you, Stafford, and then after lunch Sergeant Lane and I will commence our interviews of everyone in earnest. But before we do that, I think it only fair to let everyone know that we are investigating a murder, it may have some bearing on the statements they give us.'

Chapter Twenty-six

Rose felt restless. It was all very well to stay in her room with the door locked, but she had nothing to do save for to relive the awful events of that morning, which she was trying hard to forget. With the door locked, she felt relatively safe, but horribly restless and besides she could not concentrate, no matter how hard she tried. Her mind kept wandering off to the policemen in the library two floors below. Were they any nearer, she wondered, to finding out who had done it?

It was no good. She could not stay a moment longer cooped up inside this room wondering what was happening. She crossed to the window and the vibrant gardens that stretched out before her, coupled with the glorious sunshine, seemed to beckon her. But it was too risky, she concluded, to walk in the formal gardens by herself. She was still in danger and it would be too easy for some-one to join her on her walk through the grounds. It was then that she thought of the kitchen garden. From what little she had seen of it the day before, with its fruit trees and vegetables, it seemed that it would be an ideal place to take a stroll. It also had the added advantage that it was unlikely that any of the guests would go there and there was bound to be a servant or two tending the garden or picking herbs and the like, to ensure that she was safe. Indeed, if she remembered rightly, there was a little rickety old bench by the entrance that she could sit on. If she felt so minded, she could even pick some fruit and eat it there and then.

The more Rose thought about it, the more it appealed to her. Quietly she unlocked her door and ventured out. No-one seemed to be about and she felt engulfed by the silence. She hurried down the two flights of stairs as quickly as she could, all the time afraid that she would encounter someone; visions of Lord Sneddon looming up out of the darkness kept her going. She raced across the hall into the drawing room, which she was grateful to find unoccupied, and out through the French windows. She ran along the perimeter of the formal gardens, wondering what people would think if they spotted her from a window, running like something possessed, but not caring enough to stop. She continued through the courtyard garden until she got to the kitchen garden where she collapsed out of breath on the wooden bench. Looking around, she was relieved to see the gardener's boy tending the vegetables nearby, who stopped momentarily from his task in hand to give her a surprised glance before resuming his work.

It occurred to her afterwards, what with everything that had happened to her that she must have been exhausted and it had only been adrenalin that had kept her going. Whatever it was, the peacefulness, the feeling of safety or her own tiredness had lulled her unwittingly to sleep and so she did not see or hear the person approach her until they began to speak.

'Miss…'

'What!' Rose was at once fully awake her heart beating fit to burst. 'Oh, Edna, it's you. You did give me a fright, I must have fallen asleep.'

'Sorry, miss, I didn't mean to startle you,' said the little scullery maid apologetically, hovering before Rose looking awkward. 'I just wanted to make sure you were all right after what happened to you this morning, and I wondered if I could ask your advice on something.'

'Sit down beside me, Edna, you look half worn out,' said Rose, patting the bench.

'Well, all right, miss, just for a minute, but I daren't let Mrs Palmer catch me having a rest and talking to a guest to boot, she'll have a fit.'

'Well, then I'll just tell her I asked you to sit down, that I wanted you to be here in case I fainted, because I still felt quite shaken.'

'Thank you, miss, that's awfully good of you,' said Edna, sitting down. 'But how do you really feel? We were awfully worried about you, we was. Mrs Palmer too, she was ever so cross that Sir William didn't send for the doctor to see to you.'

'I'm feeling fine now, Edna, thank you, just still a little bit dazed, but that's to be expected.'

'You weren't at all well, miss. You won't remember, but you kept babbling some nonsense. We didn't think anything of it, though.'

'Really, what did I say?'

'You kept going on about it all being your fault that Lady Belvedere got done in.'

'I see.'

'But we didn't think nothing of it, miss, really we didn't. We knew as how you was in shock, like.'

'Yes, I suppose I must have been. I don't remember saying that. I suppose I just meant that Lady Belvedere wouldn't have been out in the woods to be shot if she hadn't wanted to talk to me.'

'Yes, I expect that's it, miss.' Edna looked relieved.

'Now, what did you want to ask my advice on?'

'Well, it's like this, miss. I overheard a conversation. I didn't mean to eavesdrop or anything, but I overhead it just the same. Mrs Palmer suddenly realised that she hadn't any rosemary for the pork, so she asks me to go out and pick some, but it was such a nice day, that I thought I'd just stretch my legs a bit, seeing as I don't get to go outside that much, being stuck in that kitchen all day −.'

'Yes, yes,' prompted Rose, somewhat impatiently, having just realised that she must have been asleep for over half an hour and that surely her absence from the house must have been noted by now, to say nothing about lunch which might already have been served, for all she knew.

'Well, I went as far as the croquet lawn, miss, and I heard Mrs Torrington talking to −.'

'Yes, Edna, I heard that conversation too,' said Rose with a jolt. She thought back to yesterday morning. It wasn't really that surprising after all that Edna had overheard the same conversation as herself. Hadn't she come across Edna only moments later crying in this very same garden? The scullery maid must have heard the first part of the conversation whereas she had heard the latter part. She was tempted to ask Edna about what exactly she had overheard, but didn't. She still felt haunted by the strange conversation that she had had with Edith earlier that morning and couldn't help feeling that she had already done her a great wrong by telling the police about their conversation over lunch, when Edith had declared her hatred for the countess and that she wished her dead. To ask Edna now to divulge further details of Edith's illicit conversation with Sir William, would be an even further betrayal.

'Did you, miss?' asked Edna, sounding surprised. 'Oh, I'm so glad. I've been that worried with not knowing what to do. I didn't know whether I should tell the police or not and I was trying to pluck up courage to tell Mrs Palmer −.'

174

'No, don't do that, Edna,' Rose said, sharply. 'Don't tell anyone, not the police, not Mrs Palmer. No-one needs to know. It hasn't got any relevance to what's happened. Better just keep it to yourself, that's what I'm going to do.'

'Well, if you're sure, miss,' said Edna, not sounding totally convinced.

'I am, Edna. No good can come of it. Now, you'd better run on back to Mrs Palmer and I'd better return to the house before we're both missed.'

Luncheon was a very sombre meal. It seemed to Rose that everyone stood around rather awkwardly, not knowing quite what to say to each other. Lavinia sat there, eyes red rimmed from crying, staring into nothing, while Lady Withers patted her arm affectionately but ineffectively, every now and then. Cedric stood behind his sister, his hand on her shoulder, which he squeezed and his father stood a little way apart looking out of the window to the gardens beyond. Edith stood by the table picking at her napkin nervously and Sir William was opposite picking at non-existent crumbs on the tablecloth, throwing her an occasional concerned glance from downturned eyes. Lord Sneddon, very much apart from everyone else, was busy pacing the room, rather in the manner of a caged tiger. The food lay mostly untouched on the table. One or two of the sandwiches had had a bite taken out of them before being discarded and a couple of the guests had tried the soup. Sir William looked longingly over at the whisky on the sideboard but, like the others present, made do with coffee and water.

Rose's arrival in the dining room seemed to cause a welcome distraction. Lady Withers let go of Lavinia's arm and came over, eager of an excuse to busy herself in her role of hostess.

'How are you feeling, my dear? How very awful for you. Really, I did say to William that he must call for the doctor but he was most insistent that you speak to the police first. A typical man, that's what I say, and you still looking so peaky too.'

'Lady Withers ...Constance, I'm so very sorry –.'

The door opened and all faces turned immediately to the new comers, who were strangers to many there present.

'Good day,' began Inspector Deacon, 'my apologies for disturbing you. I appreciate that this is a very sad and difficult time for you all, and my commiserations go particularly to Lady Belvedere's family. However, I am afraid that I must ask you all a few questions, and it is my intention to call you one by one to be interviewed in the library. I think it is also only fair to warn you that we have established without a doubt that Lady Belvedere's death was not the result of a tragic accident, as some of you might have been led to believe,' the inspector paused a moment to look reprovingly at Sir William, 'but was the result of wilful murder.'

There was a gasp amongst the onlookers. The cup and saucer that Lavinia had been holding slipped from her hand and smashed on the floor, coffee spilling everywhere. Albert, the footman, dashed forward to attend to the mess. Lady Withers' hand had gone to her mouth as if she were attempting to stifle a scream. Cedric seemed to totter slightly, his face having gone very white. Rose longed to go to him, but she was afraid that the others would consider such a move inappropriate. Instead she turned and glared at the inspector. How dare he shock them like this? He should have waited and broken the news to them individually and gently. As if reading her thoughts, Deacon's eyes met hers for an instant and she realised then that his intention was to unsettle them so that they would let slip what otherwise they might have kept hidden. He wanted also to prepare them in advance of their interviews that the questions he would be asking would be probing and intrusive. He would expect, and want them, to reveal their suspicions and provide alibis. Rose looked around at the stricken, down turned faces. The enormity of the inspector's words had not been lost on anyone. They were all suspects now, they knew it as well as they knew that they needed air to breathe. And they knew something else, something far more terrifying; they knew that one of them was the murderer.

Chapter Twenty-seven

'My lord, do come in,' said Deacon, as Lane ushered the peer in to the library. The inspector indicated a chair in front of the desk of which he was seated the opposite side, and the earl sat down, as beckoned. The inspector was impressed that, despite everything, the Earl of Belvedere did not sink in to the seat and slouch dejectedly or broken, but instead sat upright as if to attention. Deacon suddenly remembered something that his mother had once told him about good breeding would always out, which he had dismissed at the time as pure nonsense.

'Firstly, I should like to express my condolences for your very great loss. I realise that this must be a very difficult time –.' Deacon was interrupted from continuing his prepared spiel by the earl holding up the palm of one hand to bid him to stop.

'Enough, Inspector, I appreciate your kind words, but they aren't necessary. I know that you have got a job to do and would like to get on and do it, and I myself, although shocked by this morning's events, am not devastated by them.'

'Indeed?' The inspector eyed the earl with curiosity. Whatever reaction he had been expecting from Lord Belvedere, it was not this. To his mind, the man looked remarkably composed as if they were sitting down to discuss the weather or a business transaction, certainly not his wife's untimely death, and her murder at that.

'Well, in which case, my lord, I'll get straight down to business, and if you would be so good as to give me full answers to my questions, then I do not think I will have to detain you for too long. Firstly, I should like to ask whether to your knowledge your wife had any enemies, or anyone who might wish her harm.'

'I imagine ... no, I know for a fact, that my wife was disliked by many people. She had rather an unfortunate manner, Inspector. She tended to rub people up the wrong way. But actual enemies, people who would want to do her actual physical harm, I think not.'

'And yet someone did kill her deliberately.'

'You are sure, Inspector, it couldn't have been an unfortunate accident?'

'There can be no doubt, I'm afraid. It was definitely a premeditated act; your wife was murdered, my lord. Late last night, or in the early hours of this morning, someone deliberately broke into Sir William's gun cabinet by forcing the lock. His shotgun was then removed, used and returned, the fingerprints wiped clean.'

'The fingerprints were wiped from the weapon, you say?' queried the earl.

'Yes, they were deliberately wiped from the gun either by the murderer himself,' said Deacon, slowly, 'or by someone else not wishing a member of the household or one of the guests to be incriminated. Whichever scenario, Lord Belvedere, I'm afraid that the murderer is in this house.'

'Yes, I see,' agreed the earl, 'as you say, there appears no room for doubt.'

'I appreciate this may sound rather intrusive, sir, but would you be so good as to describe your relationship with your wife. From what you have said, you were not particularly close?'

'No, we weren't, Inspector, but it was hardly surprising or a cause for distress. A man in my position needs above all to marry a suitable wife and Marjorie was that. Her family was rather disgustingly wealthy and her aim was to marry a man of title and estates. What was more, she was prepared to do whatever was necessary to retain her position. When she was young she was remarkably beautiful and managed to keep the more unattractive qualities of her character well hidden. By the time she had revealed more fully her true character, we had both become settled in our ways, our own separate little worlds, I in my library with my books and she with her charitable works. So you see, Inspector, we managed to rub along quite well.'

'And, if you don't mind my asking,' said the inspector, rather apologetically, 'now she is gone?'

'I expect my life will go along very much on the same lines as before. I doubt whether anything will very much change, Inspector, other than that my children might come home to Sedgwick more often.'

'I see. I'd now like to ask you what may seem like a rather strange question. Are you aware that your son appears to have formed a certain attachment to Miss Simpson?' enquired Deacon. 'Suppose, just

178

hypothetically you understand, they intended to marry, what would your thoughts be on that?'

'If you suppose that I'd be shocked or that I'd do everything in my power to try and put a stop to it, then I'm afraid I must disappoint you, Inspector,' replied the earl, firmly. 'Miss Simpson appears, from what little I have seen of her, a very personable young woman. True, she does not come from the class of woman I would be expecting the wife of my son to come from, but her head appears firmly screwed on and I think she is probably likely to make Cedric as happy as any woman can. And thanks to my wife's family there is no need for my son to marry into money as I was obliged to do.'

'I see, thank you. Just two more questions, if I may. Firstly, as a formality you'll understand, we are of course asking for everyone's movements this morning. So I would be grateful if you could oblige me by telling me where you were this morning, between say nine thirty and ten thirty?'

'That's easy, Inspector, I was in the library. I breakfasted early as usual and retired there to have one last go at Sir William's books before we left for Sedgwick. And before you ask, there is no-one to my knowledge who can vouch for me and say that I was there all that time. I am most insistent that I am never to be disturbed when I'm cataloguing books. And unfortunately I did not open the door once so did not see anyone go into the study to return the gun, and I also had no idea that my wife intended to go for a walk with Miss Simpson this morning.'

'Thank you. Now just one last question, if you please. Whose idea was it to come to Ashgrove this weekend?'

'My wife's, Inspector. She'd got wind somehow that Lavinia would be here and she insisted that we come down and that I accompany her; she wouldn't take no for an answer in fact.'

'He's a bit of a cold fish,' said Lane as soon as the earl had departed and the sergeant had closed the door firmly behind him. 'He didn't show any emotion at all; strange if you ask me, not natural. His wife's just been bumped off and he acts as if nothing untoward has happened.'

'He's been brought up to keep his emotions bottled up, Lane, stiff upper lip and all that. And he admitted himself that he and his wife weren't particularly close. Although he didn't say so in as many words, I would hazard a guess that he didn't like her very much and that her death comes as a bit of a relief.'

'Disliked her enough to kill her, do you think, sir?'

'I wouldn't go so far as to say that, Sergeant. I'm minded to believe him when he says that they muddled along quite happily with each doing their own thing and seldom the twain meeting, so to speak. Unless he's got some woman stashed away, I can't see what he'd particularly have to gain by getting rid of his wife.'

'Pity,' said the sergeant, looking despondent, 'nine times out of ten it's the spouse that's done it.'

'Well, it looks likely that he'll be the one out of ten that didn't. But it's not all doom and gloom, Lane, at least your Miss Simpson's in the clear.'

'How do you make that out, sir?' asked the sergeant clearly interested.

'Well, now that we as good as know that Sir William's shotgun is the murder weapon, Miss Simpson can't possibly be the murderer.' The sergeant still looked in the dark. 'Think, man. She would have had to bring the gun back to the house and return it to the study before the maid discovered that the gun cabinet had been broken into. Unless she had an accomplice who brought the gun back for her, she couldn't have done it. She wasn't carrying a gun with her when young Sid escorted her back to the house, was she? And anyway, she had no opportunity to put the gun back in the study because she was never left alone. First she was attended to by the servants and then Mrs Torrington sat with her. From what we've been told, nobody thought she was in a fit state to be left by herself.'

'You're right, sir,' said Lane, brightening considerably. 'She couldn't have done it. Well, I thought as much, didn't I, sir, a nice girl like her.'

'Appearances can be deceptive, as you well know, Lane,' cautioned the inspector. 'Well, I suppose we'd better get the next one in; Lord Sedgwick, I think, and then his sister.

'You're not inclined to bring in this Mrs Torrington first, sir, given what Miss Simpson said about her trying to stop her from coming to talk to us?'

'No, I think we'll let her stew a bit, don't you?'

The Earl of Belvedere returned to the dining room looking tired but composed. Lavinia immediately ran to him and he gave her a brief hug before moving on to Cedric.

'Your turn, old man,' he said. 'That inspector seems a jolly decent sort, nothing to worry about. Just answer his questions and you'll be back here in no time.' He turned back to his daughter. 'And then I expect he'll want to talk to you, my dear. As I've just said to Cedric, there's nothing to worry about, he's quite the gentleman. I'm sure he'll treat you gently, he appreciates what a dreadful shock this has all been for all of us.'

'Lord Sedgwick, do take a seat. I appreciate that this is an awful time for you, but I'm afraid that I must still ask you a few questions.'

'Yes, thank you, Inspector,' Cedric sank heavily into the chair. He has no concerns about slouching, thought Deacon, and his mother's death has clearly left him very shaken.

'What you said in the dining room, Inspector. Is it true? Was my mother really murdered? Uncle William seemed to think it was an awful accident, you know, a poacher or something.'

'I'm sorry, my lord, but that's quite out of the question. Your mother was quite deliberately murdered. Someone broke into Sir William's gun cabinet and used his shotgun to do the deed. It was returned to the cabinet after it had been used.' The inspector waited a moment for the significance of his words to sink in. 'I understand, my lord, that the majority of you went to Sir William's study last night to see a couple of antique duelling pistols that he had recently acquired?'

'Yes, but I already knew where my uncle kept his guns, if that's what you're getting at, Inspector. We all did. Well perhaps not Mrs Torrington, although she has stayed here often enough so she might have been aware of where they were stored, and of course Miss Simpson wouldn't have known before she was shown the pistols. But no-one could possibly think that a girl like her would –.'

'What about your sister, my lord?'

'Lavinia?' Cedric was clearly shocked at the suggestion. 'Well she'd have known where the guns were kept, of course, and she's a mighty good shot although you wouldn't think it to look at her. But absolutely not, Inspector. She and I may not have got on that well with our mother, in fact we may even have gone so far as to actively avoid her if at all possible. But my sister would certainly never dream of doing such a horrendous thing, as indeed I would not.'

'I wasn't suggesting that, sir, I was just trying to ascertain how familiar she was with the guns Sir William had and where they were stored. Now, I'm afraid that I need to ask you where you were this morning between half past nine and half past ten. Just a formality, you understand; we will be asking everyone the same question.'

'That's easy, Inspector, I was with Lord Sneddon. And,' Cedric took a deep breath, 'I might as well tell you before someone else does, that I was reiterating what I had said to him the night before. I was telling him in no uncertain terms to pack his bags and go.'

'I see, sir. I take it that this relates to his propositioning of Miss Simpson on the staircase last night?'

'He did more than that, Inspector. He threatened her. He was prepared to take her by force. If I hadn't been there, I dread to think what would have happened. Anyway, I didn't want someone like that in my aunt and uncle's house, I can tell you. He was supposed to be my friend. The sooner he leaves the better, and I hope never to set eyes on him again.'

'I'm afraid that won't be possible, not for the time being anyway. I'll be asking you all to stay on here at Ashgrove for a day or two, until we're further on with our investigation. Now, tell me, were you with Lord Sneddon all that time?'

'Yes, he was being jolly difficult. Refusing to go and all that. He accused me of trying to scupper his chances with my sister. As if I'd stand back and watch her marry someone like him. I will do everything in my power to make sure that she is left in no doubt as to the sort of man he is. She won't want to touch him with a bargepole once I've finished speaking to her, I can tell you. And he was being very insulting about Miss Simpson too, Inspector. I hardly want to tell you but he pretty much said that she was doing all the running, had led him on, would you believe, was toying with both of us. As if a girl like Miss Simpson would do that, she's an absolute angel, Inspector, a jewel. He went so far as to say that he was saving me from her, showing me what sort of girl she really was.'

'What were your mother's feelings about your fondness for Miss Simpson?'

'She was not very pleased, Inspector. She wanted me to concentrate on my studies and then marry someone from the aristocracy. She tried to warn me off Miss Simpson, said she was only interested in my money and

182

position, but I was having none of it. Although I suppose she only had my best interests at heart,' he added rather wistfully, 'but it didn't seem like that at the time, I can tell you.'

'Indeed?' Deacon looked at Cedric sharply and Sergeant Lane stopped writing for a moment.

'I meant, Inspector that I had made up my mind to marry Miss Simpson and had no intention of listening to my mother's arguments on the matter.'

'Is that what she wanted to talk to you about yesterday afternoon?'

'Yes, she called us all in to see her one by one, me, Lavinia and Sneddon, although why she wanted to speak to him, I can't imagine, unless she wanted to find out his intentions towards my sister.'

'Was there anything she could do to stop you marrying Miss Simpson?'

'No, I don't think I was about to be disinherited, if that's what you think; my father would never have stood for that. But my mother could have made things pretty awkward, particularly for Miss Simpson. She had a great knack for humiliating people and making them feel inadequate. She regarded me as her golden boy and had great plans for me. And, of course, Miss Simpson didn't feature in those plans.'

'Were you aware that your mother intended on going for a walk with Miss Simpson this morning to warn her off, so to speak?'

'No, of course not,' Cedric looked slightly uncomfortable. Deacon looked up and caught his sergeant's eye. Good, he had not imagined it, there had been the briefest of pauses before Lord Sedgwick had uttered his denial and Lane had picked up on it too.

'Do you really think, Inspector, that if I had any idea that my mother intended interrogating poor Miss Simpson in such a way I would just have stood back and let her get on with it?'

'No, I don't, my lord. I think you would have tried to put a stop to it.' Cedric looked the inspector in the eye for a few seconds before he looked away. Deacon noticed that the young man had the grace to blush slightly. He's not used to lying, he thought, I hope he doesn't play poker.

'According to Miss Simpson, your mother spoke to her very loudly last night after dinner about going for a walk this morning. She was quite sure that your mother must have been overheard by a lot of the people present. In fact she thought that was her intention. But you say that you didn't overhear her yourself?'

'No I didn't, Inspector, I can't have been standing near her at the time.' Strange, Deacon thought, he could have sworn the young man was speaking the truth. But if he didn't hear about the walk then, then when did he?

'You didn't go down to breakfast this morning?'

'No. I breakfasted in my room and then, as I told you, I went to speak to Lord Sneddon about his leaving.' Cedric looked slightly shameful. 'If you must know, Inspector, I wanted to see Hugh's face. I punched him rather hard last night. It occurred to me this morning that I might even have broken his nose.'

'And had you?'

'No, although you'll see his face is quite badly bruised.'

'Well, it sounds to me that it's no more than he deserved, my lord, and I'm sure that you'll have gone up in Miss Simpson's estimations. Right, just one last question if you please; can you think of anyone that might have wished your mother ill?'

'No, I can't, Inspector. I may not have got on that well with my mother, or even liked her that much as a person, but she certainly didn't deserve to die the way she did, and I can't imagine that there's anyone who can think she did. Please, Inspector, I beg you. Find out who murdered my mother, I want them to pay for their crime.'

'Don't worry, my lord,' Deacon said, 'we will, I assure you.'

'Well, Lane,' said Deacon, as soon as the door had closed behind Viscount Sedgwick, 'what do you reckon? Is Lord Sedgwick our man?'

'I wouldn't say so, sir,' said the sergeant, getting up from his seat to stretch his legs. 'Seems like a thoroughly nice chap to me, not the sort of person at all to bump off his mother, I'd say. He obviously didn't like the woman, but we've yet to find anyone who did. It seems to me though, that he didn't even have much motive. Lady Belvedere couldn't stop him from marrying Miss Simpson and she must have known that when he inherited the earldom, if she was still alive, she would be dependent on his generosity. It seems to me that, although she huffed and puffed a bit about it, there was nothing she could actually do.'

'You're right, of course, Lane, but Lord Sedgwick may have been worried about what she might say to Miss Simpson. It seems to me that the countess would not be above using a little emotional blackmail and he might have been worried that she would play on Miss Simpson's feelings for him. You know, say what a social disaster it would be for him to marry her and did she really feel so little for him that she was prepared to stand by and watch him ruin his life over her. I think he would have been concerned that his mother would change Miss Simpson's mind, that she would make her feel that the only right thing to do was to end all contact with him.'

'You may be right, sir,' said Lane. 'Although I don't think Miss Simpson would have been so easily swayed by what Lady Belvedere said.'

'No, but Lord Sedgwick was not to know that, was he? And there is something else that is worrying me, Sergeant.'

'What's that, sir?' enquired Lane, looking interested.

'He lied to us, Lane. Deliberately lied to us about not knowing that his mother had requested that Miss Simpson go on a walk with her this morning. I believe him when he says that he didn't know anything about it last night, insomuch as I don't think he overheard his mother telling her. But that's what worries me most, Lane.'

'How so, sir?'

'I think he only found out this morning about the walk, and that wouldn't have given him much time to stop and think what to do before he did it. He seems to me just the sort of young man who might be persuaded to do something on impulse and then only afterwards think about the consequences of his actions. Look how heavily he's fallen in love with Miss Simpson. He only met her for the first time two days ago and already he's set his mind on marrying her. Suppose he finds out about the walk only when he knows that they're already on it. He has no time to waste as far as he's concerned before his mother turns Rose against the idea of marrying him. What's he to do? I doubt whether he even thinks straight. He goes to Sir William's study, breaks the lock on the gun cabinet, snatches the gun and loads it and then sets off. Perhaps he's thinking of only giving his mother a shock. He takes aim, probably at something only a little way from his mother so that he can give her the necessary fright to put a stop to her conversation with Miss Simpson.'

'So what went wrong, sir? It seems to me that a man like Lord Sedgwick would be a good shot. He's probably gone out shooting regularly since he was a boy. Do you think he may have changed his mind, decided when it came to the crunch that it might be a good idea to remove his mother from the equation for good?'

'No, I don't, Lane, I think it was a mistake. The moment he raised his gun to fire, Miss Simpson stumbled and fell. He was distracted for a moment wondering whether she was all right, but unfortunately he had already pulled the trigger and so the damage was done.'

'Yes,' agreed the sergeant, 'it could have happened that way.'

Chapter Twenty-eight

'Lady Lavinia, please sit down. I appreciate this will be something of an ordeal for you, so I'll try and keep it as brief as I can. Firstly, can I say how sorry I am for your loss; it must have been a great shock.'

'Thank you, Inspector. Yes, it was rather.' Despite everything, the awfulness of her mother's death, the realisation among them all that one of them must be the murderer, from the moment Cedric had returned to the dining room and blurted out the news that the gun that had shot their mother had come from Sir William's collection, Lavinia could not help but notice how good looking the inspector was. Not her usual sort of man, of course, but even so quite handsome, probably due to that air of authority that he had about him associated with his job. Awful really for her to be thinking like that when her mother lay cold on a mortuary slab, a bullet through her chest. But there it was, she couldn't help it, it must be the shock ....

'Please sit here, if you will. I only need to ask you a few questions and then you can go back to your father and brother.' Deacon had mistaken her hesitation for confusion arising from deep sorrow and shock; it did not occur to him for one moment that she might be evaluating his looks. He on the other hand was appraising her. He had known from the society pages that she would be a great beauty, but he had not been prepared for how very beautiful she was. The red rimmed eyes and red nose, outward signs that she had been crying, could not disguise the fact; if anything they added something, a certain fragility which was appealing and made her appear less cold and aloof. Even so, it was not lost on him that not once did she turn to acknowledge the presence of his sergeant; it was as if the man was invisible or perhaps not important enough to register.

'Is what Cedric says correct? That it must be one of us because of Uncle William's gun being the murder weapon?'

'Yes,' Deacon said, gently, 'I'm afraid so, it –.'

'Then it must be Rose.'

'I beg your pardon, Lady Lavinia?' The inspector was not often taken aback by things said by witnesses and suspects, but this was one such occasion. Even Sergeant Lane had looked up with an appalled expression on his face. It was not just the words themselves that had shocked them, but the way she had said it so dismissively and yet with such certainty that her manner demanded no contradiction.

'What makes you say that exactly, Lady Lavinia? In our view she is the only person here who could not possibly be the murderer.'

'Because she hated my mother, that's why.'

'Did she actually say that she hated your mother?'

'No, of course not, Inspector. She's not that stupid; she just told me that she didn't think my mother liked her very much. And, of course, my mother didn't because she saw right through her from the start. I'm afraid I've always been rather a trusting person, Inspector. It's my greatest flaw. I assumed that Rose liked me for myself. I never imagined that she had only become my friend so as to secure herself a decent husband, a man of means and social standing that she would never have met had it not been for my decision to work in the same dress shop that she worked in.'

'You got all this from your mother, Lady Lavinia?'

'Yes, oh and from Hugh too, Marquis Sneddon, you know. Apparently she made a play for him once she knew that he was heir to a dukedom. Awfully embarrassing for him, of course, he didn't know what to do.'

'Lord Sneddon told you this?'

'Yes. He didn't want to, of course. Not with Rose being my friend, but he thought it was his duty to. Apparently he told mother as well, that's what she asked to see him about when he went to see her yesterday afternoon. She got wind of it from one of the servants; the servants here are awfully protective of us, you know, Inspector.'

'How do you know that's what your mother wanted to see Lord Sneddon about?'

'Hugh told me. He was awfully glum when he came back from seeing Mother, and I wouldn't let him be until I'd found out exactly what she had said to him.'

'I see. But why exactly do you think Miss Simpson would go so far as to shoot your mother? It seems a very drastic thing to do in the circumstances.'

'Because she saw my mother as the only thing stopping her from marrying Cedric, of course. Although hopefully with everything that's happened my brother will see sense. She must have known that my mother would never have stood by and watched Cedric waste his life. And so she got rid of her, just like that.' Lavinia's bottom lip trembled and Deacon was afraid that she was going to cry, but she managed to pull herself together at the last moment. 'Oh, if only Uncle William hadn't shown us his stupid pistols and Hugh hadn't asked where he kept the ammunition, then this might never have happened. Of course, if my stupid brother hadn't decided to come down then it wouldn't have been an issue anyway. I can't bear it.' The tears that had been threatening to fall exploded, and Lavinia sobbed bitterly, and very beautifully, into a small lace handkerchief that she held clutched in her hand for the purpose.

The two policemen sat there awkwardly, wondering how long they should give her to weep before they tried to continue with their questioning, knowing all the time that each second that passed was precious to the investigation.

'I don't wish to trouble you, Lady Lavinia,' Deacon began attentively, ' I can see how distressing this all is for you, but if you could bear with me just a little longer and answer a couple more questions, then you can go to your family and hopefully we won't need to trouble you again.'

'Very well, Inspector, I'll do my best,' Lavinia dabbed at her eyes very prettily with her handkerchief.

'Apart from Miss Simpson, is there anyone else that you can think of who might wish your mother harm?'

'No, no-one, Inspector. My mother was very well respected. She did a great deal of charitable work, you know. She could be a bit harsh at times if things didn't go her own way, but she always had everyone's best interests at heart.'

'I see. Now, if you wouldn't mind telling me where you were this morning between half past nine and half past ten. We're asking everyone for their movements, you understand.'

'Well, I was in bed, Inspector, with a very bad headache. I think it was all the worry about Rose's conduct.'

'Can anyone corroborate that, Lady Lavinia?'

'Well, I suppose Martha can to an extent, she's the parlour maid that's acting as my lady's maid while I'm here, Inspector. She brought me in a cup of tea. Oh, but wait, silly me, that was much earlier, about eight o'clock, I think. I sent her away then, told her I didn't want her to run my bath or put out my clothes until eleven. So no, no I don't think after all there is anyone that can vouch for me. Is that a problem, Inspector?'

'No, not at all, Lady Lavinia. Now, just one final question. Did you know that your mother intended going on a walk with Miss Simpson this morning?'

'Yes, of course, I heard her tell Rose last night.'

'You didn't consider trying to stop it from taking place?'

'No, of course not, Inspector, I thought it served Rose jolly well right.'

'Well, she's a nasty piece of work, and no mistake, sir, notwithstanding that she's the most beautiful woman I've ever seen,' said Lane, indignantly, as soon as the door had closed behind Lavinia. 'Fancy her saying what she did about Miss Simpson, and her being her friend as well. Makes you wonder, doesn't it, sir, why she ever invited Miss Simpson to spend the weekend with her aunt and uncle if she thought so little of her.'

'I think Lady Lavinia's used to being the centre of attention, Sergeant, and doesn't take too kindly to the crown being taken from her,' said Deacon, getting up and stretching his legs by pacing the room. 'She's remarkably beautiful and the only daughter of an earl to boot, so there can't be that many occasions when she finds herself outshone by someone else and she must find it particularly galling to be outshone by a shop girl. I imagine she considered Miss Simpson her own special friend and resents the fact that her friend and her brother are so obviously besotted with each other. Notwithstanding all her privileges and accomplishments, I bet Lady Lavinia has got few of what you'd call true friends and that she considered Miss Simpson to be one.'

'That's all very well, sir,' said Lane, not easily appeased, 'but it was awful what she said just now, trying to implicate her friend in her mother's murder.'

'She's probably afraid of the alternatives, Sergeant.'

'What do you mean, sir?'

'Well, assuming she didn't do it, unless it was Miss Simpson or Mrs Torrington, Lady Belvedere's murderer must either have been one of her own family or the man Lady Lavinia hopes to marry. Not very palatable alternatives for the girl to swallow, I think. What do you say to that Lane?'

'Well, sir. I think as she might have done it,' answered the Sergeant, smugly. 'You'll agree that there is a possibility that the intended murder victim was Miss Simpson?' The inspector nodded. 'If Lady Lavinia thinks she's been used and that Miss Simpson's been making a pass at her beau and at the same time she doesn't want her to marry her brother, well, it stands to reason that she might fancy taking a pot shot at Miss Simpson herself, either to warn her off, or to kill her. Well, Lady Lavinia's own brother let slip as to what a good shot she is and she admitted herself that she knew Miss Simpson was going on a walk with her mother. And she's no alibi to speak of. Let's suppose that she had the young lady in her aim, and then Miss Simpson stumbles just as she pulls the trigger and she kills her mother instead. It would have been an awful shock for her, and like as not she would have blamed Miss Simpson, so stands to reason that she'll want to implicate her somehow.'

'I like your logic, Lane,' admitted Deacon, stroking his chin, 'you may have something there, although I'd like to keep an open mind for the time being.'

When Lavinia entered the dining room, she found it difficult not to feel guilty when she caught Rose's eye and received a sympathetic smile from her friend. It really was too bad, all this. She didn't want Rose to hang for her mother's murder, certainly not, but what else could she do but throw suspicion onto her friend? The alternative was too awful to contemplate. As it was, the newspapers were already going to have a field day. How much worse would it be if a member of the aristocracy was accused of the murder? No, she really must protect *him*. She was sure it was what her mother would have wanted. She just had to keep her nerve; she was sure that everything would turn out all right in the end, it had to.

'Good afternoon, Lady Withers, if you could take a seat just there. Ah, Sir William, have you something further to add?'

'I hope you don't mind if I sit in with my wife, Inspector,' Sir William said, rather apologetically. 'This has all been a dreadful shock for her and my wife is inclined to be a bit absent minded and vague at the best of times.'

191

'Not at all, Sir William,' replied Deacon, although he would have preferred to interview Lady Withers without her husband present. 'I would ask you, however, if you would be so good as not to interrupt.'

'Of course, of course, Inspector, I understand fully.' Sir William seated himself beside his wife on the settee and patted her hand affectionately.

'Well I must say, this is jolly exciting, Inspector, I've never been questioned about a murder before,' said Lady Withers, sitting up straight and placing her hands primly together in her lap. 'Obviously, it's jolly sad and I would have much preferred to have been interviewed about someone else's murder besides my sister's, well, not yours, of course, darling,' Lady Withers said, bestowing on her husband a very bright smile.

'Do stop rambling, my dear,' Sir William said, looking embarrassed. 'The inspector will think that you didn't care at all for your sister.'

'Oh, but that's not true at all. It's only because I'm still in shock. I'm sure the inspector understands, he must be used to interviewing people like me, aren't you, Inspector.'

'Indeed, Lady Withers. I appreciate that this will be an ordeal for you, but if you wouldn't mind answering a few questions. Let's begin with your sister's visit. Am I right in thinking that you weren't expecting her this weekend that in fact she invited herself down?'

'She didn't exactly invite herself down, Inspector, she just got her butler to ring up Stafford to announce that she was on her way. Most inconsiderate, but that was always her way, I'm afraid. For all she knew, we were going to have a very large house party this weekend, and there wouldn't have been room for everyone. She'd probably have sent us down to sleep in the stables and taken our rooms, don't you think, William? It's just the sort of thing she would have done. Why, when she was staying with Lady –.'

'My dear, I really don't think that the inspector is interested in all that. To answer your question, Inspector, neither my wife nor I were expecting my sister-in-law and her husband this weekend; it was quite a surprise.'

'Where were you this morning, Lady Withers, between say half past nine and half past ten?'

'I was breakfasting in bed, Inspector. My lady's maid brought my breakfast in to me at about twenty past nine, just scrambled egg and marmalade on toast, you know, but not the same toast you understand for the egg and marmalade, different slices because really they don't mix, do they?

And then I had two and a half cups of tea as I always do. And then Crimms ran my bath. It always takes her a while to get the temperature just right and I must have splashed around for a little while and then got dressed, at which time I suppose it must have been a quarter past ten or so. How am I doing, darling?'

'Very well, my dear, if anything a little too much detail but I doubt the inspector minds that too much; much better than too little, what, Inspector?'

'Yes, indeed. Very comprehensive, thank you, Lady Withers. Now tell me, are you aware of your sister having any enemies?'

'Oh I expect she had loads, Inspector. In fact, I think you'd have a job finding anyone who actually liked her. I know she was my sister and all that, but she could be very unpleasant and unkind, couldn't she, William? I've often said that –.'

'Yes, thank you, Lady Withers,' interrupted Deacon, hurriedly, 'but were you aware of any specific enemies?'

'Not as such, no, Inspector, although I have to admit there was one occasion when we were children when I was very sorely tempted to push my sister out of the window myself. She'd just pulled the legs off my favourite doll and cut its hair, and all because I wouldn't play a game of snakes and ladders with her. Well, as I was saying, the window was open and she was leaning rather unwisely out of it, and it was just so tempting. It was all I could do to resist the temptation to pull her hair and push her out. Quite a nasty drop it would have been too.'

'I'll take that as a no, shall I, Lady Withers? Sir William, I don't think I asked you what you did after you had finished breakfast, did I, Lane?' Deacon looked to his sergeant who thumbed through the pages of his notebook and shook his head.

'That's easy, Inspector. I went to the drawing room and read the paper,' said Sir William, sitting back in his seat, 'I was expecting that one or other of our guests would join me in due course, but no-one did. I stayed there reading until Stafford came to find me to tell me about the shooting.'

'Thank you. Now Lady Withers, did you happen to hear Lady Belvedere tell Miss Simpson last night in the drawing room after dinner that she would like her to go for a walk with her this morning?'

'Of course I did, Inspector, I expect everyone did, although perhaps not William as you can be a little deaf, can't you, darling?' Lady Withers said, raising her voice rather unnecessarily considering that her husband was sitting right next to her.

'Nonsense, my dear.'

'Well, how do you explain, darling, that you often don't hear a word I say to you about things and so I'm forced to repeat myself until I'm quite blue in the face, not to say bored. Why, I was telling you only the other day all about the very juicy gossip that I had gleaned at Mrs Atherton's about Lady Belington's niece, when I went there to sort the things out for the village bazaar, and a more strange assortment of donations I couldn't imagine, but anyway, if you remember, you didn't hear a word I said, I had to repeat myself at least twice.'

'I'm afraid, my dear, that my hearing is sometimes rather selective where you are concerned,' admitted Sir William, rather apologetically. 'You know I don't like gossip, it sets a very bad example to the servants. But as it happens, I didn't hear your sister mention going on a walk with Miss Simpson. If I had, I'd have put a stop to it, I can tell you, Inspector,' he continued, looking at the policeman and sounding indignant. 'I'm blowed if I'd allow any guest of mine to be bullied in my own house, I can tell you; not on at all, I'd certainly have put a stop to it if I'd known about it.'

'Yes, yes, I'm sure you would have,' said Lady Withers, patting his knee in what she intended to be a soothing manner. 'But I expect everyone else heard. I'm afraid that I think that was Marjorie's intention, to humiliate the poor girl, which really wasn't very fair. I mean you can't blame the girl, can you? It's not really her fault if she wants to better her position, I'm sure I'd have done the same in her place.'

'You think Miss Simpson was after Lord Sedgwick?'

'Well, of course she was, Inspector, any fool could have seen that. But the surprising thing is that she seemed to be having some success. I mean the poor girl is such a plain little thing, isn't she, William, she definitely was last in line when looks were handed out. But Cedric obviously saw something in her, although what exactly I can't quite think, I mean the boy's surrounded by loads of beautiful young women, being as he is so eligible and everything, so why he would choose little Miss Simpson –'

'Really, my dear,' protested Sir William. 'I think you are being most unkind about Lavinia's friend.'

'So do I,' mouthed Lane silently, from where he sat scribbling, totally unseen by Sir William and Lady Withers, but catching the inspector's eye.

'All I'm saying, William, is that you can't really blame the poor girl for shooting my sister, can you? I mean to say she was provoked. Goodness knows Marjorie's provoked me often enough with her unkind words. It's just fortunate for me, isn't it, that Miss Simpson got in there first. Otherwise it could've been –.'

'Constance!' Sir William sounded shocked. 'Please, Inspector, ignore what my wife's just said, she doesn't mean it at all about Miss Simpson or herself. I'm afraid she's just said it for effect. Really, my dear, if you're not careful, the Inspector will take what you've said seriously.'

'Oh, but I am being serious, William, the inspector knows that. I know she's awfully young and it's a great shame, but really the only person who could have done it was Miss Simpson. It can't possibly have been anyone else, it's just not the sort of thing we'd do.'

'Well, I'm afraid that I'll have to disagree with you there, Lady Withers,' said Deacon, looking at her rather sternly. 'In our opinion, Miss Simpson is the only person who couldn't have done it. Well, not without an accomplice, anyway.'

'Oh dear, how very inconvenient,' said Lady Withers, sighing. 'Well, in that case, I suppose it must have been Lord Sneddon. How unfortunate. It does make it so awkward, doesn't it, when a member of the aristocracy commits a crime. And he's heir to a dukedom, oh dear. I told you, didn't I, William, that there was something about him I didn't quite like? And now I've been proved right. How very inconsiderate of Cedric to bring a murderer down with him, although I suppose he wasn't to know, was he that Lord Sneddon was going to pop off his mother.'

'What makes you think Lord Sneddon is the murderer, Lady Withers?' asked Deacon, not anticipating a very sensible answer.

'Because he was up and about last night, or the early hours of this morning, Inspector, when the rest of the house was asleep.'

'What makes you say that?' asked the inspector, sharply. Sergeant Lane had stopped writing and was looking up expectantly.

'Oh, because I saw him wandering about downstairs when I went down for my night time snack, Inspector.'

'Night time snack?'

'Yes, Inspector, my wife often feels a little bit peckish at night and so Mrs Palmer always leaves a little something out for her in the kitchen,' explained Sir William. 'Really, my dear, that was a very large dinner that Mrs Palmer gave us last night; I'm surprised you had room to eat anything else.'

'Well, I only picked at my food last night, darling. If you remember, there was such a terrible atmosphere as if everyone knew that something was going to happen, that it quite put me off my appetite. And then I woke up in the middle of the night and felt hungry. I tried to ignore it and go back to sleep, but I couldn't. So I thought I'd just get a little something to tide me over till breakfast.'

'Where did you see Lord Sneddon, Lady Withers?' asked Deacon.

'In the hall, Inspector. I assumed that he'd been feeling peckish too and had just come from the kitchen, but I suppose he might have just come out of your study, William.'

'Was he carrying anything, Lady Withers?'

'No, I don't think so, Inspector, but he did have a very murderous expression on his face. Really, he did look most frightening and I remember thinking at the time that it would be a great pity if Lavinia married him, because he didn't strike me as a very nice man at all.'

Chapter Twenty-nine

'That was all quite draining, wasn't it, William? I don't know how you managed it, darling, being interviewed twice, so to speak,' said Lady Withers to her husband as they returned to the drawing room, where the others were awaiting their return eagerly, keen to ascertain if there had been any developments. 'Ah now, here you all are. I told the inspector that we simply couldn't all be kept cooped up together in one room, first the dining room and now this one. He quite understood how we felt, didn't he, William?' She turned towards her husband to get his confirmation. 'Really, he's not too bad for a policeman. He says we're free to move around the house and the gardens as long as nobody tries to leave or go up into the woods. Apparently the constables are still searching there for evidence or clues or something like that. Speaking for myself, I can't imagine ever wanting to go there again; the sound of every twig snapping ...'

Lavinia started to cry and Lady Withers went over to comfort her.

'There, there, my dear, how very inconsiderate of me, what was I thinking? Now have a good little cry; it's far better to let it all out, you know. You're bound to feel better if you do.' She turned to face the others. 'I thought some of us might be beginning to feel a little bit hungry as we all rather picked at our food at luncheon, didn't we. I know I did and that I'm beginning to regret it now that the shock's begun to wear off. So I've asked Stafford to arrange for some afternoon tea to be brought out to us on the terrace. I think the sunshine will do us all good. That, together with some food, should lift our spirits a bit, don't you think?'

'Really, my dear,' said Sir William, sounding a little shocked. 'I think it's going to take a lot more than a good tea and some sunshine to do that. This has been an awful tragedy for all of us. But I think the inspector was keen to take a break from interviewing. Lord Sneddon, Edith, he asked if you could stay near the house as he's still to interview you.'

'Really,' said Lord Sneddon, looking irritated. 'I don't mean to sound unreasonable, but surely I should have been one of the first to be interviewed rather than one of the last. Does he know who I am? This is all damned inconvenient, I can tell you. I really do need to be leaving.'

'If it was up to me you would have left already,' retorted Cedric, angrily. 'But is it too much to ask that you show some consideration and have a thought for what the rest of us are going through? My mother was murdered this morning and all you seem concerned about is how it might impact on your plans.'

'I think the inspector was keen to talk to Lady Belvedere's family first,' said Sir William, hastily, eager to avoid an argument erupting between the two young men.

'My dear,' said his wife, looking at Lord Sneddon with sudden interest, 'whatever has happened to your poor face? You look as if you have walked into something. Oh dear, I'm sure that the police will be very eager to ask you all about it. Don't you think so, William?'

Lord Sneddon glared at everyone in the room and went outside.

'I thought you'd want to do all the interviews before we took a break, sir,' said Lane, getting up and stretching his legs again, 'though I must say I could do with a cup of tea and another slice of Mrs Palmer's delicious cake to keep me going.'

'My thoughts exactly, Sergeant, I thought we could both do with a break. I know that I'm getting rather tired and bored of asking the same questions of everyone. I was keen also to get your views on Lady Withers. What did you make of her?'

'Well, to tell you the truth, sir, she seemed to me to be a little bit odd. I mean she was quite excited by it all, as if it was all an adventure, even though we were talking about her sister's murder. Very strange if you ask me; do you think she's a bit simple, sir? She was awfully vague and rambling, wasn't she? Half the time she was talking a lot of old nonsense.'

'Oh, I think she was very much all there, Lane,' said Deacon, laughing. 'If you ask me, it was all an act. I expect she behaves like that all the time because it puts everyone else at a distinct disadvantage; they don't know how to take her, whether she's being serious or trying to be funny, or just happens to be like that. Did you see how anxious Sir William was about her, how he kept leaping in to clarify what she meant? I think he was very worried about

198

what she might say. I wonder whether he was afraid that she might incriminate herself.'

'Well, she did a bit, sir, didn't she?' said Lane, eagerly, beginning to warm to the idea. 'She admitted that there had been no love lost between her and her sister and that she had even half-heartedly thought about killing her when they were young. You never know, she may have been harbouring murderous thoughts all these years. Although I don't know how serious she was being, do you?'

'Actually, I think she was being very serious. I was just wondering whether it was all rather a double bluff. What I was particularly interested in though, Lane, was that she was keen to deliberately try and implicate Miss Simpson in the murder and then when that didn't work, Lord Sneddon. What does that tell you?'

'That she doesn't want the murderer to be a member of her family, sir, which I suppose is understandable.'

'Oh, I think it tells us a bit more than that, Lane. I think it tells us that she definitely knows, or thinks she knows, who the murderer is and that he or she is someone close to her who she is keen to protect. I think she's deliberately trying to divert suspicion from that person by accusing someone else.'

'Rose will you take a walk with me in the garden?' Cedric disentangled himself from his sister and walked over to her. It was the first time he had taken any apparent interest in her since it had all happened, and Rose could not help her heart from leaping, even if it seemed somewhat inappropriate given the circumstances.

'Cedric, do be careful.' Lavinia caught at her brother's arm and gave Rose a contemptuous look; Rose stood there awkwardly, feeling miserable. She felt her cheeks grow hot and began to blush, conscious that everyone else was witness to her humiliation. Cedric, glaring at his sister, said nothing but took Rose by the arm and together they walked out onto the terrace and on into the formal gardens.

'I'm sorry about all that, Rose,' Cedric said, after they had gone a little way.

'Surely Lavinia can't think I did it?'

'I think she's more concerned that I did it and that I might tell you so.' They stopped walking abruptly and he took both her hands in his. 'I don't know what to do, Rose, what to think. Part of me can't even believe that this has all happened. I keep expecting my mother to appear any moment and start lecturing me as usual. I don't think I can have quite taken it all in yet. I will never see my mother again and I don't feel anything yet, just numb.'

'It's just the shock of it all, I'm sure it's normal to feel like that.' Rose stroked his cheek, gently. She did not know what more to say. What was one expected to say in such a situation? The usual words of condolence one uttered on hearing of a bereavement seemed superficial and shallow when dealing with a death arising from a murder.

'Oh, but listen to me. I have gone on about myself and not for one moment have I asked after you,' Cedric said, sounding disgusted with himself. 'How are you feeling? You were with my mother when it all happened. It must have been awful for you. You saw her be shot and then you had to deal with her dead body all covered with blood, oh, I ....' He covered his face with his hand. 'I'm sorry, Rose, I can't even bring myself to think about it, and yet it must have been so much worse for you, actually being there.'

'It was awful, yes,' admitted Rose. 'And I'm finding it hard to get the image out of my head. I keep reliving it again and again. But I just feel so useless, I don't know what to do. I feel that I am just in the way and that somehow it is all my fault, that if your mother hadn't wanted to talk to me and insisted that we go for a walk, then all this might not have happened and she would be here now.'

'Rose, you mustn't blame yourself. If anyone is to blame it is my mother. She should not have tried to interfere. She had no right to try and make you leave. You were my aunt and uncle's invited guest, not her. I cannot tell you how much I admire you for standing up to my mother. If I had known what her intention was this morning, I would have stopped that stupid walk from taking place. If only I had overheard her telling you last night. Why didn't you tell me about it after that business with Hugh on the stairs? We were quite alone then, you should have said. I could have put a stop to it right there. I could have gone to my mother's room and had it out with her there and then.'

'I was embarrassed,' Rose said, miserably. 'And then when you told me your feelings for me, well, it all went completely out of my mind. I recall

200

that I did mention that I did not think she would let us be together, but you said that it was all right, that you would do whatever it took.'

'Yes, and I meant it.' He suddenly clutched her almost painfully by the shoulders as if a sudden thought had come to him. 'Rose, tell me, you surely don't think I meant ...' He could not bring himself to say the words to finish his sentence. Instead he looked at her beseechingly. 'You don't believe for one moment that I could do something like that, do you? Not to my own mother ...'

'No, of course not,' Rose said, hurriedly, 'no, of course I don't,' and as she said it, she realised with relief that she was being sincere.

'I can't imagine how anyone could have done it and yet someone must have. When Uncle William put forward the theory that it must have been a poacher who had shot my mother by mistake, well, of course it was tragic, but it seemed to make sense somehow, an accident, an awful accident. But it can't really have happened like that, can it? Not now that we know that my uncle's gun cabinet was broken into. It must have been one of us; I can't get that thought out of my mind, it was one of us! And do you know what the worst of it is, Rose? There is a part of me that doesn't want to know who it was, who doesn't want to see justice done, who wants the murderer to go free because I can't bear to find out that it is someone I care about. But it won't do, because the more I think about it, the more I realise that the murderer must be caught, whoever it is. If they're not, I don't see how we can all go on with our lives. They'll just stand still with everyone suspicious of everyone else, wondering whether it was them. You do see that Rose, don't you, the murderer has got to be caught.'

Rose nodded slowly. She longed to tell him of her suspicion that she had been the intended target and that Lady Belvedere had simply been shot by mistake at the crucial moment because she, Rose, had stumbled and tripped. But the police had asked her not to divulge this theory to anyone connected with the case. It was tempting just to tell Cedric and swear him to secrecy, but the basic instinct for self-preservation made her hold her tongue.

Shortly afterwards they had returned to the others to take tea on the terrace. Cedric had left her apologetically to go and comfort his sister, who was standing beside her father, looking dejected. Only Sir William came over to enquire whether she was all right, although she noticed that the earl threw her the occasional concerned glance in his usual shy way. Lady

Withers was busying herself issuing instructions to Stafford, an occupation which seemed to calm her and bring a surreal sense of normality to the proceeding of afternoon tea. Every now and then, Sir William went over to Edith to ensure that she was coping with what for everyone was a difficult situation to find themselves in. Edith in turn looked over at Rose as if she wished to join her but was unsure of her welcome given their previous conversation. Lord Sneddon stood away from them all, clutching a cup of tea. Occasionally he cast a glance in Lavinia's direction as if he wondered whether he should go over to her and offer his condolences or try to comfort her, but was clearly deterred by the presence of her brother by her side who was forever scowling at him. In addition, it was unclear how he would be received by Lavinia herself. For not once, as far as Rose could tell, had Lavinia looked in his direction.

Rose helped herself to another sandwich and a cup of tea. She still did not feel like eating and had to almost force herself to swallow, but she knew that she must keep up her strength in order to face the ordeal before her. Cedric was right, she knew, the murderer must be identified and brought to justice for any of them to be free of this situation. Until then none of them would be able to get on with their lives. It did not matter that in life Lady Belvedere had been such an utterly unpleasant person, deserving of such a fate if anyone did. In death she would blight all their lives unless the culprit was caught, Rose could see that. And yet she was scared to discover who had done such an awful deed. She had told Cedric that she knew he could not be capable of such a thing, and yet he had a motive, as did she. Did she really know that he was innocent? She hoped he was, of course, it was essential to her own happiness that he was and yet …

There was nothing for it. She must find the identity of the murderer herself and before the police did. And if she found that it was Cedric, well then she could take a view as to what to do about it. She felt that she could not send him to the gallows; she would rather die herself than do that. And it was not just that she must solve the murder so that they might all escape untarnished; she must solve it because there was a possibility that she had been the intended target and, if that was the case, her life might still be in jeopardy.

Rose looked over to where Lord Sneddon was standing, dark and aloof and disgruntled. In a certain light, and when he was less brooding, he looked handsome, but he did not now. It would be easiest for them all if he were guilty. Indeed, the way he had behaved towards her the previous night, she almost wished that he was. She shuddered to think what would have happened had Cedric not appeared when he did out of the shadows. Yes, she did not feel that she would be sorry to discover that he killed Lady Belvedere. In fact, she could argue a highly plausible case for him being the murderer. He did not strike her as a man who would take too kindly to being humiliated or refused. She thought he was entirely the sort of man who would stop at nothing to get his own back by whatever means were at his disposal, and that if those means be murder, so be it. He had been humiliated twofold by her rejecting his advances and by Cedric punching him and demanding that he leave. He had threatened last night to get his own back. What better way than to kill her and ensure that Cedric did not get the woman he loved and who loved him in return, but who had made the mistake of spurning the advances of his friend.

Lord Sneddon must have become aware that she was looking at him, for he turned and caught her eye. Rose was ready to look away immediately; she could not bear to see the contemptuous way he would look at her, the ever present sneer. But when she looked at him, she saw that he was afraid, and when the constable came to get him to take him to the library to be interviewed by the inspector, she saw that his hands were shaking as he put his cup and saucer on the table and was led away.

Lady Withers cast a quick look at her husband and guests gathered around in twos and threes on the terrace having tea. Good. They all appeared engrossed in what they were saying or doing, except for that friend of Lavinia's, Miss Simpson, who was however sitting far enough away so as not to be in a position to overhear her conversation with Stafford. Just to be on the safe side she would point to the garden or pick up a sandwich so it would look to the casual observer as if she were discussing its filling or the quality of bread. She knew she could rely on Stafford to play along; even if he thought something was amiss he would not let it show in his face. Whatever would she do without her butler? He was such a calming influence, so reliable in this time of grief and disaster. Really, he was the very rock of Ashgrove, without him the world would fall apart.

'Stafford, I wonder if you could tell me something.'

'Certainly, m'lady, if it is within my powers to do so.'

'This morning, when Sir William was being interviewed by the policemen, you came to fetch him on a matter of urgency, did you not?'

'Yes, m'lady.'

'Don't worry, Stafford, I'm not going to ask you what that urgent matter was.' The briefest flicker of the butler's eyelids was all that indicated that he was pleased to have Lady Withers' reassurance on this. If truth be told, he always felt uncomfortable if he thought his loyalties were being split between his master and mistress; on the odd occasion when this happened, he found that, often as not, he sided with Lady Withers even though it was Sir William who paid his wages.

'You wanted to speak to my husband urgently,' Lady Withers continued, picking up a sandwich at random and pretending to examine its filling, 'but he insisted on stopping first to talk to someone in the drawing room, didn't he? Can you tell me please who it was he wished to speak to so particularly?'

'M'lady, I'm afraid I don't recall, I –.'

'Nonsense, Stafford, of course you do, you remember everything. It's no good trying to spare my feelings. The truth will out and I'd rather hear it from you than from the inspector or his smug sergeant.'

'Well, m'lady, I think I do recall now. It was Mrs Torrington, I believe. The master caught sight of her on the landing as we were crossing the hall. I think he had the idea of finding out from her how Miss Simpson was doing. If you remember, it was agreed that Mrs Torrington should sit with her because it was not felt that she was in a fit state to be left alone.'

'Thank you, Stafford that was all I wanted to know. I thought as much, but I just wanted to be certain.' Lady Withers turned her face away, but not before the butler had caught sight of a tear in her eye.

Chapter Thirty

'My lord, I must apologise for keeping you waiting,' Deacon said pleasantly, as Lord Sneddon walked purposefully across the floor and took the chair indicated. 'But I'm sure you appreciate that it was necessary for us to interview Lady Belvedere's family first.' Lord Sneddon, who had entered the library intending to complain in the strongest terms about not being one of the first to be interviewed, found himself nodding.

'Right, now let's get straight down to business, shall we, so that we detain you for as little time as possible.'

Lane smiled. The inspector had definitely got the measure of this young man, he'd taken the wind right out of his sails by uttering an apology before a complaint was raised. And now, if he were not mistaken, Deacon would lull him into a false sense of security before he pounced.

'Right, you are a friend of Lord Sedgwick's, I understand, and you both decided to come down this weekend to Ashgrove. Why was that?'

'Cedric, Lord Sedgwick, knew his sister would be down, she had written to him to that effect, and we were both rather keen to find out how she was getting on with this working in a shop lark. Neither of us could imagine that she'd like it, not her sort of thing at all,' Sneddon laughed rather nastily, Deacon thought. 'I can't see her being any good at it, I'm amazed that she's managed to stick it out for as long as she has. And, of course, we were rather intrigued as to the friend she'd made in the shop. We thought it would be a bit of a hoot to come and see what she was like. Cedric's aunt really is a dreadful snob and we couldn't imagine them hitting it off at all. I wanted to see old Stafford's face too, he's a bit of a stickler you know for etiquette and tradition and although he'd be absolutely horrified at having to wait on a shop girl, I can tell you, he'd be doing his utmost not to show it.' He laughed heartily.

Nothing Lord Sneddon had just said had done anything to make him go up in the estimations of the policemen. Lane sat glowering behind him scribbling down his words; he hoped fervently that this gentleman would be found to be the murderer because he thought he would experience a certain sense of satisfaction to see him dangling at the end of a rope. Deacon himself wondered how this man and Lord Sedgwick had come to be friends and concluded that the younger of the men was impressionable and probably apt to assume the best in people. Certainly he had now been thoroughly disillusioned as shown by the bruise on Lord Sneddon's face.

'What happened to your face, my lord?' Lord Sneddon had the grace to look down at the floor and squirm slightly in his chair as his mind worked furiously trying to explain away his injuries.

'I fell over last night in my room, tripped on an edge of the carpet which happened not to be securely fastened down and banged the side of my face on the chest of drawers. It hurt, I can tell you.'

'I'm sure it did,' the inspector said, slowly, all traces of pleasantness gone from his voice, 'but we have been given another explanation for the state of your face this morning, which somewhat differs from your account.'

'If you already know how I got this,' retorted Sneddon angrily, pointing to his injured cheek, 'then why bother to ask me?'

'I was interested to know whether you'd tell me the truth,' replied Deacon. 'It is always useful to determine how truthful a suspect is, if one can.'

An uneasy silence filled the room as Lord Sneddon digested the words and tried to wrestle with the need to make a clean breast of things against his feelings of superiority towards the policemen.

'Look, if you must know, I'm not proud of myself for how I got this, which is why I made up that story about tripping and striking my face against the furniture. I know it's no excuse, but I was quite drunk and I thought I was doing the right thing to try and save my friend from himself.' He looked up suddenly and smiled. 'Besides, I was just following orders.'

'Indeed, whose orders?' Deacon tried to keep the excitement from his voice.

'Lady Belvedere's.' Lord Sneddon laughed at the surprised expression on the policeman's face. 'Oh, I'm not actually saying that she asked me to seduce Miss Simpson, no, Inspector, even a woman of her character would not demand that, well not in so many words, anyway. More she implied it, or rather she indicated that she would see it as a great favour should I take whatever measures I deemed necessary to bring down Miss Simpson in her son's estimations. Ruining her reputation so to speak seemed a good way of doing that. Oh dear, Inspector, I've shocked you. I can tell from your face, although you are trying very hard not to show it.'

'Why would you want to follow Lady Belvedere's orders?'

'I want to marry her daughter, Inspector. Well, want may be a bit too strong a word. A man in my position needs a wife, although I must say I have been putting it off for as long as possible. But there it is. I need a suitable wife, and dear Lavinia fits the bill, so to speak. As only daughter of an earl, she comes from the right sort of family, is beautiful and quite amusing and, even more importantly, Inspector, her family is very wealthy. What more could I ask for in a wife?'

'When did you and Lady Belvedere discuss all this?'

'Yesterday afternoon. She summoned me as she did afterwards Lavinia and Cedric. It was quite funny really, she was used to getting her own way in all things, you see, but on this occasion it happened to suit me, otherwise I wouldn't have obliged, I can tell you. She wanted to discuss my intentions towards her daughter and I was happy to inform her. You must understand, Inspector, that a man in my position has a very big net from which to draw a wife. There are not that many heirs to a dukedom who are as eligible as I am in age or, all modesty aside, in looks and accomplishments. Lady Belvedere was keen to secure me for her daughter. And while I freely acknowledge that Lavinia is very beautiful, she is getting on rather. She has a number of seasons behind her and she's quite headstrong, take this shop work lark as an example, so I assume the countess was all too ready to get her off her hands and have her settle down.'

'Yes, but what I don't understand, my lord, is why she would even consider asking you to do such a dreadful thing as to try and take Miss Simpson by force. Whatever would make her think that you would even contemplate doing such a dreadful act and, even more surprisingly from where I'm sitting, is that you agreed to do it.'

'Now, hang on a minute, Inspector,' Lord Sneddon said, quickly, 'who said anything about taking any one by force? Lady Belvedere wanted me to seduce Miss Simpson, I admit it, but that's all she wanted me to do. There was no talk or suggestion about taking the girl against her will. Besides there was no need, she would have been agreeable, I would have won her around in the end.'

'Indeed, as you did on the Friday night? Presumably you had not received your instructions from Lady Belvedere by then?'

'No, I just thought it would be rather fun, that's all. Plus I was concerned that Cedric seemed a bit too fond of her. I thought he was likely to do something rather rash, like propose to her or something equally stupid. She seemed to me the sort of girl who would egg him on, so I thought I'd put a stop to it. And I would have done, as well, if that nosey old butler of Lady Withers' hadn't interfered.'

'It wasn't due to jealousy then, you weren't jealous that Miss Simpson preferred Lord Sedgwick to yourself?'

'Of course not, Inspector, what interest could I have in a common little shop girl, and a mighty plain one at that!'

'Well, I thought she might be exactly your type, my lord. I understand that you have rather a thing for servant girls and women from a lower class than yourself. In fact, I understand that you have built up quite a reputation for yourself amongst the country houses.'

'It is hardly my fault, Inspector,' said Lord Sneddon, colouring visibly, 'if women from a certain class have a tendency to throw themselves at me. What's a man to do, I ask you? Some of them are jolly pretty and good fun. I just do what any hot blooded man in my position would do, I –'

'… take advantage of them,' said Deacon, finishing Sneddon's sentence for him, his eyes suddenly cold. 'Oh, I don't doubt for a moment, my lord, that you exploit every opportunity for your own advantage. But you still haven't answered my original question. What hold did Lady Belvedere have over you that you would do what you did for her? And I'm afraid that whatever you say I'm far from convinced that you would have hesitated to use force against Miss Simpson, a belief that both she and Lord Sedgwick share, I might add, which might explain Lord Sedgwick's subsequent actions towards you.'

Sneddon's hand shot up to touch his injured face, and there was another silence which neither man seemed inclined to break. Lord Sneddon sat glaring at the inspector with obvious dislike. Deacon in turn returned his stare with as impassive a look upon his face as he could muster, which was an impressive feat as he realised that he thoroughly detested the man before him. The ticking of the clock on the mantelpiece seemed suddenly audible and unnecessarily intrusive in the quietness of the room. Even Sergeant

Lane, half hidden from view a few feet behind Sneddon, felt the oppressiveness of the silence in the room and found himself hardly daring to breathe least all eyes be turned upon him.

'Come, my lord,' the inspector said, eventually, 'You can refuse to answer my questions or give me a pack of lies, if you will, but it will only serve to hinder our investigation temporarily. I can assure you that we will discover the truth in the end. Why not save yourself and us a lot of time by telling us now. The truth invariably comes out in the end; much better that you tell us yourself now, in your own words.'

'Very well, Inspector,' said Lord Sneddon, sighing deeply, 'I will, although it has no bearing on Lady Belvedere's murder, I assure you. She and I were after the same thing, after all, that I should marry Lavinia. Indeed, it appears that as soon as Cedric and I became friends, the countess recognised the benefit that such an acquaintance might have on her daughter's prospects and began to scheme. She knew that I would be spoilt for choice when selecting a bride and decided that the best way around this was to employ a private detective to see if he could uncover anything unsavoury about me that she could use to force my hand.'

'Lady Belvedere attempted to blackmail you?'

'Blackmail is an ugly word, Inspector, and not one that I think the countess would have used. I think she viewed it more as gentle persuasion. She informed me that her private detective had uncovered one or two things which I would not wish to have banded around and one thing in particular that I do not wish to become public knowledge. I hope, Inspector, that if I disclose what it is, I can rely on your discretion?'

'That you have a tendency towards seducing servant girls?'

'Alas, I fear that is already well known in certain circles, certainly if this house is anything to go by. The butler here has put every hindrance in place to ensure that I am quite unsuccessful in my quest while I remain at Ashgrove.' Lord Sneddon chuckled as if he found the whole thing amusing rather than annoying but Deacon, watching him closely, was not deceived.

'What the countess discovered, Inspector, is that my family is rather in need of ready money. We have assets aplenty, but little immediate finances on which to call on to grow or maintain them. To be frank, we have rising debts and no way of satisfying them other than to commence the selling off of parts of our estates. So what it really boils down to, Inspector, is that Lady Belvedere knew full well that I was badly in need of a very rich wife.'

'And Lady Lavinia would be that?'

'Indeed, she would. Lady Belvedere assured me that I could expect a very large dowry if I were to marry Lavinia. But she applied certain conditions. I had to stop my womanising and undertake whatever measures I considered necessary to discredit Miss Simpson in Cedric's eyes. She did not say as much, but her tone implied the steps that she anticipated that I would need to take.'

'And did you find this disagreeable? I understand from one witness that you returned from your interview with Lady Belvedere quite out of sorts.'

'I did not find what was expected of me particularly disagreeable, as you put it, Inspector, but what I did resent was being ordered around as if I were employed to do the countess's bidding.'

'I see. Can you tell me please what you were doing wandering around downstairs last night, or in the very early hours of this morning, after everyone else had gone to bed?'

'I assume you have a witness, Inspector, so I won't try and deny it. If you must know, I went on the search for food.'

'Not servant girls?' enquired the inspector. 'You didn't by any chance during your travels go into Sir William's study?'

'No, Inspector, I did not and I didn't take Sir William's shotgun either, if that's what you're getting at.'

'But you knew where Sir William kept his guns along with his ammunition? You knew of the existence of the gun cabinet in the alcove behind the curtain?'

'You must know full well by now, Inspector,' said Lord Sneddon, beginning to sound irritated, 'that I do, as do most of the other guests here, I might add. Sir William took us to his gun cabinet last night after dinner to show us a pair of antique duelling pistols that he had recently acquired.'

'You asked him where he kept his ammunition.'

'Did I? I forget. If I did ask about it, then it was only for something to say. If I am perfectly honest, I was frightfully bored and was trying to make polite conversation to disguise the fact. As it happens, Sir William is one of those fellows that if you start them talking about something they go on and on about it; don't know when to stop.'

'Where were you between half past nine and half past ten this morning, my lord?' Deacon asked suddenly.

'Ah, the fateful hour,' retorted Lord Sneddon, looking unfazed. 'Well for at least fifteen minutes of the time in question I was being lectured at by Lord Sedgwick. Actually, shouted at would be more accurate a description.'

'What exactly did Lord Sedgwick say to you?'

'Oh, something along the lines of his being totally incensed at my conduct towards Miss Simpson last night, that he no longer considered me to be a friend, that he wanted me to pack my bags immediately and leave, and that he would do everything in his power to prevent my marrying his sister, something along those lines, I think.'

'I see. Where exactly did this conversation take place? Presumably neither of you wished to be overheard?'

'No, indeed not. Cedric practically dragged me out of my room, up the stairs and onto the next floor. We used one of the empty bedrooms there. Lavinia and Miss Simpson were the only occupants of that floor and we concluded that they'd be having breakfast so we'd have the floor to ourselves.'

'Tell me, did you know that Lady Belvedere intended going for a walk with Miss Simpson this morning?'

'Yes, of course. I expect everyone knew. I mean, she announced it loudly enough last night. I have to admit, I felt a bit sorry for little Miss Simpson. Not nice being humiliated in public like that.'

'Lord Sedgwick told us that he didn't know about the walk.'

'No, he didn't, he must have been at the other end of the room, or something. He didn't know about the walk *then*.'

'What do you mean,' asked Deacon, sharply, 'he didn't know about it *then*?'

'Well he knew about it this morning, because I told him about it while he was berating me. I suggested that instead of wasting his anger on me, it would be better spent on his mother who, I had little doubt, was at that very moment instructing his darling Rose to pack her bags and leave Ashgrove.'

'You told him that this morning?'

'Yes, and I'm afraid that I was that annoyed that I let slip what Lady Belvedere had asked me to do regarding Miss Simpson, you know, so as to prevent their romance from developing.'

'And what did Lord Sedgwick do?' asked Deacon, unable to stop himself from leaning forward.

'Why, what any other fellow would have done in his position,' smirked Lord Sneddon, clearly enjoying himself. 'He turned on his heel and fled down the stairs.'

'What time was this?'

'Oh, about a quarter to ten, I should imagine. Plenty of time I expect to catch them up and undertake the ghastly deed.' He removed an invisible piece of fluff from his trousers. 'And now, Inspector, I think I have answered enough of your questions, don't you? Especially as I may have given you the murderer. Goodbye.' With that, he got up and left the room, Deacon and Lane still reeling from what he had just said.

'He's an evil whatsit and no mistake,' said Lane. 'Do you think he did it, sir? Lord Sedgwick, I mean, sir, not Lord Sneddon. Although I'd much rather it was Sneddon.'

'I hope not, Sergeant, I rather liked *that* young man, although, like you, I can't say the same of the one that's just left. If Lord Sedgwick is guilty of his mother's murder then I'm damned if I'm not going to get Lord Sneddon on a charge of incitement to murder.'

'I know how you feel, sir. What was worse was that he seemed to be enjoying it all as if it were all some sort of game.'

'Well, he was definitely relieved to be able to shift suspicion on to someone else.'

'But was Lord Sneddon ever really a suspect, sir?' enquired Lane. 'I can't see a motive. True, he probably resented being told what to do by Lady Belvedere, but they both wanted the same thing, didn't they, for him to marry Lavinia?'

'I agree, but you're forgetting something, Lane.'

Am I? What's that, sir?'

'The countess may not have been the intended victim. Miss Simpson might have been and, if so, our Lord Sneddon had a very good motive for wanting to do away with her. She turned down his advances, something which he is not used to if you believe what he says, and she was instead enamoured by his friend. Lord Sneddon was a man spurned and he does not seem to me the sort of man to take such a thing lying down. Plus I would imagine that he's the jealous type. He probably also felt humiliated by being

212

punched in the face in front of the girl. And he did after all say that he was going to get his own back. Also, we only have his word for it that he told Lord Sedgwick what he said to us and at that particular time. Still, if what he says is true, it would help explain something that's been puzzling me.'

'What's that, sir?'

'Why Lady Lavinia was so eager to accuse her friend.'

'And why was that, sir?' asked Lane. 'Although I thought at the time it was a particularly mean thing to do particularly to someone like Miss Simpson.'

'You and Miss Simpson, Lane, you are quite blinkered where she's concerned. But to answer your question, Lady Lavinia, I think, was eager to accuse her friend in order to divert suspicion from her brother. Remember what Sneddon said. The two men had their argument in one of the empty rooms in the corridor in which Lady Lavinia and Miss Simpson had their rooms. They assumed that the two girls would be at breakfast, but we know that that was not the case. Lady Lavinia was suffering from a headache and so was in her room. Given that their argument was heated and that they were probably shouting at each other, it is inconceivable to think that she did not hear at least some bits of their conversation. She would have been surprised that they had come up there in the first place, and no doubt was inquisitive to know why. She may or may not have overheard Sneddon taunting her brother, but she can hardly have failed to hear Sedgwick fleeing the room and tearing down the stairs.' The inspector was getting into his story and began pacing the room. 'She must have realised that he had set out to thwart Lady Belvedere's plan of persuading Miss Simpson to leave. Later, when she is informed what has happened and the time that the shooting supposedly took place, she is certain that her brother is the murderer. She is very close to him and is determined to protect him from the gallows; the only way she can be certain of doing that is to have someone else found guilty of the murder.'

Chapter Thirty-one

'Mrs Torrington, so sorry to have kept you waiting,' said Deacon, smiling at her disarmingly, 'do take a seat.'

'There's no need to apologise, Inspector, I quite understand that you needed to interview Lady Belvedere's family first. Such an awful thing to have happened, I can hardly believe it, I ...' She broke off suddenly to weep into a handkerchief that she held balled up in her hand. 'I'm so sorry, Inspector, you must think me very pathetic. I know everyone else has been very strong, except for Lavinia, of course, but you wouldn't expect her to be, seeing Marjorie was her mother. But it's such a dreadful thing to have happened and such a shock, it's not what one expects when one comes to Ashgrove. It's so peaceful here, you see, so untouched by anything awful, I always think of it as such a beautiful place to escape to when times get too tough to bear. It's as if it's not part of the real world. For example, have you ever seen so many servants? Everyone always complains these days how hard it is to get good servants since the war, but Ashgrove is simply teeming with them just as it was before the war. And I don't believe that Constance was affected at all by the war. She didn't lose one member of her family, can you believe it, no nephew, cousin or anything. I didn't think that was possible, I thought everyone lost someone, but not Constance, everything has always gone well for her, well, except for having a sister like Marjorie, of course, nobody would want that.'

'What was Lady Belvedere like, Mrs Torrington? At times like this it is important to build up a picture of the victim. Often as not people are liable to say what a wonderful person the deceased was, although,' Deacon added, 'I have to confess that in this case they have not. The countess appears to have been universally disliked.'

'I think that's a fairly good summing up,' said Edith, drying her eyes. 'It seems awful to say that of someone, doesn't it, especially when they've just met with such a violent death. But Marjorie really was quite an awful woman, well, she was when we were younger, and I assume she hadn't changed much although people do, so she might have, and I hadn't seen her until Friday for years and years.'

'How long had it been since you had last seen Lady Belvedere, Mrs Torrington?'

'Oh, over thirty years, I should say. We were all at school together. I'm something of the poor relation, Inspector. We're related to each other very distantly, but Marjorie and I never kept in touch, not like Constance and I did, or should I be saying Lady Withers. Oh, it's all so very complicated, isn't it, and I'm not sure that I feel up to all this and…' The inspector noticed that her hand had gone almost instinctively to her handbag, which she opened, put her hand inside and almost instantly withdrew it, an exclamation on her lips, as if she had received a sharp stab of pain.

'Mrs Torrington, are you all right?' Deacon had leapt up from his chair with concern. Lane stopped his writing and looked up in surprise.

'Oh, yes, of course, how silly of me, Inspector. Please ignore me. I'd just forgotten, that's all.'

'Forgotten what, Mrs Torrington?'

'Oh, nothing, nothing at all,' Edith said evasively, 'it really doesn't matter, Inspector, it isn't important, please go on with your questions.' There was a sudden firmness in Edith's tone which made the inspector think that, however much he questioned her about what was in the bag to cause such a reaction, she would refuse to answer or else be unnecessarily vague.

'Can you please tell me where you were between half past nine and half past ten this morning? We're asking the same question of everyone, Mrs Torrington.'

'Oh, I was breakfasting and getting up, I think. I know that I'd just got downstairs when William told me about Rose being in a state and Lady Belvedere being shot. He said that the girl was in the servants' hall but that he'd appreciate it if I would sit with her, and of course I was more than happy to help. Such a dreadful thing to happen to a young girl. You think she'll get over it in time, don't you? She seems such a level-headed, sensible kind of woman to me. Now if it had happened to Lavinia, that would be a totally different case, she'd –.'

'Excuse me for interrupting you, Mrs Torrington, but can you explain to me please why Sir William should ask you to sit with Miss Simpson rather than his wife, she was the hostess after all, and Miss Simpson her guest.'

'You've met Constance, Inspector. Do you really think she would have been any good at being calm and sitting quietly with Miss Simpson? Besides, she hadn't yet come down and William was no doubt anxious how she would react to the news, given that Lady Belvedere was her sister. For all he knew, Constance could have been very upset. One never knows how she is going to react. Sometimes she is completely over the top and at other times it is as if something barely registers. Really she is the most contrary sort of person that one can imagine. One moment she is vague and absentminded and the next, shrewd and perceptive.'

'I see. Tell me, can you think of anyone who might want to cause the countess harm?'

'Really, Inspector, it was years since I had last seen Lady Belvedere, so I really couldn't tell you. All I will say is that if her character remained the same as it was when we were girls, well then I think there are probably a fair number of people who would not weep too much at her death.'

'What about you, Mrs Torrington, are you one of those people? You were heard to say how much you hated Lady Belvedere and how she should be dead if there was any justice in the world. I think you even went so far as to say how you would quite willingly do the deed yourself, if necessary.'

'Did I really say all that? How very silly of me. I didn't mean it, of course, it's just something one says, isn't it? I'd never do such a thing, really I can't think what came over me to say something like that. It's not like me at all, really it's not.'

Deacon could not decide if she was shocked or impressed by her own behaviour. From what little he had seen of her, it seemed distinctly out of character. He knew her sort though, had interviewed many such women like her; she was the neurotic, timid type that wouldn't say boo to a goose, but if pushed too far could suddenly snap like a finely coiled spring and the consequences could be quite devastating. He looked up; Lane was looking at her keenly, a similar thought having obviously crossed his mind.

'Miss Simpson said that you were quite adamant. She said that you told her that the countess had once done you a terrible wrong and that she should pay for it.'

'I said that?' Edith looked scared, Deacon thought, as if she suddenly realised that she had let all her pent up emotions run away with her and said too much.

'Yes, you did, Mrs Torrington.'

'I didn't mean to,' she said so quietly that Lane had to bend forward in his seat to catch her words. 'Not to Rose ... Miss Simpson, anyway. It was wrong of me.'

'What great wrong had Lady Belvedere done you, Mrs Torrington?' the inspector asked gently. Such was her manner of vulnerability coupled with abject misery that he found himself almost tempted to lean towards her, clasp her hand and try and comfort her.

'I don't want to talk about it, Inspector, not to you.'

'I'm afraid that I must ask that you do, Mrs Torrington, it may have a bearing on this investigation.'

'I assure you it doesn't.'

'I'll be the judge of that, if you don't mind,' Deacon said, speaking firmly so that Edith looked up and studied his face, as if seeing him for the first time.

'I'm sorry, Inspector, but I'm not going to tell you.' She held up her hand as Deacon tried to protest. 'It's no good, Inspector, you won't make me change my mind. Even if it means that you arrest me for Lady Belvedere's murder and throw me into prison or charge me with whatever.' She flung her arm in the air in an act of desperate abandonment and caught the side of an empty teacup and sent it crashing onto the floor. She leapt up in alarm and looked at the broken crockery aghast.

'Sit down, please, Mrs Torrington. Don't worry about that, there's no real harm done. We'll get one of the maids to clear it up in a moment. Now I want to ask you another question, one I hope that you'll oblige me by answering, this time. Miss Simpson was under the impression that you were keen to prevent her from speaking to us after she had remembered something about Lady Belvedere's shooting. She claimed that you had gone so far as to actually bar her way and that you seemed overly anxious to know what she'd seen. She felt you were trying to make her promise that she hadn't seen who killed the countess.'

'That's nonsense, Inspector, of course I'd want her to tell you anything that will help you to solve this crime. She was just overwrought, I expect, hardly surprising after what she'd just witnessed. I think she just got the wrong end of the stick, that's all. She's right in that I did try and encourage her to lie down and rest a little before she came down to speak with you, but that's only because I was worried about her. She'd been through a horrible ordeal. Really William should have sent for the doctor; it was really too bad of him, the girl was in clear need of a sedative.'

'So you totally deny the allegation that you tried to prevent Miss Simpson from giving evidence to us?'

'I do.'

'Tell me, Mrs Torrington. You know, don't you, where Sir William keeps his guns?'

'Of course, in a cabinet in the alcove off his study. William makes a point of always carrying the key to the cabinet on him. He's afraid that the guns will get into the wrong hands.'

'Well he proved to be right to be afraid, because they did. Someone forced the lock, took out his shotgun and used it to kill Lady Belvedere.'

'Oh!' Edith's hand shot instinctively to her mouth and she seemed to recoil. 'So it really *was* one of us, then? I hoped ...'

'You hoped it was a poacher? No, it was one of you, as you say. Tell me, can you fire a gun, Mrs Torrington?'

'Well, yes, that's to say that I have fired a gun, but it's years ago now since I last did; I'm not sure I'd remember how to.'

'I understand that it's a bit like riding a bicycle,' said Deacon, in a matter of fact tone, 'once learned, never forgotten. Did you shoot Lady Belvedere, Mrs Torrington?'

'I ... no, Inspector, I didn't.'

'But you know who did, don't you, Mrs Torrington?' The inspector leaned forward, looking at her earnestly.

'Yes ... at least I think so, but I could be wrong.'

'I'd like you to tell me who you think it was.'

'No, Inspector, it's just based on suspicion, that's all. I wouldn't want to find that I had incriminated an innocent person, it wouldn't be fair.'

'Even so, Mrs Torrington, I think you should tell me who you think it is. We wouldn't just take your word for it. We'd have to investigate, prove to ourselves that you were right in order to build a case.'

'No, Inspector, I'm sorry, I don't think so. Oh, dear, how awful you must think me. I seem to be constantly refusing to tell you things or answer your questions. I don't mean to be awkward, really I don't, but I can't tell you.'

'If you keep this information to yourself, you might be placing yourself in danger, have you thought about that, Mrs Torrington?'

218

'Yes, and I'm prepared to take the risk, Inspector.'

'Don't you want to see justice done, Mrs Torrington?'

'Justice?' Edith almost spat out the word. 'Yes, I want to see justice done. I don't want Lady Belvedere's murderer ever to be caught, that would be true justice, Inspector.'

Chapter Thirty-two

'Well that's the last of them, Lane,' said Deacon as the sergeant closed the library door behind Edith's retreating form. 'It must be one of them, but which one, that's the question.'

'My money's on the butler, sir,' grinned Lane, 'you know what they always say about the butler having done it and in this case I could quite see it happening. Lady Withers relies on him enormously, you know, for the smooth running of Ashgrove. I imagine Stafford's just the sort of chap to do away with a troublesome guest if he thought it was in the best interests of the household.'

'Agreed,' said Deacon getting up and walking to one of the bookshelves to study a book, which he took out and examined before putting it back, 'but I think if that fine fellow were to commit a murder, he'd do it in a quiet and discreet manner so that no-one would even realise that a murder had been committed. I certainly don't think he would consider it fitting to shoot one guest in front of another one.'

'Well, who do you think did do it, sir?'

'I'd like us to go through each suspect to see if we can determine motive and opportunity. I have to say that at first glance it looks to me that while no-one appears to have much of an alibi, everyone apart from Miss Simpson seems to have had ample opportunity both to carry out the murder and to return the gun to the study unobserved.' The inspector wandered over to the French windows. 'Have you noticed, Sergeant, that there is a terrace running along the entire perimeter of the house outside and that all the key rooms in question downstairs, by which I mean the downstairs rooms which our suspects claim to have been in, the drawing room, study and this room, the library, all have French windows leading directly out onto the terrace.'

'I see what you're getting at. No-one had to use the hall to get outside or come in, where they might have been observed by the servants or other guests coming down the stairs or crossing to use the lavatory or the like.'

'Exactly, Lane. Now, with that in mind, let's go through the suspects one by one shall we. Before we start, I assume no little, eagle-eyed housemaid just happened to be looking out of the window at a crucial time and happened to see one of the household or guests on the terrace, did they? Or perhaps one of the lady's maids returned to a bedroom quicker than expected by the occupant and found it empty?'

'I'm afraid not, sir. They were all much too busy trying to keep on top of everything. The servants were severely understaffed, you see, on account of a lot of the guests having been unexpected and them not having had time to get in extra help. Plus, I understand Lady Belvedere was very demanding, which put even more pressure on them. She insisted that everything be just so and if it wasn't then everyone tended to get it in the neck, so to speak, including Lady Withers. Apparently she was always on edge when her sister came to visit, dropped things and knocked things off tables even more often than she was apt to do.'

'I expect her fear of displeasing her sister stemmed from childhood. Right, let's start with Miss Simpson, shall we? I think we can discount her fairly easily, don't you, for the reasons we talked about before. She had no opportunity to return the weapon to the study before the housemaid decided to dust the gun cabinet and found the lock forced. So, unless she had an accomplice, she can't be our murderer.'

'Could she and young Lord Sedgwick be in it together, do you think?' enquired the sergeant, rather doubtfully.

'I don't think so, Lane. They only met for the first time the day before yesterday and, although it appears from all accounts to have been love at first sight, it's quite a step from that to getting into cahoots together to commit a murder, especially when the victim is the mother of one of them.'

'I agree, sir,' said the sergeant, looking relieved. 'I wouldn't like to think that little Miss Simpson was involved in this business.'

'Right, who's next? Shall we go on to Sir William? He doesn't appear to have thought much of his sister-in-law, although I can't see that he disliked her enough to go so far as to kill her. We need to remember, Sergeant, that if we are to believe what Miss Simpson says, there's a possibility Lady Belvedere wasn't the intended victim, the girl was.'

'I can't see what motive Sir William can possibly have had to kill Miss Simpson, can you, sir?'

'No, although I suppose it's possible that she may have seen or overheard something that he doesn't want his wife to find out. He had opportunity, of course. By his own account he was the only one in the drawing room at the time, he could easily have gone out of the French windows across the gardens into the wood and he'd know the places to hide. Also, we mustn't forget that he had breakfast with Miss Simpson. Like as not he heard Crimms telling her Lady Belvedere was ready for their walk.'

'Then there's Lady Withers, sir. I really don't think she's all there no matter what you say about her being shrewd and putting on an act. She strikes me as just the sort of woman who might take it in her head to kill her sister, and we know she didn't like her much.'

'I think I'd need a better motive for her, Sergeant. And as to a motive for wanting Miss Simpson dead, I can't imagine unless she was desperate to prevent her from marrying her nephew, but like as not, she would probably have assumed that her sister would be successful in persuading Miss Simpson to pack up and leave. Still, she had opportunity. She could have slipped out onto the landing and down the stairs unobserved, if she was careful, popped out onto the terrace by the study, having picked up the gun on route, and gone off into the woods. She knew about the walk because, as she told us herself, she overheard Lady Belvedere talking about it the evening before and, like her husband, she knew the places to hide. And then she could have slipped back into the house via the study and stopped off to put the gun back into the cabinet, and no-one would have been any the wiser.'

'We've been assuming that the lock to the gun cabinet was broken either late last night when everyone had gone to bed or else in the early hours of this morning. I assume though, sir, that there's no reason why the lock couldn't have been broken just before the murder took place?'

'I don't think it was, Lane, it would have been a noisy business breaking that lock. I doubt that the murderer would have chanced it, there'd have been too much risk of being overheard by the servants who'd have been clearing the breakfast things away. Besides, for all the murderer knew, it might have taken quite a while to break the lock and he wouldn't have wanted to be any longer than necessary in the study, for fear of getting caught.'

'What about the earl, sir? I said before that the spouse of the victim is the most likely culprit and he wasn't that fond of her, was he? He said as much himself, he did.'

'You're right, Lane,' agreed Deacon, 'but my problem is that I can't see a strong enough motive. Yes, we know they didn't get on insomuch as they hadn't much in common, but by all accounts they were both perfectly happy living separate lives. And it's not as if we've got any evidence of there being another woman in the offing. Still, Lord Belvedere did have opportunity. We know he breakfasted earlier than everyone else, and that he'd already gone to work in the library before Miss Simpson had come down to breakfast. While she and Sir William were breakfasting, he could have slipped out of the library French windows and gone along to the study and climbed in those ones and picked up the gun before climbing back out again and setting off across the gardens. If you think about it, he could have made sure that the windows to the study were open earlier at the same time that he broke the lock.'

'That would have meant that he'd have been waiting in the woods for them to appear, sir,' reasoned Lane, 'rather than creeping up on them once they were already there.'

'It would,' agreed the inspector, 'and there's no reason I can see why it couldn't have happened like that. Now, if we look at what possible motive he could have had for wanting to do away with Miss Simpson, I think we need only to argue that he wasn't as indifferent to the possibility of his son marrying her as he purports to be. Whatever he says, I imagine that he'd prefer that his son marry another member of the aristocracy or at least someone with money or similar social standing.'

'In which case, our little Miss Simpson certainly wouldn't fit the bill,' said Lane, sadly.

'I'm afraid not. Now, let's move on to Lord Sedgwick, shall we? Well, it seems to me that his motive for wanting his mother dead is obvious, as we've said before, especially if we're to believe Lord Sneddon that he told him Lady Belvedere indicated that she would not be adverse to his ruining Miss Simpson. That, coupled with only finding out about the walk this morning, would probably be sufficient for a lovesick young man like Lord Sedgwick to act impulsively and recklessly. And, what is more, if we are to take Lord Sneddon's word, he did indeed drop tools, so to speak, and dash out in pursuit of his mother and Miss Simpson with a view to putting a stop to his mother's scheming.'

'He wouldn't have had a motive for wanting Miss Simpson dead though,' said the sergeant.

'No. I can't say that I can think of one offhand,' agreed Deacon. 'Now, let's get on to someone far more interesting, Lord Sneddon. I don't think either of us would lose too much sleep if we were to discover that he was the murderer. He thinks he has implicated Lord Sedgwick by saying that he dashed off in pursuit of his mother, but one could just as easily argue that it leaves him without an alibi for the time of the murder. What's to say that Lord Sedgwick didn't just go to his room to try and work out a strategy for thwarting his mother's attempts to get rid of Miss Simpson? In which case, the way would be left open for Lord Sneddon to follow Lady Belvedere and Miss Simpson into the woods and we both know that he had motives aplenty for wanting to cause both of them harm.'

'We definitely do. I say, sir, something's just occurred to me. What do you say to our Lord Sneddon intending to kill both women, but that he lost his nerve after having shot only one of them? Miss Simpson was probably screaming her heart out and his first instinct must have been to get as far away from the woods as possible before someone came to her assistance, as they did.'

'That certainly is a possibility worth considering, Lane. We know that Lord Sneddon was for all intents and purposes being blackmailed by the countess. Even though he argues that they were both after the same thing, his marriage to Lady Lavinia, Sneddon does not strike me as a man that would put up with being blackmailed. He probably reckoned that things could only get worse once he had married Lavinia. We both know his type. He's the sort of young man who will gamble away any money he has and no doubt would be looking to Lady Belvedere to give him additional hand outs from time to time to ensure that her daughter did not end up destitute, and we know she was the sort of woman who would apply conditions to such hand outs.

'He probably thought it made sense to get her out of the picture sooner rather than later. For all we know, he may never have had any intention of stopping his pursuit of young servant girls either before or after he was married, and was afraid that Lady Belvedere would decide that he was not a suitable suitor for her daughter after all and would take steps to prevent the marriage.'

'What about his motive for doing away with Miss Simpson? Do you really think, sir, that he's the sort of man who would try to kill her just because she had spurned his advances?'

'Yes, I do, Lane, I think he's exactly the sort of man to do that.' A grim expression crossed the inspector's face. 'Remember he was the duke's youngest son. Under normal circumstances he would never have inherited the dukedom because he had two older brothers in line before him. But this blessed war we've had has changed so many lives and expectations. He has unexpectedly benefited from the fortunes of war but is probably ill prepared to take on what he will inherit. Can you see him taking an interest in his estates, let alone managing them? No, I think he will be interested only in the income that they generate, not on the people who work on them and are dependent on him for their livelihoods.

'But it means that he is now finding that rich aristocratic young women who would previously have had their eyes firmly on his eldest brother have now diverted their attentions to him because of his improved prospects. And, whatever you and I may think of him, he is young and good looking and I have no doubt that he can turn on the charm when it suits him. But it won't be lost on him that he is where he is by default, and he is bound to feel a little insecure. So when a person like Miss Simpson, who he will regard very much his social inferior, makes it clear that she prefers his young friend to him, I can quite see him getting into a rage and deciding to teach her a lesson.'

'Even so, sir –.'

'Yes, I know, it does sound a little far-fetched even to me, Lane,' agreed Deacon, 'but it is a motive of sorts. Now, who have we got left? Ah, yes, the beautiful Lady Lavinia and neurotic Mrs Torrington. Let's start with the daughter of the deceased, shall we?'

'No love lost between her and her mother,' said Lane, 'still, I suppose she may have had second thoughts about Sneddon, I mean let's face it, who wouldn't? Her mother might have been having none of it. Perhaps she was trying to force her into the marriage. As to why she would want to kill Miss Simpson, well, perhaps she was just jealous. With her looks, money and social position, I'm sure she's used to all eyes being on her. She may have resented Sneddon's interest in her friend, or been afraid that Miss Simpson would become her sister-in-law, she might certainly have baulked at that, sir, being from the wrong class and everything. Of course, she didn't know that her brother would be here, but even so, I'm sure it upset her seeing Miss Simpson and Lord Sedgwick getting on so well. I bet she expected Miss Simpson's undivided attention during the stay.'

'Well put, Sergeant. I don't think I have anything further to add, except that we do know the two girls had some sort of silly falling out about it all and Lady Lavinia was overly keen to accuse poor Miss Simpson of her mother's murder. I'm guessing that after this has all been resolved those two young women won't be having anything to do with one another.'

'Unless Miss Simpson marries her brother, of course.'

'There is that, although it's possible that either the sister or brother are our murderer.'

'That just leaves, Mrs Torrington, sir. And we know she hated Lady Belvedere because of some wrong that she had done her in the past. And she won't tell us what it was. I think my money's on her. She seems pretty highly strung if you ask me.'

'She is that,' agreed Deacon, thinking, 'but whether it's the result of guilt, I don't know. We haven't really got a very good motive for her wishing Miss Simpson dead, have we? No, if she pulled the trigger, I think it was definitely the countess that she was aiming at and we may never know what she had against her, she's the sort of woman who'd take her secrets to her grave.'

'What do you want to do now, sir?'

'I think we should retire from here for the day, Sergeant, and go back to the station to think things over away from here. When we come back in the morning, I want to have another look at that lock to the gun cabinet and perhaps do a little experiment. There'll be pressure on us to solve this case as soon as possible, Lane, what with a member of the aristocracy being the victim and other members being murder suspects. Let's hope that it takes a day or two for the newspapers to get wind of it, they'll have a field day.'

'Yes, sir. There's just one thing. I'm rather concerned about Miss Simpson,' said Lane, looking anxious. 'If she was the intended victim might she not still be in danger. What's to stop someone from taking a pop at her tonight?'

'The same thought crossed my mind earlier, Sergeant,' grinned Deacon. 'You needn't worry your head about it, man. I've arranged with Sir William for one of the constables to keep guard. He'll be based in one of the

226

unoccupied rooms on the first floor, next to Miss Simpson's. As far as everyone is concerned, he's staying here in case anyone remembers anything more about the murder or are concerned about there being a murderer on the loose. In actual fact, after everyone's gone to bed he'll be keeping guard in the corridor outside Miss Simpson's room to ensure that she doesn't come to any harm.

Chapter Thirty-three

There had been talk, or more accurately, mutterings of not having dinner in the dining room that evening, but that instead the household and guests eat in ones or twos in their own rooms as they saw fit, with those not feeling up to food abstaining altogether. While Rose could appreciate that few of those present might feel comfortable at the idea of dining with an unknown murderer, she was relieved when Sir William insisted that they all dine together in the normal fashion, for it was likely to have meant otherwise that she would have been obliged to eat alone.

Dinner, not surprisingly, ended up being a very sombre occasion. No-one bothered much with small talk or pleasantries, both of which seemed superficial and wanting given the circumstances. The tension in the air was unbearable and more than one glass was dropped, with either the glass smashing or the contents being spilt over the snow white table cloth. On one occasion it had been red wine, and Rose thought that she was probably not the only one present to associate it with the blood that had been spilt earlier that day.

Lavinia had retired to her room alone as soon as dinner was finished, although her presence at table had seemed redundant for she had barely touched a morsel of food or uttered a word, instead absentmindedly chasing a carrot or bean around her plate with her fork. Mrs Palmer had purposefully prepared a very light and almost frugal meal but, even so, most of the dishes had been returned to the kitchen only partially eaten and, in some cases, untouched.

Rose made her way slowly up the two staircases, only vaguely aware of the presence of the constable who had stationed himself to one side of her door, a chair propped against the wall indicating that for him, at least, it would be a long night. She knew that she ought to go to bed and try to get some sleep, for she was sure that the following day was to prove just as draining as this one had been, but she was reluctant to do so, sure that she was still suffering from the shock of it all which would deny her sleep.

She was also very aware that she had not spoken a single word to Lavinia since the tragedy, and that, although any overtures on her part were likely to be turned down, as her friend she must at least try. She tried to pretend that the constable was not there to witness her humiliation as Lavinia sent her away but, raising her hand to tap lightly on her friend's door, she was aware of the sound of weeping, although a more accurate description might be wailing, for it sounded as if Lavinia was pouring out her very heart. At Rose's knock the crying stopped abruptly to be replaced by silence and it seemed to Rose that the whole world seemed to hold its breath, so quiet was the house. Rose felt that she waited for minutes for something to happen, although it was actually probably only a few seconds. She was just about to turn away and go to her room when the door was flung open and Lavinia beckoned her inside. The constable half rose from his seat as if he were minded to prevent her from entering the room, but a look from Rose made him sit back down again in his seat looking awkward, as if he feared that he would receive the wrath of his superiors if anything untoward were to happen to her in the room. Rose went in and shut the door behind her.

'Is he there to protect you from us in case you remember something?' asked Lavinia, sounding disinterested in her own question. She looked awful, Rose thought, in so much as her eyes were red and puffy from crying and her skin was blotchy, but she still managed somehow to look beautiful whereas in similar circumstances another woman would have looked quite plain.

'It must have been awful for you,' Lavinia continued, in a dull voice that seemed to lack all emotion. 'I realise that now, although I didn't see it before I must confess. I saw you as responsible for my mother going on the walk. I thought that if you hadn't been here, then she wouldn't have been –.'

'Lavinia, I'm so –.'

'I'm not sad she's dead, you know. That sounds awful, doesn't it? A daughter saying that about her mother, but there you are, it's true and I don't feel I have the strength to try and pretend something I don't feel, just for appearance's sake.'

'But just now you were crying as if your heart was fit to break,' Rose said, appalled by her friend's words. 'You're just in shock, you'll feel something soon once the numbness has worn off.'

'I don't think so, not for my mother. But you're wrong, I don't feel numb, as you put it, I feel everything very much.'

'Lavinia, I don't –.'

'Understand? Yes, I see that. It's not for my mother that I'm weeping, Rose, it's for my brother.'

'Cedric?' A feeling of dread came over Rose. She felt an overwhelming urge to turn and run from the room before Lavinia could say anything more to confirm her worst fears.

'He did it, Rose, Cedric killed our mother and the police will find out and then he'll hang.' Her voice had started to rise.

'Shh,' Rose grabbed her arm and dragged the girl to her bed where they both sat down, Rose turning to glance at the closed door, very aware of the constable's presence a few feet away. For all she knew, he had left his chair and moved to the door to try and overhear their conversation, eager to assure himself that she was not being attacked. 'For goodness sake, speak quietly, have you forgotten that there's a policeman the other side of the door? Do you want to be the one to send Cedric to the gallows?' She did not wait for an answer. Instead, even though a part of her desperately did not want to know, she felt compelled to press Lavinia for why she believed something so awful to be true. 'Tell me, Lavinia, what makes you think your brother is guilty of your mother's death?'

'I overheard them talking this morning, Cedric and Hugh. They were in one of the rooms on this corridor, the room the other side of yours. I pretended I had a headache this morning so that I didn't have to go down to breakfast, because I didn't want to see you, not after our argument yesterday.' Lavinia cast Rose a look, which was far from kind. 'I was still angry with you, you see, so I decided to stay in my room. Anyway, I suddenly became aware that two people were shouting at each other in one of the rooms. You can imagine my surprise as only you and I have rooms on this floor. Anyway of course I was curious, so I crept along the landing and listened outside the door. I recognised Cedric's and Hugh's voices at once and, although I found it difficult to hear clearly what they were saying, I caught the odd word here and there, enough anyway to grasp that my mother had put Hugh up to enticing you away from Cedric. Cedric, as you can imagine, was incredibly angry and then, when Hugh went on to tell him that at that very moment Mother was out walking with you just so she had the opportunity to berate you and persuade you to leave Ashgrove, Cedric tore open the door and bounded down the stairs two at a time looking as if nothing would stop him. I had little chance to hide before being caught eavesdropping, but he was so set on his mission I don't think he even saw me.'

Even though Rose had felt her heart sinking at each word uttered by her friend, she tried not to think the worse.

'That doesn't mean that he killed your mother,' she argued, clutching at straws. 'For all we know he just shut himself up in his room.'

'You know as well as I do, Rose, that he did no such thing,' retorted Lavinia. 'Do you really think he is the sort of young man who would just have stood aside and let my mother lay in to you without coming to your defence? You know he isn't.'

'No,' agreed Rose, giving up any pretence of doubt. Cedric was not that type of man. If he had been she never would have fallen in love with him the way she had. And hadn't he told her that he would do whatever it took to ensure that they were together? Hadn't he identified his mother as an obstacle to be overcome? And if she were honest with herself, hadn't she known all along that he was guilty? She remembered leaning over Lady Belvedere's body to try and stem the bleeding and check for signs of life. She remembered the words that had sprung from her own lips unbidden. 'It's all my fault'. In fact hadn't she said it again and again even when the man and boy had found her, on and on so that she was even mumbling words to that effect in the servants' hall? She had known then that Cedric was guilty and had felt responsible, that his love for her had driven him to commit the most horrific of acts. She thought back to their snatched conversation that afternoon before tea, when he had reassured her of his feelings towards her, when she had realised with utter joy that, despite everything, he still wanted her. Her heart leapt now as she remembered his very words and then, just as quickly, it sank and she was engulfed with a sense of dread. He had been there. All at once she knew without a shadow of a doubt that he had been there. He had overheard their conversation, hers and Lady Belvedere's. He had been there in the woods while they had snarled and spat at each other, he had been *there*!

Chapter Thirty-four

Rose awoke the next morning, the feeling of dread still firmly lodged in her stomach. She was prepared to swear that she had not slept above a few minutes all night, her eyelids felt sore and heavy and her head throbbed. She lay back on the bedclothes feeling sick and absolutely wretched. But she had no doubt of her course of action. As a law-abiding citizen she should inform the police of what she knew to be true. As soon as Inspector Deacon and his sergeant arrived to resume their investigation, she should demand to see them and tell them everything. But this was not the course of action that she had chosen to take and Lavinia, she realised, had banked on that. She could no more hand Cedric over to the police to be sent to the gallows than she could stop breathing. Lavinia held her responsible for Cedric's actions as she did herself. He had killed Lady Belvedere in a spur of the moment, desperate act, goaded into it by his erstwhile friend. It had been a half crazed, frenzied Cedric that had pulled the trigger, not the kind and gentle man she knew. But ultimately, although she may hold Lord Sneddon to account, she must face the fact that her very presence had been the driving force. Had she not been there that weekend and met Cedric, then the countess would be alive now, free to bully and intimidate her family it was true, but alive nevertheless. Rose had no alternative; she must stand by Cedric and do everything in her power to protect him because surely morally she was as guilty as he was, or at least she felt as if she were.

She must focus her attentions on diverting suspicion away from him. But, and this was a very big but, however could she feel for him as she had done before? If he requested her hand in marriage, then she was duty bound to give it because of what he had done to be with her, but could she really love him as she had done, knowing what he was capable of, knowing him to be what he was, a murderer? However, could she in all conscience introduce him to her own mother as her future son-in-law? Her whole life going forward would be based on secrecy and deceit, afraid always that the truth would come out. They would never be able to relax for one moment. And should she tell him what she knew? Should she tell him that she knew what he had done to be with her? Lavinia was anxious that she did not. Lavinia wanted to pretend that he was not the culprit, but if she were to adopt such a stance, would it only serve to drive a wedge between her and Cedric? Or was it better that he never knew that she knew the truth? Otherwise, when he happened to catch her looking at him might he not always be left wondering whether she was thinking back to the woodlands and the gunshot that had changed their lives.

There was no use thinking about it now, she knew, although it was so difficult to stop herself from doing so. She would have a lifetime to do nothing but think about it, but whatever happened she would have to see it through. She owed that much to Cedric. The enormity of the task that lay ahead of her suddenly struck her and she buried her head in her pillow and sobbed.

'Right,' said Deacon, as the two policemen let themselves into Sir William's study and made for the alcove, 'let's have another look at this gun cabinet, the forced lock in particular.' He pulled back the heavy velvet curtain and both policemen studied the broken lock carefully.

'It hasn't been picked, sir, if that's what you were thinking,' said Lane after careful examination, 'it's definitely been smashed. Looks as if it took quite a lot of attempts too, looking at all these marks here on the metal.'

'It was and it wasn't what I was thinking,' replied the inspector, somewhat mysteriously. 'The position of the lock, Lane, what strikes you about it?'

'Well, there being a pane of glass in the door, rather than it being solid wood, I reckon it would have been quite hard for the murderer to break the lock without breaking the glass,' said the sergeant, standing back so as to be able to appraise the gun cabinet as a whole, 'but he obviously managed it all right, didn't he, sir, because the glass is intact, not even a scratch.'

'My thoughts exactly, Lane,' concurred the inspector. 'Well, I think that answers my question. Let's get back to the library and go over everything again. Before we do that, though, I think we'll have Miss Simpson in to see if she's remembered anything else about the shooting that may help us to identify the murderer.'

'Take a seat, Miss Simpson. How are you feeling today?' Deacon looked at her kindly. It occurred to him that she appeared more agitated this morning than she had the previous day, which interested him.

Rose sat with her hands clasped tightly in her lap. It had not occurred to her that the police might want to interview her again, and being summoned to appear before the inspector this morning had definitely thrown her. It was all very well to decide not to tell the police about Cedric and keep out of their way, but quite another thing to sit before them and lie. And what was worse, the inspector seemed to know that she was on edge. The way he looked at her so intently, had he guessed that she was hiding something?

'Miss Simpson, Rose, if I may say you look decidedly unhappy to be here. Do you find the presence of myself and my sergeant here so abhorrent?'

'No, of course not.' She glanced up from looking at her hands. There was something of a twinkle in his eye, she thought, as if he was trying to put her at her ease. She hadn't noticed yesterday how attractive he was. If it hadn't been for Cedric, she would have noticed, she knew. But from the very moment she had first set eyes on Cedric, she had known that she would never be able to think of any other man. Cedric, Cedric, Cedric, oh Cedric ... She could not stop herself, even though she knew it was the very worst thing to do because it would confirm to them that something was most definitely wrong, but she couldn't help it, just saying his name to herself made her think of the awful deed he had done to be with her, how much she owed him and how much danger he was now in and that, coupled with her lack of sleep which was beginning to make her feel quite sick with tiredness, suddenly made her burst into tears. Once she had started she sobbed uncontrollably. She covered her face with her hands and was only vaguely aware that both inspector and sergeant had shot up out of their chairs in alarm, the inspector hastily passing her a handkerchief on which to dry her eyes.

'I ... I'm ... sorry,' she stuttered between sobs. 'I think everything has suddenly got a bit too much for me, it's the shock and everything. I'm just being silly –.'

'Do you know something, Miss Simpson? Something that you haven't told us about yet? Perhaps you've suddenly remembered something that you'd forgotten about yesterday? It happens like that, you know, the sergeant here and I often find that, don't we, Lane?' he indicated his colleague, who

234

nodded. 'That's why we wanted to see you this morning, in case you had remembered something else.'

Rose said nothing. She felt cornered and did not know what to do.

'I'm guessing by your silence that you have found out something about someone you care about that could implicate them in Lady Belvedere's death, am I right?'

Still Rose said nothing. If she had had more sleep, felt more refreshed, then perhaps she could have thought of what to say or do, but as it was she could think of nothing to allay their suspicions. They were going to guess, were on the very verge of guessing, she knew, and there was absolutely nothing that she could do about it.

'I'm thinking it concerns Lady Lavinia or Lord Sedgwick,' continued Deacon, looking at her closely. He noticed that she clenched her hands together when he mentioned Cedric's name.

'You've found out something about Lord Sedgwick which implicates him in his mother's death, Rose.' She noticed that he said it as a statement rather than as a question. 'I know you don't want to tell me what it is, that you've got feelings for Lord Sedgwick, but I implore you to let us know what it is you've discovered, for your sake as much as for justice's. You'll find that you won't be able to get on with your life until you do. It will eat away at you and you will always wonder if you did the right thing. Lady Belvedere was brutally killed in cold blood. If you think you know something that will help us catch the murderer and bring him to justice, then now is the time to tell us what it is.'

Silence filled the room. Once again the ticking of the clock was clearly audible. But even as she sat there in the quietness, Rose knew that ultimately she would break. She could not keep it to herself any longer. Already the knowledge was eating away at her. She had thought that she would do whatever it took to protect Cedric, but she realised now that she could not keep the truth to herself. The inspector was right, justice must be done, she was only sad that she must do it. She realised now with a great sinking feeling that a man like Deacon would never give up. He would never close the investigation until he had arrested someone for the murder. She could perhaps manage to keep silent today, but there would be other days. They would hound her, these policemen, she felt sure. They would interview her every day until she broke down and divulged what she knew.

'He was there,' she said eventually, so quietly that both men had to lean forward in their chairs to hear what she said, 'Cedric was in the woods, he heard my conversation with his mother, or at least a part of it.'

'How do you know?' demanded Deacon. 'Did he say as much to you?'

'He didn't need to. He gave himself away, although he didn't realise it, and neither did I at the time.'

'How so?'

'He referred to my being Sir William's and Lady Withers' invited guest, and not the countess.'

'Yes?' The inspector sounded disappointed, even to Rose's ears.

'I said as much to Lady Belvedere in the woods. But that's not all.'

'What else, Miss Simpson?'

'Cedric ... Lord Sedgwick said that he could not tell me how much he admired me for standing up to his mother,' Rose looked up at their uncomprehending faces. How could they not see the significance of her words?

'Oh, don't you see?' she felt herself becoming angry. They had forced her to divulge what she knew and now they were forcing her to interpret it for them. How could they be so dense? 'Nobody knew that I stood up to the countess. I told no-one except perhaps you, I can't exactly remember, but I definitely didn't tell anyone else, I know I didn't. Cedric could only have known that I did stand up to his mother if he'd been there to overhear our conversation. He was there a few moments before Lady Belvedere was killed, he was *there*!'

Chapter Thirty-five

Rose fled the library, leaving the impact of her words to echo around the room as if she had shouted them. Both the inspector and sergeant had looked shocked, although it was the breakthrough that they needed to solve the case. In a few moments they would be summoning Cedric to their presence and then they would be arresting him for the murder of his mother. She could not bear to stand and watch. She would go outside into the garden until it was all over and he had been taken away. She had betrayed him. He had done what he had done for her, and then she had betrayed him. Even if she was eventually able to convince herself that she had done what was right, she would never, she knew, be able to forgive herself for being responsible for sending the man she loved to the gallows. And he would know what she had done, they would tell him. She could imagine the hurt look in his eyes, the disbelief that she could have done such a thing. She may even have to stand up in Court and give evidence against him. She could not bring herself to do that, she would rather die than do that. The thought of having to look across the Court at his shackled and dejected figure, to have him hear her give evidence against him and perhaps their eyes would meet and then what would she see in his face? Surely hatred, she deserved that, but how much worse would it be if she saw only misery?

She crossed the hall which, to her relief, was deserted although she could hear Lady Withers in the dining room, the door of which was open, discussing with Stafford her requirements for luncheon.

'I suppose that we'll have to have just soup again, Stafford, rather than a proper meal. Will you speak to Mrs Palmer to that effect for me? I'd rather have something more substantial, of course, but I suppose it's not the done thing after a murder, is it? I suppose we're all supposed to still be off our food, which is all very well if one has just got the appetite of a sparrow like dear Lavinia, but when one enjoys their food like I do it really is rather trying. But still I suppose it would look rather insensitive to just tuck in. I wonder if Henry has much of an appetite. One would not expect a man in his situation to, of course, not when his wife has just been murdered, but I've always found that reading makes one so hungry, don't you Stafford, and that's all poor Henry ever seems to do.'

'I can't say I have much time to read, m'lady.'

'Oh, I'm sure you don't, Stafford, you work far too hard. Oh, but one thing before you go, I wasn't quite sure about those herbs that Mrs Palmer put in the soup the other day. I'm not very good at herbs, of course, find it awfully difficult to distinguish one herb from another, but I'd swear that it was rosemary, and surely that shouldn't go with anything but pork ...'

Rose hurried on past before Lady Withers had time to finish her conversation and come out into the hall. The thought of being accosted by Lady Withers and have her babble on about absolutely nothing, while she all the time would be wrestling with her conscience at sending Cedric to his death, was more than she could bear. She prayed ardently that Cedric would employ a brilliant barrister who would manage to get his death sentence commuted to a life sentence in prison. Surely there had been ample provocation, wasn't that a defence? But even if it was and the barrister was successful, would that really be a better fate? To spend years locked away, hidden from society, to grow old without having experienced any of the joys of life ...

Rose began to sob, and then, as if to make matters worse, she heard Lady Withers move towards the door of the dining room. Quick as a flash she darted into the drawing room which, to her relief, was empty. She let herself out of the French windows onto the terrace and then set off across the lawn. She did not have a clear destination in mind, just the absolute desire to get away and leave everything behind. She thought back over Lady Withers' conversation with Stafford. How could she possibly think about food at a time like this? What did it matter who would be hungry and who would not, who always had a big appetite and who didn't? What did it matter if the soup had rosemary in it, what did –

She stopped abruptly. She realised then that she had had a nagging feeling about everything ever since she had come to Ashgrove. Things had not seemed as they had appeared at first glance for the very simple reason that they were not. She had taken everything at face value when really she should have scratched beneath the surface to get to the truth.

She turned on her heel and fled back into the house, indifferent to who saw her now. She threw open the French windows into the drawing room with such a bang that Lady Withers, who had retreated there after her conversation with the butler, spun around in alarm and knocked into an occasional table, upsetting a vase of roses; water and flowers and broken lead crystal littered the carpet. These things barely registered to Rose and she ran through the room, not even acknowledging her hostess let alone offering an apology.

She sought Stafford who fortunately was just coming out of the dining room, the dishes and crockery and general debris from breakfast having now been quite cleared away.

'Stafford, Mr Stafford, I must see Edna straightaway.'

'The scullery maid, miss?' Even Stafford found it difficult to hide his surprise completely. 'Why she'll be in the kitchen, miss, helping Mrs Palmer start the preparations for luncheon.'

'I must see her at once, Mr Stafford, it's a matter of life and death. The inspector's about to arrest Lord Sedgwick for Lady Belvedere's murder and I know he didn't do it.'

The butler took in her dishevelled appearance and the desperateness in her voice and came to a quick decision.

'This way, miss, through the green baize door. It's for the servants' use, as you know, but it's the quickest route to the kitchen.'

'My lord, why did you lie about knowing your mother had gone for a walk with Miss Simpson yesterday morning? Lord Sneddon has told us all about it, so you might as well tell us the truth. According to him, you had your talk where you asked him to leave, and he in turn told you about your mother urging him to ruin Miss Simpson. According to him, my lord, you then stormed off and he assumed that you had gone in pursuit of your mother.'

'I went to my room, Inspector, to think things through.'

'I'm afraid that we know that you did not. We know for a fact that you must have overheard at least part of the conversation between your mother and Miss Simpson. We have a very reliable witness who has said as much.'

'I'm afraid I don't understand, Inspector,' replied Cedric, beginning to look uncomfortable.

'You told Miss Simpson that you admired the way she had stood up to your mother. You could only have known that if you had been present.'

'I see, Rose gave me away.' Cedric sounded absolutely dejected.

'If it's any consolation, my lord, we had to force the information out of her,' Deacon said, taking pity on the young man. 'Miss Simpson had absolutely no intention of giving you up to the police. I think she would have gone to her grave rather than disclose any information which would implicate you.'

'Bless her!' Cedric, despite the situation he found himself in, sounded elated.

'Indeed, but I'd still like to know why you lied to us, my lord.'

'I was afraid that you'd think I did it if I told you the truth,' admitted Cedric, rather sheepishly. 'I'm afraid I was being a bit of a coward. I'm sorry, I shouldn't have lied to you, but I swear to you that I didn't do it.'

'That's as may be,' the inspector said, grimly. 'But we have means, motive and opportunity. We can even place you at the murder scene.'

'But surely you don't think –.'

'I'm afraid that I –.'

'But, sir,' interjected Lane.

Deacon held up his hand and looked fiercely at his sergeant. Cedric meanwhile had gone exceedingly pale and had all but collapsed into his seat.

'Lord Sedgwick, I am arresting you in connection with the murder of your mother, Lady Belvedere…'

Chapter Thirty-six

Their emergence through the servants' door into the kitchen caused quite a stir. While the servants were used to seeing Stafford come that way, they had never seen a guest enter the servants' hall, let alone come via the servants' entrance.

'Mrs Palmer, could you spare Edna for a minute or two? Miss Simpson requires to speak with her on an urgent matter.'

Edna, who at that moment had her hands in the sink up to her elbows in vegetable peelings, although somewhat surprised by Rose's unexpected appearance, looked more than a little keen to oblige.

'Begging your pardon, miss,' Mrs Palmer said, looking completely flustered, 'but we're that short staffed and what with her ladyship changing her mind every minute as to what constitutes a suitable lunch, I really cannot spare my scullery maid until after the meal has been served.'

'Oh, but you must,' implored Rose, desperately.

'Indeed,' agreed Stafford. 'It concerns Lord Sedgwick, Mrs Palmer. Unless Miss Simpson can do something to prevent it, our young lord will be led away from Ashgrove in handcuffs.'

'Master Cedric in handcuffs! Heaven help us!' exclaimed Mrs Palmer. 'Well don't just stand there girl, take your apron off, wash your hands and take Miss Simpson into my sitting room.' She looked at Edna as if she had disobeyed an order. 'And mind you don't touch anything neither,' she added looking crossly at the scullery maid, 'any breakages will have to be paid for.'

As soon as they were ensconced in Mrs Palmer's sitting room, sitting side by side on the settee, the door firmly shut, Rose seized Edna's little hand in hers and gripped it so tightly Edna winced.

'Edna, listen to me, this is very important. Do you remember you mentioned to me that you had overheard a conversation between Edith, that's Mrs Torrington, and a gentleman on the croquet lawn?'

'Yes, miss. I told you about it and you said as I didn't need to worry about it or tell the police.'

'That's right, I did, Edna, but I think I may have made a mistake.'

'Really, miss?' Edna, Rose noticed, was beginning to look anxious.

'I assumed, you see, that you had overheard the same conversation that I had. But I'm beginning to think that you may have overheard a completely different one entirely.'

'How do you mean, miss?' Edna sounded confused.

'Well, I assumed you were referring to a conversation that had taken place on Saturday morning just before I met you. That's the one I overheard taking place on the croquet lawn. But now, because of something Lady Withers said, I'm beginning to wonder whether that's the case. You see, Lady Withers mentioned to Stafford that she thought that the herb rosemary should only ever go with pork and I suddenly remembered what you said when you were telling me about the conversation that you'd overheard, you know, about Mrs Palmer suddenly realising she hadn't any rosemary to go with the pork. And we had pork for dinner on Saturday night.'

'I'm not sure I follow you, miss,'

'When did you hear the conversation on the croquet lawn, Edna?'

'Saturday evening, miss, about six o'clock.'

'I knew it!' Rose was elated. 'I thought because it took place on the croquet lawn and because Edith was one of the parties to the conversation, we were talking about the same conversation, but we weren't. Don't you see, Edna, the conversation I overheard took place on Saturday morning not Saturday evening. Now tell me,' she clung to the girl's hand even harder, 'who was Mrs Torrington talking to?'

'Why, Lord Belvedere, miss,' answered the scullery maid, 'and it was awful, miss.'

'Why, Edna, why was it awful?'

'Because they were both crying, miss, something dreadful. They were crying as if their hearts would break.'

Rose hurried through the corridor and emerged out of the green baize door, much to the surprise of Lavinia, who had just come downstairs, having breakfasted again in her room. Rose acknowledged her presence briefly and hurried on. She had some pieces to the jigsaw, now she needed to get some more. Something vague was forming in her mind, she just needed some more bits of the puzzle to be able to solve it. She must find Edith and confront her. She wondered why she had not done so before. And she cursed herself for

242

not realising the significance of the photograph before. How dense she had been.

She was about to mount the stairs in search of Edith, who she assumed to still be in her room. However, looking up the staircase, she saw Edith was just coming down. Rose waited impatiently for her to reach the hall and, as soon as she had, she whisked her out of the front door onto the drive where they could not be easily overheard.

'What on earth are you doing, Rose?' Edith sounded somewhat alarmed.

'I want you to answer a question for me, or at least confirm what I put to you. I want to know who Robert's father was. It wasn't your husband, was it Edith? Lord Belvedere was your son's father, wasn't he?'

When they came back inside, everyone seemed to be about. Sir William was just coming out of his study, Lady Withers and Lavinia were coming out of the drawing room, and Lord Sneddon down the stairs. The door of the library opened and Inspector Deacon and Sergeant Lane came out, Lord Sedgwick handcuffed between them.

There was a collective gasp as everyone took in the scene and then Lavinia began sobbing, casting a murderous glance at Rose, who shrank back under such a venomous stare.

'Don't tell me you have arrested Cedric?' demanded Sir William, stepping forward. 'Whatever are you thinking, man? Surely you can't think him guilty of his mother's murder?'

'Out of the way please, Sir William. We're taking Lord Sedgwick to the police station where he'll be charged.'

'No, Inspector, you've got it all wrong.' Rose ran over and stood before them, trying to stop them from leaving. 'I'm sorry, Cedric, I'm so sorry. It's all my fault that you've been arrested. But he didn't do it, Inspector, he didn't do it. I swear he didn't do it because, you see, I know who did.'

Then everything seemed to go very fast indeed.

'I did it,' shrieked Edith, 'I did it. Let him go, Inspector, I killed Lady Belvedere, let him go.'

'Edith!' exclaimed Sir William, 'whatever are you saying? Don't listen to her, Inspector, I did it.'

'William!' wailed Lady Withers, clutching her hand to her heart.

'No, Inspector,' said Rose, firmly. 'None of *them* did it, they are just trying to protect each other. But I know who did do it, it was –.'

'Miss Simpson is quite right, Inspector, none of *them* did do it.' The voice was loud and commanding and cut through the din that had arisen, as smoothly as a knife. In the silence that followed, every face was upturned to look at the first floor landing, in particular the figure standing at the top of the stairs looking down on them. Rose realised that, in the throng of people downstairs, she had quite forgotten that he alone had been absent. 'I killed Lady Belvedere, Inspector,' he continued, his voice full of emotion, 'I killed my wife.'

For a moment no-one moved, and then the sergeant bounded for the stairs. Although he had hesitated only for a few seconds before making his move, the delay was enough for the earl who, anticipating what was about to happen and having made his confession to save his son, made a goodbye gesture, which indicated also his love, to his two children, and made for his room, locking the door firmly behind him. Lane banged on the door for all he was worth, but to no avail. Desperately the sergeant looked around the landing for some heavy object which might help him to batter down the door. No-one came to his aid, not even the inspector, and before he could find anything suitable, a gunshot rang out through the house, bringing the servants running. Even before they had eventually managed to break down the door, each person present, looking up in horror at the scene unfolding before their eyes, knew what the sergeant would find.

Chapter Thirty-seven

'Right,' said Inspector Deacon, walking over to the fireplace in the drawing room and turning to face the expectant faces of Sir William, Edith and Rose. 'I've brought you all here together in this room because, between us all, I think we can put together the pieces to explain why Lord Belvedere felt driven to murder his wife.'

It had been two hours since Lord Belvedere had taken the drastic step of locking himself in his room and taking his own life, thus avoiding the shame and humiliation of a trial and execution. His body had been removed from the house and Lady Withers was, at that very moment, comforting her niece and nephew in her morning room on the first floor. Lavinia and Cedric could little have anticipated that in the space of just two days they would lose both parents and under such horrendous circumstances. Rose's heart went out to them both, but she did not attempt to go to them, assuming that her presence would not be welcome, and that they might hold her partly to blame for the tragedy that had occurred.

Coffee had been poured out and distributed by the footman, and a plate of sandwiches lay largely ignored on a tray, despite luncheon having, for the first time ever in Ashgrove's history, been missed or perhaps more accurately, overlooked. It appeared that only Lady Withers had any appetite. Rose had overheard her discussing with Stafford whether it would appear very callous and uncaring of her to eat a few sandwiches in front of her nephew and niece. Stafford had informed her in no uncertain terms that it would, and suggested that she instead find an opportunity to slip into her bedroom where a plate of food would be left for her on her dressing table. Lord Sneddon, to everyone's delight, had taken the first opportunity to leave Ashgrove, departing some half hour ago.

'Sergeant Lane and I managed to put together a few pieces of the puzzle ourselves, but I believe if we pool together what we all know, then hopefully we can understand why this crime took place.' Deacon looked at them earnestly. 'I can assure you that what you tell me now will stay within these four walls. The newspapers thankfully have not got wind of this story yet, and the powers that be will want some elements of this crime to be kept out of the public domain. They will be relieved that a peer of the realm will not be going on trial for his life, accused of murdering his wife.'

'You knew, didn't you, that Cedric hadn't killed his mother?' Rose said, looking at the inspector accusingly. 'And yet you let me think he might have done. Have you any idea how wretched I felt?'

'I'm sorry, Miss Simpson,' replied Deacon, looking apologetic, 'but I'm afraid it was necessary. We had great good fortune in that Sir William's servants are so diligent in their cleaning, so that the discovery that someone had broken into the gun cabinet was made so quickly. We were able to eliminate you, Miss Simpson, from our list of suspects because you had no opportunity to return the gun unobserved. But the gun cabinet was bothering me. I had assumed that whoever had taken the gun must have done so either after everyone had gone to bed on the Saturday night or very early Sunday morning. When Lord Sneddon told us yesterday that he had practically goaded Lord Sedgwick into going after his mother, I wondered whether my theory about the gun cabinet was wrong after all.'

'And was it?' enquired Rose.

'No. The sergeant and I checked it this morning. It would have taken quite a bit of work to break the lock and probably resulted in some noise as well, come to that. Also, because of the positioning of the lock on the cabinet, it would have taken time to force it because the murderer would have had to be very careful to ensure that he did not break the pane of glass in the door.'

'So you knew it couldn't be Cedric, because if he had done the murder he would have had to break into the gun cabinet just before setting off for the woods and that couldn't have happened? According to your theory, it would have taken him too much time and have been a very noisy exercise; he would have been bound to be disturbed.'

'Exactly, but it did give me an idea. I soon realised that this was going to be a difficult case to solve, not just because almost everyone had a motive for wishing Lady Belvedere harm and had no alibi for the time in question, but because no-one was particularly concerned that the murderer be caught. I hoped that by arresting Lord Sedgwick, I might encourage the real murderer to step forward, which of course happened.' The inspector looked around the room. 'But I still don't know why Lord Belvedere killed his wife, and I want

246

to, for my own peace of mind. You two,' he said looking at Edith and Sir William, 'I think, can tell me why. And you, Miss Simpson, worked out the truth and I'd like to know how you did it.'

'Very well, Inspector, I'll tell you,' said Edith sounding almost weary. 'Goodness knows it will be a relief to have it all out in the open, if only just between these walls, as you say. I suppose you would like me to start at the beginning and the beginning is a very long time ago, some thirty years.'

'We were all friends then, Inspector,' Sir William joined in. 'Edith, Constance, Marjorie, Henry and I. The girls had all gone to school together, as had Henry and I, and we spent all our holidays together at the insistence of our parents who were keen that we should marry. Constance and Marjorie's parents were keen that they should marry men of title or social standing, and both mine and Henry's parents were keen that we should marry the Bellingham sisters due to the money that they would bring with them into such an alliance; their family really was obscenely wealthy, you know.'

'I was just the poor relation, there on sufferance,' continued Edith. 'But what they never expected, particularly as I was shy and plain in comparison with the beautiful and accomplished sisters, was that I and Henry, Lord Belvedere, should fall in love. We kept our relationship a secret because we knew it would be frowned upon. But then I found that I was with child.

'I was frantic, as you can imagine. I knew that Henry's family would be furious and my own mother disappointed, but I assumed they would let us marry. After all, I came from a good family, if a poor one. But I made the fatal mistake of confiding in Marjorie before I had even told Henry. Even after all this time, I've often wondered what made me do it. I was always far closer to Constance, you see, but Marjorie was a little older than us and always seemed sensible and worldly wise. She promised to help me, but instead she took the opportunity to use my misfortune for her own ends so that I never saw Henry again until this weekend. She went at once to Henry's mother and told her. Between them they arranged that Henry never received any of my letters, which were growing more desperate by the hour, and I in turn never received his. Marjorie told Henry I no longer had any feelings for him and she told me that he didn't want to have anything to do with me and the baby. I was distraught. I informed my mother, who took me to the continent so that I might have my baby secretly and give it up for adoption. While there, I had the great good fortune to meet Harold who, despite being

247

informed by my mother of my condition, proposed marriage and said that he was happy to bring up the child as his own. As you can imagine, I jumped at the chance to keep both my child and my reputation. We were married soon after and then returned to England, at which point I discovered, on reading my first English newspaper for months, that Marjorie had married Henry.'

'Do I take it then that Lord Belvedere never knew about the child? How did you learn of Lady Belvedere's deception?' The inspector looked at Edith, keenly.

'Her old lady's maid wrote to me about it a couple of years ago. She felt guilty for the part she herself had been made to play in the deception. She was on her deathbed and wanted me to know the truth so that she could make peace with her maker.'

'Until this weekend, when was the last time that you saw the earl and countess?'

'I never saw either of them again, Inspector, until this weekend. Our paths never crossed. I never seemed to be invited down to stay at Ashgrove at the same time as the Belvederes; I suppose that was your doing, William?' Sir William nodded.

'I guessed, you see,' said Sir William in reply to the inspector's quizzical look. 'Cedric looked far too like Robert for it to be just coincidence. When Cedric came to stay one time when he was six or seven, I looked out a photograph of Robert at a similar age. They looked identical; they could have been the same child. Henry had confided in me years before about his relationship with Edith, so I asked her outright next time she came to stay.'

'It was a relief to tell someone,' admitted Edith. 'I have never even told my husband who Robert's father was. From the very start we pretended even to ourselves that Harold was his natural father. But I knew that I could trust William to keep my secret, I knew he would never betray me.'

'When I discovered that Marjorie and Henry had invited themselves down this weekend, I tried to get Constance to put off your visit,' admitted Sir William. 'I was afraid what would happen if you all met again. But Constance wouldn't listen to me. She assumed I was concerned about your meeting Cedric, not her sister and her husband.'

'So I wasn't imagining the likeness between Cedric and the photograph of your son,' Rose said. 'And it explains some other things too. When you fainted it was because you were shocked to see Lord Belvedere there, not

Cedric, wasn't it?' Edith nodded. 'And the earl was shocked to see you here too,' continued Rose. 'Lavinia said he was shaken, as if he'd seen a ghost, which I suppose he had.'

'Even so,' interjected Sir William, 'I feel sure that he somehow knew you were going to be here and that's why he accompanied his wife down this weekend. He hardly ever visits us, he prefers to shut himself away in his library at Sedgwick.'

'Yes, he confessed as much to me on the one occasion that we spoke,' confirmed Edith. 'He wanted to know what had really happened, you see, all those years ago when I had to all intents and purposes just disappeared.'

'Lady Belvedere was afraid of you when she first saw you,' Rose said, remembering. 'She must have been afraid that you were going to tell Lord Belvedere the truth.'

'Yes, I felt quite powerful to begin with,' said Edith, 'but then I became nervous about telling Henry about Robert, and Marjorie always had a knack of intimidating people she considered weaker than herself. She began to make me feel timid and afraid, and I think she started enjoying my discomfort in the end because she began to feel safe. She didn't think I'd have the nerve to tell Henry, you see.'

'And I was worried about Edith,' said Sir William. 'I thought it was all making her quite ill. I was afraid you would get sick again, my dear. I fear, however, that my wife thought I was being over solicitous to you and misread my intentions. I will have to make amends to her.'

'It explains why there was always a tension in the air at dinner,' said Rose. 'Everyone was tense, reading things into things which weren't there, or just waiting for something to happen. On Saturday at dinner you said, Edith, that you weren't well and stood up to leave; what happened then? Something did happen then, didn't it, something that shocked the countess?'

'Henry came to my rescue and put an arm around me so that I wouldn't fall. He whispered that he was sorry about everything.'

'So Lady Belvedere knew then that you had spoken to him? I think she sensed that she was in danger. Oh, I got it all so completely wrong, you know, in the beginning,' admitted Rose. 'I overheard your conversation with Sir William on the croquet lawn and assumed you were threatening to tell Lady Withers about your relationship with her husband. I thought he was urging you not to, when all the time what he was trying to do was to persuade you not to tell Lord Belvedere of the role played by his wife in having you disappear from his life and in keeping him in ignorance about his son.'

'That explains our rather strange conversation over lunch that day on the croquet lawn,' said Edith, looking relieved. 'I thought you knew the truth having seen the photograph and overheard my conversation with William. I spoke far too freely then; I think I was rather delirious from the stress of it all. It was only when you mentioned my hating Constance that I realised you were still in the dark about it all.'

'You spoke of the hurt that it would cause Harry, and I assumed at the time that you were talking about your husband, Harold,' said Rose. 'But then I happened to overhear Lady Withers talking to Stafford about Henry, meaning the earl. I'd only ever thought of him as Lord Belvedere before, but then I realised that everything made sense if, when you'd been talking about Harry, you'd been talking about Lord Belvedere.'

Deacon had been avidly following the dialogue between the three. Now he interjected.

'I'd like to know, though, what made you, Mrs Torrington and you, Sir William confess to Lady Belvedere's murder.'

'I couldn't let you arrest Cedric, Inspector, and I knew if I didn't do anything Henry would confess. I didn't want him to do that because, you see, I felt it was all my fault. I realised, right from the very start, that he must have done it. I felt responsible. If I had only kept quiet, Lady Belvedere would still be alive today.' Edith turned her head away. 'And Henry, of course.'

'I myself thought Edith had done it, Inspector, and I didn't want to see a lady hang for the crime. And I'd promised to protect her, you see, no matter what,' explained Sir William. The inspector looked at him impressed. There was more to this man than he had at first thought, although whether his nerve would have held all the way to the gallows, he'd never know.

'William assumed straightaway that I had shot Lady Belvedere,' said Edith. 'That's why he thought up that silly story about the poacher, to try and put you off the scent. The first opportunity he had to talk to me alone he asked me why I had done it and I said I had to. I meant tell Henry, of course, but he thought that I was confessing to the murder.'

'This is all very well,' said Deacon. 'It explains why Lord Belvedere may in time have come to hate his wife, but I still don't see what drove him to murder her this weekend.'

'I doubt he would have done,' said Edith, 'if it hadn't been for the photograph.'

'And Cedric and me,' Rose said quietly.

'Yes,' agreed Edith, shooting her a quick glance, 'that too.'

'Photograph?' Deacon sounded confused.

'Yes,' Edith said. 'But before I explain, I think I'd better go back to the Saturday morning. Despite what you may have thought at the time, William, I did heed your words. I wondered if I was being very selfish after all. It was obvious to everyone, I should imagine, that Henry and Marjorie were not close, but Henry seemed reasonably content immersed in his own little world of books. I wondered what would be gained by telling him the truth. To tell him in one breath that he had fathered a son that he had never known even existed, and then in the next breath to tell him that he would never lay eyes on his son because he had died on the battlefield, seemed cruel beyond belief.'

'And yet you argued your case with me,' reminded Rose, 'even if we were talking at cross purposes.'

'Yes,' admitted Edith. 'It was when I was describing to you Marjorie's privileged background, that she'd had everything she could possibly want, and yet she had not been satisfied. She had thought nothing of trampling on me to get what she wanted. The more I spoke about her, the angrier I became and I realised that I simply couldn't just let her get away with it, I couldn't. So I arranged to meet Henry on the croquet lawn once you had concluded your game, and I told him everything. I don't propose to go into details, to tell you what we said to one another after all that time. Suffice to say that he was very shocked and sad, not to say angry; indeed there was much emotion on both sides.' Edith broke off, a glazed expression on her face as if she was back there on the croquet lawn remembering their conversation.

'And then you decided to show him the photograph of Robert,' said Rose, 'the one you carry around with you everywhere and showed me on the Friday.'

'Yes.' Edith seemed to falter, and Deacon wondered for a moment whether she would continue.

251

'She'd damaged it, hadn't she?' Rose asked suddenly. 'Lady Belvedere had somehow got hold of the photograph and done something awful to it. I think you knew it was a possibility. I remember you'd been showing it to me when the countess appeared unexpectedly; you quickly snatched it back and stuffed it into your bag. But you hadn't been quick enough, had you? Lady Belvedere saw you do it and must have guessed who the photograph was of.'

'I shouldn't have put my bag down, I shouldn't because she must have found it.' Edith's voice was rising dangerously. 'She could have just taken it out of my bag and got rid of it. I'd have been none the wiser. I'd have probably thought I'd dropped it somewhere. But that wasn't enough for her, she wanted to hurt me for threatening to upset the life she'd built for herself. What she probably hadn't reckoned on was that I would only discover the fate of the photograph when I took it out to show Henry. She'd cut it up into fifty or so little pieces and stuffed them back into my bag so I would know it was her. I was distraught. It was the last photograph I had of Robert, taken a couple of days before he went off to war. She must have known it was irreplaceable, and I'm afraid I rather lost control. I screamed at Henry, told him exactly what I thought about the woman he had married, as I tried desperately to try and piece it together so that he would at least have an idea of what his son had looked like.'

'And you told him about Cedric and me,' Rose said, her voice hardly above a whisper.

'Yes. I told him that Marjorie was going to ruin Cedric's life as she had ruined his. I told him that his son had the possibility of happiness but Marjorie would do everything in her power to prevent a relationship from developing between you, that she'd prefer for her son to be in a loveless marriage so long as it brought wealth with it. Henry didn't say anything, he didn't need to. He just looked down at the ruined photograph and studied it for a moment before turning very pale and walking away. I didn't even try and stop him from going; I think a part of me was glad that he was at last sharing a little of the pain that I'd endured. But I should have gone after him; I think I knew even then that he had decided to stop her.'

'I suppose the idea of shooting his wife came to him when you showed everyone your duelling pistols that evening, Sir William,' said Deacon. 'He'd just found out that his wife had arranged to go on a walk with Miss Simpson the following morning, presumably to persuade her to leave, and he decided to act sooner than later. It was not a spur of the moment thing, of course. He had the whole night to think it through. But even so, I think he was shocked by what he'd done as soon as he had pulled the trigger. He certainly wasn't thinking straight when he put back the gun because he hadn't even wiped off his fingerprints. It explains why he seemed surprised to hear that there were no fingerprints on the gun when we interviewed him. He wasn't to know after all that someone else had seen fit to wipe them off.' Deacon paused to give Sir William a meaningful glance.

'I'm sorry if I frightened you, my dear,' Edith said to Rose. 'I didn't mean to, I just wanted to know if you had seen something that would implicate poor Henry. I so wanted him to get away with it, you see.'

Chapter Thirty-eight

'Harold!'

Edith turned to face her husband. Except for the two of them, the house seemed unnaturally silent as if they were the only ones there, when Edith knew for a fact that Rose was gathering her things together in preparation for her own departure, Sir William was in his study, Lady Withers was in the drawing room with Lavinia and Cedric, and umpteen servants were milling around like busy ants behind closed doors ensuring that, whatever happened in the nature of catastrophes, Ashgrove, as a country house, would continue to run smoothly.

'What are you doing here, Harold?' Edith was poised on the bottom step of the stairs, her husband having just come into the hall. 'I can't come home, I can't. When you know what's happened, and that it was all my fault, you won't want me to either.'

'I know what's happened, Edith,' replied her husband, gently. 'William telephoned me and told me everything. I've come to take you home. Then I'll make the necessary arrangements so that you can divorce me.'

'Oh, must I? Yes, I suppose I must.'

'It's what you want, isn't it. I've always known that you only married me because of Robert. I hoped you'd come to love me. I loved him like my own son, Edith, truly I did. But when he died a part of you seemed to die with him. I wanted so much for us to share our grief, but I didn't know how to and you seemed to shut me out as if it was your own personal sorrow. I felt that I was intruding or being insensitive if I showed any sign of weakness. But I longed to cry for him as much as you did, truly I did.'

'Oh, Harold,' Edith leapt forward and clasped his hands in hers.

'I knew Lord Belvedere was Robert's natural father. Your mother hinted as much to me and then I saw the likeness when I looked in the society pages, between Cedric and Robert. I knew you never stopped loving him, I knew I was a poor substitute.'

'You're wrong, Harold, you were never that. I never realised until just now how very much more of a man you are than he was. I stopped loving him years ago, I realise that now, I just couldn't forget about him until he knew about Robert.'

'Then …'

'I want to go home, Harold. But I don't want a divorce. I want to be your wife, but this time I want it to be real. I want to live in the now, I'm tired of living in the past.'

'Oh, Edith,' And, with that, her husband took her in his arms, much to the surprise and delight of Lady Withers, who had just come out of the drawing room with the express intention of ascertaining once and for all from Edith her true relations with Sir William.

Half an hour later Rose descended the stairs. Edith and her husband were long departed and she was hesitating, weighing up the necessity of going in search of her hostess to thank her for her stay, against coming face to face with Lavinia and Cedric, who must surely harbour feelings of resentment towards her for the part she had played, admittedly unwittingly, in the tragedy that had unfolded. She wondered, given the very unusual circumstances, whether it wouldn't be best for all those concerned if she just left without saying anything and then sent a note. As she was considering this option, which was becoming more attractive by the minute, the drawing room door opened and Cedric came out.

'Rose! Surely you weren't going to leave without saying goodbye?'

'Oh, Cedric, I didn't know what I should do. I know you must hate me, what with my telling the police that you had overheard my argument with your mother and then your father only did what he did because –.'

'Rose, I don't blame you at all. In fact I admire you enormously for being prepared to tell the truth, no matter what. Lavinia, I'm afraid, doesn't feel quite the same as I do, but she'll come round.' He moved forward and took her hand. 'I know this is totally the wrong time to say anything. We must let the dust settle and there's likely to be some frightful publicity concerning all that's happened, although that inspector chap was jolly decent. He told me that he'll do what he can to prevent some of the more sensational aspects of this case from getting into the newspapers. But I just want you to know, Rose, that I meant everything I said. This doesn't change a thing as far as I'm concerned. No, please don't say anything now, just tell me I have reason to hope, that I –.' The remainder of Cedric's sentence was cut short due to Rose throwing herself into his arms, at which point they surrendered to a passionate embrace.

'I don't know what the world's coming to, Stafford, I really don't,' said Lady Withers, emerging from the drawing room with her butler in tow. 'First Edith and now Cedric and Rose. In my day such public displays of affection were considered vulgar. I do hope you won't get any ideas about Mrs Palmer, Stafford. I've seen the way she looks at you.'

'No, indeed not, m'lady,' replied Stafford, for once abandoning his impassive air, and instead looking visibly shocked.